THE SEARCH FOR A PERFECT DAY.

IN A PLACE EVERYONE WANTS TO BE.

AT A TIME WHEN IT ALL STARTS TO FALL APART...

All Joe Deegan ever wanted was a quiet, simple life
in a reasonably organic environment.

So naturally he comes to HEAVEN UStraylia seeking healing,
enlightenment and a little lie down on an unspoilt beach
- where it finally dawns on him that, while life could be
completely miraculous, time remained unbearably short.

And with expensive guidance from his accountant/guru
things were going really well … until the occasion of Joe's
50th birthday.

In quick succession he nearly drowns in the surf,
virtually throws away an undemanding, well paid job,
and almost destroys the perfect relationship.

When it looks as though his modest fibro cottage is about
to be swamped by dozens of pink and lilac cluster town houses,
the beautiful birthday starts to go seriously pear shaped…

33 Postcards from HEAVEN UStraylia

a novel correspondence
Paul Davies

First Edition 2004;

National Library of Australia Cataloguing-in-Publication data:

Davies, Paul, 1949–.

33 postcards from heaven Ustraylia gateway to the Rainbow Coast

1. Relationships – Fiction. I. Title. II. Title : Thirty three postcards from heaven

A823.4

Cover photograph: Suzi Rosedale
All other photographs: Paul Davies (unless otherwise credited)
Map of Heaven page 287: Tabitha Davies & Look Chook Designs
Editing, design and prepress: Gordon Balfour Haynes,
Wordsmith Services–Verbivore Services Group

Special thanks to Ken Watson, Tabitha Davies (Look Chook Designs), Peter Tapp,
Suzi Rosedale, John Shanahan and Skydive Byron Bay (www.skydivebyronbay.com)
for permission to use the image for card #18.

**The characters described in this correspondence are,
fortunately, entirely fictional and, like their setting,
bear absolutely no relation to any person or place that
ever existed at any time anywhere in any dimension.**

33 Postcards from *HEAVEN*

a novel correspondence

Paul Davies

CONTENTS

LIFESTYLES OF THE FINANCIALLY CHALLENGED AND NOT TERRIBLY REMARKABLE

Just another two of the four colourfully unreliable faces of **HEAVEN**'s solar- and lunar-powered town clock. Discover the Rainbow Coast and find a place where time can be basically…when–ever it likes.

Affix stamp here

#1 of 33 Postcards from Heaven

printed on gently mulched, plantation-grown, organic bamboo fibre using recycled greywater and bound with a biodegradable non-toxic glue

No animal or dolphin suffered in the making of this card
(apart from, of course, its author)

1

**LIFESTYLES OF THE FINANCIALLY CHALLENGED
AND NOT TERRIBLY REMARKABLE**

"…we know no more about where we come from,
than we know about where we are going…"
(Gra'eme Every Now And Zen)

12.00pm-ish, Pearly Gates Hotel, Friday 13th March

According to the town clock (and depending on which colourfully unreliable face you checked), it was either exactly…shortly before…or sometime after high noon on Black Friday when Joe Deegan felt suddenly overcome by a strange woozy feeling. Indeed, for a pretty awful moment, the incurable romantic could neither recall who he was exactly, or even what he was meant to be doing…

While sadly, such a state mightn't be all that unusual for him, Joe could see that he'd been standing, warming his tofu pie under the hand dryer in a gents' toilet somewhere; and was pretty sure, deep down, that he'd arrived where he was out of a basic desire to get healthy, reassess his priorities, and have a fairly relaxing time. Yet so far this morning his mail box had been vandalised, he'd almost drowned in the surf, and scarcely three hours later found himself menaced with a chainsaw by an unstable property developer in urgent need of serious anger management.

Most of which was quite disappointing- given that Joe generally preferred his days a lot better planned with fewer shocks. Punishing decisions often had to be made. Like, what angle to set the banana lounge? Or, how long to spend drying off in the hammock? Sometimes it was a question of coffee before, or *after* the first body surf? And on many mornings now, in a fit of pure exuberance, Joe would have a full caff skinny cap both before *and* after his first plunge into the ocean. Along with a medicinal glass of Chardonnay- but only for the pain relief. And the insight. Plus the slight odour wine gave his perspiration seemed to keep the mossies at bay. A pretty vital consideration when your humble fibro shack backed onto pristine coastal wetlands.

Joe Deegan wasn't lazy. Far from it! His time on the Rainbow Coast had been packed with strain and effort (admittedly mostly mental). It was more- that he couldn't for the life of him, imagine any compelling reason for accomplishing today, what could safely be put off 'til tomorrow.

As his accountant and best friend, Gra'eme, often pointed out: "We all know about Hell and the Inferno. Everyone's an expert on pain and suffering; but try and get people to outline their idea of eternal bliss or even true happiness, and most punters haven't got a bloody clue. Some even try to imagine a kind of endless long service leave, poor bastards- if they're lucky enough to still have such a thing."

Rising to Gra'eme's challenge, Joe would often tweak the Beautiful Day with a little 'lite' gardening, or fifteen or twenty minutes of actual work- requiring a serious Lie Down before lunch so that all the free time of the afternoon could climax with a casual stroll along Purgatory Beach towards Point Paradise. Here he might investigate the relaxing properties of a quiet smoke prior to a second or third body surf on the way home. Sometimes Joe hardly worked at all. Or needed to, really. It just didn't seem such a high priority. Indeed, there were many days that are so delightful and satisfying it seemed silly even, to stick to a sure-fire plan. On such occasions he would simply improvise as the mood took him. Going with the flow. Time in Heaven as a kind of lifestyle jazz…

Joe knew that in order to be fairly good at anything you needed to feel pretty good doing it. A great writer had to have great feelings. But right now, the only real challenge for him seemed to be: how to make each successive twenty four hours even more satisfying and delightful than the ones which preceded them. In short, Joseph Michael Deegan, veteran teledramatist and underachiever par excellence, had come to Heaven seeking Paradise on Earth, and fundamentally believed he had found it.

It was all obviously a shy, and rather pathetic cry for help.

Because, despite the natural beauty that surrounded him- the fabulous climate, unspoilt beach, healthy food and relatively clean drinking water- there was still something missing from the core of Joe's life in Heaven. Something gnawing at the gristle where his soul should have been.

But what *was* it exactly? How could the overweight word merchant put a seriously nail bitten finger on the strange unease coiled like a death adder in the midst of his own private Eden? Already today Joe was gripped by a sinking feeling that the forty ninth anniversary of his arrival on the planet was going to be one of those seminal moments in his personal journey where he wished he could just push the fast-forward button and start all over again…like preferably tomorrow.

But tomorrow his darling Barbara would be gone. Off again on one of her many trips back to Jerusalem. Where she'd much rather be. Working as a tour guide (war permitting) and surrounded by the sights, smells and people she loved (maybe not so much the smells). Joe knew he was holding back his lover from *her* promised land. And if it wasn't for him, Barbara would probably never leave her beloved Muddled East. That much was certain. This beautiful woman's commitment to him hung on a thread. And Joe knew it. And Barbara knew it. And he knew she knew he knew she knew he knew it…

Yet here Joe remained, almost half a century old, alone in a toilet with only his tofu pie and a mid-life crisis for company (a crippling complex of depression and inertia that was now entering its ninth, obstinate year). If the malaise didn't end soon he felt sure it was in danger of degrading into some sort of low level, irreversible melancholia- much like the rain depressions that exhausted Queensland cyclones slumped into every summer between January and April. Mid-life crisis morphing into late-life crisis with hardly a decent pause in between.

Sometimes it seemed as though Joe had done nothing worthwhile or tangible since Kate gave up her struggle all those years ago… Apart of course, from falling in lust with Barbara- whose bright spirit and angelic good sense rescued him from the grief that set in after Kate's long illness took its inevitable course…

FLASH BACK TO:

St. Kilda Melbourne, 9 years before…

At that time, Joe just couldn't get motivated about anything, or see much point to it all. While he remained in St. Kilda friends got harder to keep in touch with. Very few ever just popped round out of the blue. To his shame Joe never even checked his emails. Phones, at the best of times, held a certain terror for him. The idea of someone's mouth speaking directly into your ear and vice versa (however electronically separated), seemed not only a bit of a liberty, but actually technically unhealthy. Little wonder his social calendar went into a kind of cryogenic suspension. Invitations to parties, openings, first nights and other 'must-go-tos' soon dropped off from under the fridge magnet and got lost behind the stove. Besides which, it was quieter when you were by yourself. And in any city now, as Joe had come to realise and Gra'eme confirmed: "the battle against noise is nearly always lost" (see *Cars=Carnage*)…

Joe's inner recluse felt he could easily have become an Essene living in that ancient monastery Barbara took him to at Qumran near the Dead Sea. Lost in concentration in his cell all day, scribbling away at some beautiful manuscript, singing in the choir at five, perfecting really good wine from the local vineyard and living each day to an ordered routine, a spiritual template. Insulated from the loud, vulgar world. Part of a community at peace with itself. Not lonely so much as happily solitary.

Escaping Melbourne had been the easy part. All Joe and Kate wanted, as soon as she'd been diagnosed 'stage 2a', was to head north together- towards the sun. Towards some healing for both of them. To avoid the gloom of Victoria generally and that freezing drizzle which descended in early autumn like an auctioneer's hammer and didn't fully loosen its paw until the summer was just about over. Those interminable, eight or nine months of the year when your towels never quite got dry on the line and the carpet always felt like furry ice as you slithered out of the doona for another awful day's slog in the gloomy half-light of a southern UStraylian winter. Joe came to loathe Melbourne's big annual rituals: Finals and Festivals, Tests and Tournaments, Cups and Cockups, and that awful, compulsory feeling that you're going to miss out if you're not there. For him it was too hard to have fun in public. It only seemed like showing off.

And after Kate, Melbourne also contained the things that reminded him of her, their familiar haunts and habits, routines and rituals, along with the feeling that everything wasn't quite right in the world. That if someone with Kate's boundless energy and life-affirming good nature could die at the tender age of 38 then there was no justice in the world, and something fundamentally wrong with the whole box and dice…

JUMP FORWARD TO:

Utopia **Mt. Lookout! 5 years later…**

It was hardly surprising that Gra'eme (as soon as Joe came to his 'meditation retreat' for help) urged the scriptwriter to use his mid-life crisis as a 'creative opportunity' to touch base with some 'inner feelings'. But Joe, who by that stage survived mainly as a scribbler of serial drama for The Network, was already quite emotionally aware. Getting in touch with his anxieties, phobias and nervous compulsions was more or less what he did for a living. In fact, generally speaking, Joe was pretty much 'inner-feelinged' out. That was part of the complex of problems he was reeling from. There just *were* no more internal sensitivities to plumb down to. He'd gone from a person who used to be in control of his life to someone who almost always took "no" for an answer.

RIPPLE DISSOLVE FORWARD TO:

12.00pm-ish, Pearly Gates Hotel, Friday 13th March

In fact Joe's depression had become so bad lately he was finally thinking of seeking professional help- probably exorcism. Everyone in Heaven was raving about a marvelous new witch who'd just arrived from a coven in San Diego. And so here again was the message writ large: the time had come for the low-sensation thrill-seeker to take charge of his own healing and find closure on the apparently interminable illness he seemed to be afflicted with- to rescue his id from its main worst enemy: namely himself.

Joe made a mental note to look up Raiina Virago's number in the *Nirvana News'* 'Wicca Guide'. He would explain to this beautiful young woman with her lovely gypsy eyes and frisky dark hair, how his long decline had followed the classic pattern: beginning with a certain persistent lack of self worth and building up to a feeling that, in an increasingly insane world, riven by terror and lies, his life and its overall mental shape didn't actually amount to terribly much. In fact all Joe felt now was a certain laissez faire desire to become more nurturing, to express himself honestly, to plant trees, turn on, tune in and not so much drop out of, as leave happily behind whatever rat race he happened to find himself in. Which, to be honest, wasn't all that often. As with mobile phones, Joe tended to avoid rat races…

The obsessive body surfer glanced away from his tofu pie and unfortunately caught sight of himself in a mirror above the sink. Dark rings under each yellowish eyeball were sunk like drought stricken creek beds into the puffy white sand dunes of his cheeks. It looked as though some alien force had sucked the life blood out. Once glorious curls were now a mattered haywire of tangles looking less like hair and more like some badly overused copper scrubber. His belt had stopped at one minute to midnight (there was only a single hole to go)- meaning he was now within 18 inches of being as round as he was high. A truly awful sight. Something Joe's Hawaiian shirt, tattered shorts, cracked sunglasses, and dilapidated dunlop volleys couldn't hope to brighten- even if the dunnies' fraying canvas bodies and broken rubber souls were a pretty neat approximation of his own physio/spiritual state.

To make matters worse, after three decades of an unbroken love affair with wine of all colours Joe discovered his liver. (And almost immediately rather wished he hadn't.) He failed every attempt at a self-administered detox. Giving away animal products was hard enough, but life without the fruit of the coffee bush or the grapevine seemed about as impossible as it was unnecessary. In any case, the bio-chemical blueprint saturated into his pleasure receptors by food and alcohol were already locked in, clamped down and rusted on. The behavioural patterns set out long ago on the road to perdition were simply irresistible; and let's face it, 'will power' had never been one of Joe Deegan's strong suits.

He marveled that Barbara actually put up with him. He wondered, when it all boils down, what attracts a woman to a man anyway? (Or a man to a man, or a woman to a woman.) Who would want a girl who'd tolerate me? He thought, paraphrasing Marx (Groucho). It could only have been because he was pretty fabulous in bed. Which Joe was- despite the exterior decay. All three women he had ever made love to volunteered the fact unconditionally. A trio of classic Capricorns (stubborn, bossy, always spot on)- so it had to be true. He naturally assumed it was the Welsh genes on his father's side- a certain Tom Jones/Dylan Thomas/Richard Burton factor kicking in…

Joe tried to suppress his mutinous locks back into some order by scraping a claw of fingers through the congealed knots. Dandruff fell like snow. A haircut was long overdue. Although his curls were the only thing about himself Joe actually liked. Unfortunately, the almost permanent stubble underneath now made him somewhat uneasy- ever since Charlie Manson and Osama Bin Laden had given long hair and beards a bad name- effectively ending the dreams of the both sixties and nineties respectively.

So Joe gave up trawling for lice and in the end just rubbed his brow. A headache threatened, requiring either serious hydration or more alcohol- something he was reluctant to attempt as early as high noon- even if it was his birthday and he was currently standing within several metres of a bar licensed to sell many delightful beverages…where UStraylia was 2 for 407 against the Poms on the big screen. Heading for another mega victory. About which Joe could conjure as much interest as he would in the contents of a cholera hospital's faulty septic tank. So he kept rubbing his forehead and felt the subcutaneous cyst that had been there ever since his mother dropped him out of the pram all those…too many years ago. Gra'eme had told him that bumps on the head in childhood were a precursor to genius. Well, Joe was still waiting… And it struck him again how so many parents seemed to scar and maim their darling offspring in so many varied and caring ways- even without thinking. Sometimes without loving.

The couldabeen minor playwright sighed as he turned from the mirror and finally the sense of dislocation passed as he paused in relief for a refreshing glance out the gents' toilet window- panning left to right over the fibro-asbestos rooftops of Heaven's tiny commercial hub. Built on the back of a frontal dune system, the Pearly Gates Hotel was high enough for him to take in the Good News Agent, Café Celestial, St. Peter's Pizza, Martyr's Meats, the Blissed Out Bakpakah Academy, Seraphim Surf Shop, Blue Sky Bowls Club, All Hallows Hospital, Himmel's Hot Pies, and the Happy Hunting Ground Tepee- where you could be aura cleansed and cranially rebalanced (if you were totally insane).

Vasuda Devi, who ran the Tepee and was gifted with such things, once applied her skills to one of Old Frank's sick greyhounds and had the poor thing out like a candle in ten seconds- its head flopped sideways across her tarot table like a wet towel, looking anything but balanced. It was the sort of thing that tended to put you off cranial work, and Joe made a mental note never to go near Vasuda again or part with any money in her direction. (Despite the fact she had once worked an amazing cure for his recurrent outbreak of boils.)

CUT TO:

Utopia **Mt. Lookout! 3 years ago…**

Instead, it was Gra'eme who, for an immodest fee, and after almost a year of trying, finally laid out Joe's personalised recovery chart. In order to become 'whole' again, all the wanna-be screenplaywright needed to do was terminate this infernal, internal and apparently almost *eternal* war going on between his male and female personas. Joe Deegan had to accept that he was fundamentally ordinary, would hardly ever achieve anything much, and probably remain a constant source of disappointment not only to himself but others. He had to, in a sense, embrace the death of his old self, discover the inner shaman, and 'follow his bliss' (a la Joseph Campbell). But which bliss was that? Joe was as far from feeling genuinely happy right now as a politician was from thanking you for voting for him/her. Gra'eme's prescription for a cure was all very well in theory: to move forward you had to, in a sense, *murder* your old self. But how easy is it to commit a kind of retrospective suicide?

"It's like trying to smile and whistle at the same time- I just can't do it," Joe protested, resisting Gra'eme's formula for an easy cure. "I'm rather fond of that cheeky young larrikin I used to be."

"Then you'll never achieve anything," pronounced the disgraced former corporate auditor ominously.

Which was of course true.

JUMP CUT TO:

12.00pm-ish, Pearly Gates Hotel, Friday 13th March

Because now, the mere thought of a direct confrontation with anyone, the prospect of some public or productive activity generally, brought with it a tsunami of lethargy in Joe. Something seriously malignant had sapped his resolve. Beta-blocked the will to go on. And it was all very well for Gra'eme to come out with these marvelous ideas about inner shamans and personal self-advancement, but Joe's mentor (despite the bankruptcies and his long dispute with the tax department) still had enough untraceable bio-tech futures contracts and numbered accounts in small island states to buy a whole truckload of bliss. In fact many truckloads, which he had poured into *Utopia*: a technically illegal holiday resort masquerading as a 'private meditation retreat' which just happened to have two dozen self-contained cabins scattered amongst an 'income producing' macadamia plantation on the eastern slopes of Mt. Lookout! The property included a spring fed dam, hydro power, astonishing views and teak furniture.

Gra'eme (to give him his due) was certainly an enlightened person. He had written 61 'Blue' pamphlets on speculative philosophy and economic_irrationalism which alone qualified him as a kind of life coach. And bliss was a cinch within his beautifully manicured rose garden and solar-heated jacuzzi…

CUT TO:

2

THE VIEW FROM A GURU'S JACUZZI

Erect, pale and circumcised—the much over-photographed lighthouse on colourful Cape Surprise! Just another perfect spot in **HEAVEN US**traylia for whale watching, life counseling, hang gliding or finally having that complete nervous breakdown.

Affix stamp here

#2 of 33 Postcards from Heaven

printed on gently mulched, plantation-grown, organic bamboo fibre using recycled greywater and bound with a biodegradable non-toxic glue

No animal or dolphin suffered in the making of this card
(apart from, of course, its author)

2

THE VIEW FROM A GURU'S JACUZZI

"The only good thing about shaving is that it forces a lot of men
to take a cold, hard look at themselves- almost every day.
Sometimes without bleeding."
(Gra'eme *Reflections In A Third I*)

Utopia **Mt Lookout! 2 years ago…**

Joe was lounging in Gra'eme's hydrotherapy complex one day, enjoying a setting sun as it transformed the whole sweep of Purgatory Beach from the lighthouse south- past Rapture Rocks to the Three Sisters off Point Paradise…

They had already polished off a Lambrusco for sweeteners and were working their way through some late model Grange Hermitage (a little token of gratitude from one of the financial guru's insider trading mates). Joe took the plunge, literally and metaphorically, and put it to Gra'eme directly: 'following his bliss' just didn't seem to be cutting the mustard- so to speak. Okay, Joe had embraced the death of his old inner hero. He even accepted that he was fundamentally ordinary and would never really achieve anything much. But none of this seemed to be working. The scriptwriter's mid-life crisis was now becoming more or less interminable.

"My dear Joseph, you've got to see it as an opportunity to withdraw and take a serious look at yourself. Like I keep saying- freshen up your investment portfolio, opt for more risk. Act like an American. S/he who looks outside dreams, s/he who glances inwards, wakes!" (*Smart Money*)

"Yeah, but Gra'eme, it's been nearly seven years now." (And even then his guru's gender-neutral pronouns irritated Joe slightly.) "All I wanted to do when I came here was surf with dolphins under rainbows."

"And you've got that almost every day!"

"Then why do I still feel so shithouse?"

Gra'eme sighed. "I know, I know…your mother, your father, dying in quick succession and then Kate getting that dreadful tumour. You became an orphan and a widower almost simultaneously. With hardly enough time to grieve before another one got struck down."

A lump caught in Joe's throat. Gra'eme had an unerring ability to bring the tears out. And, sensitive to the general mood, the Wise One recharged his client's glass from an open bottle of the cheeky little Beaujolais which had been 'breathing' nearby in a floating pool tray.

The last dying glint of sunlight was setting up a rainbow that arched, as if on cue, right over the pale and circumcised lighthouse on Cape Surprise!. In the next moment its lamp switched on, officially separating one Day in Heaven from another Heavenly Night, shooting out twin rays from two giant lenses, spinning back to back on their bath of mercury, like whirling dervishes…beaming en*light*enment out across the wide Pacific Ocean; and then back around again, to the hillside on which Joe floated (despite the sinking feeling) in Gra'eme's spring-fed jacuzzi.

Too heavy to stop, the lenses flashed diamonds by day and golden electric beams at night. Offering guidance and welcome at all times. French crystal set in British steel, carving out another moment of infinite possibility. Fifteen precious seconds in which to discover the joy, betrayal and heartbreak of life in Heaven, UStraylia. This demi-paradise. The answer to all Joe's prayers. It was simply…breath-taking. And something you almost got used to, he realised, living where he did.

Gra'eme placed his glass on the lip of the jacuzzi's imported tile border and breast stroked across to the large cooling pool beside it. He flopped in there like a hairy walrus who'd had a bit too much of the good life, and swirled around offering another free insight: "Don't be afraid to be yourself, Joseph. You're the best one qualified. In any case you're not a total write-off. You still have some talent."

"Oh yeah, sure." Joe challenged back. Hoping for another contradiction. "Name one."

"That Irish gift of the gab, for starters. Not to mention the underlying Welsh talent for performing it. I keep telling you, Joseph, you're so naturally depressed you would've made a great stand-up comedian."

"But it's a funny word 'me'. Isn't it, Gra'eme? By definition, it means different things to different people. I mean, where did 'I' come from? Where am 'I' going? Are we just gene taxis fuelled by hormones, driven by a cabbie with few immigration papers on slave wages, with the fare covered by some higher porpoise - or similar certacean, obviously much smarter than us?"

The Life Coach let his disciple's complicated and provocative question hover over the darkening landscape as the rainbow itself started fading with the light. A final, passing cloud cast its shadow on the great curving strands of colour. Nearby gums with their wispy thin foliage were soon silhouetted two-dimensionally against the twilight as Joe glanced over towards Mars and Venus, just now rising on the eastern horizon. Soon these tiny pin-pricks of red/blue light would be wiped out again as a full moon came beaming up over that great, planet-curve of sky and sea. Its smiling, round face laying out a 'stairway to heaven': a ribbon of light dancing on waves, encouraging 'lunacy'. And sure enough, all over Nullumbah Shire, in forests and tepees, on beaches and the tops of mountains, ferals and pagans would be chanting, dancing and twirling fire sticks. Percussing really badly any drum, box, or can of dry beans that came to hand. Driving neighbouring property owners mad. Yet once again, Magick would be loose upon the landscape- thanks be to Gaia, mother of all things…

It was the perfect setting and the perfect moment for Gra'eme to finally offer his favourite acolyte the key to an entire accounting philosophy: "Joe, we no more know where we come from than we know where we're going. You're born, you're alive for a series of miracles called an ordinary lifetime, and then we just, basically…fade to black."

There was a pause as Joe struggled to come to grips with the enormity of what was actually being proposed here. He realised then that, just as some people had personal trainers, he was privileged to have his own personal philosopher/cosmologist. And all the fees he'd paid the Great Man over all the years would probably be worth it for this next insight alone (and he was right):

"The only thing we can be sure of is that, at its highest measure, 'life' consists of a series of halting, imperfect glimpses of our own personal potential. Which on a few rare occasions we actually achieve. To try and dredge up any other answer to it all is to totally misunderstand the question. In fact there are no answers, there are only alternatives. And whether you arrive here as a frivolous socialite or homeless orphan and whether you go out as a bus driver or a billionaire, you are chained to a series of moments from which there is no escape- in any direction, of any dimension. Only one thing is certain: you're always going to need friends. As many as you can reasonably bribe or emotionally blackmail. Because we are united as much by our base instincts as by the fear and hope of our next heart beat."

There was another pause as Gra'eme generously opened a West UStraylian Pinot and topped up both their chalices.

"We're born. We breed. We die. And sometimes along the way you might actually pay off the mortgage- if the banks will let you. But that's the beginning and the end of it. To try and wrench any more significance out of our curious presence on this otherwise exquisite planet is a complete and unnecessary waste of what you'll now appreciate is ridiculously precious time."

"But surely, Gra'eme, there are things that happen which we *can't* explain, phenomena simply beyond rational understanding: déja vu for example, most UStraylian television, or real estate prices in Byron Pay?"

However the Master was already smirking- like a federal treasurer about to deliver bad economic news.

"Try and get someone to describe their idea of 'Paradise'," he countered brilliantly. "Most people haven't got a bloody clue. They just don't know how to have a really good time. Some poor fools spend all their lives buying the house and passing on their DNA; then as soon as the kids leave home and the dog passes on, and they're packing the caravan for that slow drive around UStraylia...they die! I mean what's the point?"

The wannabe poet shrugged, point taken.

"On the other hand...everyone's an expert at Hell. We all know about pain and suffering."

Joe pounced on what seemed an obvious contradiction: "But, if it's just this endless black before and ever after- then what's to stop us from committing suicide right now?" His sense of familiarity with the multiverse he'd come to know and love was skewing wildly out of control. "What you're proposing, Gra'eme...is just so depressing. I mean, I'm down enough as it is."

"Well that's a very good question," the Enlightened One conceded. "For most people it probably *would* be better if they committed suicide. It'd certainly make the world a cleaner, cheaper, quieter place. I mean what is the point of most people's lives anyway? Why do so many succumb to golf memberships? Or learn to play bridge? Can there be any greater waste of time?"

Joe was reeling a little as the heady nectar of the wine again took hold of his taste buds and spat kisses straight to his cerebral cortex. "Okay, I accept there's no God. Look at the horrors of the twentieth century. Look at St. Kilda's failure to win its second grand final in fifty eight years...But, what about Angels?"

"What about them?"

"Here are these selfless, powerful creatures looking after us. Everyone with their own personal guardian. Keeping us safe- what a fantastic idea."

When Gra'eme clearly didn't agree Joe threw in some personal experience: "I'm quite convinced for example, that angels disguised as a flock of lorikeets arrived to carry Kate's soul away only moments after she died."

But the Great Teacher was already shaking his head, suppressing laughter. Losing some self-control himself. At last. "If birds are angels, devils must be flies. Sorry, mate- big mistake."

"Well, if there aren't any angels, then who shapes the clouds?" Joe retorted. Taking some moral high ground (literally). "Who creates the perfect surf when the north westerlies rustle across Purgatory Beach?

Gra'eme laughed outright. "Who shapes the clouds?"- and glanced up at a thin strand of cirrocumulus turning deep scarlet as it caught the last rays of a sun now sunk well beneath the western horizon. "I'd say that cloud for example, was shaped by a commercial jetliner. In fact, if I'm not mistaken (and I rarely am), that's the 6 o'clock Sydney shuttle limping into Nullumbah airport on one engine."

Joe looked up and could see that Gra'eme, as always, was pretty well spot on. In fact, the back end of the vapour trail left by that single functioning propeller was already wedging out and starting to break up from the south, caught by the high altitude westerly and drifting east towards the rising moon. Promising another perfect day less than 12 hours away.

As if to soften the blow, Gra'eme put a brotherly arm around Joe, literally taking him under his wing. They'd been over anointed with expensive lubricant and were now exceeding the legal limit for driving cars, if not flopping about in pools, let alone speculating on higher theo-philosophical anomalies. What followed was obviously going to be pretty significant. And it was all getting a touch sentimental Joe reflected, in retrospect, when his headache cleared some days later.

"Joseph, listen to me. The point is not to die for God, but to *live* in spite of Him. Only when the human race comes to its senses and fully realizes this extraordinary possibility can we take the next step and evolve into something rich and mature and pretty damn near perfect."

"Something post-human, perhaps?"

"In a way, yes- but without the genetic manipulation. Look, the spiritual impulse is a valid thing and always has been, deep down. As the 'god spot' in the brain so amply demonstrates. No problems with that. But if you want religious upliftment why not go out and buy yourself an old Pink Floyd record- or something by Elixir? Van Morrison never fails to give me all the 'soul/sole satisfaction' I need."

"But there have to be *some* moral guideposts," the couldabeen minor playwright protested. "Surely we need a *few* commandments to control the worst excesses of human behaviour?"

"Honestly Joe, the only sins I know of are: giving any sort of credence to tabloid journalism, paying more tax than you have to...oh and, er...actually maiming or killing somebody- unless of course, they're trying to do the same thing to you. Which unfortunately has always been used as an excuse to justify war- something that is really only legally sanctioned murder on a mass scale. But as for putting God, Thor, Zeus, Vulcan, Krishna, Allah, Baal, Vishnu, Neptune, Jupiter or Jehovah first, and respecting your parents or your current squeeze...that rather depends, I should think, on the respective merits of the individuals concerned."

"What about stealing?" challenged Joe.

"Stealing!? Gimme a break. How could something that underpins the whole operation of Private Enterprise be wrong? Forgodsake Joe, without robbers, swindlers, thieves, monopolies, privatisation and the misappropriation of funds how would anyone grow rich? And even more importantly- where else would the hard currency and untraceable cash reserves needed for high exposure investment come from? We'd be doomed without some kind of criminal behaviour going on in the commercial life of the country."

Gra'eme sighed, like it was disappointing for him to have to spell it out.

"You see, my dear friend, you make the classic mistake of assuming that religion actually teaches people how to behave. Nothing could be further from the truth. All that organised systems of belief achieve is paranoia about the mob next door- the ones who believe something different (even though it quite often involves the same Divinity). These unfortunates therefore, generally either have to be converted (if they're lucky), or wiped out (if they're not)."

Mercifully, the disgraced former corporate auditor unhitched his fraternal arm to grab the floating pool tray for a completely unnecessary glass of wine and Joe, released at last, flopped drunkenly back into the jacuzzi where he submerged briefly and thought about it. Above him, Gra'eme warmed to his theme, hardly registering his client/disciple's temporary absence.

"I mean, how do you measure love, Joseph? What keeps the heart beating? Why do women with prominent noses always have such gorgeous legs?" he demanded, surprised at his own question- just as Joe exploded back up onto the surface, like a depth-charged submarine. Gra'eme was splashing the crisp young Chardy with its peach and melon characteristics into their glasses now as if there was no tomorrow. Which there wasn't, when you took his world view to its logical conclusion.

"I mean- is there light at the end of the tunnel or is it merely the headlamp on some huge train plunging towards us? We simply don't know. There's enough electricity in the average human brain to power a light bulb and people still don't get it!"

This was pretty depressing stuff, and Joe sighed again as he glanced back over the gloomering coastline- feeling, and maybe even indulging himself in, a mixture of vague dissatisfaction and slight disappointment. On any *normal* Beautiful Day he should by now, be settling down in front of the 6.30 pm news. Enjoying the evening litany of global violence and natural disasters; or sometimes natural violence and global disasters. With the same result: an endless stream of refugees. The poor souls who lose everything and subsequently trudge dusty roads with the sad baggage of all they have in the world, their animals and possessions swept along with them by the tides of history, surfing a wave into some other desperate community. Signifying yet another war surging across another border in another decaying state, a mere handful of Loyal Traveler Miles™ away...

Again Gra'eme read Joe's mood accurately. He understood the ennui, the frail, human longing for it to be otherwise. That deep, hopelessly flawed pining for a crutch or scaffold to hang one's soul on, to wrench some meaning from life. The desire for structure, certainty and purposefulness- all mere figments unfortunately of a sadly mortal and therefore fairly fevered and unreliable imagination.

"Look Joe, you can chose to grow, or you can opt for stagnation. It's entirely up to you."

Gra'eme was keen to wind the session up now.

"To move forward, *become* your own hero. Be that individual 'you' that only *you* can be- no matter how disappointing the end result might seem. Here's another tip: get in touch with your female side. She's always there…waiting for her mate, the other half of you. This inner woman is the lightning rod between our conscious and unconscious selves, Joe. Just as a mother ushers us into the world, so too, will your anima usher you into your very own and probably not too demanding future. This is the key to becoming 'whole' again. A step that only *you* can take…"

BLUR FORWARD TO:

12.00 pm-ish, Pearly Gates Hotel, Friday 13th March

All memory of that crucial, life-workshop with Gra'eme faded again as Joe found himself hovering uncertain and apprehensive before the mirror in a gents' toilet somewhere- just as it began to steam up. Had someone left a hot tap running? he wondered, glancing round and then down at a hand dryer which still refused either to warm his tofu pie or switch itself off…

The former minor playwright, now TV hack, gazed back at his reflection just in time to see it blur behind the steam. As if his life itself had begun to smudge out. Then he felt a jab in his heart- that quick stab of pain he got occasionally (but always refused to acknowledge could be angina).

How many heart beats did he have left, anyway? And was it fog on the mirror or just scrim in some hazy reverie? A veil to be wrenched aside in order to reveal yet another horrible home truth or dangerous and probably incriminating fantasy.

This whole sad, 49th birthday event seemed merely a dream that Joe still had to Wake Up! from.

As Gra'eme so forcefully and frequently urged.

RIPPLE DISSOLE BACK TO:

EVERYBODY'S GOTTA BE SOMEWHERE

Colourful *Casa del Fibro* at # 13 Redemption Rd, **HEAVEN**.
Just another classic example of **us**traylia's unique fishing
and drinking class architecture—built on flood-prone,
only slightly radiotoxic landfill—a mere stone's throw from
pristine Purgatory Beach, with its perfect curling breakers,
low-mortality rip systems, and pristine sand (apart from the
dog droppings).

#3 of 33 Postcards from Heaven

No animal or dolphin suffered in the making of this card
(apart from, of course, its author)

3
EVERYBODY'S GOTTA BE SOMEWHERE
"Question: Why don't sharks eat property developers?
Answer: professional courtesy."
(Gra'eme *The Ten Plagues Of A Real Estate Boom*)

6.41am, Casa del Fibro, Friday 13th March

Out on Cape Surprise! the lighthouse took one final illuminated sweep and decided to blink itself off- officially marking the exact point where another Night in Heaven morphed into a brand new, Heavenly Day. Littered with tantric body surfs.

Somewhere in the distance, like a bad sound track, came the spluttering mechanical farts of a motor bike the size of a small truck as it flatulated its way up Sinners Street and round the corner into 11 Redemption Road. It was Filthy Mick, head honcho of the Utta Bastards Motor Psychle Club returning home from his nightly drinking and urinating competition- folded in now with the squeak, rattle and crash of an enormous, robotic garbage truck going about its own dawn assault on everyone's sleep.

Inside a modest fibro shack on the back dunes of the most fabulous beach in the world, Joe Deegan was dreaming of a future in which his beloved home town had degraded into some kind of low-rent Surface Paradox. A place where the mindset of developers and real estate agents had finally taken over. The 'paradox' being that a place so gormlessly entranced by its own self image could turn out so monumentally ugly. People were crammed into concrete caves like rats in a pigeon coup. The smallest space at the cheapest cost and highest altitude with no one left to blame when the lifts broke down. It was a dream of a future in which Joe wanted no part, and from which there seemed no escape. Greed had triumphed over Nature and simple Common Sense, ensuring that people had willingly built their own prisons- the kind of dreadful, nocturnal premonition Joe usually had just before Barbara went off on one of her regular commutes back to Israel.

So bad in fact, that it shocked him awake as he sprang bolt upright in bed, sweating, nervous, feeling really flat and washed out…

Barbara was jolted awake beside him. "Are you all right?" she frowned, a little worried to see him hanging there, breathing hard, holding his chest.

He turned and stared back down at her. Not quite sure where the nightmare ended and reality began. Which was no reflection on Barbara. Waking up beside her was the best start to any day Joe could imagine. Racing towards fifty herself, and still a delight to both the eye and the soul.

Finally he collapsed back down into the sheets and reached out for a little bodily contact. But Barbara withdrew, still looking concerned. It was the face of a young girl when you only glimpsed the eyes and part of a smooth cheek above the crumple of bed linen. He pushed it all away and beheld her more fully, taking in her smooth, coffee-coloured, Sephardi skin, and short stubbly hair. Barbara Solomon, the angel come to rescue and protect him.

Joe leaned in to touch foreheads, and up close Barbara's dark, almond-shaped eyes coalesced into one- like a desert pool. Mysterious and unknowable. The semitic thing always there in the background- or in her case, the foreground as well. And if the eyes were the windows of the soul, then the eyebrows must be the guttering. Up close these two arching ridges of dark fur also melded into one, Frida Kahloesque stripe. Was this where the myth of Cyclops had come from? Joe wondered. Lovers touching foreheads in the morning…

Eight years ago Kate died and less than twelve months later Barbara walked in through the wide open door where Joe's heart had gone missing in action- slamming it shut so resoundingly behind her that he Woke Up! at last! From his first bout of debilitating inertia. Right now, she was very content to be walking out again for her annual dose of tour-guiding in Israel. Joe knew he should go with her, if only for the company. If only to have her still within reach, and partake of the crumbs of her wonderful social life. But he distrusted plane travel and didn't exactly warm to the idea of abandoning his beautifully crafted lifestyle for a war zone. They would often have this awful argument about him going/not going, then a joint, then make love, and everything would be okay again…for a while…

WHIP PAN TO:

6.50am Casa del Fibro Same Morning

The sound of the garbage truck grew louder as it approached, shook, and continued on past their one-and-a-half bedroom cottage.

"Shit!" Joe swung his legs over the edge of the bed, fully awake now. "We forgot to put Otto out."

For a moment he actually contemplated grabbing the wheely bin and quickly dragging it round the front to chase after the truck but a) apart from a raggy t-shirt, he had no clothes on, and b) he could hear it was already too late.

"It's all right Joe, it's only half full. Just remember next week, okay?"

"When you're gone," he added gloomily, pouting a bottom lip, over-acting badly.

Barbara laughed and jumped out of bed as she always did. Rocketing into action with gusto and enthusiasm. If she saw a hill, Barbara had to climb it. Confronted by any dilemma she always had an solution. There was a spring in her step, a special verve as she embraced the promise of each new morning. Especially one that would bring her closer to her favourite place: the holy city where time began and where it would surely end. Barbara was never happier than stashing her bakpak for another return to Jerusalem: 'going up', making 'aliyah'. 'Ascending' to her spiritual homeland, her city of angels again. It always made Joe feel, well…frankly a bit inadequate, actually.

Enough today to cause him to collapse back onto the sheets again, weighed down by the prospect of having to have another fabulous time for the next ten or so hours. Given his life as a wORK-oF-aRT programme, it should have been for Joe too, an exciting, recurring opportunity: to bounce out of bed singing, and get on with it.

So why did he feel such dread, this…palpable reluctance to kick start the occasion of his last birthday as a forty something?

Barbara flung off her silk pyjamas and began hunting for togs.

Propped on one elbow and still mischievously refusing to budge, Joe took in her lithe brown figure- the well shaped calf muscles, the strange absence of a bottom, the lack of any curve to her waist. It was almost a male body when you added in the short, slave-like hair. In fact, Joe sometimes wondered if his love for Barbara was fuelled by an almost subliminal homosexuality. Something he might've picked up from boarding school. Or was this what Gra'eme meant by getting in touch with his female side?

"Barbara- I adore you," he declared unconditionally.

"Please Joe, you promised you wouldn't be like this…"

"I just want to hold you in my arms and grow old with you."

"That's what *I* call a nightmare!" she resisted. Putting a sensible distance between herself and Joe's hopelessly romantic arms.

"Okay- so I'm almost officially a senior citizen," he conceded. "Why not share every last minute we've got left? I can't believe how quickly the days seem to go now. Time is just rushing away."

"I'm rushing away, Julie really wants to get to a Tai Chi class before some last minute shopping."

"How can I, a lone, semi-talented individual, compete with an historically amazing, spiritually dense, ultimately unfathomable, and completely fucked up country?"

"Joe- what would I *do* in Heaven all the time? There's no work, here. You know yourself the Rainbow Coast has the highest unemployment rate in UStraylia."

"Because people come here to *be* unemployed," he rancoured accurately. Then after a decent pause: "Anyway, what would *I* do in Israel?"

It was a selfish question and Joe knew it. And Barbara knew it, and he knew she knew he knew she knew it.

"There's nothing for me here," his life partner insisted, resisting the urge to make it easy for him.

"Except your lord and master," he toadied. "The one who idolises you."

Barbara rolled her eyes, treating that sort of thing with the contempt it deserved.

He fell prey to a mad, random impulse: "Let me kiss your feet…"

Joe craned out over the edge of the bed and tried to grab her legs. Laughing, she jumped back- away from his clutches. Defending herself, kicking out at him. All those body combat classes finally paying off.

"Why can't I kiss them?" he giggled.

"My toes are too long."

"Nonsense, your feet are beautiful- fallen arches turn me on."

"They're embarrassing. Stop it!" she laughed, backing away, bumping into the wardrobe.

"Please, Barbara. Just one kiss. Let me chew an old corn off."

"Stop it, that's disgusting." Barbara was tiring of this joke. But still smiling nevertheless. He always made her laugh at the right/write moment. It was one of his few charms. A talent certainly.

"Come on, just a nibble. I'll save you a 'chopping' trip to the chiropodist," he goofed. Then slid out of bed and begged, literally on his knees, bending to within a few inches of pressing his lips onto some toe knuckles…when Barbara flicked out her beautifully shaped leg again- reflexively, to pull her foot away- and caught him straight on the nose.

It hurt. He broke off. There were a lot of stars before his eyes coinciding with a sudden searing sensation right in the middle of his face.

"Sorry- " Barbara bent over him concerned, studying the damage. The tomboy tamed.

"No, no, it's okay. I deserved it."

An initial red trickle from his left nostril was starting to flow quite freely. Joe's blood being the only really thin thing about him.

"You're bleeding."

"Ah- there's plenty more where that came from," he swaggered, "eight pints by the old measure."

A beat.

"So they reckon." More bravado.

But it did the trick. Barbara was already feeling a touch guilty.

"I told you Joe, going back to Jerusalem is just something I *have* to do." She was massaging his head, beneficially hovering over him. Her ample breasts waterfalling onto his shoulders. He didn't find it hard to remain on his knees and let her continue. In fact he began to harden considerably in all the obvious places as he remained genuflected like an altar boy, pressing one ear to her plump tummy, listening for a heartbeat. Her heart. With which his was twinned.

"Joe, I have to be there. I feel connected to Israel. I can't explain it. It's…it's an umbilical thing."

"A biblical thing?" – he craned back, gaping up at her, his hearing also starting to fail lately, along with prostate, knees, hips and eyesight. He remained blinking and curious, leaning his good ear towards her.

When she declined to correct him, Joe felt compelled to point out the unfashionable truth: "But you were born in Melbourne!"

Barbara disengaged and moved away from him, continuing to dress. "Look, it's not a religious thing, you know that. It's just that- when I'm in Israel I feel…*whole* somehow. Fulfilled. I don't have to seek distraction. Just *being* there is enough. It's the place. It's mad, I know but…I'm addicted. Life in Israel is always out there, on the edge. It calls me, Joe. What can I say?"

" 'Nobody's home?'"

"Joe…" she sighed/warned.

"Leave the answer machine on."

"Please, don't be like this. It only makes it harder for both of us."

"I love you, Barbara, you're my sole soul mate. My other, better half."

"Put it away, Joe. Not now. I promised Julie a swim before Tai Chi."

Her last day in Heaven and, as always, Barbara had heaps of classes and workshops to cram in. Even as it started, Joe's masterplan for his 49th anniversary was facing compromise and a certain disturbing aberration- like those planets that wobble round double suns- in and out of each other's orbit.

She handed him a tissue (which he quickly bloodied) and went on hunting for her swimmers.

"Gra'eme said I had to 'get in touch with my female side'," he tested.

"Not *this* female side."

"Oh please, Barbara. Just a quickie. One for the road…"

But he could see she was adamant.

"Okay, I'm sorry I fell asleep last night when we were making love…"

"You've reached a new low there." -Barbara still appalled by it.

"I slowed down, I wanted to improve on yesterday."

"You slowed down and two seconds later you were snoring!"

"Well I'm awake now."

"Too late, mate."

She was slipping into her one-piece bathing costume, putting her fabulous body beyond reach. While remaining so tantalisingly on display. Joe couldn't help noticing how taut and muscular her shoulders had become from the pump classes- despite the little embryonic pot belly which Barbara, despite her overall lean figure, could never quite shake off. It was his only comeback when she really got stuck into his intractable weight problem.

"Barbara…please, we're going to be apart for three months."

"One minute you're there, all over me, licking the mango off, next thing I know- you're dead to the world! Like I'm suddenly stuck under this beached whale."

"Not of the sperm variety, obviously."

Like Gra'eme, Barbara usually ignored Joe's feeble attempts at self-deprecation. This was way beyond being funny now and it wasn't scoring any points with her at all.

"Do you realise how overweight you're getting?"

Joe nodded his head in sincere self-loathing. He had it coming.

"It was disgraceful," he pleaded. I don't know what came over me."

His hands were spread wide, his palms cupped, facing each other, like he was trying to be honest about it– or indicate the length of a fish he'd allegedly caught. The man was genuinely trying to find the right words. Even to behave a little Jewishly.

"I…just don't have any energy at the moment. I'm so *tired*." He pinched the bridge of his nose. As usual this early in the morning, pain threatened from all sides. And it was his birthday forcrissake!

"What do you mean 'at the moment'?" she rounded on him. Angry at last. "You're almost continually worn out! Depressed and *depressing*. You're no fun to be with anymore, Joe."

There was the threat writ large. Not even implied. It was already a question of whether or not to 'be with' him.

"Forgive me."

"Joe, please."

"I'm turning over a new leaf."

"Yes- of the seven pointed variety! And you're only turning it over to dry it for another spliff."

This was a recurring sore point. Joe knew he had to cut down. Barbara was right. He smoked too much. It was as simple and as complicated as that. Dope is called dope because it makes you *stupid*. His addiction was turning her into a nagger. It wasn't a good look for either of them.

"I've heard it all before, Joe. Too many times."

"I'll do anything- anything. I'll keep the bath clean. I'll vacuum once a week…"

"Groveling does not enhance your fading sex appeal."

"I'll even come to a tango workshop."- making a really big concession.

"That includes lying."

He couldn't help noticing how Barbara's right calf muscle flexed so attractively as it went through the leg of the shorts she put on over her swimmers. The other leg was mangled in a motor bike accident. It looked as though a shark had tried to bite off her shin and made for a interesting story in the middle of the Negev desert with her British or German pilgrims. There was something about being consumed by larger animals that always tended to focus people's attention. As if a deep, atavistic fear got stirred up. Some dim, collective memory of the sabre toothed tiger looming in the jungle behind our primordial campfire.

Yet, despite this one 'blemish' (or perhaps because of it), Barbara in her late forties was growing even more good looking as the years flew by. Posing another great paradox: why a privileged few actually became more delicious with time- like a great cab sav…

Whereas, getting older for Joe already involved not only more pain in most of his joints, but an increasingly frequent and often hopeless search for either a cheap dentist or the nearest toilet.

"How come the rest of us age, while you only ripen?" he flattered.

"Stop sounding like a cheap birthday card. Come on! UP! I don't want to miss a last swim."

"But it *is* my birthday, Barbara, and you owe me. I'm almost half a century old. My life is slipping away. "

"Your brain is slipping away."

"Please, darling, three minutes tops. I'll make it quick, I promise."

"Three minutes! That's disgusting!" Barbara was appalled. Again. How could he get it so consistently wrong?

"Do you have any idea of how unappealing a proposition that is to me, right now?"

"You can have a swim and still get to *Cosmic Bodyworx* for your Tai Chi…"

Barbara's shoulders slumped. Firm, rounded trapezoids already starting to sculpt nicely from the rowing machine that *Cosmic Bodyworx* had recently installed. She knew she couldn't deny him a last tryst before leaving. It was kind of a ritual part of their parting ritual. One final, lustful embrace to sustain Joe through three months of serial bachelorhood.

"Later- Julie might hear us."

"Oh shit!"

Joe was really annoyed now. He flopped melodramatically back onto the bed, hugging his pillow like a consolation prize. Holding onto the blind hope that masturbation really *did* prevent prostate cancer.

Julie was one of several hundred people, refugees from the south, who happened to have 'popped by' since Barbara first arrived in Joe's life eight years ago. In fact, Julie was pretty close to being Barbara's oldest and dearest friend. He did his utmost to make sure the guestroom/study/library/archive was pretty uncomfortable (it was a garage after all). But still they arrived and stayed, and played havoc with his sex life. Casa del Fibro's walls were just too thin. However much these visitors kept Barbara wonderfully preoccupied, it all came at a terrible cost.

Julie, for example, was an almost permanently happy person. Unbelievably buoyant and optimistic. She saw the good in everything and everyone. So life affirming and positive about the world and all it contained that it made Joe almost clinically depressed. In fact he wanted to strangle her- but only for the relief it might bring (for both of them).

"Is she on prozac or something?"

"Joe!" Barbara's voice had that warning tone- the one he knew he had to be careful of.

"Don't go, Barbara."

"She isn't on prozac, she takes progesterone."

"I mean to Israel."

"Everybody's got to be somewhere, Joe," she decreed with a conviction that effectively closed discussion on the matter.

And the observation was so…appropriate, so poetic and wise and universally true that Joe wanted to write it down in the notebook he kept beside the bed, and maybe use 'Everybody's Gotta Be Somewhere' as the title for something. Except that, Barbara would see him do it and demand an explanation. He'd have to trust his memory- never a good tactic.

"Come on, Joe. Don't you want a body surf?" It was the only question she knew (and he knew) could really stir him.

But Joe continued to sulk, so Barbara gave up and went out to wake Julie in a mosquito-netted corner of the guestroom/study/library/archive- a lone mattress on cold concrete, loomed over by columns of teetering archive boxes and unsafe looking shelves of books.

CUT TO:

Casa del Fibro, 7 minutes later …

Realising that pre-prandial sex with Barbara was now a lost cause, Joe finally dawdled out of the tangle of sheets that had fallen with him off the bed and staggered to his feet; feeling last night's overindulgence in a cardio-protective Merlot right on the frontal lobes. Where it definitely didn't belong. He glanced through the bedroom window- across the back deck and out onto his own little handkerchief of Eden. A backyard jumble of lovingly planted palms and paw paws, wattles and grevilleas, golden cane and fish fern. Anything native and low maintenance and capable of camouflaging the Twelve Apostles- the only plants Joe really cared about (an impressive eight of them, female this year).

Beyond the back fence he could just glimpse the cool green canopy of the littoral rainforest which separated his humble, but ideally located home from Purgatory Beach. On Joe's small patch of lawn (useful for showering off after swims) an arrogant currawong looked up from its breakfast of worms and stared unflinchingly back, cocking his head to one side. Rather belligerently, Joe thought.

He turned in time to glimpse Julie emerging all puffy with sleep from the guestroom/study/library/archive. She offered him no greeting as she draped a beach towel over the banana lounge for Barbara to lie on. A moment later their house guest was mounted on top of Joe's paramour, rubbing suntan cream into those wonderfully emerging biceps. The wannabe poet slumped as he looked down at the two women having a really good time. Clearly the Tai Chi could wait if it had to.

"You know all that stuff does no good whatsoever," he announced glumly through flywire.

"Hullo birthday boy," Julie chimed around smiling. Finally acknowledging his existence. Her voice charged with a sort of breathy, just-woken-up, phlegm crackling, heavy smoker kind of effervescence.

"I wanted to get you something special, but I'm hopeless at presents so I told Barbara I'm going to cook you one of my favourite dishes on the BBQ for our party. I do fabulous things with smoked scampi."

Joe's scowl deepened. He bet she did. That was already seven personal pronouns in two sentences. Self-obsession gone rampant.

"Do you have any idea of the potpourri of chemicals dissolved in suntan cream?" he rankled, trying to spoil their bonding opportunity. "It's worse than nail polish." (Taking in the lurid aqua colour Julie had applied last night while propped in his favourite squatters chair.) "The skin soaks it up and processes the dreadful stuff straight through to your liver. You might as well slip into a warm bath of DDT."

"Don't be silly, Joe." Barbara was playing mediator/peacemaker/voice of reason. As always.

"Why not just wear a long sleeved shirt? It's cheaper *and* more effective," he persisted. "Anyway, it's too early in the day to worry about skin cancer. The sun won't do any harm at this hour and you do need *some* vitamin D- for the immune system."

Barbara swiveled round to Julie by way of explanation. "Joe has a fear of almost everything invented in the twentieth century."

They both laughed outright, the girly moment triumphant. Amused at how foolish and timid a sensitive, old age guy (a 'snoag') can look when exposed for the wuss that he really was. The same reaction Joe got when he insisted to any one of Barbara's many girlfriends that he didn't *need* Personality Realignment Counseling. As if blindly asserting your mental health was indication enough of a serious problem. Barbara and Julie knew, without bothering to remind him of it, that: a) everyone *needs* Personality Realignment, because b) we're all damaged, all injured by the people who love us the most.

Joe felt his cheeks burn. He dabbed at the renewed nasal flow with a corner of his deteriorating Chairman Mao t-shirt, quickly bloodying it. He could no more let their argument go than he could this ridiculous and now officially embarrassing pseudo-pyjama top. Like the idiot that he was, Joe just had to plough on and invite relationship danger.

"Most of what we call science today is a huge fraud," he pontificated, Gra'eme-like, still speaking through flywire, sounding like a priest from behind his confessional. One obviously under suspicion of doing nameless things to numberless children. "There's no pure research anymore. Everything has to be done on time and for a profit. Shareholding has become more important than sharing." Misquoting Marx (Karl) and simultaneously exposing his limited political understanding. "We've got to stop associating the word 'progress' with all the crap that is killing us. Our fearless leaders know the cost of everything and the value of nothing. Something like a hundred genetically-altered compounds are invented every day and absolutely *nobody* has the faintest idea what the long term effects will be!"

"But we *are* better off, aren't we? Than people a hundred years ago?" queried Julie, unconvinced of Joe's neo-Luddite stand.

"Do you *really* think so?" he cantankered.

"Well, *I* certainly think so. I mean, I may not be a scientist but as far as *I* can see most people aren't starving, we're better educated, less prejudiced, healthier, more liberated..." Julie as ever, always the optimist, slewing off more personal pronouns like ego fuelled cruise missiles.

"Better off? Are you sure?" Joe hectored back. "When in UStraylia alone, we obliterate a dozen native species every week- not all of them in Queensland. Are we really *free* when we're constantly surveiled, or have our names and addresses captured by a million corporate data banks? Every time you use an autoteller you're photographed. Did you know that? Somewhere in a giant computer, owned by people with no morality, are thousands of digital images of us taken on an almost weekly basis."

"Daily in my case," chuckled Julie, still amused by him. Letting both her class and her blatant consumerism hang out.

"Do we really want to have such a confronting, permanent record of our physical deterioration held by strangers?" he pleaded. Appealing to her vanity finally.

"Joe, please- Julie's on holiday," warned Barbara. Again. Same tone, same threat. The danger signs were flashing faster than a someone in a public place with a raincoat on and little else.

But Joe was too wound up about missing the garbage truck, and then missing out on Barbara. "What's wrong with our technology is that it's all based on war. Computers arrive because of the need to crack enemy codes. Tanks become tractors and give us the disaster of monoculture. Bomber squadrons morph into airline fleets and spawn the debacle of mass tourism. The internet comes straight out of Star Wars and puts our mind in a straight jacket as wide as cyberspace… What we need is a technology based on peace. Love instead of hatred, *life* instead of Death."

"I'm sure I don't know how you manage to get up in the morning and bear to face it all." Julie scoffed. Openly.

"Sometimes I don't," he rejoindered enigmatically, not being totally unfrank with her either.

Julie remained convinced that Joe was just another typical, arrested adolescent. Probably a passive aggressive with mild ashberger's and an obsessive compulsive disorder, with associated addictions. All clear indicators of how desperately he needed Personality Realignment. Little wonder Joe was so negative and inept. Hardly a very fashionable look. Certainly not anywhere within a latté chuck of Julie's aRT gallery in Newtown. She even felt sorry for Barbara and suddenly understood her best friend's need to escape to Israel every six months.

Meanwhile, Barbara threw Joe a look that said: 'Did you really have to go off like that on one of your interminable raves?'

He cast a look back that said: 'Sorry, I couldn't help it.'

Their mute conversation was interrupted as the olivewood chimes above Joe's hammock were caressed into life by a gentle zephyr. Barbara had picked them up from a shop in Bethlehem three trips ago (part of her 'commission' that day); and, like a kind of meteorological alarm clock, they only rang when a north westerly blew- effectively announcing that the surf on Purgatory Beach would now be curling towards perfection. Sanity and joy still had a purchase on things, Joe realised (thanks be to Gaia).

And so, and thus, despite the rocky start, a body surf was always possible and only ever just around the corner (literally). His plans for the Beautiful Birthday could always, so easily, be modified and put back on track…That was all part of their foolproof daily design.

BLEACH OUT TO:

HEAVEN USTRAYLIA

One of planet's best kept secrets, colourful **HEAVEN US**traylia boasts a near-perfect climate, mostly shark-free bodysurf, affordable real estate, excellent coffee, laidback lifestyle and clean drinking water. It can't last. (And it won't.)

Affix stamp here

PHOTO: SUZI ROSE DALE

#4 of 33 Postcards from Heaven

printed on gently mulched, plantation-grown, organic bamboo fibre using recycled greywater and bound with a biodegradable non-toxic glue

No animal or dolphin suffered in the making of this card
(apart from, of course, its author)

4

HEAVEN UStraylia

"It's as basic as the Law of Supply and Demand and as stupid as lemmings jumping off a
cliff:
as soon as people converge on a place because of its natural beauty
they invariably destroy the thing they came there for."
(Gra'eme *Prisoners Of The Imagination*)

7.04am, Purgatory Beach, Friday 13th March

Summonsed by muddled eastern chimes to an easterly beach somewhere around the middle of UStraylia, Julie, Joe and Barbara soon found themselves making the short stroll with hats and towels along Redemption Road's grassy footpath. Where the lawn petered out the track meandered on through a precious remnant of littoral rainforest- to arrive finally at the great, golden curve of Purgatory Beach. This five kilometre arc of finely grained sand ran from Point Paradise in the south with its craggy islets (the 'Three Sisters'), right up to the lighthouse- that 'great joint' (Heaven's Big Thing)- smouldering away on the rocky bong of Cape Surprise!.

The panorama always seemed to erupt like the opening of some great symphony as you hurried in anticipation up over the main dune to suddenly emerge out onto this vast amalgamation of sky and sea meeting at some point on a perfectly curved, light blue/dark blue horizon. It was almost too much, but it was always different and sometimes a teeny bit treacherous, if not actually scary. The water was warm, the sand relatively unpolluted (apart from the dog droppings), and freely available to anyone who cared to go there.

Purgatory Beach, as the name implies, was where the good citizens of Heaven went to 'pay' for their sins. Yet the only people who really suffered on it these days were the handful of pale British bakpakahs regularly scorched lobster red by a harsh antipodean sun. For everyone else, Purgatory Beach was simply…Heaven on a stick. It only really 'hurt' as it took your breath away. (Which it frequently did.)

Barbara and Julie dropped their towels and, like most visitors, made an impatient dash for the water. While Joe held off a little, as a true local should. In fact he greeted his last birthday as a forty something much like any other day: by standing upside down on the sand. The one yoga pose he felt reasonably confidant about, and which he held for an impressive forty seven seconds. Joe might have stayed up even longer this morning but the stress of supporting his weight on his head and two elbows reactivated the tear in his nasal vessels and caused the blood to reverse back down *into* his nostril this time- soon making it hard for him to breathe.

Nevertheless he could see that the Bethlehem chimes had been spot on. A gentle north westerly was already coaxing the surf up into classic glassy cylinders, with sunlight sparkling off the waves like diamonds on corrugated blue silk. Forty percent humidity, a balmy twenty nine degrees, and hardly a cloud to be seen in that great big canopy of empty sky. It was just another perfect day on the most fabulous bit of coastline imaginable.

Indeed Joe's chronic depression almost lifted as he realised there was no other place on this planet or in the cosmos generally, that he'd rather be. Obviously March 13 this year, with its calm, warm morning was already shaping up to be a three swims day- just about as good as any birthday could get.

So perfect in fact, that the addicted body surfer had to remind himself these daily baptisms were at the heart of a stress-challenged lifeplan. The low fat/high fibre diet kept him well irrigated and the surf kept him sane. Purgatory Beach was his altar, his analyst, his oracle, his chiropractor, and once (in fact in about eleven minutes), almost his downfall. Yet a dash into the waves, one roll through a big dumper, and Joe was whole again, born again, free again. Ready to face another Beautiful Day containing all the pleasure and relaxation he could cram into it.

Sometimes, when the westerlies blew white manes of spray off the back of perfectly curling breakers, a fan of dancing rainbows flared out across the top of each wave in the mist that followed. Magick was inherent in the landscape. You only had to look to find it. And here again, Gra'eme was so right when he asked: "Who needs mobile phones and unit accounts in pension funds when you had all this out your back door?" (see *Buyer Logical Warfare*)

Still upside down, and risking spinal damage, Joe rotated his head inside his elbows and let his gaze wander up the beach towards the lighthouse, taking in that fabulous boomerang of golden sand. He tried to imagine what the place must have looked like forty years ago- when the minerals had all been taken out and the wetlands behind the beach left a virtual wasteland by two mining companies…

FLASHBACK TO:

Historical Montage, Bogwater Creek, 4 decades earlier…

The swamp on which the village of Heaven now stands was originally bought 'for a song' (an old nazi marching ballad) by a cabal of Queensland property developers in the vain hope that their name change from 'Bogwater Creek' to 'Heaven' might entice some poor fools to buy flood prone land sight unseen. Thus transforming what had started as an impoverished whaling station and slaughterhouse for the neighbouring cattle industry into another version of their booming Cold Coast further north. A place so named because its twenty kilometre spread of unrestrained high rise blocked out all hope of any sunlight hitting its rapidly disappearing beaches shortly after noon.

However, no simple repackaging or blitzkrieg of roadside posters and glossy brochures could overcome the persistent rumours about Bogwater Creek's radio toxic waste dumps, mosquito born viruses, poisonous dip sites, or widespread acid sulphate contamination.

Consequently and fortunately, the boom that had gone on above and below the Rainbow Coast just didn't make it across the Nullumbah Shire border. And so and thus, mercifully, the anticipated hordes of absentee landlords didn't arrive. In fact the only people who actually did turn up were some malaria resistant surfers (self-immunised from trips to Bali) plus the occasional kombi-load of hippies still looking for the Nullumbah Aquarius Festival many years after the original grass huts and tepees had packed up and gone home.

The regular outbreaks of encephalitis and Limbo Creek fever that soon followed were correctly identified as an unnatural consequence of the sand miners having removed vast swathes of pandanus, titree, banksia, paperbarks and sheokes- trees that had helped drain the wetlands and keep the mosquito populations down- not to mention the insect devouring birds that went with them. This self sustaining, life-saving ecosystem had been bulldozed in order to excavate rare metals for the 'space race' and to make 'whiter than white' paint. So much so that the only truly original patch of native habitat left standing on the entire Rainbow Coast was that 100m wide strip of littoral rainforest standing between Joe's backyard and Purgatory Beach- effectively stabilising Heaven's entire frontal dune system. This dune system was the only thing that protected the town from total inundation- should another cyclone turn up on a king tide- which it would, given humanity's willful inability to curb either global warning or the relentless destabilisation of the earth's crust through the hunt for undersea oil.

After the original sandmining barge had been dismantled and parts of it left to rust, vast amounts of fill were brought in, water and electricity arrived, and finally the half dozen streets of 'Heaven' proper were officially gazetted and zoned Freehold Residential. This saw a score of fibro cottages lurch up, wobble in the breeze a bit, and survive their first gales- principally the spring northerlies. Fibro shells with hardwood frames were plonked straight down onto concrete slabs above a plague of white ants feasting on the buried root systems of that devastated coastal forest. In the short-lived stampede of the Rainbow Coast's first property 'boom' many houses were built illegally on patches of monazite tailings- another unfortunate by-product of the sandmining industry (as if more were needed). But it was a health hazard largely hidden from later residents because the warning signs were removed by a second wave of developers absconding from a financial disaster in Western UStraylia. These men bought the radiotoxic blocks at rock bottom prices. And promptly on-sold them at a tidy profit to a bunch of young, well-connected Brisbane professionals looking for cheap holiday investments in a place paradoxically that wasn't anything like the Cold Coast.

Certainly, the warm inner glow that suffused many residents of Heaven these days didn't just come from a bit of meditation and the fructarian diet. In fact, residing in some of the older sub-divisions of the town was only marginally more healthy than sleeping on a hessian bag stuffed with the sweepings from Madame Curie's laboratory floor. The fact that leukaemia is such a hidden, slow moving disease meant that all those who benefited from this crime pocketed their ill gotten gains a whole generation before anyone knew anything had gone wrong.

JUMP FORWARD TO:

Heaven, Present Day

All that remained of this sorry history (apart from concentrated radioactive sand with a half-life of 29 million years) was the large artificial pond where the mining barge had floated. When this body of water to the north (dubbed 'Lake Lethe' by a local comedian) was factored in with the southern wetlands around Joe's shack and you added Purgatory Beach to the east, then Limbo Creek running all along the town's western boundary- it was easy to see that Heaven's half dozen streets were built on a virtual island. In fact, dig a couple of metres down anywhere in town and you immediately struck water. The place was not only built on shifting sands, it was built on *floating* shifting sands. A kind of hydroponic landgrab sailing on borrowed time. Even with more clairvoyants per capita than any other settlement in the world, anyone who studied the map soon realised it could only be a matter of time…just one big tidal wave would do it. Heaven UStraylia, and all who resided on her, would go under again…because it had all happened before…after the last great ice age, when the curling waves of Purgatory Beach were breaking as far inland as the rocks at the base of Mt. Lookout!.

None of which stopped anybody from living there, or ravenously scrambling for its still modestly priced real estate. The Rainbow Coast was far enough north to have a swim-all-year-round climate, and just far enough south to avoid any flow-on effect from the overdevelopment of the Cold Coast. For all these reasons it was the ideal spot on the entire UStraylian mainland- if you wanted a surf that was warm, relatively unpolluted, within a stones throw of a decent cappuccino, and lacking in fatal box jellyfish.

It was even possible, when it rained, to be the only person *on* the beach. Sometimes it made you want to collapse onto its pure sand and give thanks (hoping you'd missed the dog poo on the way down). Some winter nights the air was so still and humid that the flash of the lighthouse- even if you couldn't see it directly- broke over the town like a bolt of lightning. Pulsing light through tiny droplets of mist that just hung about in the air like warm fog. The entire Rainbow Coast, with it's headlands and hinterland, its fragrant forests and golden sands, was an oasis of radiant, inner calm. As good as it gets as far as anyone could tell. Heaven, UStraylia, had to be the best place in the world to live because everyone who lived there kept saying so. For Joe it seemed almost too good to be true. (And it was.)

The only problem, as always, remained a fiscal one. Most of Heaven's diminishing real income arrived courtesy of the diminishing Department of 'Social Security' (sic). The rest of its indigenous and virtually indigent economy hinged on exploiting the slave labour of the handful of cash-strapped bakpakahs who drifted by looking for Byron Pay without realising that they'd made a wrong turn off the Pacific highway. Yet these vulnerable young foreigners were prepared to linger on in Heaven (like temporary refugees) in order to break their visa conditions and work illegally- generally for a few steamed vegies and a spare bunk in the cow bails behind Heaven On A Cone- the town's organic ice creamery.

Attracted by the low rents, there were also quite a number of 'artists' moving in. Some semi-retired. Along with the usual drifters, see-ers, healers, waiters, cleaners, no-hopers, poets, troubadours, jugglers, basket weavers, and far too many struggling but beautiful single mums with empty double beds, and triple bypassed ex-husbands...

And so, and thus, despite the odd, neo-Noosa townhouse popping up here and there, Heaven still remained basically the same kind of place it had been since its 'Bogwater Creek' days nearly half a century earlier: a small, impoverished semi-rural community, trapped inside the illusion of an about-to-happen property boom.

But for many of Joe Deegan's ilk, making a sensible property decision just didn't enter into it. He'd come to Heaven seeking healing, enlightenment and a pleasant lie down- preferably from the vantage point of his Mexican hammock, with a cooling Chardy in one hand and a not too demanding novel in the other- all within earshot of that inimitable beach...

FLASHBACK TO:

Melbourne/Heaven, 10-11 years ago...

After Kate's radical hysterectomy her oncologist was so optimistic she and Joe sold their tiny flat in St. Kilda for a small loss and headed north, seeking convalescence. They migrated to Heaven for the waters; but for Kate the miracle cure remained conspicuous by its absence. And when it was all over Joe knew he couldn't go back to Melbourne to pick up the pieces- there not being many pieces to actually re-collect, let alone put back together. His life had always been a mess and now he desperately needed to change direction, seek new horizons and find some kind of point to it all. Answers to the really big questions like: "Where do socks go?" "Is biting your nails a form of cannibalism?" and "Why *do* grown men dress up as long dead rock stars?"

So for all these reasons, and out of a kind of failure of energy, Joe stayed on in Casa del Fibro, the humble shack he and Kate had bought for the cure that didn't happen. Happy at least to hang on a bit longer in Paradise. Secure in the faith that a living income would come later. Which it did- but at a cost...always at a cost.

Joe lingered because he felt comfortable with the weather, the people, the attitudes, the range of massages available, and the altered states. It was both familiar and reassuring. He 'belonged' in Heaven. In fact he'd been born in Nullumbah, well within the Enchanted Triangle, all those too many years ago so that when he first returned with Kate it truly felt like coming home. And, reflecting on his long exile in Melbourne, Joe realised that he'd escaped the largest city in the world facing Antarctica just in time.

It was especially comforting to know that should anything actually go wrong with you in Heaven, every second house seemed to contain a nurse, drop-out doctor, practicing or retired mid-wife, pathologist, homoeopath, naturopath, osteopath, chiropractor, chiropodist, ayurvedic yogi, metagenician, breatharian, live blood analyst, re-birther, kineseologist, iridologist, acupuncturist, herbalist, crystalographer, aura cleanser, exorcist, immortalist, druid, warlock, colonic irrigationist, white witch or miracle worker.

It was that sort of place. You name it, Heaven would workshop it, lay gentle, healing hands on it, massage it, ponder it, and charge a modest fee for it. At any given moment half the population seemed to be treating the other half for some kind of ailment. This was important on a globe where people were now getting viruses that caused your ankles to swell up, or made you cry all the time. Put simply, Heaven was one of the best places in the world to break down and get sick in. The main reason why Joe and Kate had been attracted in the first place...

And why Joe had stayed…able to linger on by virtue of making it onto the active (sic) writer's list for *On Golden Sands*: an unsuccessful soap opera set in the steamy, hyperactive world of Surface Paradox's corporate elite. The Network were obviously fairly desperate for word merchants. Virtually anyone who could string a line of dialogue together would do.

After much soul searching and a clear understanding that he was truly cheapening himself, Joe decided that dealing with the vagaries of his story editor's mood disorder was a small price to pay for a job that enabled him to stay in Paradise and not only keep creditors at bay but bailiffs from the door. Besides, the narratives invented by the twitchy and unpredictable Craig Huxtable (which Joe had to find the dialogue for) were invariably the same, and endlessly repeated. It was hardly a case of undertaking anything terribly original or difficult. In fact, Joe regarded the *On Golden Sands* gig more as a kind of scribbling-for-a-living than actual real writing. Creating any 'new' (sic) episode for this show often involved simply rotating the characters' names over minimally altered chunks of dialogue. This is where several gagabytes of hard disk space came in so handy.

Joe's 'job' had the irresistible advantage of allowing him to spend most of his time on really important things: like dozing on the back deck, drinking extremely good coffee, or listening to old Pink Floyd albums. As Gra'eme so brilliantly intimated, each day was a gift from somewhere and the talented wordsmith always made sure he set aside enough time to meditate upon, graciously accept, and give thanks for such anonymous benefaction.

All this despite the recurrent ennui. Not to mention the constant flow of house guests: both the jealous and the curious, come to see just how badly Joe had bombed out… Mercifully, they eventually got the message (along with crippled backs from the spare mattress) and their numbers dwindled…

…Until Barbara entered Joe's life and a whole new set of gatecrashers arrived (as exampled by Julie now). Joe rarely had the chutzpah to say "No" and Barbara, of course, positively encouraged the rampage north. It was one of their few real arguments (apart from his intractable weight problem). In any case, who could deny Barbara anything? She loved the company and the distractions they brought. Like most women, Joe's sole soul mate made sure things got done and contacts maintained. Like a lot of men, Joe craved time alone and resented any intrusion into his carefully honed, but isolating routine.

Slim and outgoing, Barbara complemented Joe at every point. She had a zest for people, a curiosity about the world which he always marveled at but could never hope to match.

BLEED THROUGH TO:

India/Israel, 8-9 years ago…

During one of her visits to Muktananda in Gnaspuri, Barbara was given the name 'Sanmahdi'- the 'Wise One', the creative energy of Lord Shiva. Some gurus got it so right. Barbara's energy was exhausting, her wisdom in everything as clear as a teetotaller's eyeball.

Occasionally, when Joe ran out of excuses, he would allow himself to be dragged along in her brilliant wake; to stay in some tiny Jerusalem flat while she tour-guided Mormons and Evangelicals, Catholics and Welsh choirs in the footsteps of her boyfriend Jesus. Left alone, Joe would wander the streets of the Old City feeling like an intruder, yet rediscovering a kind of childhood faith in the wonders of churches as constructs, and history as a series of pavements one on top of the other…

Conquered, occupied, or destroyed 27 times (and still counting), the sovereignty of Jerusalem was clearly never a terribly fixed thing. Yet people kept trying to claim it for themselves, their faith or their empire- this place where Earth intersected with Heaven. Not realising the same thing happened on the Rainbow Coast, too. And without all the fuss.

Frankly, and much and all as he supported public transport, Joe was a bit afraid of bombs going off on the bus or in his local espresso bar. He just couldn't quite get a handle on the fear and loathing in this Muddled East where his better/other half so dearly wanted to be.

Sure, it was a great place to visit, and he and Barbara would always have the moonlight experience at Be'er Ada; but surviving a civil war and dodging rubber bullets wasn't exactly the couldabeen minor playwright's idea of a fun time overseas.

5

THREE SISTERS

Bearing a striking resemblance to the trio of Pyramids at
Giza in Egypt, the legendary Three Sisters off Point Paradise
are just another classic example of HEAVEN's many colourful
landmarks—enshrining a powerful local warning myth about
tantric bodysurfing on unpatrolled beaches.

#5 of 33 Postcards from Heaven

printed on gently mulched, plantation-grown, organic bamboo fibre using
recycled greywater and bound with a biodegradable non-toxic glue

No animal or dolphin suffered in the making of this card
(apart from, of course, its author)

5

THREE SISTERS

"People are capable of acts of great stupidity as well as deeds of the highest moral order.
Unfortunately, it's the stupidity that lingers."
(Gra'eme *The Great Forgetfulness*)

7.13am, Purgatory Beach, Friday 13th March

While Joe remained upside down he could see Barbara and Julie frolicking among some perfectly shaped waves on a sandbank they had found about twenty metres from the shore. In some ways, the two women were closer than sisters. Together since primary school, they had never lost touch (no matter where they separately went in the world). An amazing achievement Joe conceded- until you understood how Barbara was so genuinely, wonderfully open to everybody and everything; and Julie always so positively upbeat with her.

The body surfing addict looked to the maimed handful of his own acquaintances and realised, in the examples of Barbara and Julie he was staring at a couple of master socialisers. Then again, the light of Joe's life was also a great traveler. It was part of Barbara's skills base to be curious, optimistic and outgoing. She worked hard at all her personal contacts and ran up massive phone bills. But what *was* the momentum that kept these great conversations with her girlfriends going?- Joe wondered as he caught himself eavesdropping in on them, tossing up whether he could plunder the dialogue for *On Golden Sands.* Was it simply a boundless, insatiable interest in each other, and each other's most intimate relationships with all their difficulties and heartache? A willingness to explore your dearest friend's deepest feelings and elicit startling inner confessions? The fact that women always sat around the campfire gossiping while the men went off (singly) to hunt...

The disturbing thought now arose in Joe like gas from a stomach disorder that perhaps Julie had also come to Heaven seeking some sort of cure? Was Barbara aware of a hidden agenda to her oldest and closest friend's visit? Information Joe couldn't be trusted with? (Quite rightly.)

As Barbara pointed out: "A crisis is only that which brought out the best (or the worst) in a person."

And bringing out the worst in Joe was always too easy.

Yet how could Julie be inwardly suffering and still sound so pleasant and reasonable? It wasn't just that she painted her toe nails or carried that slight sense of south-of-the-harbour, Sydney-centric superiority. It couldn't be merely the black clothes or the empty, indifferent, inner-city lifestyle. It was more that (dare he admit it) Julie in her own way, cut Joe off too. Their mutual dislike wasn't simply rivalry for Barbara, it was pretty much a clash of egos that would have happened anyway. And no doubt jealousy *was* involved. Julie was there because of Barbara. And Barbara was there for Julie. And Joe and Julie really had nothing in common (apart from Barbara). And Julie knew it, and Joe knew it, and she knew he knew she knew he knew she knew it.

Nor was there all that much for Julie and Joe to talk about really. Her gallery in Newtown contained works that Joe, for the life of him, could no longer fathom. Piles of dirt on the floor, or obscure slogans in neon tubing said very little to him. Odd bits of car parts welded together to look like domestic pets or prehistoric creatures left him baffled and slightly uneasy. Plain, carrot-coloured canvases made Joe simply want to return the favour and throw up.

But sometimes life was like that, and as Gra'eme so shrewdly pointed out: "There's no point wasting time on people who will never waste time on you." (*Practice Random Acts of Sarcasm And Senseless Brilliance*).

Joe flashed back to that evening (nearly three weeks ago!) when Julie first arrived. It was during pre-dinner 'sundowners' on the back deck. He recoiled at the way she lit a cigarette without permission and draped her admittedly fairly attractive leg over the arm of his favourite squatters chair. He was already wondering how long she'd stay this time. Hoping it would be short, being too polite and middle class to ask.

And although Joe couldn't deny it *wasn't im*possible, he was still yet to meet any truly intelligent woman who painted her toe nails- or man for that matter. To be honest…and completely gender neutral about it.

REWIND AGAIN TO:

7.14am, Purgatory Beach, Friday 13th March

Finally, after 47 seconds upside down, the bleeding in Joe's left nostril became so bad he was forced to roll out of his headstand and kneel facing the sea (paying his respects); before leaning forward and resting his head on two vertically aligned, clenched fists- enjoying a good neck stretch and soaking up that smell of old rope and burnt thong mixed with a hint of wet dog that always wafted across Purgatory Beach's fine, golden sand.

Then he squatted back on his heels and, as on just about every morning of his life now, felt the pain in his knees, then let himself fall victim to the spell of the beach…this beach, his little daily ration of bliss. Following Gra'eme's prescription, Joe wrapped his arms around his ribs and gave himself a good hug. Almost feeling happy. Again.

"You live where you do because of some fantasy about 'going to the beach' left over from childhood," Gra'eme chastised him once. "Time to move inland, Joseph. Buy a block of land at least 200m above sea level like my little patch up on Mt. Lookout!. It's the only insurance against any collapse of the West Antarctic Ice Shelf, or the coming meltdown of Greenland's glaciers. All thanks to the coal and oil lobby and weak willed (or corrupt) governments' inability to stop them. If the car doesn't kill you quickly in an accident it will drive you off your land in a drought and eventually pollute all the air we breathe. Did you know, every twelve months now nearly a million people die in car accidents around the globe and almost nothing is done about it? That's a city bigger than Adelaide wiped out every single year. Although, in Adelaide's case, who'd notice?" (see *Cars = Carnage*)

While the collapse of the any Antarctic ice shelf or the sudden reversal of the Gulf Stream (and the consequent permafrosting of Europe and North America) were always a bit of a worry; and even though it would be great to have a block of land with a view at last, Joe knew he couldn't wrench himself away from living within a casual stroll to these waves and that perfect, two-blue, true blue horizon.

However, Gra'eme was certainly spot-on (as always!) about Joe's beach fantasies left over from childhood. The ritual escape to 'the coast' every 'Sun'day with his parents was the one bright spot of any boarding school week. And in a sense his whole life since *had* been a kind of hankering to get back to the simple pleasures of shooting down waves on surf-o-planes and trench warfare with sandballs. Of cutting up jellyfish with cuttlefish, or sipping sarsaparillas in the shade of the family umbrella on a beach so wide your *hav-a-heart* melted before you could get from the milkbar back to your towel. Migrating to Heaven was obviously an attempt by the failed minor playwright to recover some notion of real happiness left over from an otherwise pretty comprehensively damaged childhood.

And yet the whole point about Purgatory Beach (Joe reminded himself) was simply that nobody owned it. And hardly anyone died on it. Apart, of course, from the almost ritual, New Year's Eve drownings of young, skinheaded bovva boys from Bristol or Leicester. Out for a lark on their trip 'down chunder'. Hooning about as they staggered into the surf at 3 am. All laagered-up and legless, weighed down by their Doc Martens and tartans, and years of bad eating, never to expectorate again on the opposition at a soccer match. Gone with the tide, and only their broken mums in some decrepit council flat back home to mourn them.

Joe glanced away from a couple of kids flying kites under the lighthouse (where these semi-tragedies would often occur), back to the stretch of beach in front of him. Barbara and Julie were catching some fabulous right hand breaks off that distant sandbank. It was time to stop hugging himself and join in the fun.

The talented lover actually ran the last fifteen metres and plunged in, getting that slight cosmic jolt as he body-bombed water the temperature of chilled champagne, paddling furiously for the first few seconds to blast the cold aside...until again, Joe was like a kid on Xmas day. Letting himself be lifted up by a wave and suddenly dropped down, copping the snatch of salt up the nostrils (rinsing out the bleeding a little this morning) as he crash dived towards the bottom. Quickly followed by the scrub of sand on skin- Neptune's loofer, exfoliating blackheads and other grit as he was pushed shorewards against the ocean floor on a pulse of energy that had come thousands of miles across half a planet.

Sometimes Joe deliberately dumped himself inside a wave and felt its wet fist hammer into his back like an invisible but divine chiropractor- crunched by half a ton of water dropping straight onto him. Then he'd stretch against the current, letting it tug him this way and that, getting the aqua yoga thing happening. It was tantric surfing as total body workout, swimming as dynamic meditation- guaranteed to lift the soul. You saw the effect on anyone who went into the water around here. They always emerged smiling. It was the best high of all. That sense of wholeness, completeness and enrichment beyond imagining. Something to which Joe was both willingly and willfully addicted.

Occasionally, a wave would tumble him end over end, like an odd sock broken loose from its partner during the wash cycle, never to be seen again...before spitting him back up onto the sand. Feeling regurgitated and Jonah-ish. Baptised and ready for more. Wave after wave, over and over, leaving him convinced that a day as good as this could never end. And for Joe it almost didn't.

Julie and Barbara were swimming a little further out, also caught up in the sheer pleasure of it all. Joe threw himself in front of another dumper and, turning to catch more, noticed the two women drifting a bit. They were bobbing up and down, obviously no longer in contact with the sand underneath. He waved at Barbara to come in, back towards him. At first it was just a vague feeling they were going out a touch too far. Nothing to get terribly excited about...

Barbara waved back and Joe frowned. Even from where he now stood, on the edge of the sandbank, he could feel the rip tugging at his legs.

"Swim over this way," he called, louder for emphasis.

Barbara sort of frowned. It wasn't clear she'd heard him. Concerned, and not quite sure why, Joe allowed himself to drift out towards them. It just seemed sensible not to lose contact.

"Barbara, come back in, there's a strong current!" Joe yelled across about thirty metres of turbulent water: an area where the waves were flattened by the strength of the rip as it sucked water away from the shoreline. Julie was drifting even further out than Barbara.

"Julie, swim this way!"- Joe shouting now, urging her back towards the beach with a wave of his hand. But of course, it was hopeless to make any headway against a current this strong.

"I can't." Julie started to panic and kept making futile efforts to paddle out of it (as you do); but she was only going backwards- away from the shore.

Being a strong swimmer was the one useful legacy Joe had from a Rainbow Coast childhood (something to offset the potentially fatal skin damage). So even at this stage he could have made for the edge of the rip and caught a wave back to the beach further down. For weaker swimmers like Julie the only option was in fact, to go with the flow and either wait for rescue, or drift out of the rip where it finally lost its strength some distance from the shore. The important thing was not to burn up energy fighting it. But leaving the women to their own devices in these circumstances, just didn't seem quite the proper thing for Joe to do. And where would he go for help anyway? This end of Purgatory Beach was practically deserted. That was the whole point of why they came here.

It felt a bit scary to suddenly find yourself unable to touch bottom- bobbing around like a loose cork in some large, turbulent gutter. And of course the rip gathered strength, just when you were least capable of dealing with it. How quickly great fun flips over to life threatening struggle, Joe realised. Two seconds of Heaven Time about as far apart as it was possible to get.

There was no other option for all three of them now but to attempt to stay afloat and wait for the rescue helicopter. Assuming a) someone had noticed their predicament and b) had access to a phone- or a helicopter. The elderly pensioners staggering along the beach hundreds of metres away with their rheumatoid arthritis, raging tinnitus and five barking dogs didn't seem like a promising option. Besides which, like a currency speculator in a bull market, when you're being sucked *out* you just want to get *in*!

Attempting to tread water, Joe felt a certain lethargy take over. They'd only just *started* getting into trouble and already he was exhausted.

"Julie, swim towards me!" he pleaded, hearing his voice turn croaky with emotion- something that didn't exactly inspire confidence in either of his interlocutors. Besides which, Joe was starting to swallow water, and for this reason alone it seemed a pretty good idea to keep his mouth shut.

"I can't !" Julie yelled- just before she disappeared under another huge wave, as pale with fear as the ghostly white foam that enveloped her. And seemed to want to swallow her. Would she come up again…?

…after twenty nine agonising seconds she did. But looked terrible, on the verge of collapse. Joe was sick to the pit of his soul (or it's equivalent- depending on whether Gra'eme or Father Murphy was right). Either way, the odds were shortening on the distinct possibility that they were all going to drown.

Great, thought Joe, just the sort of thing to totally fuck up my birthday.

Like a car accident, you can see it coming but are powerless to avoid that slow slide towards the edge of the cliff or some oncoming truck. The machine no longer responding to your control. A greater, disobedient fate having taken over. Paralysed within a fragment of time, everything now seemed to be drifting into a weird, slow motion for Joe. A sort of hopeless, helpless, mental torpor. A bad dream he couldn't wake from. A silent movie that won't stop going over the same simple sequence. Like a film loop caught in the projector. The mere effort of treading water suddenly required an enormous output of energy. And the harder it became the less reserves Joe, Barbara and Julie seemed to have- which in Joe's case wasn't a lot to start with (despite the daily bike ride). What's more, his angina started kicking in again, like the stubborn mule that it was, making its presence felt via an intense shooting pain down his left arm.

Faced with the distinct probability that they were now spending the last waking moments of their cruelly shortened lives, an overload of things started banging around Joe's head. A rush of nostalgia for all the things he'd never done or ever said to people but wished he hadn't. (And a few things he wished he *had* said to people but was too intimidated, or not witty enough to manage at the time.) He remembered this was how his father went- tipped out of a small dingy, at night, in a storm. And not so much drowned, as killed by the heart attack brought on in the ensuing panic. A silly little accident- just like this one. His father who hated boats (probably out of some kind of premonition) yet went on one last fishing trip with his mates. This was all too impossibly coincidental. It seemed absurd.

Fortunately however, only witches died on their birthday. And despite certain unfortunate personal peculiarities, Joe was no warlock (white or otherwise). But how typically neat and symmetrical of him. Living *exactly* forty nine years! He should've seen it coming of course, because 4 plus 9 equals 13! Killed by a combination of his own fatal clumsiness and numerological bad luck. Life may or may not have been meant to be easy, but it certainly wasn't meant to be this concise either.

How absurd for Barbara and Joe who knew the beach so well to be so easily suckered by a rip. Joe (especially) who swam here two or three times a day. In all conditions, all year round. It was silly. It was crazy. It was such a waste and so unnecessary! It had to be Julie's fault…

He looked back in time to see another huge wave crash down over her. They had finally drifted round the back of the rip into a big, rolling Pacific swell two hundred metres out. And as Joe speculated on whether Julie would come up this time, he still believed he could make for the beach himself- maybe even tug one of the women along with him. Get her arms around his neck, and go dogpaddle style. But now even his blood (despite its overall thinness) started to accumulate like lead in his veins, and it already felt as though a couple of car axles were chained to each limb. Plus, his heartbeat was already up around 195 beats per minute- at which point the frontal lobes of the brain start to shut down and a more primitive, reptilian, mid-brain takes over- effectively removing all rational thought. Just when you most needed it!

Julie was already starting to look like a lost cause. Yet it was so selfish and so obvious that Joe would try to save Barbara first. Something Julie seemed to sense herself as she began screaming. Her shrill cries loosened Joe's grip on things generally and almost made him want to give up too. It could only be a matter of minutes anyway- for all three of them. Just a few more waves. Julie's panic would guarantee she'd be the first to go, with Joe and Barbara not far behind. He felt such an idiot. To have drifted (literally) so casually into it! Like the fool that he was.

Joe floated up close to Barbara and could see she was barely coping. The light of Joe's life believed that a person died the way they lived and in her own case she was absolutely spot on, as always and probably for the last time.

He glanced towards the receding beach, then back out to Julie another twenty or so metres further east. When he touched Barbara gently on the shoulder he was careful not to add any extra weight.

"You okay?" It was an absurd question.

But she nodded, pretending otherwise- just before another big dumper crashed over them, plunging them down before popping them out the back, gasping.

"You've got to get in, Barbara." he urged.

"I don't know if I can." She was dogpaddling aimlessly, trying to float. Gravity- the common enemy. Honesty always her policy.

"You've got to, it's your only chance. Catch the next wave, let it take you."

"I don't think I can…" She was clearly exhausted.

"Just try!" he yelled, hoping to shock her into action as another three metre giant came building up behind them. "You can make it Barbara, you have to. Catch this one now!"

Joe grabbed her around the middle (that strange absence of a waist) and tried to kind of, propel her forward.

Amazingly, Barbara managed to keep rising on the face of the wave, using her last reserves and paddling hard to put her centre of gravity in front. The big dumper lifted her, and as it curled over at the top she dropped down with it and started shooting forwards, landwards. Towards a beach on which still no one seemed aware of their mortal struggle- barely four laps of an Olympic swimming pool away. So close and yet so impossibly out of reach…

Joe watched Barbara go and to his immense relief noticed that even as the wave spent its force she was still making some headway against the outer edges of the rip- getting round it somehow. He swivelled back to Julie. Should he use his last reserves to save himself? Follow Barbara with the next wave? A moment of awful truth. Julie was going under again. He lingered only to see if she would solve the dilemma for him…

…but she came up. And Joe could see in the way her arms struggled to ape a swimming motion- barely lifting themselves out of the water- that she wasn't going to make it.

He cast a last glance towards Barbara as her feet touched firm sand again and she waded, gasping, back across the gutter to the shore. Barbara proved it was possible. He dearly wanted to join her. But some impulse that Joe couldn't fathom wouldn't let him abandon Julie. He drifted out closer to this rival for his lover's affections, and realised the horrible final irony: that he was now going to die in the arms of someone who didn't even like him very much. And vice versa. A drowning womin and her last straw man.

While Joe struggled to hold Julie's head above the water a torrent of nostalgia suddenly flooded through him as he flashed back over 49 years in 49 seconds. That much was true about a watery death- even if Joe wouldn't survive to confirm it. He revisited all the projects he hadn't finished, and quite a few he'd talked about but never started. His all-too-brief and fairly mediocre career. For some bizarre reason he even thought of the photo that Barbara got the bouncer at Shangri La La Land to take of the three of them last night. An image which now would be the final record of him and Julie. He could imagine his darling de facto grieving over it tomorrow. How much for him, how much for Julie, remained a moot point. And not one Joe really wanted to go into right now.

Nevertheless time, the world, nature, experience, other people, the work we do, the people we love, the idea of consciousness itself, pulsed through him like a rush of current through an innocent man in the electric chair. This vessel of existence- his body (which presently seemed so unimportant and useless in the overall scheme of things)- was going to very soon cease its proper functioning. Certainly, it seemed incapable of saving him right now, and intent only on separating itself out from whatever might be left of him after it went. (Again assuming there was some spirit of Joe distinct from his corporeal form.)

It made him finally realise that it *was* ridiculous to hoard all those boxes of paper 'archives' and illegible jottings: the manuscripts, letters and verbal doodlings of a not very remarkable (or terribly lengthy) lifetime. Barbara had every right to burn it all as soon as possible. A bonfire of the banalities. Why should she be tied albatross-like to them. As Joe had been. So foolishly in retrospect.

He knew this day had to come. Such was the great lesson of seeing his parents and wife die in quick succession. Thirty eight was far too young for Kate, but forty nine was hardly a full innings for him either. The enormity of it hit home as painfully as a blow from Brother Carol's reinforced leather strap. Joe knew he had squandered the promise that the Brothers and Father Murphy had placed in him. He'd been Dux of his class but had failed the only important test. He had given less than he had, and taken more than he needed. And no matter how hard he tried, his Beautiful Day and carefully crafted lifestyle- if that was his crowning achievement- could make no real difference to anybody outside of himself. (Except as some kind of strange, not to be imitated, example.) Joe had achieved very little for himself personally, and even less for others. It was a shameful record to go out on.

And so, and thus…as the incurable romantic and lesbian gallery director held each other in what was rapidly becoming a final, fatal, culturally conflicted and sexually mis-matched embrace, it struck Joe that despite life's mysteries and its curious brevity, its haphazard nature and the grand inconsequentiality of it all- we somehow *still* cling to the meagre ration that we're given. And no matter how desperate or how rough life's knocks were, it always seemed better to be conscious than not exist at all- however meaningless and unaccomplished such an existence may be. It was all Joe had and all he knew he needed. It was familiar. It was *his* life after all. And in line with his general nostalgia for everything he wanted to keep it too…please! Gaia. (And whoever else might be listening- in case Gra'eme *was* wrong.)

Joe felt Julie's hands tighten around his neck. Her incandescent fear was now strangling the only thing keeping her above the waterline- namely himself.

"Don't panic, Julie. We're going to make it," Joe lied, hoping to remind her subliminally that he needed his throat open to speak as well as breathe. "You can float in salt water if you keep calm. It's okay, we're out of the rip now."

The fact they were also about half a kilometre from the shore didn't get a mention. They both knew it was beyond either of them to make it back by themselves.

Joe allowed himself one last, lingering, farewell glance over towards Barbara, a thin speck on a beach too far- safely catching her breath and unable to decide where to run for help. Torn between going and staying. Not wanting to lose sight of them. It was lucky Joe did look because Barbara noticed it first. And she pointed, yelling a warning he couldn't hear. Frantically drawing his attention to something out behind them.

Could it get worse? Had Barbara seen a shark? Joe swivelled and realised to his immense relief that she was indicating a board rider even further from the shore. It was Joe and Julie's Guardian Angel. And unfortunately it took the form of Wayne Wilson, a tree vandal from Sinner's Street. Often seen skateboarding through the Kingdom Come carpark, terrorising pensioners. Joe too, had felt Wayne's indifference for the adult world generally; but hated the way he tried to twirl the board up in the air, right in front of you, risking ankle injury- just to really piss you off. In fact Wayne was currently doing something similar with his five foot ten *Aloha* on a wave off to the right, heading towards Point Paradise.

Joe waved frantically- drowning *and* waving.

"Help! Please help us!" he squawked, doubting he could project that far. Yet somehow Joe's pathetic plea travelled out with the breeze. Loud enough for Wayne to hesitate and look vaguely over in their direction, not sure what all the yelling was about.

Joe was almost sobbing now. It was so pathetic it held Wayne's attention deficit disorder long enough for the penny to drop, and finally the young lout deigned to paddle over. As soon as his *Aloha* cruised within arms length, Joe grabbed Julie and tried to push her up onto it. Wayne obligingly slid off. But getting Julie physically above the water line was too much- just yet- for all three of them. So Joe and Julie simply held on to gather strength, and get their breathing back to something resembling normal. Hold on to the most wonderful slab of ditoxopolyphenalcarbate in the world. Something that defeated gravity absolutely. (And any natural attempts to biodegrade it over the next 740,000 years.)

But at last! Joe felt the adrenalin rush receding- despite his angina kicking in again, reminding him (if he'd care to listen) that there were always other problems looming. And how could you be sure about anything anyway, if all of us were only ever a heartbeat away from oblivion every waking and sleeping moment of our lives?

Wayne was treading water beside them, not helping directly, but allowing them to touch his precious surfboard. Too unsure of himself to make a formal offer of rescue. But sticking with them nevertheless, floating alongside just in case- despite being slightly amused (bastard) by it all. Joe was relieved to see some colour returning to Julie's face.

"We got caught in the rip and were just too buggered," was all Joe could manage by way of explanation. Not that explanation was called for. Wayne seemed more concerned that he was being drawn away from some pretty fabulous right hand breaks out the back.

With Julie now half astride the board, draping one attractive leg over, Joe eventually felt the sandbank beneath his feet again, and knew they had made it. Barbara was coming back out across the gutter towards them, anxiety personified. In fact they emerged from their ordeal a good two and a half kilometres south of where they had left their towels. Here Julie and Joe collapsed back onto the sand, feeling like Noah's family, grateful for the miracle of dry land. Sensing another chance at life slowly seep back through every pore of their watertight but (slightly) heavier-than-water bodies.

Joe felt born again- literally baptised out of the sea. A new life, the possibility of a second half-century stretching before him. At least another decade or so in which he could do things, and be with Barbara and enjoy opening a reasonably quaffable Shiraz at sunset.

"You okay now, mate?"

The Archangel Wayne was hovering, leering down at them, holding his life-saving instrument, wanting to get back out to those near perfect wave breaks, waiting to be dismissed. The faint smirk still curling his lips, amused at how breathless and hopeless and old the three of them looked. It was as if the cheeky brute really had no understanding of what he'd just achieved- without hardly trying.

Joe wondered about offering Wayne a slab of Carlton Light or at best some mid-strength XXXX. But how many stubbies were two lives worth? Just to put a figure on it seemed rather shabby and a bit boganish in itself. In a sense, Joe and Julie owed Wayne... everything. But the equation of life with money (let alone beer) was absurd. And something that would be wasted on their impromptu lifesaver's limited capacity for abstract thought. So all that came out from Joe was:

"Yeah, we're okay thanks, mate."

Blokey, familiar, down-playing, 'Straylyin… Wayne considered himself dismissed and sidled off with his synthetic *Aloha* back out to the surf, as if none of this was any big deal. Although he would laugh about it with his mates over a few bongs later.

All Barbara could manage was "Geezus." and "That was incredible."

And for a while the three of them just lay exhausted on the beach, struck dumb by intimations of mortality.

While Joe gathered enough strength to be able to stand, he sat and stared blankly at the sea's edge only a few metres away: shallow water nibbling at the shoreline, continuing its argument with the beach, calculating how much territory to claim on this afternoon's high tide- and from this angle no threat to anybody.

Then it hit him. The irony! It was there- staring him in the face and he hadn't paid attention. Joe glanced south to Point Paradise and the three islets of its broken cape: sharp, triangular pyramids of rock- like a family of large sharks cruising by. These were the fabled 'Three Sisters' of the Nullumbah nation. A story set in stone from the dreamtime. Of three girls who'd been swept to their death by an evil current, on this very beach! Like Barbara and Julie and Joe had almost been. Two sisters became caught in the rip and a third went to save them. All three drowned and were turned to rock- as symbolised in the islands today. And while, admittedly, Joe wasn't a 'sister' as such- in the technical sense- he was certainly an incurable romantic, as well as a bit of a wuss, could barely drive a car safely, and was not good at sums, or reading white goods manuals, let alone assembling DIY furniture. Added to which he always felt a certain, almost sibling rivalry whenever he, Julie and Barbara formed their peculiar emotional triangle. In any case, the Three Sisters legend was clearly a vital tale that parents had used to frighten their offspring with for thousands of years around here: "Beware of the rip, you silly kids, or you'll get turned to stone- like those three sisters…"

And stone sinks! Just like we do, Joe realised with a sudden flare of insight, demonstrating frontal lobes back on track and mid-brain persona receding. Stone sinks just as surely as the sun rises. And for the same gravitational reasons.

And so here, this morning, Julie, Joe and Barbara had, in a sense, *become* the myth. Re- enacted it. As it must be re-enacted. For all our sakes in every generation. And maybe that was the point. If you lived anywhere inside the Enchanted Triangle long enough you became caught up in its spirit dreaming. Captured by its magick and held as if in thrall.

Because today's near-drowning, so inconsequential in the overall scheme of things (especially given the lives involved), was also clearly part of a much larger tapestry. What had happened before would happen again. There was no escaping it.

And as if out of the blue a voice deep inside immediately urged Joe to "Leave. Leave now. You are healed."

And for a scary moment he wondered where the hell that had come from. What 'voice' was he hearing now? Was it his id finally telling him something he didn't already know: that this near-death experience was exactly the sort of shock therapy he needed to end the decade-long depression? It seemed to be both an offer of hope and a warning…

7.31am, Casa del Fibro, Friday 13th March

Barbara, Julie and Joe strolled the hundred metres home through the rainforest and along Redemption Road's grassy footpath to Casa del Fibro in silence. As if they still couldn't quite believe it. Frankly they were just too buggered to talk. The experience of almost dying simply too overwhelming. Leaving each lost in his/her own thoughts. Of what might have been. And how easily it can happen.

And in the back garden as they showered off under a hose, there was a moment when again, nothing was said.

Then they just broke off what they were doing and, as if in a daze, hugged each other, forming a scrum. Reassuring themselves, with this primordial holding-on, that they still existed. No matter that the world knew nothing of their ordeal. A hug reinforced the obvious: that being alive was about having a body that could feel and touch and still get goose bumps. And that was really as close as you got to anybody anyway- while you still could. It was what separated us absolutely from the inanimate world- the cosmos of waves and stones.

Finally, Julie laughed and broke off, standing back a little. "If this was town, people might think we were a bunch of Pathsandras."

Joe and Barbara laughed with her. The devotees of the Smiling Swami seemed to spend quite a lot of time holding each other up in public. Almost as if, whenever they met, instead of shaking hands Pathsandras fell into this deep embrace, forgot where they were, and sort of…went to sleep, gracefully, in each others' arms. It was something Joe always caught himself sniggering at and now thought it was the funniest thing he had ever heard Julie say.

JUMP FORWARD TO:

6

'ON GOLDEN SANDS'

Just another 'big' Easter crowd on popular Purgatory
Beach—enjoying a colourful bodysurf in crystal clear water
the temperature of chilled champagne. Come to the Rainbow
Coast and discover a place where the hardest thing to bear
is that stab of awe you get as its pristine beauty simply takes
your breath away.

*Affix
stamp
here*

© paulmdavies@bigpond.com.au

printed on gently mulched, plantation-grown, organic bamboo fibre using
recycled greywater and bound with a biodegradable non-toxic glue

No animal or dolphin suffered in the making of this card
(apart from, of course, its author)

6
'ON GOLDEN SANDS'
"It's irritation that produces the pearl."
(Gra'eme *The Bloke Who Spoke In Jokes*)

7.40am, Casa del Fibro, Friday 13th March

Joe's hand still trembled slightly as he sprinkled fat busting lecithin (mother nature's little internal detergent) on chilled mango and passionfruit. An industrial strength, double caff, whole milk cappuccino was already on its way- straight after the wheatgrass and Echinacea (for that extra 'private' health insurance).

He was even tempted this morning to ditch the low cholesterol cheese in favour of some real camembert on sour dough- both to 'toast' his survival, so to speak, as well as redress the feeling-smug factor from having sacrificed so diligently (for nearly a whole year now) at the altar of his body temple. Too much of a good thing had to be bad for you, Joe reasoned in a Gra'eme-ish sort of way, convinced now that there was no need to be a slave to blooming good health all his life.

Since it was also the last birthday of his middle-middle age, Joe was wisely toying with the idea of starting a daily aspirin regime- as recommended by his GP, Dr. Beanland. But decided to hold off for another year and perhaps do it on his next birthday: the big 5-Oh! Opting not to risk the digestive problems and kidney damage aspirin would bring with it- for the moment at least. Figuring his decaying cardiovascular system could take it on the chin for another 12 months, no probs.

Alas, nothing could have been further from the truth.

That aspirin was needed now! Along with copious amounts of whatever cholesterol lowering drugs Joe might reasonably get hold of. Because, thanks to the hyper anxiety of nearly drowning this morning, a tiny particle of plaque (ancient fat cemented together with smoke, salt and sugar particles) had just broken off in a blood vessel near his groin and was currently making its life-threatening journey through hundreds of kilometres of ravaged veins and arteries.

As soon as this foul globule reached his heart a myocardial infarct could virtually be guaranteed. Effectively, a biochemical time bomb had just begun ticking inside Joe of which the overweight hypochondriac was blissfully unaware. From this very moment, Joseph Michael Deegan of 13 Redemption Road, Heaven, UStraylia, sex god and couldabeen minor playwright, was living on borrowed time. One more serious fright or sudden bit of bad news and the Joe Deegan story would be in the remainder bin. The prospect of him exhibiting witchhood credentials in the timing of his life's entrance and exit was firmly back on track.

Yet, because it *was* his birthday, Joe falsely believed that he had licence to let his hair down. More so than usual. He'd survived a potentially fatal drowning, what else could go wrong? If there were any little twinges of angina rearing their ugly head he would always pretend it was indigestion and even (catastrophically) console himself with a 'cardio-protective' glass or three of red wine before lunch- all unadulterated, self-deception. As was the idea of an early joint on account of feeling so good about things generally. (More ammunition with which to shoot himself!)

In the self interest of his body temple Joe tried to follow a high carb, low fat, quasi-vegetarian regime with minimal dairy products. The general idea being to try to live as long as possible in the most robust condition achievable, somewhere within breathing and drinking distance of a clean environment. There was no point finding Paradise on Earth if you couldn't enjoy it. And while the camembert today was a minor relapse, here again Joe was only following Gra'eme's general prescription of: "All things in moderation- including moderation" (see *'Minding' The Body Temple*)

"And some things," Joe would add, smiling.

"And other clichés," retorted Barbara whenever Joe tried to use it as an excuse for his many shortcomings in this regard.

The TV hack also liked Ronnie Rainbow's ayurvedic approach, believing that it didn't really matter what you ate as long as you did so under relatively stress-free circumstances. Such as could easily be wiped out by an argument with Barbara (involving an updated litany of all the many things he still did that were bad for him).

…Or by the radio news, which at breakfast this morning was not particularly calming. It appeared that a chicken was singing like a quail after scientists had transplanted part of a quail's brain into the chicken's head. Why this was news or even necessary remained troublingly unclarified. Elsewhere, in some poor blighted corner of the 'developing' (sic) world, escaped convicts were returning to their cells after a mass break out. They'd quickly come to realise that liberty in a state of rampant market forces was far worse than being locked up in prison. The only trouble now was that their guards had also fled and there was no food left in the prison (whether good for you or otherwise).

Joe killed the radio, went out to his guestroom/study/library/archive, and promptly booted up his computer, as always, on the dot of:

FLASH CUT TO CLOSE UP OF CLOCK SHOWING:
7.47am, Casa Del Fibro, Friday 13th March

…where Joe is putting on his metallic vest and turning the screen at a slight angle to avoid the full carcinogenic effect of its electromagnetic field.

Barbara and Julie, having missed their Tai Chi at *Cosmic Bodyworx* opted for Plan B and had already driven off in Rusty to a Yogalates session, allowing Joe to get on with his daily half hour of actual 'work' (sic).

Of course he could easily have given himself a day off (it was his birthday after all). But switching on the computer at 13 minutes to 8 was the one disciplined element in an otherwise pretty loose routine. And half an hour was usually enough time to write a couple of scenes for *On Golden Sands.* Which netted (before tax and after his accountant's retainer) the princely sum of 100 sad looking, if not actually depressed Aussie doleurs. This was approximately what Joe needed to pay the bills, keep the mortgage bound and gagged, and maintain for himself what Gra'eme claimed was a 'revenue neutral' situation. Not a large sum by any means, not even an average income by most people's standards (despite its untested legality). But sufficient to keep body and soul together in Heaven. Which only proved, yet again, that you can't *buy* happiness. It's an attitudinal thing. Besides which, contentment in Heaven was an essential part of the town's social amenity. And that meant it came for free.

Nor was scribbling soap operas likely to win anyone the Nobel Prize for Literature. In fact it was only marginally better than writing sitcoms where you could hear the ghost of the joke committee behind every line. But soaps happened to be the only thing Joe was any good at- apart from body surfing and making love. In fact, he'd penned so much crappy dialogue since Kate died that his actual handwriting could now officially be described as 'missing in action'. Virtually indecipherable. Something that came in handy at *On Golden Sands* script conferences where the frustrated wordsmith often seared his dissatisfaction with Craig Huxtable into his note pad, committing actual venom to paper while appearing to be dutifully taking notes.

Such jottings eventually joined the millions of pages slipped into folders in his filing cabinet until finally transferred out (when the cabinet became full) into the hundred or so wine cartons stacked unsafely around the walls of the guestroom/study/library/archive. These pages were a direct by-product of carrying, at all times, a small notebook in the top left-hand pocket of his Hawaiian shirt and pouring every snippet of idea or overheard fragment of conversation into it (not trusting his memory).

The accretion of paper from this obsessional behaviour now took up nearly half the cubic volume of the guestroom/study/library/archive. Thus banishing 'Rusty', their ancient Datsun, to weather Heaven's corrosive salt air out on the footpath. Something Barbara wasn't terribly happy about. She needed the car to facilitate her social life and threatened, quite openly, to burn most of this *'stuff'* as soon as he died (Joe, not the car). Always assuming of course, that a) Joe would go before her (and Rusty), and b) that the army of white ants marching up from the murdered forest under the slab floor didn't get to Joe's pearls of wisdom first. Which they now were, having already found the damp lower boxes at the back- the ones against the wall where the leak from the broken gutter was growing worse. Boxes Joe hadn't actually sighted for nearly a decade.

As Gra'eme so wisely pointed out- it was 'Leisure' that had fashioned 'Civilisation' in the first place (see *An Excessory After The Fact*). Culture couldn't happen unless people had a lot of time to sit down and think, listen to good music, drink great coffee/wine and engage in humorous, idle chit-chat on a back deck with terrific views.

But none of this was getting today's workload shifted. Not a big ask, Joe realised, as he glanced over the storyline handed down to him by Craig Huxtable and Carmel Savage (Craig's senior script editor). Thirty minutes of adding dialogue to that lot was about all it should take. And Joe was a realist when it came to calculating time needed for anything. He had to be. Because Time was the rough clay from which he shaped each Beautiful Day. His one enduring, if selfish masterpiece.

On Golden Sands was the saga of a bunch of unfaithful, and invariably tanned young fashion designers, merchant bankers, life savers, interior decorators, hairdressers, fashion models, golf pros and meter maids- the sort of movers and shakers (people in linen suits, panama hats and gold bikinis) who had made Surface Paradox what it was today: a shameless quagmire of built environments and very little that is natural apart from some of the more disturbing fungal growths inside its myriad air conditioning systems. The tragic and toxic outcome of a decades-long stampede by various battalions of the get-rich-quick brigade.

One of the more positive reviewers called *On Golden Sands* "A hopeless hodge-podge of dreadful acting, ludicrous plotlines and sleazy direction with atrocious dialogue. So bad it wasn't even laughable. In short- appalling television."

As for the actual sands of this once golden Cold Coast- these were not only pretty permanently in the shadow of that unrestrained spread of highrise, but had to be mechanically replaced by an offshore barge as soon as there was any kind of storm. At considerable expense to the current rate payers. The original 'developers' having long since disappeared along with their vast profits. It was strange and fairly character building to discover that a place so narcissistically entranced by its own self-image could have turned out to be so monumentally ugly.

Nor was it any real surprise for Joe to discover that the characters in *On Golden Sands* were unanimously good looking, immaculately groomed, mobile-phoned, shoulder-padded, empty-headed and completely ruthless. By the time he'd received his first contract from Craig, all of the dozen or so main characters had slept with, stabbed in the back, menaced, cheated, lied to, emotionally abused, denigrated, detested, shamelessly manipulated, cursed, or comprehensively betrayed every other character in the show- at least once. In other words, the narrative content was a fairly accurate mirror, even an almost documentary record of the moral behaviour animating the team that produced it.

Fortunately, nothing in the tide of human affairs has ever gone completely according to plan. Not even a Network programmer's. Doubt still had a purchase on things. We were fallible mortals after all and our fantasies of order and control always came unstuck. Monarchs, Corporations, Empires, Religions, Philosophies, Scientific Orthodoxies, Time Share Deals and even Soap Operas all eventually folded or sued for bankruptcy. Thank Gaia, thought Joe.

For example, inside the slick, unreal world of *On Golden Sands* a troubling uncertainty had recently entered the narrative equation. The problem was quite simple: having exhausted their spite and vented their spleen on each other (in so many fascinating, degrading and amazingly destructive ways), the limited range of plot possibilities in a universe as morally constipated as the one peopled by the corporate elite of Surface Paradox was such that, basically, and at a very fundamental level, these shameless monsters suddenly had nowhere else to go! There was little more that the principals could say or do to each other that hadn't already been done or inferred, insinuated or bellowed across a dining or boardroom table. Unless, of course, everyone just returned to the plot-line of episode one and started filming themselves backstabbing each other all over again.

Smirk as one might, for story editors like Craig Huxtable this was not beyond the realms of possibility. And indeed, in their desperation, Craig and Carmel had even pitched the idea of a repetition strategy to the Suits Upstairs, the cabal of former car salesmen who actually owned The Network. These men however, while sorely tempted by the possibility of eliminating writers altogether and just rehashing old scripts, couldn't quite bring themselves to embrace anything so…obvious. Plot recycling seemed just a bit too dodgy- even for the Suits- and would likely get them into a deep, contractual hell with the writer's union. So, The Network, in their wisdom, rejected the idea. (Obviously ignorant of the fact that this was what happened in all soap operas most of the time.)

Which left the *On Golden Sands* crew with only two options: either halt the bloodletting, call it a draw, and let the actors drift back to the various Reality (sic) TV series from whence they had come. Or make the characters actually behave nicely to each other. Deal with people in a positive, ennobling, uplifting sort of way and approach the world from a position of charitable concern, sweetened by an interest in the Common Good.

However, just throwing away the show (and the sets and the expensive props and costumes) didn't seem like a terrifically cost efficient option. Not to mention the investment in the 'stars' publicity campaigns. Despite the critical thumbs down the Men In Suits knew that *On Golden Sands* captured an important demographic: namely, the wretched insomniacs prepared to wait up until the show's 11 pm or post-midnight timeslot. Such viewers were obviously the social misfits, wired loners, burglars, taxi drivers, shift workers and drug addicts who needed the softer beds, more powerful depressants, and all sorts of appalling fast food with which the *OGS* ad breaks were peppered.

Just *when* exactly, *Golden Sands* went to air largely depended on the footy game or sporting event preceding it. Occasionally, if the match went overtime, the show didn't appear at all. It was *that* highly regarded by its owners.

Still, The Network's wish was a story editor's command. And consequently, Craig Huxtable, forced to find the basic good in people, proceeded to have a very loud, very expensive, and very nervous breakdown.

RIPPLE DISSOVLE OUT TO

IGNORING MT LOOKOUT!

Nestled in the colourful Limbo Valley and extinct as a volcano for 29 million years, **HEAVEN**'s magnificent Mt Lookout! contains at its core the southern hemisphere's largest crystal—an appropriate cornerstone for the Enchanted Triangle and a direct source of so much of the Rainbow Coast's cosmic healing energy.

Affix stamp here

#7 of 33 Postcards from Heaven

printed on gently mulched, plantation-grown, organic bamboo fibre using recycled greywater and bound with a biodegradable non-toxic glue

No animal or dolphin suffered in the making of this card
(apart from, of course, its author)

IGNORING MT. LOOKOUT!

"If music be the food of love then doof and fairly mindless percussion
must be the broken wind that follows"
(Gra'eme *Towards A Stock Exchange Of Principles*)

8.03am Casa del Fibro Friday 13th March

Joe had crossed swords (pencils? keyboards?) with the tormented mindset of Craig Huxtable over many years of frontline scriptwriting. Craig had a background in sports journalism and valium dependence and was still lunching off the kudos of having devised the most watched and most *hated* game show on Scottish television.

Yet here was a man, desperately needing to be put out to pasture, and still getting migraines from the awful tripe he had to dream up in order to keep the *On Golden Sands* juggernaut lurching along in a vaguely forward direction while pulling ratings the Men In Suits could live with. Up till now it had been a matter of finding ever more improbable acts of human malevolence and bastardry. From now on it would have to be acts sweetened with the milk of human kindness. And, given the characters available with locked in contracts, that prospect was truly daunting. In fact, Craig's long-term hopes for the show were now collapsing faster than penthouse prices during one of the Cold Coast's many 'market corrections'. It was around this time that Joe started to lose his initial enthusiasm for *On Golden Sands.*

Fortunately, The Network couldn't explain what it wanted from any given set of characters. It couldn't concoct a credible storyline or tell a writer what, or how to write. Which, thank Gaia, was why scribblers-for-a-living like Joe were still necessary. (And until computers developed souls he believed would remain so.) All the Men In Suits wanted was another huge, nation-wide success. Yet nobody could predict (despite some feeble computerised attempts), exactly where the next million-dollar riff of setting and characters destined to fire up the remote controls in Western Sydney and Eastern Melbourne would come from. In theory at least, anything was still possible.

But the Men In Suits knew what they *didn't* like- and they didn't like it just as soon as a writer gave it to them. Then they knew they hated it. What to replace *that* with however was the eternal structural flaw inherent in the whole television script equation. Usually it meant that most episodes of any drama series got feverishly rewritten by teams of in-house script editors in a hopeless attempt to meet production deadlines and keep the cameras and their expensive crews in some semblance of motion (and away from the bottle shop before lunch). Thus had scriptwriters become merely a kind of point scout for a creativity-by-committee exercise. This was the brave new world of future yarn spinning for massed medias in which Joe Deegan soiled for his living.

And like most of his peers, the wannabe screen playwright absorbed the humiliation and meekly faxed off his invoices. Swallowing his pride along with all the other artificial stimulants and pharmaceutical crutches needed to get through another brain and eyesight damaging half hour in front of his alzheimic computer.

The Suits, for their part, hated the fact they were dependent on anything. Especially such an unruly, untamed and congenitally anarchistic bunch of dialogue crunching substance abusers. But there was even a larger fear troubling them and one which, in their dull way, the Men In Suits probably weren't even fully conscious of. Namely: that writers were also a bit of an embarrassment to the whole process.

The Suits would have preferred audiences to believe that their overpaid performers made up the dialogue themselves- which to anybody who knew anything about actors or writing was a pretty laughable proposition. Almost all 'stars' were barely capable of forging their own Logie award nominations- let alone entertain something so delicate and complex as an actual dramatic idea. One only had to look at the abysmal failure of most improvised film/theatre to realise, Joe realised, that this was an idea whose future was about as limited as the concentration span of a Network Programmer - the sole link in the chain even dimmer and more paranoid than the Suits themselves.

And here again, was another great paradox: why, despite the flood of magazines dealing with the subject, so little real information filtered through to the viewing public about what actually went on in television. Amongst the endless nonsense about the actors 'personal lives' and who was sleeping with whom or what, almost nothing of any substance was conveyed about anything (see Gra'eme's *The Dis-information Age*).

In any case, the Suits needn't have worried, because most audiences *did* believe the characters made up the words themselves. (Thank Gaia again, thought Joe, who would have hated being recognised in the street all the time like some poor actors he knew.) All of which suited the Men In Suits just fine. In fact, they aided and abetted the anonymity of their writers, freezing them permanently out of the lime light. The Network certainly didn't want a second tier star system built around rum swilling, pot smoking, pill popping, caffeine addicted scumbags. As far as stardom went only actors need apply- preferably ones with magazine cover good looks, limited self knowledge, and tame agents.

Consequently, having to suffer through a script conference with Craig Huxtable was a bit like being trapped in some endless car journey where the radio was permanently stuck on Redneck FM. Here was a man who had crafted programmes which people *loved to hate*. And, stressed out by this looming crisis of having to find uplifting stories, whenever Craig couldn't get his way in a script conference these days he tended to get down under the plotting table and howl like a dingo.

Which meant he tended to get his way.

Although, whenever the barking started, the girls in the production office (who actually ran the show) began to wonder if a stint in the Script Department was the sort of career move they really wanted. The last time Joe witnessed Craig sucking the lino and whining under the table he also began to wonder what *he* was doing with his life- to his sense of self respect, by working here. Excuse me? Was he missing something? Why had he again put himself through the ritual humiliation of a job in television? After such a promising start with Kate in a theatre where he could say what he liked and get paid very little for it.

Joe could have been a minor playwright and still intended to pen the great UStraylian Feature Film. Yet here he remained, frittering away what little was left of his talent (and his eyesight), patching together dialogues for shallow characters in a competition-driven, two-dimensional world. The only convincing excuse he could find as to *why* he persisted in demeaning himself like this was, well... frankly, that he was doing it for the money. And any hard currency (Joe had to agree with Gra'eme) was a peace treaty in the war that constantly lies in readiness beneath the veneer of any 'civilised' society (see *Smart Money*).

Although he also believed- again with Gra'eme's whole hearted consent- that war was unnatural and that deep down, humans didn't fundamentally want to kill each other (unless they were fundamentalists or killers- frequently both). And that, for any other species to do so was tantamount to pretty rapid extinction. Gra'eme went on to point out that money also actually allowed one to obtain certain goods and services without having to bludgeon them out of any potential supplier by a greater show of force. A symbolic acceptance of the need to be *nice* to each other. (see *Nail Biting For Cannibals*).

Gra'eme went on to argue that money had also (thanks to its offspring, 'Leisure') allowed 'Culture' to flourish, and as such, had been humanity's greatest invention- even more important than fire, the wheel, internal combustion, or the banana lounge.

"There's nothing intrinsically wrong with having cold hard cash," agreed the disgraced former corporate auditor, "except that, the pursuit of loot is also the direct cause of most people's downfall. Thus establishing the curious paradox that the more we got of the stuff the less content we seemed to become. In fact, all that great fortunes really produce are debilitating anxieties about how to keep them." (see *12 Steps To True Happiness)*

And avoiding any kind of anxiety, as far as Joe was concerned, was now what his main goal in life basically boiled down to. As Gra'eme constantly reminded him in their many workshops: "The line between wealth and happiness is always a fine one, but still worth pursuing. Everyone has their price, Joe…few are called, but many are cheapened."

And so, and thus, as soon as Joe re-read Craig's crazy plotline and contemplated the creative task confronting him on his forty ninth birthday (the scene where Jason and Samantha, the happily married investment banker couple, explore their rivalry for the new lifesaver Damien Prendergast, in all its gory detail- prior to separately betraying him shortly afterwards), the couldabeen minor playwright was hit by a sudden feeling that earning a living today would take slightly longer than the allotted half hour (broken down into two 15 minute sessions separated by some Lite Gardening and a Little Lie Down).

Three wordless minutes later Joe put the computer to sleep, took off his protective metallic vest and gave up on Jason, Samantha and Damien's complex sexual dilemma. Resolving their ludicrous problem required a little Smoko In The Hammock. It was the only place Joe could feel really good about himself again. He took a pre-lunch stubby from the back fridge, rolled a small spliff, and settled into his favourite piece of furniture with all the familiarity of a hermit crab returning to its shell. Besides which, while drugs in sport may well be a 'no no', drugs in writing were virtually a compulsory pre-requisite. Like it or not, hearing dialogue in your head and channeling it onto paper was, on the face it, a pretty mentally hazardous occupation. And looked a lot like schizophrenia (from the outside).

And so, and thus, as he lit the smoke and kicked off from the edge of the deck, swaying back and forth, Joe felt about as comfortable as a lawyer taking a retainer from a vexatious litigant. He couldn't help harking back to a time when having a birthday was something you actually looked forward to. And he appreciated, yet again, how little had gone wrong with his childhood- apart from his parents, his over eating problem, the recurrent boils, and just about everything to do with his boarding school. Was it the security of growing up in a home where buying Arthur Mee's *Children's Encyclopedia* could somehow be seen as a genuine investment in a child's future?

Pulling Volume Eleven down recently from a bookshelf in the guestroom/study/ library/archive and glancing through it again after 38 years, it all seemed so end of an era- so flags of vanished colonies and merchant navies and great steam engines thrusting across wide superior bridges built to a meccano precision. All that Shakespeare and English nursery rhymes; all that weird old Anglo Saxon world order so out of date now on a planet where the sun quite frequently set on the British Empire.

In 1961 (the year you could write upside down), the largest building on the Cold Coast was the two storey Surface Paradox Hotel. Most of the town's permanent dwellings at that time were simple fibro cottages of the classic box shape. Their basic rectangles and low, sloping asbestos roofs, an honest expression of fishing-and-drinking-class architecture. And when Joe thought about it, he realised this was precisely the kind of house he had ended up in himself- strangely enough. Mainly because 13 Redemption Road was so cheap; but also because it had been implanted there in his subconscious- as a thing worth having, perhaps? A rusted-on cache of nostalgia for a happy time. Precious 'sun'days when you could still stroll down virtually any street in Surface without getting mugged.

Not surprisingly, after nearly half a century of unrestrained boom/bust growth the glittering yellow sands of this Cold Coast were now almost gone; and the once golden tans now playgrounds for melanomas. The original string of beachside villages had become one vast, under planned, badly resourced, overcrowded megalopolis: a place of purple fountains, themed shopping malls, and hundreds of high rise buildings perched precipitously on its precious frontal dune system.

At least in Nullumbah Shire there was still a coast worth saving (and mercifully, no building over three storeys high). Yet it was also curious how Joe's life kept going round in circles like this. Curious that he had ended up living in a place so close to the ocean, writing soap operas set in his long vanished, childhood arcadia. A place he visited with his parents many times. And now a seaside fantasyland where the tyranny of the concrete cave and the architect's set square had gone mad. Where sirens in high heels and little else called families to their doom in some dodgy time share scam: the ultimate unReal Estate. As if buying or selling, let alone 'sharing' time, was cosmically possible, or even desirable.

And as he rocked back and forth in his hammock, puffing quietly, Joe flashed on a future where Gaia would have her just revenge on this vapid Cold Coast. A time when nearby Woolumbin (dormant as a volcano for 20 million years) eventually re-erupted and spewed out purgative lava, turning the Venice of the Southern Hemisphere into its Pompeii; completely obliterating this shabby Sodom by the sea and burying its buyers and sellers of time inside a geological 'time capsule' available for much later archaeologists to marvel at and deplore.

What *would* future generations make of the imitation, full-size plastic replicas of Renaissance masterpieces standing so incongruously with their figleafs in the middle of muzak washed plazas? Of the monorail to nowhere? Of the huge expanse of underground car parks? Of the eight lane highway cutting right through the middle of the place, not to mention the 45 storey dwellings with imitation chimneys and gable roofs on top?

Fortunately, Heaven was safe from that kind of mega over-development. For the time being at least, its residents believed that their general low profile, lack of services, or any proper public infrastructure- along with rumours of its toxic past, would keep the Rainbow Coast safe from a virus that contained purple fountains and pointless monorails. In their simple country way, the green warriors of Nullumbah Shire firmly believed the infection could be stopped around Kingscliff or Pottsville- just south of the Queensland border.

However, as Gra'eme also understood and so eloquently pointed out: there's nothing 'real' about real estate anywhere." (*Guilty Bystanders*)

BLUR OUT TO:

8

MEN WHO WANT TO MAKE A COMMITMENT

Just another visiting couple enjoying the colourful
health benefits of **HEAVEN**'s demineralised sands—the
valuable radioactive elements having all been extracted
by sandmining many years ago and concentrated in toxic
stockpiles on only a few public areas. (**NB:** Limited exposure
to radioactive sites during normal holiday visits is unlikely to
have long-term health effects.)

*Affix
stamp
here*

#8 of 33 Postcards from Heaven

printed on gently mulched, plantation-grown, organic bamboo fibre using
recycled greywater and bound with a biodegradable non-toxic glue

No animal or dolphin suffered in the making of this card
(apart from, of course, its author)

8

MEN WHO WANT TO MAKE A COMMITMENT

"If evolution's so great how come fish still get caught ?
Can't they *see* the hook inside the bait?
Haven't they WOKEN UP! yet? "
(Gra'eme *Save The Shark*)

8.21am Casa del Fibro Friday 13th March

It was only after Joe had ashed the spliff and made a third, industrial-strength, triple cream, maxi-caff cappuccino, that he realised the cavortings of young, thirty-something yuppies along with their artificially crazy and fractious sex lives, was slipping well beyond him; and that he would probably find it difficult, if not impossible to keep writing this stuff in his fifties. It was time to admit defeat and pack it in for the day. This was his birthday after all. Samantha, Jason and Damien's ridiculous *ménage a trois* would have to suppurate until Joe was good and ready for it. Fortunately, creativity (or in this case, regurgitated dialogue) couldn't just be turned on and off like a tap. But such a pleasant thought was shattered by an unwelcome intruder:

"Anybody home?"

It was Onecoat Kev, scratching his head and smirking down at Joe with barely suppressed innuendo.

"What's going on?!" Joe spluttered as he quickly rolled out of the hammock, almost spilling his coffee, flustered by the sudden invasion of his privacy. He could easily have been still puffing the joint.

A good mate of Sergeant Doreen Harris, Kev was known to dob in people with plants. It was the stickybeak in him that lead Onecoat to his part-time postal career in the first place. An under-achiever of an order even higher (or lower) than Joe, the all-purpose handyman had never come across a wall, ceiling or floor that needed two coats of paint. And like most tradies, Kev was unparalleled in his ability to take longer than any one else to either, a) arrive for a job or b) go, when it was finished. His excuse that too many days of the week started with the same letter just didn't wash with Joe anymore. Even if they learnt that sort of excuse as apprentices.

"Sorry to disturb you, mate," Kev lied, "but your mail box seems to have been decapitated."

Joe nearly had his heart attack there and then, dislodging a wedge of badly digested toast. The mailbox was a small, hollow gnome called 'Larry'. Joe had sawed a hole in Larry's mouth to fit letters through and taken a patch out of his backside to retrieve them from. Bewildered and incredulous, he hurried around the front of Casa del Fibro (keen to draw the prying postie away from the barely disguised 12 Apostles)…and sure enough, right on the pedestal Joe had built for him, there remained only Larry's body from the neck down.

"Three boxes got vandalised in Sinners Street last week." Kev smiled, warming to his role as the bearer of ill tidings. "We don't have to deliver if there's no actual receptacle on the property- but I knew you wouldn't want to miss your latest masterpiece from *On Golden Sands*."

Joe glanced down at the large parcel Kev now placed in his hands- the 'release' script of an episode he had written many months ago. But its author was still reeling. A headless gnome is an appalling sight.

"I don't get it!" Joe stammered. "Why would anybody *do* this? To a mailbox fercrissake? "

"Kids probably," speculated Kev. "Or somebody from the Gnome Liberation Front."

"The what?" Joe was still reeling.

"Well they don't like people vandalising gnomes by sawing into their mouths and backsides. They're fanatics, Joe. They'll do practically anything to free a gnome from a cruel owner." Kev looked reprovingly at what was left of Larry.

"Geezus !"

"Probably kids though…" Kev tried to reassure him. "Usually happens during the holidays. They get bored, of course. With Easter just around the corner the single mums sort of give up and let the boys run wild- like last Halloween- when Mrs. Geogharty had to be taken to hospital."

Kev was scratching his head again, staring at his thongs, resting his restless hands in the pockets of his footy shorts, not up to wearing a postie uniform even- apart from the cap with its fluorescent yellow band.

"So…what? Some bloody juvenile delinquent, with no father figure to instill any discipline, comes up and mutilates your mail box and that's it?" Joe couldn't fathom the complete mindlessness of it.

"Yeah, I guess UStraylia Post is like a kind of…I dunno, an authority thing to them? Something they can lash out at?"

Kev slid back his cap, scratching his head again. Reaching the limits of his knowledge (which wasn't very far). "Like the government or big companies and all that …"

Joe tried to look blank. What the government or megalithic and often dehumanising global corporations had to do with Larry's headlessness would be opening Kev, unqualified tradesman and right wing conspiracy theorist, up to an interminable and lunatic discussion which Joe, at this point in his Beautiful Birthday, was completely uninterested in pursuing.

"I don't think it's got anything to do with Larry personally," the incompetent postie speculated. "Sometimes I think the little buggers just have a bad day at school, you know?"- still trying to rule out unilateral intervention by the Gnome Liberation Front.

Then Kev shrugged as if there could ultimately *be* no logic to it. "Anyway, it makes my job easier. We don't have to deliver if there's nothing to put the mail in,"- repeating it, making it sound like he was doing Joe a really Big Favour and wasn't just using it as an excuse to poke his nose into another person's backyard.

Joe was stewing over the fact that he would now have to waste as much as half an hour locating and organising a new mailbox.

"I liked the scene where Jason and Samantha get married," Kev lingered, trying to look on a brighter side, indicating the parcel Joe was still absently holding. "Fancy a gay bloke shackin' up with the show's resident princess. That's brilliant. I'll bet he falls for that new Damien fella… "

Then a spurt of inspiration:" what if Samantha fell for Damien too? Geeze that would set the cat among the magpies… I reckon I could write that show, mate. What do you think?"

As if to make a point Joe took the rest of the junk mail Kev was holding out and dropped it straight into Otto's recycling compartment (still standing there beside the front shed, unclaimed and unemptied).

Then, about to turn back inside, Joe used the opportunity to download a problem which had been nagging him for months: "Kev, that information about the show in the release script is supposed to be confidential. We all know you read our mail, that's okay- so long as you put it in the right box. But please, think of my position if the soapie magazines got wind of what was going to happen next week in *On Golden Sands*. I could lose my job." Joe pleaded, not unreasonably. Unaware that it was about to slip from his grasp anyway.

Kev stared at the ground and shuffled a little, looking sheepish and feeling a touch guilty. But not really. "Sorry, mate," he repented, assuming a familiarity that didn't exist. Then on a brighter note: "I've got a cousin who's a chippie, could whip you up a nice new mail box in no time- same colour and shape as your house. Trev takes a photo and makes a small replica. They're very popular over in Nullumbah." Kev malingered in the driveway like a Telco salesman who can't believe you're knocking back their fabulous Special Deal.

But Joe was too angry to even bother answering. What should have been another pleasant morning was turning into something of a pain in the arse.

'Find a new mail box'

would now have to go up on the corkboard containing the list of all the chores he was supposed to carry out but rarely got around to. It was amazing how easily 'urgent priorities' got relegated sideways to columns headed 'sometime soon', or 'maybe next month', or 'this year, definitely'.

"Oh well, better make like a nut and bolt," Kev chuckled as he finally got the message, climbed back into his ute and drove next door to Old Frank's place to have a few beers and a bit of a chat with Filthy Mick- where he would lose the rest of today's undelivered mail as the Utta Bastards checked all the rest of the envelopes for cash (especially anything that looked like a grandparent's birthday card.)

The disturbing thought now clouded Joe's mind that Kev and his carpenter relative might be perpetrating some kind of mailbox extortion racket (recruiting vandals like Wayne Wilson to hasten the need). But Joe realised instinctively this was going to be rather difficult to prove. Assuming there *was* some sort of scam going on... Unless he was just being paranoid... Always a worry after you'd had a smoke. But then, as Gra'eme pointed out: "Who's to say that in an increasingly illogical, dispassionate and digitised world, the hyper-suspicious and fearful aren't always pretty well spot on?" (see *Just Because You're Paranoid Doesn't Mean They're Not Out To Get You)*

SLAM CUT TO:

8.30am, Casa del Fibro, Friday 13th March

Joe stormed back into his guestroom/study/library/archive where he had been trying to work until interrupted by, firstly the desire to have a smoko in the hammock, and then Kev. Here he stared glumly at his precious archives: the wall of wine cartons that contained virtually everything he had ever committed to paper and which tottered dangerously over the uncomfortable guest mattress. Various articles of Julie's clothing were hanging all round the place- tucked into crevices in the columns of boxes like messages to God at the Wailing Wall.

The couldabeen minor playwright paced up and down in the narrow strip between the mattress and his stacks of paper (trying not to slip on Julie's scattered rolls of lipstick), stewing over the fact that somebody would actually bother to mutilate Larry.

Eventually he sat down at his computer again, pausing briefly over the view out through the side door, which had banged open again after he'd tried to slam it shut. Inspired and settled by the leafy green coolness of his humble backyard, Joe determined finally to put this stupid imbroglio with Jason, Samantha and Damien behind him and get on with the rest of his life.

While the computer was waking up! again, a chainsaw started low in the background, its constant dreary whine soon overwhelming the kookaburras and currawongs as they screeched back at the noise in intense disapproval. Oh great, thought Joe. He always found it impossible to work with any sort of mechanical noise going on and turned instead to the release script of episode 1113 that Kev had just given him. It seemed like ages since Joe had penned Jason and Samantha's ludicrous marriage vows. But was it really that long ago- or just so forgettable?

Out of a kind of idle curiosity (not at all related to ego) Joe skimmed over the cover page with his name on it, and then glanced at the opening scene, figuring his short term memory must be getting worse than he'd realised. Absolutely *none* of the dialogue in the first three pages was at all familiar- from *any* of the *two* whole drafts he'd been compelled to write by Carmel.

And, despite the ridiculous changes she demanded, Joe still took a lot of effort with episode 1113 as it was his first paying gig on the show- spending as much as an hour a day crafting a couple of these early scenes. What's more, although *On Golden Sands* wasn't exactly a comedy (until you stood outside it and saw it for what it really was), he'd even thrown in a couple of one-liners. Just to keep the 'zing' thing happening. To leaven the absurdity of the situations the characters (and their creators) found themselves in. Believing, as Gra'eme did, that comedy was "always about that sudden flash of truth buried inside the mundane." (see *The Man Who Lived Without Television)*

Strangely, not one of these jokes seemed to have made it to the release script. As he read on, Joe could hardly recognise any of the dialogue at all! It soon became obvious that, despite all the effort of him going through two whole rewrites, Carmel Savage had virtually changed the entire script- *again*- herself! Unfortunately, she was so deeply shallow that her knowledge of the common human feelings on which all soap opera thrived was about as limited as her insight into the plight of a family that had just been downsized by one of her father's many corporate take-over vehicles. Savage by name, savage by nurture.

Joe fumed and resumed pacing. How could Carmel understand that a lot of what a writer does is invisible? That a script is something going on in your head all the time- like an unshakeable tinnitus. Writing was an endless and sometimes exhausting internal debate. You were always adding, cutting, pre-empting, listening, reading, shaping and note taking. Writing is obsessional. And like all illnesses, patently damaging. The act itself had beginnings, middles and ends, with high palpitations and great rushes of creativity in between. Huge outpourings of words onto paper were followed inevitably by the dreaded 'Block'- not to mention those uncertain and troubling intervals when you think you're over the malady, but never are. So you backtrack a little and relapse into the fever again and you lose faith and you wonder who on earth could ever possibly be entertained by it? Let alone distracted by it long enough to sit still 'til the next ad break. Because, of course, the ego *is* involved. There's all that investment in research and feeling. All that personal expression. All the conflict, betrayal and deception that has to be imagined and dealt with tastefully. And you never quite get it out of your system- until it's irretrievably committed to the screen or the published page. And even then it lingers like a curse of what-could-have-been; if only you'd risen to the occasion. Or risen that day at all really…

Nor was it, of itself, so unusual that a script editor would come along at the end and completely change everything. A television hack had few rights in the matter. And you either got used to the fact and accepted it, or gave up. But Carmel Savage's final redraft of Joe's original version of Craig's appallingly vacuous storyline for Episode 1113 of *On Golden Sands* was so palpably awful, so lacking in sparkle, that even in Joe's hands, at the end of it's strange journey, it felt like a drab, mangled, stillborn thing. The dialogue had lost the wit and flair Joe poured into it. Carmel's end result was nothing more than a plodding regurgitation of Craig's very silly starting point. From whence Joe had tried to resuscitate it and breathe some semblance of life into it. He came to loathe the sight of his name on the front page. People would actually think he had actually written this chaff!

Not the audience of course. Thankfully, nobody watching television ever took the slightest notice of a writer's credit. But if Ronnie Rainbows was right and all our electromagnetic broadcasting would eventually be picked up by civilisations across the other end of the galaxy (millions of years from now), then these recurrent nocturnal emissions were a kind of radio-borne, electronic time capsule of who we are…and someday, were. It was chilling to speculate on what intelligent life forms far, far away in both time and space would make of Jason, Samantha and Damien's brainless mating dance.

Joe's place in the multiverse was at stake.

JUMP CUT TO:

Casa del Fibro, 11 minutes later…

Barbara and Julie returned from their Yogalates session in time to cop the full brunt of Joe's considerable sarcasm. On top of the near drowning barely an hour ago, his Beautiful Birthday was now being pretty comprehensively undermined by a full realisation of just how demeaning his 'job' really was.

"Look at this crap!" he thundered (unaware it was what Craig himself had said on first glimpsing Joe's second draft- before Carmel made it worse).

"I could have been a minor playwright. Savage and Huxtable have absolutely no idea."

For once, Barbara actually looked concerned. "Joe, calm down."

…While Julie went in to have a shower, not wanting to get involved. The whine of the chainsaw could be heard a bit further off in the gap of silence.

Barbara continued to study Joe. "It's all right, darling. Nothing matters, remember. *Golden Sandshoes* is crap anyway." She was being brutally frank and basically honest (but only in order to be kind- even if she couldn't get its title right).

"I know. But some things *do* matter," he insisted.

"No they don't."

"Yes they do."

"Not really- deep down- when it's all said and done," she sensibly pointed out, Sanmahdi-like.

"I can't accept that. That…that's just throwing it away," he whinged.

"Throwing what away?"

"All sorts of things that *do* matter."

"Bullshit."

"You can't believe that, Barbara. *You* matter…" He allowed a slight pause for dramatic effect. Then added: "…to me."

"Joe, look at me," she said; and he did, and fell in love with her all over again. *"Nothing* matters. Got it? In the overall scheme of things. You said it yourself: the Universe is unfolding perfectly, and there's not a single thing you or I, or anyone else can do about it."

Joe accepted defeat. Barbara was right. As always. And not only because she was re-quoting Gra'eme indirectly through something Joe had paraphrased to her earlier.

"Remember last New Year's Eve?" she reminded him. "Standing on top of Mt. Lookout!? We decided to 'let it all go'."

How could Joe forget that precious moment- even with his compromised memory. They'd made the three hour climb before dawn and as soon as the sun rose the fog lifted from Elysium Valley in great steaming columns, looking for all the world like ghosts swirling up and coalescing into dense mist- forming a cloud that soon covered the whole mountain. Confirming their resolution, sealing their deal.

"And you agreed, Joe. That's what we'd do: we'd let it *all* go. *On Shifting Shores* isn't worth having a heart attack over."

This was always a slight worry for Barbara. For both of them. But all Joe could see right now was the damage to his fragile sense of self worth. He even ignored the fact she *still* couldn't seem to get the show's title right.

"They've rewritten my entire episode."

"So what else is new?"

"But my name's on the script, Barbara, and I really made an effort with the first one."

"So take the money, honey, and run. You get paid handsomely for it."

'Handsome' wasn't quite how Joe would have phrased it. Paid 'plainly-with-no-make-up-and-looking-like-you-had-bad-acne-as-a-child-and-were-coming-down-with-some-rare-skin-disease' might have been nearer the mark. But he didn't want to get bogged down in semantics or actual dollar amounts.

"The point is, Barbara, they didn't even phone, you know, just to say 'by the way we're changing it'. No reasons, no consultation. It's like…writers…our work is constantly undervalued. We're just some kleenex tissue to be used up and thrown away."

"So try another TV show with more integrity."

"What makes you think there's any of them left?"

Barbara just threw him one of those looks- one of the ones he knew he had to be careful of. He was indulging his tendency to pessimism in all things. Taking the Irish view. Again. And Barbara knew it. And Joe knew it, and she knew he knew she knew he knew it.

So he tried to back peddle a bit by explaining: "I've sold my talent to the devil and I still can't get anything I've actually written on the screen! How fucked is that?"

"Then ring this Huxtable person and *tell* him how you feel." Barbara was impatient and somewhat distracted by Julie's shower which was running longer than a bad musical. Faint sobbing could be heard under it. Joe anticipated Barbara's concern and selfishly tried to deflect her attention back to *his* problem.

"I'm afraid of what I might say," he humbugged, whimping out as usual. Of course he baulked at the prospect of actually ringing a producer to register some dissatisfaction. Demanding any sort of rights in the matter could, of its very nature, ensure a self invitation onto the dreaded *Golden Sands* blacklist. But would it make any difference? If the universe was unfolding perfectly? And there was nothing anybody could do about it?

Given that what he was holding was the release script, then this bumpf was already in production, rendered immortal and about to make its electromagnetic way out into the cosmos towards the drama critics of Alpha Centuri where they would pay no royalties for watching it. Certainly nothing that Joe or his heirs and beneficiaries (if he had any) could get their hands on. The couldabeen minor playwright was certainly angry enough to make the call. But what would this achieve at such a late stage? Credibility? A small stand for individual hacks? A modest, halting shuffle forward for writers generally? Was it even worth trying if nothing mattered- ultimately- in the overall storyline of the universe?

"You can't put your emotions in a bottle, Joe. You said so yourself- that's how cancer starts," cajoled Barbara, reading his fears accurately.

Cancer was always a worry. It was splashed all through the gene pool on his mother's side; and ever since nursing Kate he'd seen the 'Big C' at close hand. He'd rather die than go through what his wife had to. Far, far better to go quickly in an accident, like his father- as seemed most likely. Especially given Joe's chronic clumsiness and underlying heart disease.

Meanwhile, Julie's shower kept up its record breaking run, the sobs more intermittent now. Barbara cast an anxious glance towards the drain pipe Joe had rigged to take grey water from the back shower into the garden- specifically via the 12 Apostles to Kate's poinsettia, which was now looking a trifle flooded. Julie was using a hell of a lot of one precious natural resource- even discounting the flood of tears she added to it. They were already on level 4 restrictions. Mid March this year and still no end to the drought.

"If you don't let The Network know you're unhappy, then how are things ever going to change?" Barbara added with that irritating talent she had for going straight to the obvious point. But Julie's unhappiness, on such vivid display, had a much greater claim on her attention. So Barbara went back inside to make the mid-morning, liver cleansing, dandysoychinos…leaving Joe to ponder his options.

With all this excitement another Little Lie Down was definitely called for, prior to the distinct likelihood of an early lunch involving at least a demi-carafe of quaffable red.

At which point, the distant chainsaw broke back into life again, making any sort of rest fairly problematic. Nevertheless, Joe climbed back into his hammock to make some plans. Any blue with Craig and Carmel over Ep. 1113 would severely curtail his brilliant career. But even if Joe didn't phone back straight away he would have to say something at the next script conference. To salvage some modicum of artistic credibility. On the upside, finding himself ungainfully employed again would certainly be the Wake Up! call he needed to get a Real Job. To make his mark and do his own thing at last. He'd forget television and go for that feature screenplay. Finally!

Or should he call a spade a bloody ugly implement for moving dirt and officially retire? Liberate that fifteen or twenty minutes of every Beautiful Day currently wasted on earning a living?

It was a tempting proposition. But unfortunately, after a career spent hovering from contract to contract, Joe had no super, no holiday pay, no 'entitlements' whatsoever to fall back on. Television scriptwriters never received any real royalties- apart from the minimum amount, paid out on signing the contract. Leaving the Men In Suits to clean up in perpetuity. In any case, as far a show's revenue profile went, the Network accountants always made sure that no local drama ever earnt more than it cost. Joe realised he had to invest in his own copyright for a change. Create his own 'royalties' - be the 'king' of his own income stream. Yet, whenever he attempted to broach the idea of 'investing' in some 'down time', his accountant was scathing:

FLASH BACK TO:

Utopia, **Mt. Lookout! A year or so ago…**

"My dear Joseph, if a person pulls up stumps and chucks in the towel at any point after their mid forties- either stops working voluntarily, or loses their job- it's statistically inevitable that s/he will *never* be offered a full time position again."

Gra'eme may have been (statistically) correct, but such a prospect seemed so wasteful of the collective human talent pool. Joe felt that, on the cusp of 50 himself, he was just reaching a certain creative peak (along with a fair amount of accumulated personal insight).

"Gra'eme, you know I value you enormously as an adviser and a friend," Joe flattered, "and I don't want to sound immodest, but at 48 I feel I'm just hitting my straps as a writer. I did the apprenticeship thing in my 20s. Almost established a 'voice' with the plays in my 30s. Then stood back and saw the faults (had a small nervous breakdown) in the early 40s. And now I feel more capable than ever- despite, or even perhaps because of, this whole mid-life shambles. Why should I be forced onto the scrap heap at the peak of my own personal golden period? Just when I've finally worked out what's it all about…"

Joe left a gap for Gra'eme to throw in a few complimentary remarks supporting that. When he failed to do so, the couldabeen minor playwright further prompted with: "I'd be throwing away the experiences of a lifetime…"

Gra'eme only shrugged, still not a 100% in agreement. But, after another embarrassing silence (from Joe's point of view), the Great Man finally felt compelled to offer something (since his latest invoice to Joe was currently in the mail):

"Look, I agree with you, Joseph, absolutely. I'm not saying it's a *good* thing that people are cut off in their prime. It just happens to be yet another example (as if more were needed) of how we're dooming ourselves as a species."

RIPPLE DISSOLVE FORWARD TO:

9.02am Casa del Fibro Friday 13th March

For all these reasons, Joe didn't make the call to Craig or Carmel. But just to be firm about it, he swore a pact with himself *never* to work for *On Golden Sands* ever again. If they offered him another contract he would tell them where to shove it, and given his gift for metaphors that would not be a pleasant place.

He kicked the hammock into a swinging motion and felt good about himself for the second time that day, breaking the news to Barbara as soon as she brought the dandysoychinos out onto the back deck. And he was absolutely delighted to find her onside for a change.

"Good, hooray at last! Now you can do that feature film you've always been talking about. The one where the earth stops."- Barbara, as always, looking for the upside, the positive spin.

But Joe's spirits sank. He knew getting a film 'up' was practically impossible in UStraylia. Only a poker machine or some televised lottery had worse odds.

"Make a commitment, Joe, to something really worthwhile. Create a project you can finally be proud of. This is the perfect 'Heaven sent' opportunity. Let the whole television thing go. Before it kills you. Write that Big Idea you know you've got churning away inside you."

Churning didn't seem quite the right word, either. Stabbing pains from an intractable stomach ulcer or broken down pancreas might have been nearer the mark. So, when he didn't look too sure, she conciliated with:

"Or do your book of poems at last."

"Musings, ramblings …"

"Whatever - "

"There won't be any money in it," he predicted accurately.

"So?"

Barbara's question hovered between them in its own, immensely reasonable way- like a beautiful but doomed butterfly. There would be very little money in anything Joe did from now on. Why shouldn't it be poetry? He sipped his dandelion coffee and slumped back into the hammock. Writing a book of idle reflections in rhyming couplets would now go onto the cork board of things he still had to do and would probably never get round to. He was *that* depressed.

Meanwhile, Barbara had to intentionally restrain herself from breaking in on Julie's audible distress. The sobs now segued into one continuous wail of misery.

"Barbara, I've got bugger-all chance of getting anything made," Joe deflected again.

Julie's sobbing was really quite unnerving.

"You've seen the filing cabinet. The rejection slips fill two whole drawers! I don't have the contacts. I don't have the chutzpah. I don't go to the right cocktail parties in East Sydney."

"A turtle only moves forward by sticking its neck out."

"So who wants to be a turtle!" he rancoured unnecessarily and immediately regretted it.

"Sorry, Barbara, sorry. Shit. Why am I yelling at you? I should be more worried about what Gra'eme will say."

"Who cares what Gra'eme thinks? *Finally* you stand up to be counted."

"… out." he quipped, bleakly.

"Great. So you make a commitment to *some*thing, Joe. It's about time!

He winced. "Nearly drowning this morning…it makes you realise how short life really is. Any of us could die virtually any moment of the day from any number of causes…"

"Don't get mad- get even madder," she urged him. "*Then* get even. Produce something important for a change. A story that surprises people. That makes waves. Takes their breath away…"

Barbara's faith in him was touching, but again he slumped at the effort required.

"With what? No funding body would risk a cent on someone like me- even if they had anything to give away. We all know they're just remedial work schemes for unemployable bureaucrats and cultural gate keepers."

"Let me worry about the funding for a change,"- open hearted and generous to a fault. As always.

"No way."

"Think of it as rent," she persisted.

"I can't let you give me money Barbara, you're my…"

There was an embarrassing pause as he searched for the right term. 'Spouse' seemed way out of date, 'wife' wasn't strictly technically correct, and 'de facto' sounded like an unsavoury legal put-down. What *was* it that they actually had together? This serial bachelor/spinster-hood thing? An intermittent coupling? A mateship, friendship, through-thick-and-thinship sort of arrangement? Too much of their 'marital contract' was tacit. Built on faith in each other and little else.

"You know I want you to be with me here. Rent doesn't come into it," was all that emerged, rather inadequately, from him.

"But it's your house. You and Kate paid for it. And I get to use it."

"Occasionally." Joe was curling his bottom lip, bunging it on again.

Barbara tensed. "Please, Joe, we don't have to make it any more difficult than it already is," she concluded as:

Joe glanced across again at the poinsettia under which Kate's ashes were buried. If she hadn't died his life would have been completely different. He'd still be writing plays. He'd have integrity. Poor but honest. Well- he was poor either way. But if Kate was alive his name would still be appearing in luke warm reviews in a handful of free local newspapers. At least a small scattering of people would know he had written *some*thing, even if the critics hated it. In television nobody had a clue a writer even existed. On the flipside to that: if Kate hadn't died he would never have moved to Heaven, and would never have found the necessity (or the opportunity) for Barbara.

What strange twists a life can take, he thought. When you stand back from it and truly see it for what it is: an individual's halting, erratic journey through time, accompanied by a growing realisation as to what it's all about, deciding it was all too difficult to understand, and yet still staggering on, however tremulously, towards our separate destinies- if we were lucky enough to have one…

And so and thus, as they waited for Julie's lachrymose ablutions to end Joe put his dandysoychino aside, rolled out of the hammock again, and felt a crazy urge to engage in a little Lite Gardening- to kick some mulch and a bit of lime into place around Kate's poinsettia. The plant under which he had placed her ashes all those years ago, unable to fling them off Point Paradise into the great sink of the Pacific ocean- as Gra'eme had so sensibly urged. Unable to make the final break- to let go…

Instead, Joe had kept them close by, in the backyard at 13 Redemption Road, barely seven metres from where his wife's sole soul had been taken away by lorikeets.

CROSS FADE TO:

Euphoria (poinsettia) Pulcherrima
6

Just another one of the many tens of native plants that flourish in the colourful backyards of **HEAVEN**'s ideal subtropical climate—creating a virtual Garden of Eden in Gondwana's ancient heart. Visit the Rainbow Coast and smell the flowers.

Affix stamp here

#9 of 33 Postcards from Heaven

printed on gently mulched, plantation-grown, organic bamboo fibre using recycled greywater and bound with a biodegradable non-toxic glue

No animal or dolphin suffered in the making of this card
(apart from, of course, its author)

9

NAKED GARDENING BY TORCHLIGHT

"The world is mainly divided into those who receive
and those who serve."
(Gra'eme *The Outer Game Of Tennis*)

Casa del Fibro, 9 years ago ...

Straight after he got back from the crematorium Joe dug a small hole in their backyard and made a 'pot' in the sand with sheets of newspaper (to retain the moisture). Then he tipped Kate's ashes in and placed the poinsettia on top, giving the young shrub a good water. Not so much ashes to ashes, as ashes to life again. Poinsettias were in flower that month- so it seemed appropriate. It would be an annual reminder.

At first, however, the plant failed to thrive. Its leaves turned a sickly tobacco colour, the flowers didn't seem to want to happen, something was eating it. Joe began to fear there may have been *too* much ash and he'd gotten the whole acid/alkaline thing somehow out of kilter- bad farming *and* bad kharma.

He consulted all the local nurseries, but refused of course, to pollute the hallowed ground with herbicides, pesticides, snail pellets, and all the other synthetic chemicals the 'experts' at Hosanna's Herbarium urged upon him. In fact, Joe became so obsessed with having Kate's plant survive organically that he would often stagger out in the middle of the night naked as the day he was born, with torch in hand and garden fork in the other- to mulch up the earth around it, or add some extra bit of compost. Perhaps even catch a bug doing its leaf eating thing and promptly pulp the poor creature (unBuddhist-like) mid-meal, turning the act into its last supper.

On those nights when the Utta Bastards were out scoring bakpakah chicks at the Pearly Gates Hotel and Old Frank had some peace in his house at last, the failed gambler and greyhound breeder would sometimes glance over his side fence and notice Joe's torch beam flashing around the neighbouring yard. Old Frank would shake his head sadly, wondering (like Onecoat Kev) whether Joe, in his birthday suit, staggering amongst the fish fern, wasn't going a little sub-troppo.

And were they wrong? Did Joe Deegan, loner and chronic worrier, in fact need Personality Realignment Counselling? Despite his naive belief that there was nothing a shrink or counsellor could tell him about himself that he didn't already know?

"And how *would* you know unless you saw one?" Barbara countered in any one of her many sensible attempts to get him to embrace Personality Realignment.

BLUR FORWARD TO:

9.29am, Casa del Fibro, Friday 13th March

It was already early autumn of this drought year and the poinsettia was only just starting to flower (red bracts surrounded by small greenish-yellow flowers); reminding Joe that the ninth anniversary of Kate's death was only a few weeks away. Almost a dog's lifetime. The years had simply galloped by. Like a dream. If that was another one gone his life would be over in a minute. Time in Heaven exacting its cost. Speeding wildly downhill, out of control- like the stubborn unruly thing that it was.

Joe nudged another divot of mulch back into place under the poinsettia with his frayed old canvas sandshoes while Barbara gave up waiting for Julie and came over to join him, taking his hand in hers. He was grateful for the physical contact, the recognition that Barbara knew what he was thinking; grateful that she had walked into his life when he most needed her...

They stood looking down at Kate's bush for several minutes with only some hysterical kookaburras, the distant chainsaw, and Julie's sobbing to drown out the eternal sound of the beach through the rainforest: that one long, continuous whoosh of waves, wind and leaves, sometimes like a train roaring past, sometimes like an angel's sigh.

For a while now nobody had said anything about Julie.

"It was touch and go there for while…" Joe was sure he'd probably told Barbara this before. "I thought the whole plant had actually died. The problem was mostly water. Now it's finally made contact with the lake underneath and I don't have to worry so much anymore."

Barbara looked up and glanced around the backyard. She always suspected he had made the whole thing a kind of shrine, with the poinsettia as its focus. Unconsciously perhaps. But that's what it amounted to. A sacred garden. In a way a kind of secret garden with the 'Twelve Apostles' camouflaged in amongst the fish fern, budding nicely, almost ripe for harvest and difficult for any police helicopter to spot (although Onecoat Kev remained a worry on that score).

Joe followed Barbara's gaze, surveying the fruit trees that had sprouted willy nilly from the compost- along with the golden cane, the Norfolk pines, the shrubs and flowers he had planted. Gardening: his hobby, his relief, the only thing worth doing really. Creating life. Much more important in the overall scheme of things than writing inane, plot-driven, formula-bound scripts for television.

"You watch all these trees struggle for a few years until their roots reach down the two or three metres it takes to meet the water table then…they hit the jackpot and just take off. Like skyrockets. Look at those Bangalows! They're racing away…"

He was indicating two giant palms he was particularly fond of. Then he turned back to Barbara and smiled. "Like you."

She sighed at his tired old argument. "I'm only going for a few months, Joe."

Barbara accepted that these melodramatic pronouncements were the price she had to pay. He knew there was nothing he could say that would stop her going- apart from feigning some terminal illness. And he knew she knew he knew she was never happier than on the cusp of boarding some plane, train, or camel with all her worldly possessions in a single bakpak. Off on another adventure, the wind tickling her feet…

Joe never suspected bi-polar disorder until much later.

"Anyway, we need a break," she decided, already looking forward to being out of here. "Just remember how good it is when I come back."

This was true. Her returns were like a serial honeymoon, failing in love all over again. And lately, to be perfectly honest, there was a little more failing than succeeding when she came back. A little more baggage. A growing resentment and vague dissatisfaction. More doubt about giving up Israel for him.

Then it hit her. An elegant solution. "You can come with me now… Why not? "

"Barbara…"

"No, really, what's stopping you? If you aren't going to work on *Drifting Sands* anymore."

It annoyed him that she still couldn't get a proper grip on the show's title, and that she had started by emphasising the negative. Fortunately, they both heard Julie cutting the shower scene from Casa del Fibro, and Joe was relieved to hear the ticking water meter fade from the soundtrack.

"I can't take a break, Barbara. Groveling letters to producers will have to be written. My CV dusted off and redrafted in a hopeless attempt to make itself look attractive. It's too hard doing your own thing."

"I told you- *I'm* going to be your funding body."

It was that simple. And that beautiful.

She took his hand again. Her hand in his. His grip had gone sort of limp- like his soul.

"I've got faith in you Joe. Even if nobody else has. We'll rent a flat in Nahlaot. Near the market. You can write all day long when I take my groups up to the Galilee."

"We'll be burgled, Nahlaot's where all the junkies hang out."

"Not more than five minutes from a great cappuccino, I promise. You know the wines from the Golan are really good now. Even if they're politically incorrect." (Since the Golan Heights was occupied land.)

"Walking distance?" he queried, obviously pretty tempted, now that he'd taken a principled decision never to write crap again, and therefore in urgent need of unencumbered down time to generate some pitchable ideas.

"Of course. Seven minutes walk to the Jewish market, fifteen to the Old City, tops." (All, tragically, sites of terrible violence and devastating bomb attacks, including the local coffee shop- none of which anybody needed to go into right now.)

"*Make* that film happen, Joe. Before the senile dementia sets in." She was only half joking.

"Barbara, nothing I do will ever get made. It's a waste of time. I've lost the spark."

He was being brutally honest, and also fairly accurate. In fact, he knew he was being pretty well appalling, but sometimes he couldn't help himself.

"You'll have *millions* of ideas in Jerusalem. You know the buzz you get over there, Joe. What's stopping you? You'll never have to deal with the likes of Craig Huxtable or Carmel Savage again."

That was a given. Even if it meant sacrificing his best shot at a proper living. And just how long Joe would go on 'living' in Israel remained a moot point- given his overall bad luck. That unerring ability he had to be in the wrong place at the wrong time...

"Let it go, Joe." Barbara was sub-texting to Kate's poinsettia and here too, she was right. "Let it all go... Mt. Lookout! remember? You, me and the ghosts swirling up? Nothing matters."

What Joe remembered was the first time he'd gone over to Israel with Barbara, just after their relationship started, to see what this other half of his better half's life was all about. She wanted the experience to be as extraordinary for him as it had been for her when she herself first arrived there. She was hoping anyway, that perhaps he would want to stay. And he was trying to give it his best shot. He really was.

WIPE ACROSS TO:

Latrun, Israel, 8 years ago...

Straight from Ben Gurion airport Barbara drove Joe to the ruins of an ancient monastery near Latrun in the Judean foothills- just off the main highway going up to Jerusalem from the coast. They sat amongst the rubble of what had once been a Crusader chapel a thousand years ago. Here she broke bread and sprinkled salt and welcomed him like Abraham had been welcomed by the Canaanites (just before his own biblical land grab). Then Joe and Barbara made love on the picnic blanket she had brought; watched he was sure, by a security guard with binoculars from the nearby army barracks. They were in a war zone after all- it was the first 'Intifada' and there was no place to hide. Not even for post modern lovers.

Afterwards, they drove on up to Jerusalem and over to the house she was sharing at that time on Mt. Scopus with her friends and fellow tour guides, Amnon and Dinah. Joe was struck by Amnon's pistol lying so casually in its holster on the kitchen table and wondered how people could bear to live so permanently in a state of- not so much fear- as heightened alert. The pistol never more than a few seconds from Amnon's grip. Every house in Israel still had its 'sealed room' left over from Gulf War I- a refuge from rocket attack with chemical weapons. It seemed an apt metaphor for a country of sealed roads and sealed hearts. Trust had long since disappeared in this part of the world and with it went hope.

So the 'gun' was everywhere, slung over the shoulder as casual as a tennis racket or set of golf clubs. The wild west of the Muddled East with the same American accent. Joe couldn't quite get used to the sight of ordinary people carrying M16s or Uzis, especially in bank queues. Tanks on huge trucks lurched past on every highway. Enormous military helicopters were constantly overhead, their pale underbellies bristling with machine guns and rocket launchers. When jets broke the sound barrier it was like a bomb going off, rattling windows, and giving Barbara's pilgrims serious palpitations- while they still came. Once, during a desert hike, her group saw a jet fighter suddenly scoot out from the side of a mountain, as if hidden there against surprise attack. Like a miracle... Or something from Armageddon. A nuclear deterrent mutually assuring destruction.

Meanwhile, at that time, soldiers and civilians continued to die every other day in southern Lebanon. Occasionally, a bomb would go off in the centre of Jerusalem or on some bus. The number 9 was hit twice- the one Joe caught from Mt. Scopus to central West Jerusalem. Every now and then someone would be stabbed in broad daylight, often at bus stops. It seemed like a war on public transport. The terror was there too in the eyes of the Arab kid who passed Joe in a street near the Old City and glared back with such incandescent hatred that if looks could kill, Joe felt sure he would have been sliced open as expertly as a lamb's throat at a wedding. Because he looked a little bit Jewish? Was that it?- with his curly Welsh/Roman locks, olive skin, and broken nose from an old football injury. It didn't seem fair. Joe wasn't occupying anybody's land. And didn't want to. In any case, as the Nullumbah nation could have told the kid and all those oppressing him: nobody owns the land- the land owns us...

There was another kind of look in the lifeless expression of the Israeli border guards-young women mostly, who interrogated you before you could be allowed into Israel, mixing a sort of tedious suspicion with that faint, superior air of boredom they cultivated so effortlessly (they could stop you getting on the plane after all).

Questions like: "Where did you come from? Where are you going? Who do you know? What do you do?- queries that Joe had neither philosophical nor practical answers to (thanks to Gra'eme). And then the clincher: did the person who sold you that bottle of perfume know you were on the flight to Tel Aviv?"- illustrating a paranoia approaching brilliance. The strategies of the horrorist knew no bounds and had to be met by an intelligence of equal daring. These young guardian angels may have looked inexperienced, but already they'd seen off enough boyfriends to pick insincerity a mile away. It was a clever tactic to use them as a screening device (as it was to then put them on the plane with you). They had to get it right for all our sakes.

A more defeated air of boredom was there too, in the sad faces of the old men who inspected your bags whenever you went into any department store or cinema or public place. These Israeli grandfathers waited like we all waited. For something to happen. For the suicide bomber, the martyr, to come through the door- their door! Constantly reminding you that nothing had been resolved. That where there was no peace there was no sovereignty. In a place already conquered and occupied 27 times. But did it matter? If nothing matters? And who's counting anyway, if the universe was unfolding perfectly?

CUT TO:

Deheishe, Same trip to Israel, 8 years ago...

Barbara took him to visit a family she was trying to help in a refugee camp near Bethlehem. Deheishe was a walled compound sealed with sheets of tin and barbed wire, and off limits to Israelis for obvious reasons. But Barbara had no fear of her Palestinian friends and took little notice of military pronouncements. She even knew a secret way in, avoiding the constant IDF patrols. After three generations of continuous occupation the camps had become de facto prisons. Effectively villages without land and little to gainfully occupy its community- apart from a honing of their hatred for the circumstances that had put them there.

After 40 years in limbo the original refugee tents had become concrete buildings piled, unplanned and under-resourced, one on top of the other. Like a Cold Coast highrise, at a hundredth of the price and without the plumbing. Each generation of sons and their families had nowhere else to go but up. So there was never any final roof in place, only rusty spikes sticking up, ready for the next pour of concrete- for the next crop of martyrs.

While Joe and Barbara were in the home of the family she had come to visit, a platoon of soldiers in bullet proof vests suddenly burst through Deheihse's main gate in a convoy of jeeps and started arresting boys randomly- anyone old enough to throw stones would do. A group of girls raced in to tell Barbara. She was Israeli. She could somehow, maybe, restrain the events now erupting throughout the camp...

Joe and Barbara followed the girls along a dark, narrow laneway with its half starved wild cats and fetid sewer water- the cause of so much ill health in the place. They turned a corner and ran headlong into the oncoming platoon; and while the kids dropped back the soldiers braced themselves. Taking aim, expecting stones to fly.

At which point Joe realised he could die. He and his lover stood alone in a kind of impromptu de facto no man's land. And if the little Davids behind them *did* start pelting rocks, then the Goliaths in front would have no hesitation in opening fire. Whether with rubber coated bullets or not wasn't going to make a whole lot of difference at twenty paces. It was a visual cliché seen a thousand times on the news. Only one that Joe and Barbara were now firmly in the middle of. This lovely thing called Joe Deegan would soon cease to exist. "The facts speak for themselves." (see Gra'eme's *Life's Too Short To Drink Bad Coffee).*

Joe would end up as worm fodder and that was all he knew and all anyone could be certain of. It seemed such a waste. His life gone in an instant. In absolutely the wrong place at a catastrophically bad time. Something he had literally stumbled into. Killed by his own fatal clumsiness- combusted with Barbara's tendency to always push the envelope and help complete strangers.

A tall, blonde officer with piercing blue eyes like Paul Newman in *Exodus*, detached himself from the uniformed column and came forward, speaking Hebrew with a South African accent. Which at least explained the eye and hair colour, while lending the scene certain unfortunate historical ironies. In fact, it suddenly struck Joe that this little encounter was like a micro version of the Boer War all over again- only 100 years later and at the other end of virtually the same continent. However, this time the Afrikaaner was the one in uniform and the USsie irregular dressed guerrilla/civilian style.

All Joe could think of blurting out was: "Don't shoot, I'm UStraylian. I play Rugby..."

The words fluttered in the air between them like a sick joke. But it did manage to throw Lt. Nathan Zambon off his stride long enough for him to get really pissed off. Nobody quite expected an overweight, disheveled tourist, wearing an Hawaiian shirt, tattered shorts, cracked sunglasses and dunlop volley sandshoes, to suddenly appear in the middle of a Palestinian refugee camp. Especially one who played half back for St. Patrick's College Nullumbah (Second Fifteen).

Then again, UStraylians in more presentable clobber had also been in this neck of the woods before- the strategically vital land bridge between Africa, Asia and Europe. Sometimes in major concentrations. In those days they were the ones wearing the khaki and riding the jeeps (or light horses). Of the 27 conquests, occupations, and/or destructions of Jerusalem, two of them, a generation apart, had been carried out by diggers. It was not, therefore, a totally foreign battlefield for someone of the likes of Joe's blended ethnic background.

Lt. Zambon demanded his passport. Cool, clipped, acting really angry. Used to being hated. Only wanting to get through this appalling shift and be home in Haifa before three stars in the sky tonight announced the arrival of the Sabbath.

Joe was about to explain that he didn't have any ID on him, coming as he did from a lucky country where IDs weren't necessary (and ids were a worry)...when Barbara waded in with a torrent of abuse in holy Hebrew. Accompanied by much hand waving and classically beautiful Jewish outrage. She tore into the Israeli-Afrikaaner and almost blamed him personally for the abuse Palestinians had suffered over half century of tragic struggle. What did *he* think *he* was doing here? These were children he was trying to arrest! Where were *his* documents? What gave *him* the right to demand anything? How long would this oppressive occupation continue to destroy the souls of both peoples...?

But of course, there was no easy answer to any of Barbara's questions. Nobody present at this tiny confrontation would realise that the conflict here in Israel was already flaring out into the Third-World War sane people had always dreaded: stretching from Chechnya and Bosnia near Europe and linking up with all the other little wars right through north Africa and the Muddled East, past the nuclear stalemate of India/Pakistan and on across to Indonesia on the rim of the Pacific. Half the planet now engulfed in some kind of meltdown. While the other half stood back and did nothing more than throw fuel on the fire. (Or oil as the case may be.) Gaia wouldn't stand by and let it continue…There would be a reckoning. And very soon (if Gra'eme was right).

However, Lt. Zambon was barely aware of his tiny part in this coming global catastrophe, and even less impressed with either Barbara's arguments or Joe's appearance. As a result the unlikely couple were summarily 'escorted' to the local headquarters of Shin Bet, Israel's internal security force. Here, in one of the ugliest buildings Joe had ever seen they were detained for several hours while Barbara's papers were thoroughly gone through and marked down for further attention. Eventually, they were released on condition she never go near a Palestinian camp again. Something Barbara chose to ignore completely. Joe was lucky not to have been deported. While the boys they'd come to arrest got to sleep at home one more night…

RIPPLE DISSOLVE FORWARD TO:

9.47am, Casa del Fibro, Friday 13th March

PULL BACK FROM

Kate's poinsettia to discover Joe and Barbara still standing in front of it, looking down.

"I'd love to travel with you Barbara, I really would…" he is saying, his hands in the same tatty shorts' pockets, wearing the same fraying Hawaiian shirt with less buttons, "…but I'm not organised."

He knew there was no way he could just jump on a plane with her the day after tomorrow and leave Heaven for possibly half a year.

Further discussion was derailed by Julie's renewed sobbing. Loud enough now (without the shower running), to be an unequivocal call for help.

Joe frowned towards Barbara, at a loss, unable any longer to ignore it. "What's going on?"

"It's all right, Joe, just don't draw attention to it." Barbara was being her usual, inscrutable self. "You don't need to know."

"I can be discreet."

"No you can't. I can't tell you anything."

This was perfectly true. Unfortunately. Among his many shortcomings Joe was a serial blabbermouth. All part of a writer's natural attraction to gossip, bad news, and peoples' flaws generally. But Barbara couldn't help herself sometimes either.

"Julie's pregnant."

Joe was shocked. It didn't seem possible. But before he could say anything embarrassing Barbara joined the main dots: "Libby and Julie found a gay guy willing to make a donation. The girls were going to bring the child up themselves. Then Libby met someone in the Women's Circus…" Barbara shrugged. "Now it's all up in the air. Julie's a mess, that's all. It's why I wanted her to have this holiday…where I could keep an eye on her."

"Geezus." Joe felt genuine sympathy. Some poor souls seemed to attract unhappiness and disaster like lone strollers down a back street in Surface Paradox. Mugged by circumstance.

"I might have to stay in Newtown for a while. Get her through the pre-natal bit."

"Pre-natal depression?"

"I'm not putting labels on it."

"What, delay your trip?" He could sense another mission of mercy coming on.

"She needs me, Joe, there's no one else."

"Julie's got plenty of friends."

"No she hasn't."

82

"Do you ever wonder why!?"

ECHO SOUND AND
FREEZE FRAME ON:

Joe

He didn't have to make his evident jealousy of Julie quite so obvious. But he'd been genuinely annoyed and mystified by Larry's strange decapitation and depressed at having to take a principled stand and draw the line under his humiliating but financially useful job- not to mention the stress of nearly losing his life to save Julie's barely two hours ago. Plus, there was something about her dopey self-obsession that irritated him enormously.

MOVE FORWARD AGAIN ON:

Barbara

She is saying:

"You've got no sympathy at all, have you?- for anything outside your own, narrow comfort zone." Quite angry with him now. And rightly so.

"Does that mean you won't be able to do the stopover in India...?" He was still making it hard for her, stressing the angle that would needle Barbara the most.

"I can skip the ashram and go straight on to Jerusalem- when Julie's back on her feet." She shrugged, letting it all go.

"St. Barbara." declared Pope Joe, canonising her on the spot.

"Stop it."

"You can't help yourself, Barbara, when there's a mother with a kid in trouble."

The call for help from Julie was stuffing up all his plans for the afternoon. This was already an atrocious start to any Beautiful Day, let alone a Beautiful Birthday.

As soon as Barbara went off to minister to her best friend, Joe noticed a couple of currawongs return to the lawn, scratching for morning tea. He envied their liberty. Birds didn't have to worry about jobs or mortgages, or wars, or kids without fathers, or even who to vote for. He suddenly longed for a currawong's options. The freedom to travel anywhere, anytime. Always looking down on the world. No ticket or Loyal Traveler Miles™ required. But then he didn't want to live on a diet of worms either...

Without including Joe or noticing him in any way, the two women went back into the kitchen for an exhausting heart to heart- set in fluid motion by a cup of chai.

Joe seized the opportunity to reclaim his guestroom/study/library/archive and finish work for the day. In fact, to finish with work full stop! He began to take down the various little inspirational quotes he'd scattered around the wall above his computer and blu-tacked onto the boxes of paper archives. Stuff like:

'keep it real - no bullshit'

(impossible on a show like *Golden Sands* anyway), and,

'don't get it right, get it written'

(bad tactics in retrospect), and,

'have fun doing it otherwise no one will have much fun watching it'

The last quote was from Jean Genet, it read:

'a writer has to want to change the world...'

It fluttered into the waste paper bin with all the other prompts Joe would no longer be needing now that this part of his career was finally behind him...

Maybe, on second thoughts, he'd keep the Genet.

Joe reached down and refiled this scrap of paper under 'Next' and put it in a new box beside the 100 or so others that contained everything he'd ever written or had rejected.

"My life as a first draft," he sighed (finally talking to himself out loud and perhaps cracking up at last).

All this work and so little to show for it! All those tedious hours of main stream drama fabricating and hardly more than a few minutes of it worth skiting about. Only the television stuff ever got made and sometimes broadcast; but by the time it reached the small screen in a hundred thousand living rooms (where it minimally distracted the masses while they waited for the next ad break), it bore so little resemblance to what he'd written anyway that it hardly seemed worth mentioning- even in a CV as generally barren and undistinguished as his truly's.

There were scripts, notes, poems, diaries, letters, and sketches for stories that had all come to nothing. He wondered what it all amounted to- all this *paper*? This self-perpetuating mausoleum now closing in on him. Almost forcing him (and Barbara's guests) out the guestroom/study/library/archive's door. A complete written record of an ordinary, conspicuously unimpressive and suboptimal life.

"Big Deal", as Gra'eme would say. "Go tell someone who cares."

So why *was* Joe hoarding it all? Was it just ego? *Would* anybody else be remotely interested? Not Barbara, that's for sure. She'd been at him for *years* to compost the lot. Barbara the nomad, whose accomplishments were not measurable on the material record. Her legacy lay in her numerous, deeply held and highly valued relationships- along with the passion, heartache, and effort she poured into them. Lasting emotional bonds. Recorded only in the huge telephone bills that followed. Barbara knew, almost instinctively, that the most permanent account of anything was in the memory of friends and loved ones…at least until the Alzheimer's set in...

She, who travelled constantly and produced little that anyone could point a finger at. He, who in order to produce too much, stayed in the one place and achieved…not a great deal- when it was all said and done. Life can be many things but it was always short. And as Barbara's wonderful example proved: you have to seize it with both hands. *Carpe Diem. Carpe* Heaven Time…

Joe wondered, in fact, if he shouldn't just pile the hundred or so wine cartons into a big pyramid over the BBQ hotplate and inaugurate a bonfire of the inanities. Something to celebrate his semi-official, private retirement. But of course he couldn't let go. Could he? Not right now. Not yet.

"Not ever," Barbara would taunt.

Joe wandered back into his 'work' (sic) space and picked up that week's copy of the *Nirvana News* (lying next to his computer). Like everyone else in Heaven he turned immediately to the only page worth reading and discovered that Riuyku was urging Pisceans this week to "put their money where their fishy mouths were and go for the 'dream plan'- the one you've been talking about for years. Act now," she prophesied, "and your innermost Neptunian heart's desire is sure to come true…"

It was quite uncanny how Riuyku sometimes, somehow (like Gra'eme, like Barbara), also seemed to hit the nail so squarely on its head. Of course, the proposition that the whereabouts of stars at the time of your birth had something to do with your inherited personality or private destiny was patently absurd. Occasionally though, Riuyku just seemed to sync so beautifully with what was actually going on in Joe's life. And it *was* weird but, having just survived a near drowning, he *did* feel as if a new door might be opening and could almost hear the creak of a larger wheel turning…

So alright then. He would start the 'great work' Barbara had so beautifully urged on him. Today. This very afternoon…

…Probably after a power nap and a second body surf followed by a serious lie down (best to get the energy levels pumping on full throttle). Why postpone it a moment longer? He'd call the film *'Nothing Matters'*. An unheard of thing for an UStraylian feature, it would be about normal characters who care for each other and commit acts of moral heroism. It would even be uplifting for those who saw it- dealing only with issues that people felt really passionate about…

And for that reason alone (and especially given that it wouldn't include a serial killer)…it would probably…never get made.

Joe slumped. He knew he would have to run all this past Gra'eme. Which involved not so much a spiritual, as a financial reality check. Perhaps there might even be a tax advantage? Invest in *himself* for a change, buy some time as a freelance screen playwright? At last.

INTERCUT WITH:

10.01am *Utopia* Friday 13th March

"You idiot !" exploded Gra'eme from his mobile tractor on his mobile phone. He was spraying toxic insecticide amongst those wonderfully useful, 'income producing', tax deductible, 'organic' (sic) macadamias.

"You can't possibly let that television job go! Do you realise how much provisional tax you're up for this year?"

"Well, no. That's why I need you, Gra'eme." (Joe was going to say "pay you, Gra'eme"- but thought the better of it.)

"Have you put *any* money aside?" he demanded.

"It's not due till April is it?"

"I thought so," the Great Teacher sighed. "When will you ever learn?"

"What about that alpaca farm in the Cayman Islands? Weren't we going to buy shares or something?" Joe pleaded with fading hope.

"Forget about the fucking alpacas. Just hold onto that *Golden Sands* job like your life depended on it. Which it partly does. If I've told you once, Joseph, I've told you a thousand times! Lose an actual paying gig anytime in your late middle age and you *will never work again!*"

Joe was middle aged all right. Like the sun was middle aged: 5 billion years old with 4 and a half billion years to go. At the end of which it would explode in a last blast of exhaustion and atomise everything that had ever existed (so far as earthlings knew). And that included Joe's 100 or so boxes of written archive (but not his episodes of *On Golden Sands* which by then would've have slipped through a worm hole and come out into a parallel universe where they might finally make some kind of sense). After which cataclysmic event, our malignant sun would hang around filling a quarter of the sky like a huge, pale blue moon. Not that anyone would be left alive on planet Earth to see it. No thanks to Gaia.

But the thought of crawling back to Craig Huxtable after the contempt he and Carmel had demonstrated for Joe's brilliant version of Ep. 1113, along with the prospect of further humiliation to come, was incentive enough for him to stand his ground and never submit to such personal and professional humiliation again. Besides which, the stars (as outlined by Riuyku at least) were on his side.

"I just can't write that crap anymore, Gra'eme. It…it's like it's poisoning my soul."

"Forget your frigging soul and start worrying about poisoning the relationship with your bank manager. You can't eat *soul*. You can't drink *soul*. *Soul* won't pay the electricity bill or the car reggo."

"But I just can't do it, Gra'eme. *On Golden Sands* is not even something I want to put on my CV. After all, nothing matters…"

Joe was trying the New Resolve out on Gra'eme, but could already hear a reproachful groan coming down the line, and for a moment his guru/accountant just hung there, with tractor idling, weighing up Joe's options- if not his actual viability as a self-managed shelf company; including his complex integration into the dense web of tax avoiding trusts Gra'eme had set up to placate, stall and obfuscate all of his clients (including the Departments of Internal Revenue of several countries and small island states).

Finally, the Wise One proclaimed: "We'll have to workshop a new financial plan at *Seventh Heven*. My float's at eleven thirty. Book yourself a tank in the Ghandi Room. This is going to require radical action."

Joe didn't like the financial sound of that already, but wanted to appear grateful. His cheque would be in the mail.

"Thanks, Gra'eme. I really appreciate it," he sucked.

And promptly hung up, not wanting to waste anymore of his financial adviser's expensive time. The reaction, while half expected, was still something of a shock. But that's why Joe stuck with Gra'eme- to face stark realities, to weigh the odds, to understand the complex accounting software. It was such a relief to know that his shaman was on the case. Joe even thought of booking himself a massage straight after the float and was about to dial Helen Strongfeather's mobile…when he realised the morning was almost gone and he hadn't even had a Proper Lie Down yet. This was seriously appalling. At the very least another smoko in the hammock was long overdue. Time to salvage something of the Beautiful Day from the debacle thus far.

Besides, Joe had to clear his mind before he made any more life-altering decisions…

IRIS OUT TO:

10

Endangered rainforest—Elysium Creek

Endangered flora and fauna (along with their vital habitat) take a back seat as this colourful bulldozer makes way for yet another classic, 13-storey, pink-and-lilac cluster townhouse development—right in the heart of **HEAVEN**'s 'protected' Elysium Creek rainforest. Discover the Rainbow Coast and see some of the last remaining examples of certain species before it's too late.

Affix stamp here

#10 of 33 Postcards from Heaven

printed on gently mulched, plantation-grown, organic bamboo fibre using recycled greywater and bound with a biodegradable non-toxic glue

No animal or dolphin suffered in the making of this card
(apart from, of course, its author)

10
A FOOL'S GUIDE TO TREE HUGGING

"Why is it called a Goods and Services Tax when so many 'goods'
these days are so obviously very bad for you?"
(Gra'eme *There Are No Answers, Only Alternatives*)

10.10am, Casa del Fibro, Friday 13th March

While Barbara spoke wisdom and simple common sense to Julie, making her see all the obvious steps she had to take to convert her current life predicament into an opportunity for growth and renewal- allowing for some genuine Personality Realignment, Joe settled back into his interrupted session in the hammock- keen to invite a little R&R into the day. At last.

However, just as the swaying smoko approached the nadir of its arc and slowed towards near perfect stillness, the calm was again shattered by that fucking chainsaw! Only much closer now, and quickly followed by the crack of a large tree crashing groundwards.

Frowning, Joe ashed the spliff early, swung his legs over and rolled out of the hammock- drawn by the thumpt of another old growth giant as it hit the dust- or in this case mud. He began to feel a kind of growing concern, if not actual alarm, mixed in with a certain, typical, pre-emptive powerlessness. When he stood on his cold BBQ hotplate (just in time to see a huge sheoke falling about twenty metres away), he knew something quite awful was happening to the pristine rainforest separating his back fence from Purgatory Beach.

Joe was pretty sure some of those trees must be over a hundred years old. He also knew there was a patch of private land somewhere in the middle of the forest and that one day, in the hazy future, a house or two might probably be built there. Yet, when Bryce Keitel first showed Casa del Fibro to Kate and Joe, the UnReal Estate agent stressed the fact that, although it had been virtually totally devastated by sandmining, this bare patch could never be used for development because it was quote, 'ringed by an unbroken stand of rainforest,' unquote. And that quote, 'all trees in Nullumbah Shire over three metres high were automatically protected,' unquote. So there was no way quote, 'anybody could physically get legal access to subdivide this last area of private land directly adjoining Purgatory Beach,' unquote.

FLASH BACK TO:

Heaven, 10 years before...

Bryce, to give him his due, was a pretty nifty salesman. Within minutes of Kate and Joe gawking at the photos in his UnReal Estate agency window, he had bundled the two innocents from Melbourne into his late model Jaguar and out on an inspection tour of all the properties for sale in their price range (which was pretty low). Bryce took them straight to the blocks of medium density townhouses he and 'some investors' had speculatively built on what used to be Heaven's public golf course. But these were all glaring examples of the pink-and-lilac cement/brutalist virus that was already devastating places well beyond either Noosa or Surface Paradox.

When it was obvious where Joe and Kate were coming from, Bryce (hiding his disappointment) finally relented and showed them #13 Redemption Road. He was down to bedrock by his own account since this embarrassing fibro shack was the cheapest house in one of Heaven's more ordinary streets- which just happened to be only 100 metres from the most fabulous beach in the world. It was all Joe and Kate cared about, or needed to know. The icing on the cake had been this bit of wild bush out the back, including that developer-repelling stand of littoral rainforest with all the birds, frogs and reptiles residing there. Not to mention: the bikepath that meandered all the way through it into town. Add all this to Casa del Fibro's cheap asking price, Café Celestial's excellent cappuccinos (even then), and of course, the complete peace and quiet of Redemption Road generally (still a gravel track) Kate and Joe had no hesitation. It was more than they could have hoped for. Bryce looked directly into their dilated pupils and knew he had a sale.

On the drive back to the office to open champagne and exchange contracts, Joe was keen to clarify the point about the trees- more out of a need to have something to talk about, than the fact that he doubted Bryce's word, or would change his mind.

"So, what you're saying, Bryce, is: 'no private developer could gain lawful access to that land at the back of our place- because they'd have to cut a road through the trees first?"

"Spot on," Bryce over-assured them. "No one can touch it."

Clearly, weaving certain fictions around dubious facts was as much a part of his job as it was of Joe's. And Bryce was delighted to hear the scriptwriter already calling it 'our place'.

"They'd have to get a Tree Protection Order just to lop off a branch. And there's *no way* Nullumbah Council would let anyone do that- certainly not in an otherwise untouched bit of bushland right next to the coast. 'Your' backyard, Joe, is looking out on the last surviving patch of littoral rainforest between Brisbane and Sydney."

"Sounds funny, doesn't it?" popped in Kate from the back seat. "A Tree 'Protection' Order that allows people to chop trees *down*."

It wasn't the only contradiction she and Joe would encounter in the real politik of the Rainbow Coast and its Enchanted Triangle.

Bryce just smiled, sort of agreeing, before adding some overkill: mentioning the school that would never be built, the soon to be upgraded shopping centre (that never happened), the 'possibility' of an aquatic complex with heated salt pools, the 'proposed' medical clinic, tennis courts, sports fields, covered bus stop, town bypass, second (competitive) stupormarket and new gym- none of which ever got off an architect's drawing board either. In any case, the school bit was lost on Kate- who at that stage was still recovering from her radical hysterectomy.

In fact the only things the citizens of Heaven ever saw built were more private golf courses and more cluster townhouses crammed onto smaller and smaller blocks, as whole ecosystems succumbed to ego systems and the Rainbow Coast at last found itself on the long hoped for property boom. But without any proper spending on public infrastructure to back it up. Something had to give.

(And it would.)

CUT FORWARD TO:

10.19 am, Casa Del Fibro, Friday 13th March

It was hardly surprising to discover that nine years later, the aforesaid adjacent rainforest was not only being 'touched', it was in fact being fairly *totally erased*. Joe could already see enormous tree trunks lying everywhere dead on the ground. The piercing mechanical whine of the saw was bad enough, what it actually achieved was even worse.

He'd have to *do* something. To act somehow. He'd have to jump over the fence and complain to someone. It must be a mistake. You couldn't do this! Joe surmised. No letter had arrived from Council warning them this going to happen (thanks to Onecoat Kev). Joe *had* to protest.

Yet disputes weren't part of his Piscean nature. For fish like Joe, Riuyku ordained a warm, talented, generous, confused, aimless, mechanically incompetent, sexually powerful, right-brain oriented soul. Confrontation or hard business dealing didn't come into it.

Joe considered rousing his neighbour, but this late in the morning Old Frank would still be recovering from last night- as would be his tenants: Filthy Mick and his even dirtier mates. Out cold all of them, lying spread eagled around the lounge room floor- where they'd passed out, semi-comatose a few hours previously. In any case, wanton destruction was a big turn on for any Utta Bastard- especially when it came to trees, or any other living thing for that matter. Joe would have to call the police, and turned back to do so… But pulled up short, remembering that Sgt. Doreen Harris came from an old logging family. Arboricide was structured into her DNA. She'd buck pass it all back to Council anyway. And no one ever saw a Nullumbah Shire Ranger or Compliance Officer turn up for work much before mid-day…assuming they did turn up that day and/or could be found.

Yet clearly, *some*body had to act before any more trees were lost.

Because a forest was greater than the sum of its parts. Without trees the water table salts up and there would be no shade, no birds, no koalas and little rainfall. Trees were our prehistoric home. Kids always hankered to climb back into them. And more than a few of Heaven's adult population still lived in their branches. Everyone gravitated to a tree's shade in summer- back to where we descended from. Just as we would finally, descend down into the earth surrounded on all sides by slabs taken from them. (Or burnt with them in some furnace.) Trees were beautiful and grand and uncomplaining. Their trunks encapsulated the history of our climate and told of other extinctions and ice ages. Warnings we ignored at our peril. And here were hundred year old sheokes, banksias, paperbarks and titrees crashing down a mere bomb's throw from Joe's back fence.

Almost without thinking (certainly without weighing up the risks involved), and in a kind of fog of outrage, Joe gathered up his small reserves of courage, catapulted from the top of his BBQ over the fibro fence…and saw to his horror that it was Lech Da Groot doing the damage.

Tall and thick, with long, shoulder-length hair, mean snake-like eyes, an IQ shy of his shoe size and a heart of pure road base, this sub-optimal example of humanity generally was as ugly as a hills hoist and nowhere near as useful.

"What's going on!?" Joe demanded with as much authority as he could manage- not a great deal, given the uncontrollable trembling in his legs.

One advantage of playing half back for St. Pats Second Fifteen, was that, like all small boys Joe had taken on a healthy respect for people much larger than himself. Being a half back he also knew, instinctively, that his best defence was attack (combined with quite a bit of evasion and a lot of frantic side-stepping).

"Fuck off," was Da Groot's fairly succinct reply as the enormous Hungarian simply continued chainsawing. Not about to be intimidated by some pseudo-greenie like Joe.

"You can't *do* his!" Joe speculated, going for broke. Assuming more than he knew.

No response. No let up in the chain sawing.

"This forest is protected," the short, chubby writer stammered, trying to recall the detail of Bryce Keitel's decade-old assurances.

"Bullshit. It's private land. Trespassers die!" The big galoot made a threatening gesture with his saw towards Joe then snagged it sideways, straight into the next tree and went right on cutting through it as if Joe didn't exist. Which he wouldn't, should the large banksia in question fall the wrong way.

The stress of which caused Joe's nose to bleed again. He was uncharacteristically lost for words. And the blood flowing onto his top lip gave the appearance of him having lost the fight before it started. There was another sickening crack. Joe shot a horrified glance up and dived sideways- just as the banksia crashed right next to him. The bastard had aimed it deliberately!

Da Groot laughed out loud at Joe's sudden mad scramble for safety- like it was the funniest thing he'd ever seen- a primitive, mocking, baboon-like screech. Humiliated, Joe slipped sideways in the mud as he tried to disentangle himself from the many branches that had broken off the main trunk and fallen around him. The wannabe screen playwright was wishing he'd brought a camera. Something with which to document this flagrant breach of Council regulations- evidence that could be used later- hopefully in the Property With Little Amenity Tribunal. If that's where justice might be found (which it probably wouldn't.) In any case Joe should have been better organised.

He tasted anger, impotence and blood all at once as he cut in front of Da Groot to stand protectively before another grand old banksia, about to be sliced off at the base.

"Look, you bastard! You've got to have a permit to remove these trees!" the fearless, tree hugger stammered.

But Da Groot just moved round the other side of the trunk and kept on sawing. If Joe stayed where he was he'd either be crushed in the ensuing fall, or sliced in two by the chainsaw. This effectively reduced him to his singular talent for abusive dialogue (honed so beautifully through those long half hours on *Golden Sands*).

"You're a criminal, environmental vandal you fucking nazi lunatic and you're not going to get away with it!"

But the enormous, ex-Stasi torturer just lifted the chainsaw and aimed it directly at Joe, coming forward and holding it over his skull, making as if to finally separate the luckless wordsmith's left and right hemispheres from their interminable, internal debate.

Joe reared back defensively, tripping over more broken branches, feeling about as useful as a barber in a shop full of bald men.

Da Groot's triumphant hilarity rang like a cold stone in Joe's heart as he made a shambolic and humiliating retreat, slipping over broken tree trunks lying everywhere, oozing sap- like Joe himself with his bloody nose.

CUT TO:

10.37am, Casa del Fibro, Friday 13th March

Ego in tatters, on the brink of nervous collapse, Joe pulled himself back over his flaky, corrugated fibro fence and finally retreated to the relative sanctuary of his own private property- where he paced up and down in the backyard.

While a mere fifty metres away, old growth rainforest continued to fall…

Barbara emerged from her Realignment session with Julie and immediately thought Joe had been beaten up. But it was only the bloody nose she had given him earlier.

"What's the matter?"- looking genuinely perplexed at his agitation, having missed the whole confrontation.

"Lech Da Groot's chopping our forest down," he whimpered, on the verge of tears, mopping the blood with a corner of his Hawaiian shirt, claiming a title over the affected land that was more moral and social than real. "It's not right. He can't do this."

Barbara glanced in the direction of the noise. "Well ring the Council! What are you waiting for?"

There was little else anyone could do. Joe dialled the number of a Green Councillor who he thought might be sympathetic. Christabel Eaton could hear the chainsaw from Joe's end straight away.

"Oh dear," she exclaimed, "when will it ever end?!"

Christabel was sounding worn out already by the constant struggle to protect Heaven from this new surge of overdevelopment that (after years of economic doldrums) was now beginning to seem unstoppable. Her pessimism wasn't an encouraging start- if she was the main democratic hope.

"We know Da Groot has joined forces with Carlos Mondeigo. They've just put in a Development Application for twelve beach units on the degraded area in the middle of that forest. But no one should be able to cut so much as a leaf in there until there's Council approval."

Joe's heart sank. A dozen units! Over his back fence. Geezus! Why hadn't anyone officially informed him? This smelt corrupt already. Nothing had come in the mail. (Still unaware this was largely Onecoat Kev's fault.)

"I'll call the Compliance Officer and suggest he get down there to see what's going on," she promised, semi-hopefully, as she rang off.

'Suggest' didn't seem like a hugely encouraging start. Especially when giant sheokes, banksias, pandanus, paperbarks and titrees continued to fall. It seemed, for the moment, that nothing could save them- or all the biodiversity, endangered species, climate balance, mosquito control and salination protection that went down with them.

CUT TO:

WWW.ECONOMIC_IRRATIONALISM.COM

HEAVEN's brand new Creators' Art Centre. Here tomorrow, gone today! Just another one of Nullumbah Shire's many colourful community landmarks currently undergoing a highly professional and very caring makeover. Visit the Rainbow Coast and discover a place where the ideal of 'letting go' can now include any treasured or publicly-owned icon.

*Affix
stamp
here*

#11 of 33 Postcards from Heaven

printed on gently mulched, plantation-grown, organic bamboo fibre using recycled greywater and bound with a biodegradable non-toxic glue

No animal or dolphin suffered in the making of this card
(apart from, of course, its author)

WWW.ECONOMIC_IRRATIONALISM.COM

"Umbrellas, like sunglasses, are made to be forgotten."
(Gra'eme *Touching Base With Your Inner Puritan*)

10.46am, Casa del Fibro, Friday 13th March

While Barbara drove Julie off in 'Rusty' to get some rescue remedy from Vasuda Devi, Joe noticed that their ancient Datsun was smoking more than he did. This wasn't a good sign (for either of them). And didn't augur terribly well for the car's reggo check in three weeks' time. Another galvanized iron nail in Rusty's coffin (as if more were needed). The poor thing seemed doomed, like most vehicles in Heaven, to a slow dissolve in the corrosive, metal-eating salt spray that constantly washed over the place. And made it so wonderful to live in.

Joe retreated back to his guestroom/study/library/archive feeling completely awful and hemmed in now by events spiralling wildly out of control. Indulging the hemmed-in thing, he paced up and down the narrow corridor between his teetering columns of paper archive and Julie's uncomfortable mattress- still failing to avoid trampling on her scattered bits of makeup, and stewing over the fact that he'd been so unprepared. A camera at least would've rescued the moment from history and exposed Da Groot's vandalism to the harsh light of day. Perhaps even provided the basis for a story Joe might be able to sell for a pittance to the *Nirvana News* or *Valhalla Times.*

WHIP PAN BACK TO:

St. Patrick's Boarding College, Nullumbah, 35 years ago…

Joe hadn't been so physically humiliated since he was frog-marched by the ear from Brother Carol's Latin exam and immediately thrashed out on the verandah. In full hearing of two other classrooms. He couldn't remember what for, or with, exactly. It might have been for smiling during the 'Hail Mary' that preceded every class at St. Pats. And it could have been with any number of the many blunt instruments that came to a Brother's hand- not just the official whale-bone reinforced leather strap, but also heavy wooden rulers, books and missals (as missiles), rosary beads with solid metal crucifixes (drawing a lot of blood), and once even a covered tennis racket that sent Joe's best mate, Dennis Hogan, deaf.

In a true act of piety, Dennis's parents didn't complain. And neither did the Archbishop of Canterbury, the Pope, Amnesty International or the International Red Cross- despite the many letters Joe wrote to all of these worthies on Dennis's behalf. At least the young lad was treated at the Brothers' expense by an ear nose and throat specialist, given a free hearing aid, and the whole matter (like so many other 'unfortunate lapses' at Joe's boarding school) hushed up as quietly as the world poor Dennis was to forever inhabit.

CUT SOUND AND BLACKOUT TO:

Blessed Boulevard, Three and a half decades later…

According to Joe's plan for the Beautiful Day he should, by now, be having his Second Tantric Body Surf prior to the Bike Ride to town along Blessed Boulevard- a tree-shaded gravel track running behind Heaven's frontal dune system and through parts of its remaining coastal rainforest. The bike path was well clear of traffic, and inside a landscape so untamed Joe would often (almost) run over a deadly brown snake, some small marsupial, or one of the feral cats that chased ducks and pelicans around the filtration ponds of the South Nullumbah Sewerage Treatment Plant.

Joe imagined that if only half the world travelled by bicycle most roads would again resemble simple beautiful paths like medieval trails through leafy cool forests. How quiet and de-stressed towns and cities would become, how free from toxic fumes. How narrow and cheap the tarmac that connected us all. With heart disease and gym memberships a thing of the past. Was there anything sillier than a stationary bicycle or jogging treadmill? Joe wondered. When you could be out in the fresh air for nothing? What *was* it about the real world that people seemed so afraid of? He asked himself rhetorically- without getting any proper answer.

The daily Bike Ride was also an opportunity for Joe to stop at that creaky old wooden bridge over Limbo Creek for a quick swig of filtered rainwater and a glimpse down at the schools of tiny fish concocting into weird hieroglyphic shapes as they twirled and grazed in the shallow brown, titree waters below. Joe cycled in order to shop and therefore to eat. It was at the 'heart' literally, of his Longevity Plan- thanks again to Gra'eme.

In order to acquire calories Joe first had to expend them. He cycled therefore he *was*- literally. And happy to let Barbara have Rusty as much as she liked. Because, as Gra'eme's blue pamphlet so brilliantly explained: 'Cars equalled *car*nage'. They simply weren't natural. And when you factored in the soaring insurance costs, global warming, pollution, and oil wars now joining up to form the long anticipated 'Third World' War, then cars were the one human artefact most likely to bring the whole species down- not even counting the million human road kill every year.

CRASH CUT FORWARD TO:

10.55am, Casa del Fibro, Friday 13th March

"Burn fat, not oil," Joe manifestoed out loud to his now seriously compromised back garden. While Da Groot's hideous chainsaw continued its arboreal massacre. Only a few arrogant currawongs (soul brothers to the Utta Bastards) were there to hear it. And the birds didn't care two hoots about Joe, his absurd mailbox, pathetic job, or crumbling relationship. All they cared about was the unpaid and un-unionised worm workforce in his compost heap.

For all these reasons today was turning out to be a somewhat less than perfect example of Joe's essential daily masterpiece. A birthday should, by definition- as he kept reminding himself- have been a really fun time. Where a little well earned self-indulgence must be pretty high on the agenda. With even less to worry about than normal.

Instead, here Joe was, more than halfway through the morning, and not only had he abandoned any hope of a second surf, he now had urgent, expensive business with his accountant in town; and fat chance of getting there in time on his trusty Malvern Star. Because Barbara had to take Julie over to get ripped off by Vasuda Devi!

CUT TO:

11.00am, Redemption Road, Friday 13th March

Fortunately, Ronnie Rainbows cruised past in his solar powered automobile just as Joe put his thumb out to hitch into town. *Perpetual Motion* may cost Ronnie nothing to run but lacked certain basic qualities- such as a floor and a roof (apart from the two solar panels)- 'optional extras', according to its owner/inventor since weight was a critical factor in the performance of any self sustaining, self propelled vehicle. Indeed, Ronnie regarded the gap where the floor should be as a kind of bonus air-conditioning.

CLOSE ON:

Four spinning bicycle wheels

Widen to discover two bicycles welded parallel to each other inorder to support a couple of plastic chairs in the gap between them. A solar panel provides current to a small car battery dangling below one of the chairs- only inches above rushing bitumen. This in turn powers a small 12volt motor.

TILT UP TO:

Ronnie Rainbows

- who is sitting, steering *Perpetual Motion* with one handle bar- half turned to Joe in the chair beside him, listening attentively as the writer downloads his angst about Da Groot's chainsaw.

"Well, you're taking on a huge shit-fight there, comrade- if you want to tackle Mein Führer Mondeigo and his sidekick Herr Goebbels Da Groot." Ronnie concluded. "You know they've got access to unlimited funds, and will sue the house off anyone who's crazy enough to stand up to them. That's how come you never see anything written about Mondeigo in the *Nirvana News* or *Valhalla Times*. Most people don't even know what Carlos baby looks like, Joe. It's the low target strategy. That's also why the mayor, the shire manager, and half the Council staff rubber stamp anything he wants. They all know he'll sue into bankruptcy anybody or anything that stands in his way."

Joe couldn't believe local corruption and/or intimidation would be that blatant.

"What? You're saying our mayor, honest Bruce Phelan, and Wal Piper, a senior public official, are in league with developers?"

"Nothing's written down. You'll never prove it."

"But…that's outrageous!" protested Joe.

"Of course it is. What else is economic_irrationalism all about?! We're talking win/lose situations here, comrade. Basically, the developers win, you lose."

Joe was hoping Ronnie wasn't talking that personally. "You mean the community…?"

"Welcome to Development Wonderland, where it's open slather all year round." Ronnie was indicating *Avalon Meadows* a recent subdivision of Mondeigo's through which they were now passing. It looked like a barren quarry (which it had once been) with tree-less brick veneers already baking in the fierce, late morning sun. Early autumn, but still hot.

"Carlos José Mondeigo, the penniless second son of a Portuguese count, arrived in here as an 'economic refugee' in 1975- fleeing the socialist government that had just confiscated his family's robber baron estate. He spent most of the money his old man had syphoned off into Swiss bank accounts buying himself an UStraylian passport via a very dubious immigration agent in Sydney. By the time Mondeigo reached the Rainbow Coast all he had left was a clapped out Falcon station wagon, half a tank of petrol, and ten dollars in his back pocket. Now he owns not only the Pearly Gates Hotel, but also St. Peter's Pizza, Shangri La La Land, and Heaven On A Cone- where he accommodates bakpakahs in the old cow bails behind the shop- the ones he recruits illegally for his various building projects and pays peanuts to (literally- or macadamias as the case may be)."

"Mondeigo always sounded pretty suss to me," Joe had to agree. Remembering a rare article in some city paper about how the developer had once been charged with medical fraud after passing himself off as a doctor.

"Of course he's suss!" Ronnie exploded. "Count Carlos The Younger took one look at Purgatory Beach and realised it was the last slice of untouched coast south of Brisbane. He drove straight back to Sydney where he posed as some sort of cancer specialist and began conning elderly widows into thinking they had some awful terminal illness- especially ones with their own homes and few, preferably no, close relatives. Or at least ones that cared. Nobody's saying the bastard actually bumped anybody off mind you, but it's funny how he suddenly seemed to 'inherit' a crumbling old Balmain terrace with a pile of fabulously valuable antique furniture, and then a pet shampoo business and a chain of hairdressing salons. He traded the lot in for that old quarry underneath Saviours Shoot- just before Wal Piper used his Shire Manager's discretion to quietly rezone it from Wasteland/Industrial to Freehold Residential. *Avalon Meadows* is where Carlos Mondeigo, Bryce Keitel and Lech Da Groot really cleaned up. At that time the rednecks on Council were falling over themselves to let anyone subdivide their exhausted dairy farms as much as they liked. Some of Mondeigo's recent house blocks are barely big enough to put a caravan on."

Joe was astonished that such obvious corruption could take place in his adopted home town- effectively demonstrating how little he knew about what really went on in the place.

"Look Ronnie, I don't actually care so much about Mondeigo's past- more about what he and Da Groot are doing *right now*, over my back fence! Did you know they're planning to put twelve townhouses right in the middle of our rainforest? It's not right. It can't be allowed to happen."

"Says who?" Joe's chauffeur demanded, playing devil's advocate. "It's private land zoned Freehold Residential. They can do whatever they like down there. Once the zoning is decided, the damage is done. You see, Joe, you can't win with these blokes. They know the rules backwards. In fact they made most of them up in the first place- before any of the rest of us even got here. The bastards cranking up Heaven's current property boom have been laying their devious plans for a very long time."

What? To suit themselves ?"

Ronnie rolled his eyes. "Gee, you're quick off the mark."

Joe let the sarcasm ride right over. He was that agitated.

"Trouble is," Ronnie continued depressingly, "it's not just Mondeigo, Da Groot and Bryce Keitel that you've got to worry about. The plot, as they say, really congeals when you realise there's a Mr. Big behind even that sinister trinity- some really heavy-duty mafia type prepared to crush anybody or anything that stands in his way. And I emphasise the 'body' part. Sorry comrade, but stand between a developer and an untouched parcel of pristine bush in a rising real estate market and your prospective life span is about equal to one of the endangered species it contains. All you can do is close your eyes, order spare kneecaps from your local orthopaedic guy, and hope the bulldozer phase doesn't last too long. If it happens during the spring northerlies you're fucked. Your house will be covered in a thick layer of weed and fly-larvae carrying black dust from all the fill they'll have to truck in."

"I can't believe anyone has the right to tamper with that rainforest."

"Neither do I! But they'll just say we're Nimbies, Joe. Only concerned with our own backyards."

"So if you can't stop it right where you live, then where the hell *do* you draw the line?"

Ronnie sighed. This argument was getting neither of them anywhere. Nor were *Perpetual Motion's* solar panels once a cloud came over and Ronnie's oil avoiding masterpiece struggled uphill again.

Joe reeled off some 'facts' he had read in the *Valhalla Times*: "The forest is smack up against the whole Limbo Creek estuarine system, a vital fish breeding ground. Bryce Keitel told me himself, it can't be touched. It's an essential wildlife corridor."

"Bryce Keitel told you that and what…you believed him!?"

Ronnie laughed and Joe simmered. If the truth be told it was this suckering by Keitel ten years ago that annoyed him the most. The humiliating realisation that he'd been fed bullshit and had actually fallen for an unReal Estate agent's assurances.

"Anyway, it's not just about native fauna," Ronnie preached to the converted, "I know for a fact that even Mondeigo's tame environmental 'expert' (sic) found 5 plant groups on the critical list in there. There's *got* to be acid sulphate once they start digging foundations and roads and stuff, plus the whole area's flood prone. Everyone knows that."

Well, nobody should be allowed to build on a flood plain. That's the bottom line- literally."

"But like I said, Joe: he'll just bring in fill and push the problem onto some other poor sod's property," Ronnie predicted, also speaking literally- as it could turn out.

"Oh great, so now we're looking at *years* of noisy earthmoving equipment and trucks skewering the kids who play in the street (because there's no parks or footpaths), making thought impossible…" Joe got angrier the more he went over the detail.

"Mate, 'round here- you pay the price, you load the dice. Know what I mean? In fact Mondeigo and Co don't even *have* to bribe a whole lot of Council staff. Most of our local town planners actually think that what they inflict on us is real 'progress'. They regard *us* as holding back the tides of history."

Joe shook his head. It was his birthday. He didn't need to hear much more of this.

"But we elected a *Green* council, Ronnie," The deluded romantic was harking back to that grand day 18 months before when the long suffering residents of Nullumbah Shire naively thought they'd voted their troubles away.

"Look Joe, no matter who you vote for the bloody government always gets in! And nothing changes. There's already been two State 'Inquiries' plus a Federal Royal Commission into corruption in Nullumbah Shire Council, and they found zilch mud sticking to anybody. Mondeigo and whoever pulls *his* strings are teflon coated. And you know why? Because they never write anything down. It's all worked out over margaritas on Bryce Keitel's back deck. Everything's done with a nod, a wink and a handshake while the bribes are distributed via a winning formula at their monthly poker game.

The basic attitude to anyone who doesn't agree with them is that you need to be 're-educated'- a lovely phrase don't you think? 'Re-educated' to their way of thinking. In order words, you'd have to be almost clinically insane and stark barking mad to want to hold up their bulldozers. Failing which, they'll use every expensive, tax deductible QC in their little black books, and every stalling tactic they and their tame town planners can dream up in order to get round the Common Good in favour of their own Private Self-interest. I tell you, Joe, *nothing* stands in the way of these people and a 'real estate opportunity'."

"But surely the Green Councillors can do *some*thing..." Joe couldn't accept it was that hopeless.

"Okay, say you *do* take on Mondeigo and Da Groot (and whoever really controls them). No matter what you do, mate, no matter how many petitions and objections you lodge, or public protest meetings you organise..."

Joe wasn't thinking of going quite that far.

"... the bloody council staff will *still* recommend it. And before you can say 'packets of cash in plain brown envelopes', there'll be thirty or forty townhouses looking down on your dope plants."

Joe gulped. "Thirty or forty townhouses? I thought it was only a dozen?"

"Only!" Ronnie was shaking his dreadlocks, suppressing guffaws and sprinkling tiny dark creatures onto his shoulders. Joe hoped they weren't parasitic.

"Sorry mate- in your dreams. It's more than twice that."

"But the Councillors can over-ride the bureaucrats. That's what democracy's all about...isn't it? They can still stop corrupt town planners when it comes to a vote."

"In which case Mondeigo will fire up his winebar full of clever barristers and take our near bankrupt Shire Council straight to the Property With Little Amenity Tribunal- where, surprise, surprise, 98% of the decisions tend to favour the developers."

"What do you mean 'bankrupt'?"

"Don't you read the local papers?"

"Only the stars."

Ronnie was losing his patience. "Well you've got to catch up, Joe. Our so called 'Green' Council can't even afford the legal fees to defend the few, half-hearted constraints they've tried to put on recent developments. Let alone bring Mondeigo and Co to book for the damage they've already caused by breaking their consent conditions throughout years of profit making. The developers always underspend on the roads, power and water that they're supposed to put in. Council's legal team made sure there were enough loop holes in the consent conditions to drive a bulldozer through- literally."

"I suppose they're in league with the developers too?" Joe queried limply, already guessing the answer.

"Of course! Council's solicitors set all the rules up to favour development in the first place. That was their brief: to promote open slather. More development equals more rates. It's the only responsible thing for a half broke Council to do. And if the State Government sacks our local representatives for financial incompetence and appoints an unelected administrator, or worse- forces Nullumbah to merge with one of the cowboy shires further inland, then you're back *behind* square one, Joe. There'd be no brakes on anything."

For a few moments both of them were too depressed to add anything more to this dreadful scenario. And as the sun re-emerged from behind a cloud *Perpetual Motion's* small sail was lowered and they were able to contemplate the rather bleak future confronting their chosen paradise as Ronnie and Joe continued to drift silently and petrol-less towards its bustling heart.

"Joe, believe me, no matter which way you turn you're going to lose. The individual, acting alone, has no hope."

"Then I'll act collectively."

"Good luck, comrade, firing up the Nullum' Protection Society." Ronnie was being his usual, sceptical, yet fairly realistic self.

"But there's a whole ecology at stake here, Ronnie! Fish, birds, trees, plants, animals. Ultimately, the water we drink, the air we breathe!"

"Joe, whatever steps you take, Mondeigo, Da Groot, 'Mr. Big', Bryce Keitel, the Mayor, the Shire Manager, Council's planners and the Property With Little Amenity Tribunal…have got you checkmated, mate. As Gra'eme says, 'the only trouble with Heaven is that suddenly a lot of retiring baby boomers and a thick slice of the foreign bakpakah market are starting to confuse the place with it's namesake.' We all know it's not that great living here. And I'm not just talking about the left over radiation from sandmining. It's the mosquito born viruses, the lack of proper roads and that chronic problem with the sewerage plant…"

As Ronnie continued to list all the things that were wrong with Heaven, he swung *Perpetual Motion* left at Repentance Roundabout drifting from Saint Street into Angel Avenue. The solar car coasted down Heaven's main thoroughfare aided now by a light northerly. Joe looked over at the 28 lot subdivision Mondeigo had just finished on what used to be the old public golf course (virtually given away by Wal Piper at a firesale price). As soon as they passed this gated community with its *Holy In One Estate* billboard plastered with triumphant 'Sold' signs, Joe realised the economic forces ranged against him were not only corrupt and irrational, but also clearly irresistible.

"You see Joe, the worst part is: they sneak up on you with a little tree line nibbled away here, and a small subdivision springing up there, and then a bit of Limbo creek getting shunted into pipes underground over yonder. And here a new road, and there a land resumption for what was supposed to be the new medical centre (but will instead become yet another overcrowded, fire prone, bakpakahs' hostel). And slowly, inevitably, all the planning requirements and strict environmental guidelines get watered down, loophole precedents are established that will stand up in the Tribunal, and then whammo- suddenly Mondeigo's thirty eight townhouses are smacked straight down onto the allotment adjoining your backyard."

Joe was flabbergasted. "Thirty eight!? You said thirty just now. Don't give me a heart attack."

"Thirty to forty."

"But you're guessing right? You don't know for sure. Christabel Eaton told me only a dozen, Ronnie. That's what it says in Mondeigo's Development Application."

"She obviously hasn't checked her in-tray. There's a late amendment to the DA that says thirty eight, definitely." Ronnie shrugged. "Council's Development Control Plan for most of Heaven allows anyone to subdivide private land as much as they like."

"Even though it's smack bang in the middle of a pristine coastal rainforest?"

"What difference does that make? 'Rainforest' is just a hippie word for 'jungle', Joe. Something with heathens in it, usually of the wrong colour."

Ronnie re-hoisted *Perpetual Motion's* small sail and they literally 'breezed' the rest of the way down Angel Avenue towards his shop: *The Alternative Everything.*

For a fleeting moment Joe entertained the idea of inviting Ronnie to his birthday BBQ on account of the free lift and all this (depressing) inside information. But he wasn't exactly *that* close a friend, and Barbara had gone right off him on account of Ronnie ashing his cigarette butts in the wheatgrass patch at last year's party. Joe had to admit that aspects of the clever inventor's personal behaviour *were* rather offputting. Other friends of Barbara's also wouldn't talk to him since Ronnie was on the wrong side of several of the various feuds with which most small towns are blighted. Not a good look for any attempt at a socially pleasant time. So Joe censored the generous thought and in any case, before he could've made the offer, Ronnie volunteered:

"By the way, I meant to say, Joe…are you all right?"

"How do you mean?"- Joe frowning.

"You look pretty shithouse, mate."

Always ready to believe the worst about himself the ex-TV hack was comprehensively taken aback. "Well, I nearly drowned in the surf this morning!"- defensive, put out.

"Oh, right," Ronnie backed off. "That must be it. Grey and ashen from the aftershock."

Grey and ashen? Joe was reeling. "Plus, I've just been threatened with a chainsaw," he exaggerated only slightly.

"'Course, yeah…right," Ronnie avoided, as *Perpetual Motion* pulled to a silent halt outside his extremely mixed business. *The Alternative Everything* was one of the more curious shops down the quiet end of Heaven's main street. And looked a lot like a permanent garage sale, full of junk nobody wanted- like poetic licences and wooden banana straighteners.

Ronnie opened the front door and went straight to the solar oven sunning itself in his front window. Here he handed Joe a complimentary tofu pie ('to fortify his body temple for the struggle ahead').

"You sure you don't want to see my latest little experiment?" beckoned Ronnie, keen on demonstrating it to a potential customer.

"What is it?"

"I'm calling it 'Bubble Magick'. You connect the outflow from your washing machine to a sprinkler in the back yard…

"Yeah and…?"

"Well, you get rainbow coloured bubbles as you recycle your grey water…"

Joe declined the opportunity of witnessing anything so sensible, useful and beautiful, and indulging his mood, took the pie rather bleakly, even somewhat ungratefully. Then just sort of…wandered back out into Angel Avenue again- with lunch in hand but profoundly more worried than when he'd left home.

Joe turned to check his external symptoms in the window of the Seraphim Surf Shop next door. Did he look more awful than usual? It was hard to tell. His reflection was both distorted and distracted by an anorexic store dummy trying to make a length of knotted string look like an expensive bikini.

In any case, Joe needed a proper mirror and probably a comprehensive series of medical tests to be sure. Either way, Ronnie's offhand comment snapped Joe back to the real world. In all the morning's excitement he'd completely forgotten!

Lacking a watch (as always) he checked the town clock standing at the other end of Angel Avenue where it intersected with Salvation Strand above Purgatory Beach. His annual dental checkup (designed to coincide with his birthday) was supposed to happen 11 minutes ago – or 8 or 15 or 20minutes ago (depending on which face you checked).

Shit! Even if Gail Divine's waiting room wasn't packed (as usual), he'd barely have time to squeeze this appointment in before the more important one with Gra'eme. The day was truly getting out of hand.

PANIC CUT TO:

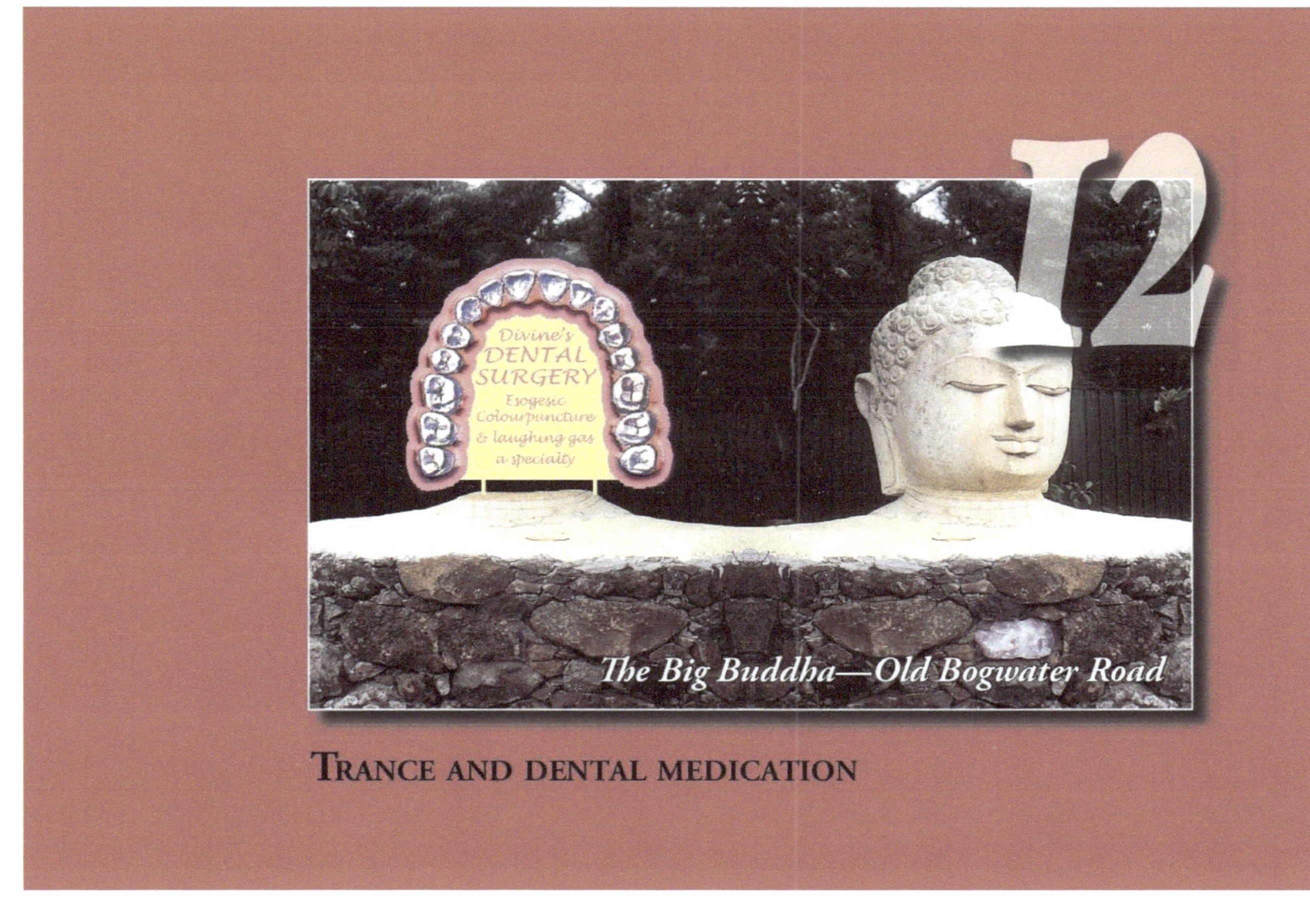

TRANCE AND DENTAL MEDICATION

The Big Buddha on Old Bogwater Road. Just another one of **HEAVEN**'s many colourful 'big things'. (See also the Big Surfboard, the Big Kombi, the Big Bakpak and the Big Pathsandra With His 16-Year Old Childbride.) Proudly sponsored by Gail Divine's Dental Surgery—esogesic colourpuncture and laughing gas a specialty.

Affix stamp here

#12 of 33 Postcards from Heaven

printed on gently mulched, plantation-grown, organic bamboo fibre using recycled greywater and bound with a biodegradable non-toxic glue

No animal or dolphin suffered in the making of this card
(apart from, of course, its author)

12

TRANCE AND DENTAL MEDICATION

"Life's a journey - usually in a broken down car
with a lot of burnt bridges behind and too many potholes ahead."
(Gra'eme *Acting The Mongrel*)

11.11am, Downtown Heaven, Friday 13th March

Running late, Joe hurried back up Angel Avenue, past the Post Office and saw that the queue was already snaking out of the building- as far as St. Peter's Pizza (and it's blinking, neon sign of the Apostle standing with halo and staff- urging customers to 'come along and eat before we both starve').

The girls behind the counter in the Post Office were cracking bad jokes again. This was not a good sign with the invasion of Easter less than a fortnight away. The queues were sure to lengthen and it could only get worse for them.

At the top of Angel Avenue, where it met Purgatory Beach, Joe swung right in front of the colourfully unreliable town clock and headed south along Salvation Strand- which ran parallel to the beach, its magnificent stand of giant Norfolk Pines effectively stabilising the frontal dune, just where the town needed it most.

CUT TO:

Divine Dental Surgery, Five minutes later...

Joe is trying to ignore the frightening posters of diseased gums and broken teeth glooming down from the walls around him. He didn't have to be reminded that this annual checkup was important. The pudgy writer wasn't a total hypochondriac, just someone who believed you owed it to yourself to hear your body talk- because nobody else would. Unless they were your mother. And that alone, made it harder for orphans like Joe.

Yet this is the very reason why Kate and Joe had come to Heaven in the first place; and why Joe had stayed: for the healing thing. Not realising that you as soon as you were cured, local wisdom insisted that you were obliged to move on- or suffer the whole debilitating illness that you came there with all over again. Which may well be the best explanation yet for the apparent interminability of Joe Deegan's mid-life crisis.

He took the opportunity to double check his star sign in this week's *Valhalla Times* lying beside Gail Divine's pile of trashy women's magazines. Since it was a Pisces birthday week, Krystal Astarte predicted that: "A dark 'stigma' will come to settle on the fish's bright spirit on the 13th, making them pine for cool seas and lost oceans. But pleasure and pain and bliss and suffering share the same home, and all dance to the same cosmic rhythm..."

Joe sighed again at the uncanny ability of astrologers to get it just *so* right. He felt pain certainly, and had had his share of suffering already this morning. But bliss and pleasure remained conspicuous by their absence. In fact, all Joe really felt right now was tired. Soul-drenchingly weary. He worried that this lack of energy might be an early sign of chronic fatigue syndrome, or late-onset diabetes; and mentioned these fears to Gail a few minutes later as she plucked away at some molars down the back. Joe was sitting in anticipation of pain, gripping the hand rests of her deceptively comfortable operating chair, fully expecting bad news.

"It's not chronic fatigue or diabetes you should be worried about," Gail's little pick was lingering over and worrying what seemed like a definite hole.

"Haf vu vound thomething ?" he asked, unable to speak properly while her mirror rested against his tongue. She found it a useful tactic with nervous patients like Joe. Mainly to stop them crapping on.

"I von't haf xth-rays, Gail."

She knew it was pointless to argue with him about the minimal risk from ionising radiation in current medical Xray practice, so she merely went on pricking her way along his lower molars.

"Then why not try Esogesic Colourpuncture?

"Whath that eggsaktlie?"- Joe as always, prepared to suspend judgment on any new therapy until presented with the 'facts'- however empirically impossible they might be to produce.

"Colourpuncture concentrates vibrating light on certain chakra points. It can restore tooth enamel and even strengthen the gums."

"Ith it kuvurd bi Medicar?"

"Get real Joe, we're talking cutting-edge healing therapy here."

Gail was expressing mild irritation so Joe backed off, promising to think about it. Not wanting to cloud her emotions while her pick lingered. As soon as she released his tongue he tried to lighten the atmosphere with an old joke: "Don't forget your working on a prize winning smile there, Gail."

Which almost worked. At least she wasn't doing her usual frowning and wincing bit as her instruments now plucked their way along the upper left hand side of that almost famous grin.

The Smiling Competition at the Vogue Picture Theatre Nullumbah forty four years ago was the only thing Joe had ever won- establishing for him at a very early age the fascinating connection between pretending and receiving an actual cash reward. In this instance a pound note so crisp and new he dared not spend it- despite the urgings of all his new found friends in grade two at St. Mary's primary school. Sadly, the intervening decades had seen that cheeky leer sculptured away to a ghost of it's former glory by nocturnal grinding- evidence of genuine internal strife, even at the end of days planned so carefully.

In fact, in hovering over Joe's mouth now, Gail Divine looked down into the desperation of a dozen different dentists who had drilled and sanded and plugged and patched away at Joe's teeth in a rear guard effort to save them. And, being human, they were all capable of making mistakes which Gail often had to over-rule and hack into. A record in Joe's mouth of the egregious errors of her profession. At the same time, she thanked Gaia that there were still people as old as Joe with fluoride-free childhoods. Otherwise, she'd be reduced to gum work and the odd emergency call from the local footy team. As precarious as it may seem, people like Joe were people like Gail Divine's future. She wanted to see him live as long as possible- at least until some serious bridge work became necessary. Joe's dentist certainly wasn't going to short change him on any shonky New Age Kure. She really did believe in Esogesic Colorpuncture.

Then, just as Gail thought her luck with Joe this year might have run out, the little pick hit paydirt and almost disappeared inside one of Joe's wisdom (sic) teeth. She experienced a thrill not unlike that of an archaeologist falling through the roof of some fabulously intact, but long concealed and richly decorated ancient tomb.

"Uh oh," she gloated, realising she could now afford that trip to Port Douglas after all. "You're not going to like what I have to say…"

Joe hated it already as he swivelled sideways to get the 'big picture' on her Dentalcam monitor. How many years had he sat in Gail's deceptively comfortable operating chair and watched the sad parade of his cracked and failing fillings pass before them both on this very screen? All that pain and expense, trying to salvage and patch together the impossible.

"How bad is it?"- Joe wondering whether he could conjure another extension on his credit card.

"It's a crown I'm afraid. That filling is compromised beyond belief." There was genuine scorn behind her tone. "Who did this work?"

Joe was tempted to say that she had done it herself, but since her memory was undoubtedly better than his, he had to admit defeat. "A dentist in Melbourne."

When her lip curled derisively, Joe pre-empted with: "Look, he was very reasonable…"

"You pay peanuts you get monkeys."

It was time to cut to the chase. Joe couldn't stand any more sarcasm.

"How much?"

"There's another large filling right alongside it that looks like it won't make your next birthday. It'd be cheaper to do the two crowns at the same time."

She always offered him these impossible choices. "Great news on the day I give away my job, Gail."

"Well- extraction *is* the cheapest option," she offered, knowing full well he'd never part with anything.

"How long will the second one last?"- hoping he could squeeze at least another year's worth out of the not-so-bad filling.

Gail shrugged and shook her head. "You bite something hard: a macadamia nut, a crusty roll- it could crumble next week. Then you'd be back for a another three hours in the chair. (Whereas) we can always get a discount from the lab if I order two crowns at the same time.

"What are we talking roughly?"

"A thousand minimum."

"For both!"

"Each- assuming there's no root canal work."

Joe's heart sank. But before he could properly do the sums, his dentist's expression grew even darker.

"How long have your gums been bleeding?"

"Bleeding?" For a hopeful moment he thought it might only have been his nose again.

"Haven't you noticed when you brush your teeth?"

Joe had, but put it down to over-anxious flossing.

"There's something very nasty happening to your gums, Joe."

"Nasty ?"

There was that word again. The one health professionals always used when they meant something really serious, probably life threatening.

"There are all sorts of viruses that get into your mouth through bleeding gums, you know: hepatitis, meningococcal, golden staph, HIV, cholera…"

"Geezus" Joe was reeling. As if he didn't already have enough to worry about.

"Gum infections are also a risk factor for heart disease- especially for someone like yourself who's had rheumatic fever. It's called 'endocarditis'. Your heart valve could become infected and seriously compromised."

Her examination successfully concluded (from her point of view), she tipped back the little miner's light on her forehead and returned the pick- her magic money wand- to the autoclave machine.

"Are you saying I should be worried?"

Joe rinsed out his septic mouth spitting into the round sink beside her chair- and felt a touch dizzy as he watched bloody water swirl round the lip of the bowl. It was another wobbly moment in a day soon to be peppered with them.

"Well… " she paused pregnantly lifting her shoulders, "You could feel fine one minute, then…" she let her shoulders drop. Joe's remnant optimism plummeted with them. "The fact is, a heart attack can come on at any time of the day or night, even in your sleep." And having softened him up with that much, she turned to her diary, moving in for the kill. "I may be able to squeeze you in to a cancellation next week. We'll need three sessions, the middle one will take several hours. Would you like hypnosis or laughing gas?"

Joe favoured the gas. Of course. It's also why he preferred Gail over Bernie Lipscomb in Nullumbah. But other problems intruded on this pleasant prospect: "Maybe I should book my gums in as well?"

"You'll need a periodontist for that."

Joe could hear the disappointment in her voice.

"But…given your family history, your father and two uncles dying of heart attacks, your double figures cholesterol reading, the bottle of wine every night, the tendency you have to worry all the time, and most of all the smoking!"

"But I cycle every day, Gail. I'm in the surf morning, noon and night. I eat *lots* of fruit and vegies. I *love* mangoes."

"Look, Joe, the thing about a heart attack is: 85% of them come on completely out of the blue. You could feel in the pink of health one minute, an ultra marathoner say, with arteries as clean as the water pipes in a brewery, no family history of cardiovascular disease, a near zero cholesterol reading, and then pow! Suddenly a bit of plaque breaks off inside an artery and you're history. Maybe stress *is* a factor. Who knows? Blood vessels are all part of the nervous system too, and in your case we're talking more nervous than normal."

Again she shrugged, signaling the limits of her expertise, leaving his personal survival up to him. "Barring some accident, I'd say…you might be lucky to see the next Olympic games."

"See them?! I expect to be competing," he swaggered.

"In what? Competitive Bullshitting?" they both laughed as she pressed the foot pedal that brought Joe up from a reclining, banana lounge position. Effectively ending the session.

"There'd be too many politicians ahead of me in that field," Joe predicted, relieved to discover she was joking about this depressing prognosis.

Actually she wasn't, but he didn't know that. And instead, Joe unburdened himself of another awful premonition:

"Funny you should mention the Games though Gail, because I had a dream about the opening ceremony a few nights back. The flock of peace doves were blown off course by a freak gust of wind and flew straight into the Olympic flame where they were instantly barbequed and dropped onto the horrified crowd below like so many wood-fired chickens. Nobody took it as a good omen for the new millennium."

Unimpressed by that, Gail Divine flicked off her disposable rubber gloves and hurried to a conclusion. "Joe, I'm not a cardiologist, okay? But go see one, get a stress ECG and possibly an angiogram, just to be sure. Then try the Esogesic Colourpuncture. But forgodsake, stop smoking! Give yourself a fighting chance."

He liked it when she was angry with him. Call it kinky, but if he was going to have to endure pain from a dentist, Joe much preferred it be a woman. That's also why he opted for Gail over Bernie.

About to complete his exit however, the incurable romantic hesitated. Because strangely, he suddenly found himself on the point of 'discharging'; and didn't want to dissolve into tears in front of her crowded waiting room. It wouldn't be a good look for either of them.

"Is there something else?" she asked, frowning. Unable to just push him out. (Much as she'd like to.)

"I don't know, Gail. I…feel I'm just not cutting the mustard anymore. I should be the happiest person alive. I own a modest property in the most beautiful place imaginable. Barbara is the light of my life. She *saved* my life… " He was raving, stifling sobs as:

Gail's reliable clock continued to tick out unproductive dental time.

"But …" she prompted, finally losing both her patience and now, potentially, some of her patients as he opened the door and they all rotated towards him, looking up, wondering what was going on- while Joe remained rooted to the spot, unable to move forward. This was weird. He had no idea what had come over him.

"Why is it so difficult for me to even express it?" he expressed, hovering in her surgery doorway, on show in front of people waiting to succeed him.

"Explaining how characters feel is what I do for a living. Often in pretty awful soap operas."

"Let me hazard a guess," his dentist offered, also acutely aware of clients watching. "Your life, Joe, despite its superficial wonderfulness, lacks a certain sparkle, right?"

Joe took a deep breath as another rogue tear ambled off the tip of his nose and dropped down to mingle with the growing pool of red fluid in the dimple above the centre of his upper lip. His nose was bleeding again- from the pressure. The spectacle was getting worse. And less hygienic.

She quickly handed him some tissues. He was grateful and pathetic at the same time.

"Ever since Kate died I haven't done anything that I could seriously claim as mine." Again the tears threatened. "Nothing remotely interesting has left my computer in all that time… I've lost it, Gail. I really have. Without Barbara there's nothing. Zero. Zilch."

Gail Divine again felt as impotent as she was impatient. "Joe, I don't have any simple answers. I don't even think there *is* a simple answer. Try the Esogesic Colourpuncture. Get a potion from Raiina Virago. The occasional salt gargle will help with the gums. I won't give you antibiotics because they've been so over prescribed they basically don't work anymore. Above all, stop living so much in your head! Be grateful and look on the bright side: the more boring your life becomes the longer it will seem to last."

Joe nodded, sighed, and finally began moving again- out through Gail's astonished waiting room. His life was certainly boring- despite its ideal location. There was no doubt about that.

"Try smiling," was his dentist's parting advice. "They've done a study, Joe, it's true: laughter *is* the best medicine. People have cured themselves of cancer just by watching old Marx Brothers movies. And you know why? Because it takes 87 muscles to frown and only 4 to smile,"- appealing directly to his lazy side. (If he had one- which he did, sometimes.)

"Yeah, thanks, Gail, I'll give it a try," he mumbled as he paid for the examination with a seriously depleted credit card, and emerged out of the Divine Dental Surgery back onto Salvation Strand. Where he soon found himself blinking over at the crystal clear breakers off Purgatory Beach, absorbing again, and marveling at, the sombre yellow light of another late morning in early autumn.

Here Joe tore himself away from the idea of a quick body surf, and turned left instead, heading towards the confused and misleading town clock at the top of Angel Avenue, bracing himself against a future that was looking distinctly more uncertain than when he'd left home less than an hour ago…

WIPE ACROSS TO:

ALWAYS TRY TO SMILE

The ever-changing face of the Man In The Moon at Luna Park, St Kilda. Just another colourful, cheap, crazy, mixed-up beachside village about to be overwhelmed by its own laid back success. And only 29 million Loyal Traveler Miles™ from Nullumbah International Airport. Gateway to **HEAVEN** us traylia. Capital of the Rainbow Coast.

Affix stamp here

#13 of 33 Postcards from Heaven

printed on gently mulched, plantation-grown, organic bamboo fibre using recycled greywater and bound with a biodegradable non-toxic glue

No animal or dolphin suffered in the making of this card
(apart from, of course, its author)

13
ALWAYS TRY TO SMILE

"Sticks and stones may break your bones
but deep mocking laughter always hurts."
(Gra'eme *My Chiropractor Always Cracks Me Up*)

11.27am, Downtown Heaven, Friday 13th March

Joe Deegan drifted along Salvation Strand in a kind of blur. His teeth were killing him-literally. His jaw wobbled like he already had a full set of dentures and the springs at the back were rusted out from too many body surfs. He somehow managed to stagger fifty metres (as far as the intersection with Angel Avenue where Heaven's dysfunctional clock tower overlooked Purgatory Beach), feeling about as far from smiling right now as a newly elected government was from keeping a non-core promise.

On the upside, a smile didn't cost anything. Nor would it need translating. A cheerful, open set of pearly whites was the same in Hebrew as it was in German, Italian, Japanese, Flemish, Spanish, Danish, Dutch, Portuguese, French, Welsh or Canadian. And consequently pretty handy on any street in Heaven these days.

Like the curtain being drawn aside in a down market theatre, Joe unleashed his crooked front teeth on the world. Letting go. Widening the lips to a sick, loony grin…

One visitor from Coolangatta caught it front on and quickly dropped his head, hurrying past, clutching his wallet, hoping police assistance might be nearby. Little realising that it wasn't. And never would be if Sergeant Doreen Harris had any say in the matter. (Which she did.)

Discouraged by this unpromising start, Joe turned and shambled on down Angel Avenue seeking some sort of 'Big Picture' from the Beatification Beauty Parlour's front window. Alas, it was nothing like the prize winning smile produced so effortlessly at the Vogue Picture Theatre, Nullumbah, almost a lifetime ago. And of course, the dreadful leer looming back at him was bad enough; but the hollow, fearful eyes above it gave the game away completely.

He put his card in the Heartless Bank's autoteller machine. It was rejected. A printed receipt said:

"Your credibility's exhausted."

That was a bit personal, thought Joe. Even for a ruthless financial conglomerate. If his mortgage repayments had been up to scratch, and he hadn't just privately thrown away a perfectly well paid job, and the queue wasn't already a mile long behind the Heartless Bank's only human teller, Joe would have stormed straight in and complained to the manager…

None of which was calculated to keep him smiling. Nor did it jog any memory of the looming appointment with Gra'eme. Which Joe had effectively forgotten about in all the anxiety produced by Gail's depressing prognosis.

Attempting, against the odds, to feel happy in himself (dentist's orders), Joe risked a shy smirk at a couple up from Newcastle. Something seemed to work. They actually smiled back. As did two Viking virgins from Reykjavik- provoking no residual fear of Vikings generally in Joe's Irish genes.

In fact the low sensation thrill seeker soon found himself on a roll. His award winning grin still worked! Most people in Heaven *were* smiling back. It was obvious: a happy face said that you weren't a threat. You wished strangers well. You were relaxed about things generally and there was nothing to worry about. A smile was not only a release, but a declaration of hope, an elimination of all threatening behaviour. Gail Divine was brilliant. Laughter *is* the best medicine. Send in the clown doctors…

Joe's mood lifted considerably as he beamed at the homeless, lonely surfer who always sat on the footpath with his carton of Milo and board full of dings, staring up at the videos set into the wall of the Seraphim Surf Shop, watching the swell of oceans meeting beaches on coasts that were far far away. Joe moved on and grinned at another bakpakah from Brazil, then two more eco-refugees from the Cold Coast (who all smiled back). He became so caught up in the moment that he almost tripped over a grubby old blue heeler, tied up outside Heaven On A Cone, looking more in hunger than in hope at each ice cream coming out.

As Joe regained his balance and moved on to Martyrs' Meats two doors up, he smiled at Brian the Butcher arranging 'today's special' in his shop window: 'calves hearts'.

Joe's happy mood rapidly evaporated.

Here was his dentist's warning laid out on a plate, so to speak. He stared in new fascination at what was, after all, just a small nub of muscle the same colour and texture as a leg of lamb, with arteries splayed along the outside: the left anterior descending (LAD) and the right anterior descending (RAD) and the Circumflex Artery (CA) that went all the way around the back. In humans as in cattle, hearts were the same. All mammals together, Joe realised, convinced now that it would be easier than he imagined to give away animal products altogether and become the vegan he had long promised himself.

Because, that's what the heart came down to: a muscle pump; light greyish-red when drained of blood and on display like this in Brian's window. The butcher smiled in expectation of a customer: but Joe was too depressed to return the favour. He wouldn't be buying any meat today, thank you, Brian. In any case, Barbara had already stocked up on too many saveloys for his party…

But what kept the heart beating? What made us want to go on? Joe wondered. What pushed us forward into the next moment? Was it just that heart cells, when they were cloned in a petri dish, started beating of their own accord? Working all our lives without a single break. Until they stopped. And then you did…

Joe wandered on, amazed that anything inside him could be so energetic. Something that kept working every single waking (and sleeping) moment of his life. He had reached Repentance Roundabout and swung round and round it- eventually heading back up towards the beach again. Letting the sun warm his face as he climbed the last bit of Angel Avenue up onto the grand esplanade of Salvation Strand- from whence he'd started the next stage of his life only a few minutes ago. Feeling the sunlight taking on a deeper golden ochre as the days became short again and the nights longer…

Too preoccupied by intimations of his own demise, Joe still failed to remember the vital appointment with Gra'eme and swung left at the confused clock tower, this time drifting north along Salvation Strand- in the vague direction of the Lighthouse…

He got as far as the Lifesaving Club, and just sort of hung out on the footpath. Dazed and wondering: about how long he might have left? About how long did anyone have? About why life was so fragile- despite its apparent fecundity? And why did some store dummies have their heads copped off? And what was the point of ironing? And why was such a dull low scoring game as soccer so popular. And where the hell was he going, anyway? When he'd just meandered aimlessly all over town!

Not that we're talking such a big area here, except that, there was no proper direction to any of it. Eleven minutes ago Joe had sat, on the verge of tears, in Gail Divine's comfortable operating chair. Now here he was, leering away at people like the village idiot. Which he technically was at this very moment. Certainly he was the town's pre-eminent current example. And on any given day in Heaven that was no mean feat. Joe's own village seemed to attract idiots like flies to dog manure on Purgatory Beach.

Certainly, he was hovering on the brink of some kind of mental collapse- right in front of the Life Saving Club- recalling (for no particular reason) that it was in the St. Kilda Lifesaving Club where Kate had first broken the news to him.

IRIS IN TO:

St. Kilda Lifesaving Club, 11 years ago…

They were doing a play about the tensions among lifesavers preparing for a big surf carnival- using the clubhouse itself as a location for the production. Kate's company of actors had stumbled across the bright idea of staging plays in the places were they were actually set- such as lifts, trams and boarding houses. Partly because they rejected the whole stale idea of the proscenium arch. Mostly because they couldn't afford a proper theatre. It was to be the last decent thing Joe ever wrote- because of all that was to follow…

The fact that Kate had cancer at all seemed incredible. Being aware of your body was what being a performer was all about. The only instrument she had. Kate was meticulous about having all the relevant tests and smears, as and when required. But the pathology lab (or her GP) got it wrong. Now Joe and Kate's ordered, ordinary life would be thrown into chaos. A long grind of 18 months of specialists and radiologists and drug programmes and surgeons and pain and apparent recoveries and waiting in hospital corridors for doctors who couldn't find a vein to put the drip in. A year and a half of mainstream cures and alternative therapies and praying for miracles. But neither love nor angels, nor lifesavers could save Kate. And all were needed in large amounts.

IRIS OUT TO:

11.36am, Downtown Heaven, Friday 13th March

More than a decade after that first diagnosis and Joe stood there on the footpath in front of Heaven's Lifesaving Club, quietly imploding. This was where random smiling got you. Right back to where your depression started. He swung away from the clubhouse, glancing up and down Salvation Strand. Then out over the late morning glory of Purgatory Beach, vaguely realising where he was. (Which put him ahead of Gra'eme in this respect who had by now been fuming impatiently for a full six minutes in his float tank at *Seventh Heven*.)

The couldabeen minor playwright did actually look up at the town clock once, but only registered that the morning was (probably) almost gone (depending on which face you took as being closest to the real time). And here he still was, confronting demons from his past, knowing he had to pay attention. Or be lost. Which more or less described both his current mental and geographical state.

For no particular reason, Joe turned again and headed south, back along Salvation Strand- away from the clubhouse- then suddenly lurched right at the clock again in front of the Pearly Gates Hotel, and cut down into Angel Avenue a second time, before swirling left into Saint Street at Repentance Roundabout. He stopped traffic at the pedestrian crossing (feeling the power) and did an about turn, turning round and round the roundabout. It seemed odd to find himself suddenly travelling in both physical and metaphysical circles. He felt light headed as a result, along with a sudden urge to sit down (or throw up- whichever came first), wandering without any particular direction or knowledge as to what he should be doing. Overtaken by a strange dislocating feeling. Again.

Joe sailed on past a tabloid headline outside the Good Newsagent gloating that a: "Misfit Kills 15 At School." As if 'fitting-in' was some sort of achievement! I'm a misfit, Joe reasoned, standing back from his hopeless, chaotic life for a moment. Seeing it in some sort of perspective at last, in the middle of a birthday, in the middle of Heaven's main street. And not liking terribly much what he was presented with.

He began to worry that he might have fatally damaged his always fragile 'reputation' with that misguided stint on *Golden Sands*. In the fickle world of commercial television you were only ever as bad as your last worst show. Now everyone would know how Joe had been called and truly cheapened.

He passed a young feral with a thirsty fire stick, begging for kerosene money- thin as a rake, his hair matted into defacto dread locks from too many nights spent sleeping on muddy rainforest floors. A teenage hobo in a vinyl waistcoat. You could see he needed food more than fuel. And a dry roof for the night. But he wanted *fire*! Joe understood why and rummaged in his pocket, handing the poor lazy soul an equally lazy dollar.

Now he really had to sit down, if only to stop the street from spinning. It already felt like Gail's predicted coronary coming on early. But as soon as Joe reached for a bench in Arcadia Park it moved away from him- like a wooden horse on the edge of some merry-go-round. No matter how hard he tried, he just couldn't reach out and climb on. Joe was stuck with the organ in the centre. Calm down mate, he tried to reassure himself, echoing something sensible such as Barbara might say: "it's obviously only a mild panic attack."

He was clearly overwrought by the prospect of thirty eight townhouses full of Cold Coast types gawking over his back fence. Not to mention Larry's mutilation, the confrontation with Da Groot, and Barbara's imminent return to Israel. It was all compounded by re-living Kate's illness, and flashes of a childhood stolen from him by the Brothers.

Or was it just a birthday thing? His last as a forty something. Getting overly sentimental at the idea of facing a sixth! decade. Definitely the end of whatever might have been youthful about him. Part of the late middle years. Giving the lie to the fantasy that he was capable of anything- if only he could find the motivation to kick his life forward. If only he could find a place for a Little Lie Down. Perhaps this is where it ended for him anyway: a hobo on a park bench, with soiled trousers, mind half gone, and dribbling...

Because he gave a dollar to a young stranger, suspecting an angel in disguise, and whack! A moment later here he was, reeling in a park, like some hopeless derro. Could it be the dope? Affecting his brain like some dreaded acid flashback? Joe knew he smoked too much, but drugs were there- in the biosphere- all around us. As useful as they were natural and necessary. They satisfied an urge to remove oneself *from* oneself. Who needed reality the way it was? A quiet smoke replaced what was missing. It got you through the day, and if you were lucky and could stay awake that long, the night was well. Because everything else had broken down. Once again Gra'eme was right: we were *all* prisoners of the imagination...

But why *did* Joe feel such an intractable disquiet about the 'real' world? Why had simply earning a living become so demeaning for people generally? He couldn't bend his soul to the task anymore. Because there *was* something missing in his life: Kate, Barbara, his parents, the children he would never have, the fabulously successful screenplays he would never write. He needed a purpose, a sane community to live in, where every tree was holy, every leaf and animal had a place and a soul. Where people finally related to each other for the bumbling, hopeless, astonishing creatures that we really were, thanks be to Gaia.

All he'd ever wanted was a straight-forward, self-sustaining lifestyle. What Joe got were feelings of entrapment and being cut off. If he had done injury somehow obliquely, to anyone, say by being the descendant of a master colonial race who had been cruel and wrong, and evil, then he was sorry. Abjectly, unreservedly, deeply sorry. Mea Culpa apologetic. Mea Maxima Culpa. And he would have to try and do something to redress the balance.

Because there comes a point, always, where you finally *have* to do *some*thing. You have to act, to draw a line in the sandwich and cut to the mustard. Joe realised he could oppose Mondeigo and Da Groot and 'do his bit for the environment'; but was Ronnie Rainbows right? Was it only because Joe's own backyard was affected? Forests the size of some small European countries were being erased every day in various feats of wanton environmental vandalism. Not all of them in Queensland. So what if 50 odd species were exterminated at the same time? Why didn't Joe do something about *that*!? Or the billion children in the world hovering on the verge of starvation? Was it simply easier to act locally? Less of a strain? Or just more selfish?

The inactive one finally contained a bench in Arcadia Park, pulled it towards him and sat down. The mist in his head cleared while the feelings of nausea subsided. Barbara *was* right: you only truly discover a place by first getting lost in it. You had to abandon yourself into somewhere inorder to see it fully for the first time. Israel was where she longed to be. And ditto, Heaven, for Joe. So be it. Let it all go. Even Barbara. The last great love of his life...

Right on cue the sun came out from behind a cloud and again warmed his skin. It felt good. Ultra-violent and potentially carcinogenic, but good. He was becoming too internal, too head driven. His isolating, writerly habits and meditative lifestyle were demonstrably unbalanced. This was not conducive to good health. It hardly needed a dentist to tell him that.

Gra'eme had urged Joe to "Look inside and wake!" Okay, the former hack scriptwriter made a mental note to get out more. Invite a few people over for dinner occasionally. Without Barbara around his days had become too same-y. One (admittedly usually pretty fabulous) day followed the next in a soothing, unchanging pattern. Half the time he couldn't tell any given day of the week from another (and he chastised tradies like Onecoat Kev!). The world, time, events were swirling past without him. (Much like the benches in this park.) 'The Main Event' trundling on like the impervious, over arching steamroller that it was, effectively leaving Joe far behind. He had ceased to be a participant. It would soon be over and he would have nothing much to look back on. Let alone leave behind.

The ancient Greeks knew there was a time that was measurable and one no clock could keep track of (even one as erratic as Heaven's). Like the time that happened inside a car accident where everything slowed down as you drifted inexorably towards the impact. There was even a third kind: Cosmic Time. Great Wheels of Time encompassed in the life spans of universes. Time in Heaven, Gateway to the Rainbow Coast, capital of the Enchanted Triangle, was a transitional thing too. Between the 'Now' and the 'Here-Ever-After. A moment of which could contain everything…and nothing. Like the moment Joe was experiencing right now, in Arcadia Park.

As Gra'eme proposed, and Joe's life mostly demonstrated: the 'Present' was the only thing we could effectively affect- the only temporal niche in which anyone had an influence. If we had no more grasp on the future than we had on the past, then the 'Moment' was all we had, and of course, we had it ALL the Time! They came one after another. These myriad little eternities inside everyone's life span. We shaped our personal journeys with a thousand nano decisions made every single day. Small choices that eventually accumulated into a tendency here, an attitude there, a feeling or insult left behind- like cigarette butts thrown out of a passing car window- sometimes to lie dead and neglected amongst the discarded stubbies and chip packets, sometimes to start a devastating bush fire…

Bang! You give a dollar to a dreadlocked, potential angel, expecting blessings and one moment, one day, one year, one decade of your life is gone. Five decades in Joe's case. Flash, cut, over and done with. That's a wrap. Blackout.

BLACKOUT TO:

Complete Black, No Time, No Place

Nothing happens. Nothing can be seen or heard. Utter blankness.

FADE UP TO:

11.45am, Arcadia Park, Friday 13th March

Even thinking about it was exhausting. The Beautiful Life had slowed and dulled Joe, left him way behind in the achievement stakes. Yet we were all potential time millionaires because we all started from the same bottom line: Now. Today. This moment from which we could basically do or ignore (or eat or drink) whatever we liked.

But still we shied away from the gift of the Eternal Present and all its potential. Afraid of the freedom it contained for us. Afraid of what might happen if we threw off our familiar shackles and embraced *all* that was possible. Afraid of life without some crutch. Unable to cope without dope, certainly without hope.

Well it was time for Joe to rouse himself from all that crap. Time to shake off amotivational syndrome once and for all. To stop looking outside dreaming, and to start looking inwards and WAKE!

CRASH CUT TO:

14

LOSING THE PLOT

Heaven by night

Just another colourful moonrise over captivating Cape Surprise!—jewel in the crown of **HEAVEN US**traylia—where every night is party night because when the sun goes down the fun begins (usually at home, alone, with one, or at best two, channels of free-to-air television where the reception is borderline bearable.)

#14 of 33 Postcards from Heaven

No animal or dolphin suffered in the making of this card
(apart from, of course, its author)

14
LOSING THE PLOT

"What was lost will be found,
what was deconstructed will be reconstructed."
(Gra'eme *Overcoming Your Fear Of Fearing Fear Itself*)

12.00pm-ish, Pearly Gates Hotel, Friday 13th March

It was just on, around about, high noon in Heaven. And (depending on which colourfully unreliable clock in town you checked), either exactly halfway through Joe Deegan's birthday…or shortly before…or sometime afterwards- when the lover and scriptwriter was suddenly overcome by a strange, woozy feeling. Indeed, for a pretty awful moment Joe could neither recall who he was exactly, or even what he was meant to be doing…

He seemed, for some unaccountable reason, to be holding a luke warm tofu pie under the hand dryer in a gents toilet somewhere- with no firm idea of how he came to be there.

The day was turning out so badly now, he began to worry that he might have become the subject of some vile Reality (sic) TV show- with hidden cameras secretly capturing and broadcasting all his worst, private moments out to a sniggering world.

Straining every available neuron (and to be brutally frank we're not talking large numbers here), Joe Deegan attempted to recapture the last few minutes, the last few hours, the balance of that hazy, chaotic morning…

Fifty already, and so far he'd lost his mail box, his job, possibly his nerve, was clearly squandering the last great love of his life, had nearly drowned in the surf, been threatened by a psychopath, and only moments ago was informed by his dentist that he may have a potentially life threatening biochemical reaction going on inside his hardening arteries- thanks to his decaying gums. Half a century old and his mid-life crisis was now entering its 10th bewildering year. So far, just another Beautiful Day in a cut rate paradise without all the fuss…

Oh shit, hang on-

He was forty nine wasn't he? It was his *forty ninth* birthday…?

For a desperate moment Joe couldn't be sure… Then it hit him like a sore throat on a freezing Melbourne morning: fuck! he *was* fifty and he hadn't even realised! He'd made a mistake with the sums again. There were too many thirteens in play, and too many numerological versions of eleven when you looked at times and dates.

But…in which case, Barbara would surely have organised a proper party- not just the stock, standard BBQ, with its usual suspects: his guru/accountant and a maimed handful of casual acquaintances. Short term memory blasted to shreds. Had Joe just blanked out there for five minutes or a whole year? This wobbly feeling was getting him down.

He turned the pie over to warm its bottom side, trying to get a larger grip on what was actually happening. Then Joe glanced up and accidentally caught sight of himself in a toilet mirror. The sad, ravaged face glaring back at him seemed much older than fifty. Was this the manifest failure of self control he presented to the world? Geezus! It was time to just turn off the lights and lie down in a grave somewhere. Indeed, hadn't Joe already, in a sense, walked out on himself? Left, and never come back. If he looked this decrepit it couldn't be more than another decade at most anyway. Definitely much closer to his end now than his beginning…

The poor soul in the mirror gloomed back, looking as though some vampire had sucked its life blood out. Joe felt like the *Portrait of Dorian Grey* (at the end of the story when the dissolution was complete). Clearly, the older you got the more obviously your shameful excesses were on vivid (sic) display. The face as a map of one's life-altering mistakes. For some unaccountable reason the ex TV hack wanted to get angry. But who to blame except himself?

Unshaven and blotchy skinned, the dark rings under each eye were sunk like dead river beds into bloated, puffy cheeks the colour of stale custard. The once glorious curls were a mattered haywire of tangles looking less like hair and more like some cruelly overused copper scrubber. He marvelled that Barbara even put up with him. Who'd want a girl who'd want me, he questioned not unreasonably- sort of quoting Marx (Groucho).

The tofu pie was barely lukewarm. Joe turned it over again and juggled it from side to side. Only his hands were getting hot. (It was a hand dryer afterall.) He tried to suppress the mutinous hair back into some order by scraping a claw of fingers through, the dandruff fell like snow…

Joe pulled up short. Snagged by a truly awful thought: hadn't he done all this before? The pie, the mirror, the glance out through the toilet window- over the fibro/asbestos rooftops of the town…

Like today already ?

WHIP PAN TO:

12.08pm, Pearly Gates Hotel, Friday 13th March

The couldabeen minor playwright panned left, overtaken by a paralysing sense of déjà vu. But as he stared out over Heaven's tiny commercial heart, instead of seeing the familiar Good News Agent, Café Celestial, St. Peter's Pizza, Martyr's Meats, Blissed Out Bakpakah Academy, Seraphim Surf Shop, Blue Sky Bowls Club, All Hallows Hospital, Himmel's Hot Pies, and the Happy Hunting Ground Tepee where you could be aura cleansed and cranially rebalanced (if you were totally insane)…there was now only a pink and lilac concrete highrise full of unrentable offices and cheap, one bedroom holiday units- blocking out what had once been an entire panorama of downtown Heaven!

What was going on?

Had Joe blacked out for a moment and forgotten not only where he was but *when* he was? (let alone *why* he was or even *how* he was!). It would seem Barbara's early morning kick to the head had given him some form of concussion or even mild brain damage- more than the self inflicted daily dose. Because here he stood, imposing old landscapes on new ones. Like the fool that he was. Expecting things to remain the same. Never a bright idea for anyone living in a small coastal community on the cusp of becoming a dreaded 'development opportunity'.

Joe was tired. He was hungry. He didn't feel terribly well and it now appeared he'd been caught in some dreadful time warp. Had the needle arm on the record player of his mind which used to spin out that hit musical *The Joe Deegan Story* jumped over a whole track called 'My 49th Year' and moved on another twelve months? Leaving Joe older but hardly wiser and with nothing to show for it except an apparently interminable mid-life crisis, as if nothing had changed and yet…EVERYTHING had changed!?

Joe *knew* that what he needed was a Little Lie Down and a cooling stubbie in the hammock. But home was two and a half kilometres away, along a delightful bikepath. And Joe had no means of getting there, because Barbara- wherever *she* might be right now- had taken Rusty with her. She always had the car. That much was certain. While little else was.

Like the giant crystal lenses in Heaven's historic lighthouse, Joe's progress through the day seemed to be one of going round and round in never ending and slightly infuriating circles. Like UStraylian television. Round and round. Going nowhere.

"Thanks for nothing, Gail," he rankled. "This I definitely didn't need right now. On top of all the other things that have conspired to ruin my birthday…"

Then it passed. Another few lighthouse turns: thirty, forty-five seconds of stability and eventually the toilet steadied or Joe steadied, something steadied, and the panic attack (if that's what it was) subsided a little, and he surrendered himself to another:

SLOW FADE TO:

Black, No Time, No Place

Again complete emptiness. No movement. No sound. But only for a moment…

QUICKLY IRIS OUT TO:

12.17pm, Pearly Gates Hotel, Friday 13th March

When Joe re-opened his eyes again it all seemed okay. Felt okay. Was okay.

A case of badly over heated hands drew him back to the struggle for an edible lunch. He rolled the tofu pie over and flick passed it from hand to hand, simultaneously trying to warm *it* and cool *them*. He tried the pinch test on his left arm and it hurt. Good. This was progress. It proved that this whole woozy episode wasn't just another bad dream. Sadly, it was actually happening.

…Unless, of course, Joe was only *dreaming* that his arm hurt. Dreams were like that. They fooled you into thinking you were WAKING UP!- when in fact, you were still away in slumber land. In dreams you could dream you were dreaming. Joe knew that, and Gra'eme confirmed it, misquoting Jung.

The wannabe screen playwright turned away from the hand dryer back to the gents' toilet mirror. Only to find the same ravaged face, scraggly hair, crumpled Hawaiian shirt and cracked Ray Bans. No clues there as to dreaming or waking. Moral and financial ruin certainly. Physical decay- it went without saying. State of consciousness? Forget it.

Joe knew he had to reconcile with Barbara, even harbour warm thoughts towards Julie. But most of all he knew he had to get out of this toilet before the record of his life condemned him to being stuck in the groove of this endlessly repeated scene in the Pearly Gates Hotel!

The short, chubby wordsmith almost ran back out through the beer garden and, as soon as he reached the footpath on Salvation Strand, glanced north west- towards Mt. Lookout! Letting the sensation of ganja vu slowly, mercifully, go… Eventually, he felt his pulse return to something any cardiologist would be happy with.

Directly in front of him, beneath the lengthening shadow of the demented town clock, wave breaks were curling into a perfect, low-tide, body surf. And as Joe loitered on the edge of the beach, contemplating joining the board riding class from the Blissed Out Bakpakah Academy for a quick mid-day tantric, he allowed himself the luxury of knowing that there were no aliens, ghosts, or other universes at the end of wormholes. And whether there was one Big Bang or many, life was simple and things unfolded one after the other, in a fairly unbroken series. We all yearned for a little comfort from time to time and as Gra'eme's masterpiece proved: there was nothing wrong with that. (see *Instant Gratifications*)

Just as we all waited for…something to happen. And happen it would at the end of a logical, mathematically demonstrable (but not repeatable) sequence of causes and effects. 'Time' amounted basically to one thing occurring after another inside a pretty mono-directional process. Despite attending several of Gra'eme's *Prophecy For Dummies* workshops, Joe tried to reassure himself that any foretelling of events to come was mere coincidence and/or good/bad luck. Besides, he'd been under a lot of pressure lately. The Beautiful Day wasn't calibrated to accommodate this much uncertainty.

Only one thing was clear: today remained Friday the 13th of March. And all over the world it was pretty much the same date (albeit at different times). Tonight another full moon would rise and after that the sun would come up too. The universe was unfolding perfectly and there was nothing anybody could do about it. What lay ahead of us might either be a delectable prospect or a fearful uncertainty; but consciousness as most people understood it, was a fairly straight forward affair…thanks be to Gaia.

Joe panned across the beach back to the lighthouse again, the house of light, the dwelling where guidance resided and safety was offered. Reduced during the day to a thousand twinkles as its rows of crystal prisms flashed on a brilliant autumnal sun, (s)weeping out another quarter minute of Heaven Time. Fifteen unrepeatable moment/seconds; blending one into the other, in and out and round and about until…here it comes again. And again… And again… That roundabout round about feeling. The giant lenses whirled in a circle, over and over, sweeping you along with them…before beaming out beyond the bluest of two blue horizons where the ocean glinted back a million more sparkles off its constantly restless water. Dark and light, day and night, round and round, the lenses went. Linked like siamese twins, turning back to back. Tethered forever to a common, insomniacal destiny. Too heavy to stop and therefore turning endlessly on their bed of mercury, eternal mercury, elixir of the gods (or so the ancient Chinese believed). Forever and ever, amen. (And awomen.)

It all ran automatically now, without need of an actual human Light Keeper. Another job with a house and family attached, that had been downsized by economic_irrationalism .com. Abolished in favour of the many en*light*ened ones wandering the dusty streets of Heaven below. Had the torch passed (literally) from the symbolic but real lighthouse to the labyrinth of illuminati and see-ers, gurus and grunge artists, archangels and anarchists residing in the town below? Keepers of an inner light. Who guided spirits instead of ships, and soothed storm tossed souls caught in life's treacherous rips…

WHIP PAN TO:

12.26pm, Salvation Strand, Friday 13th March

Joe turned from the grand sweep of the bay and walked back down the slope of Angel Avenue for a third time that day, to touch base with reality again at the intersection of Saint Street. Staring mystified at Repentance Roundabout. Enthralled by its ability to swirl cars into orbit and spin visitors and locals off towards their separate directions and destinies- just as the lighthouse swirled warnings and welcomes out to the ocean.

One face of the town clock told him it was nearly half past twelve. Either all the watches in the *Alternative Everything's* window were slow, or this was the fast face. It was too hard to tell without standing around waiting…And Joe had no intention of wasting one more nanosecond of his life waiting for anything ever again.

Besides a stopped clock was still right twice a day.

And did it matter ? If nothing mattered ?

Not in any gateway to a Rainbow Coast, or capital of an Enchanted Triangle.

WIPE ACROSS TO:

SAY 'HULLO' TO A GOOD BUY

Just another colourful example of **HEAVEN**'s many orange-and-cream brick veneers. Mass-produced from a template created by 'professional' architects, dazzling Dreamtime Beach Estate is located like some glittering jewel within a pristine wetlands containing acid-sulphate soil and Limbo Creek Fever-carrying mosquitoes. All only a mere stone's throw from Purgatory Beach and just listed at a price you can afford. (This is no gimmick). Buy off the plan. Give **BRYCE KEITEL**'s **UNREAL ESTATE AGENCY** a call now.

Affix stamp here

#15 of 33 Postcards from Heaven

printed on gently mulched, plantation-grown, organic bamboo fibre using recycled greywater and bound with a biodegradable non-toxic glue

No animal or dolphin suffered in the making of this card
(apart from, of course, its author)

15
SAY 'HULLO' TO A 'GOOD BUY'

"All prisons in the future will be mental.
In the present, some already are."
(Gra'eme *Weapons Of Mass Distraction)*

12.35 pm, Café Celestial, Friday 13th March

Halfway back down Angel Avenue, Joe stalled around the Café Celestial and idled out on the footpath, contemplating a nerve-settling, industrial-strength, full-cream, triple-caff latté. He was surrounded on all sides by bad footwear: appalling velcro sandals and overpriced runners made by underage children in some Third World hell factory where it would take them three lifetimes to earn what the CEO of the corporation makes in a single day.

Already the sun was past the meridian and he still hadn't had a proper lunch yet- containing at least a fair bit of complex carbohydrate and a lot of fibre. As he lifted his gaze and let it wander over the assembled crowd, assessing which conspiracy theory to join today, Joe realised that virtually Heaven's entire 'A list' was in attendance.

Something was obviously going on…

"It is important to remember," Gra'eme reminded anyone privileged to be within hearing distance, "that coffee, apart from being the second-most traded commodity in the world, had also lubricated Europe's finest reformations and revolutions. Coffee was the drug of the En*light*enment. It opened the voice chakra, which in turn ensured the re-opening of theatres and parliaments- a tonic to the soul, and a plus for humanity generally." (see *Life's Too Short To Drink Bad Coffee*)

And while there were other cafes in Heaven with equally good lattés and cheaper food, Café Celestial was where the real cognoscenti hung out; and where the most effective, destabilising rumours started. Joe was about to join Max, its owner, at the main table, when he noticed to his surprise and delight, that Barbara and Julie were already there, tucked away down the back, in earnest discussion with Christabel Eaton.

His darling Barbara, the still point of Joe's turning world. (Turning frankly, a bit too much this morning.) How lucky he was to have her, he realised, for those rare interludes when she wasn't in Israel and he could bask in her shadow and share with others the benefits and blessings of her prodigious energy. Watching her networking now, Joe knew that, after all the trauma of the last few hours, everything would be all right. His better half was on the case. Mondeigo and Da Groot didn't stand a chance. Bastards.

"Hi!"- Joe approached their table, confidant, relieved, beaming out his best, prize-winning smile, almost feeling good in himself again. Determined to grin his way out of trouble. It was turning into a perfect autumn afternoon. Life was beautiful and there was always hope for some kind of balance in the world. Besides, if he was going to have to spend another two grand on new crowns he figured he might as well keep putting the investment to good use.

The three women looked up as if slightly put out by an intruder. There were building plans, engineering reports, glossy brochures, statistics, lies and half-truths scattered amongst the empty cups, flourless orange cake and crumbs of macadamia-choc biscuits on the table in front of them. All the complexity of a development application and a mid-day coffee in Heaven.

"Hi Joe."

Barbara's face remained turned up towards him and he greeted it with a soft peck on the cheek, followed by a short hug, placing a familiar arm briefly around her lovely firm shoulders. Making contact. One of the last chances he'd have to actually touch Barbara before she caught the *Nullumbah-Sydney Aurora* tonight. Unless Julie suddenly disappeared off the face of the earth…

"Hi Julie."

"'Joe."

Julie remained subdued. Nothing like her normal, ebullient, ego-centric self. Joe put it down to the aftershock of this morning's near disaster in the surf. In fact, Julie had hardly employed the personal pronoun since her lachrymose shower. She took the opportunity/excuse of Joe's arrival to continue with some last minute shopping. There were already several bags of stuff from *Mystic Medicine* and *God's Glass Blowing Studio* piled high on the ground around her.

Their eyes didn't meet as Joe moved aside to let Julie out, readily taking her place at the table. Where he was impressed to hear that Christabel had already organised a stop-work order on Da Groot's impression of an enviro-nazi. What the great oaf had been doing was completely illegal. It was such a relief for Joe to discover that the torch had passed from his hands.

"I just felt so…impotent," he shrugged, still at a loss, hoping Christabel wouldn't take that too literally. Her lovely green eyes were really quite striking. Joe figured they'd have Ireland together somewhere in their respective genetic backgrounds. She brought him up to speed:

"As soon as Gus (Council's Compliance Officer) confirmed what you'd told me, I confronted Wal Piper in his office and forced him to sign a temporary injunction against the chainsawing. Piper didn't like the idea, but he had no choice when the rules are being broken so blatantly. Even a corrupt Shire Manager has to act eventually. Nothing's been approved on Mondeigo's property yet. Da Groot had no right to touch so much as leaf in that rainforest."

"Absolutely," agreed Joe, already inspired by Cristabel's strategic grasp of the situation. Glad to discover not only that the word was out, but that it had reached the highest levels- where it needed to go to set wheels in motion and heads rolling; or at best, wheels rolling and heads in motion. Joe's shrill whistle-blow had already been wildly successful. You just had to pick up the phone and let the right people know, he realised. At least the first battle was won- not the war, of course. But this was an encouraging opening salvo for the Common Good.

"When I bumped into Barbara I thought I'd pass on the good news," Christabel continued. "We've stopped them just short of cutting a road corridor right through the forest. Now there's only a thin line of sheokes and banksias (a thin green line) stopping them. As long as we can save those trees, there's no way anyone can push ahead with these plans,"- indicating, distastefully, the Development Application for *Dreamtime Beach Estate* spread out in front of her.

Joe turned to Barbara with boundless admiration. She was just fantastic at this sort of stuff: ringing people up, hassling them, forcing the action. Not that Christabel needed much coaxing, she was the one Councillor genuinely onside. Joe knew that he, they, 'The Cause', would be lost without people like her- without either of these tremendously effective women.

Unfortunately, Christabel wasn't sharing Joe's boundless optimism.

"We might've saved the rest of the forest- but only for a moment," she warned. "This is the fist battle in a war of attrition that could go on for years."

Joe slumped. Years! He may not have that long. Barbara however, wanted to get the facts straight: "So it's only temporary- the stop work order?"

Christabel nodded. "Pending Council's approval or rejection of their DA. You can be sure that this is when Mondeigo and Da Groot will get their legal team to really bully Council staff- the ones they can't blackmail or bribe. It's Bryce Keitel who makes sure all the relevant palms are greased. We know for sure that the three of them work in tandem most of the time. And no matter how many local objections you raise- and even assuming Council is brave enough to knock it back- the Property With Little Amenity Tribunal will still green-light it further down the track. At great expense to the community of course, since Council then cop all the legal costs- when the developers win. Which they always do. "

"Does anyone know what their final plans are? The DA rarely tells us, right?"- Joe, as always, anxious to hear the worst. So he could get the worrying out of the way. Or in place as the case may be.

Barbara indicated a thick, spiral-bound document, her voice had an edge of resignation "Christabel just got the DA from her in-tray at Council. It was re-submitted with amendments this morning."

"Say 'hullo' to a good buy," quipped Christabel mirthlessly as Joe flicked open the first page and cast a quick, inexpert eye over it.

"Say good-bye to Heaven," sighed Barbara. "This will kill the town off in one fell swoop. You can forget about that colourful little beach community we've come to know and love. Nobody will be able to afford to live here."

On the front cover of the DA, looking like a Garden of Eden, was an 'artist's impression' of the proposed *Dreamtime Beach Estate-* painting it as a veritable forest wonderland. On opening the first page however, Joe was confronted by Mondeigo's real plans. All he could see were dozens of tiny rectangles indicating: dreaded pink and lilac cluster townhouses- *scores* of them! It was the cement-box/brutalist school of architecture rearing its ugly head again. The same building style developed for nazi bunkers during World War 2 from some old Gestapo drawings found under a cellar in East Berlin- where virtually nothing organic or natural would be found amongst the construction materials. Joe shuddered at the nightmares that would be dreamed in *Dreamtime Beach Estate.*

Barbara was trying to choose her words carefully: "It's ah…a bit worse than we thought."

"Ronnie Rainbows reckons as many as thirty eight." He informed them. Depressed by the size.

"Double it and you might be getting close," decreed Christabel, looking defeated herself.

Joe frowned and turned to her, searching her lovely Celtic face with its hint of freckles, for some sign that she might be joking, then back down at the leggo blocks, counting wildly.

Christabel cut to the chase: "Basically, Mondeigo wants to build ninety four 'luxury' (sic) cinder block 'beach units' in medium density clusters of eleven or thirteen."

"Geezus, Ninety four!" exploded Joe "'Beach units'! 'Luxury'!" His potentially damaged heart sinking again. The well planned, quiet lifestyle vanishing before his eyes. He couldn't believe it. The word 'cluster' conjured images for Joe of cluster bombs, or ridges of boils conglomerating to form carbuncles. (As they did last time on his right buttock, before he got that marvelous potion from Vasuda Devi.)

"That just about doubles the population of south Heaven in one sub-division. I mean, Kerrist, even the possibility of a few *dozen* was too much."

Christabel was nodding, but added: "I'm afraid they've snookered us on this one, Joe. Under the old Council, the Development Control Plan for your part of Heaven was changed to allow medium density housing just about anywhere a developer wanted." She shrugged, like it was obvious: "Who wouldn't go for this last bit of prime beachfront?"

"That's insane!" cried Joe, drawing a few head turns from some of the A list in their various conspiracy theory workshop groups. "It's an untouched remnant of pristine, littoral rainforest. The last sub-tropical example left on the entire coast between Brisbane and Sydney."

"But it's on private land, zoned 'Freehold Residential'," Joe's sympathetic councilor explained. "If Mondeigo and Da Groot go through the pretence of following all the rules about setbacks and building footprints and minimum allotment sizes, they can basically do whatever they want with that bare patch in the middle. The only problem is access. Obviously Da Groot was hoping to chainsaw their way out of that minor technicality before anyone noticed. Lucky for us, Joe, you were on the ball this morning."

Christabel shot him a grateful look and glanced down at her watch. Other problems threatened. Having run out of cheap coastal land everywhere else, developers were beginning to converge on the Rainbow Coast from all sides. Christabel had other bushfires to put out.

Because it was becoming abundantly clear that every year now, thousands more tourists trooped up and down the east coast of UStraylia seeking a real alternative to the Cold Coast. And the more damaged and dysfunctional Surface Paradox became, the more ravenously the Slavering Greed Brigade focused on places like Nullumbah Shire. Eager to relieve its overseas and interstate visitors of both their foreign currency and their illusions. While those unfortunate enough to live in Heaven paid the real price.

"Of course, it's been impossible for Council to actually amend the planning rules to contain development and get an outcome that locals can live with," Christabel went on. "The developers themselves made sure of that years ago. I'm afraid Barbara's right. What we're witnessing here is the end of that colourful, weird, beautiful, eccentric, multi-talented, crazy, healing community we all know and love,"- shrugging, having almost given up herself. "So far as I know, a moratorium on over development of any coastal community has never succeeded anywhere in UStraylia."

"I thought we'd elected a green Council?" Joe pleaded.

"Well we did- sort of. But some of them turned a funny shade of brown afterwards. In any case, does it matter who sits on Council when Wal Piper and his planning department run the show ten to three, Monday to Thursday? They slip through things we haven't got time to look at and bury crucial facts at the bottom of a paperkrieg of documentation. Their jobs are permanent, Joe, ours are at the mercy of a fickle and easily manipulated electorate."

"But…you *are* elected, Christabel, that's the whole point!" He challenged, trying to rouse her. "Councillors get the final say," Joe insisted. Then a doubt. "Don't you?" His voice was rising in the opposite direction and conversely proportional to his hopes. Barbara threw him a warning look.

"Only over the rules as they come down to us," their elected representative pointed out.

Joe didn't quite seem to get it. Christabel tried to elaborate.

"Look , Council can't just rezone the land to what it should be: 'Endangered Habitat' and protect it for all time, without paying Mondeigo and Da Groot a huge compensation bill. Which this community clearly can't afford right now because we can't even service the development that has already *been* approved. Let alone bank roll all the cases that developers constantly bring against us in the Property With Little Amenity Tribunal. As everyone knows, it seems to be physically and legally impossible to change the Development Control Plan for Heaven to something low key and sustainable. The control (sic) plans that do exist (allowing open slather) all got worked out years ago- before Heaven started to become popular with bakpakahs and anyone realised what Mondeigo and Da Groot were really up to. In fact, they barged their way onto the resident committees set up to consult with Council and cynically manipulated the future planning rules to suit themselves. Making sure all their properties got rezoned Freehold Residential in the meantime."

This sad history of deception and devious cunning was of course, a well known facet of the town's colourful history. But Joe still couldn't accept that these greedy bastards were going to get away with it.

Again Christabel tried to put it as simply as she could: "If Council says 'No' to *Dreamland Beach Estate* then Mondeigo will go straight to the Property With Little Amenity Tribunal, claim Council's own Development Control Plan allows him to do whatever he likes (which it does); and the judge will simply over-ride, yet again, the Common Good in favour of the developers' own Private Interest. Effectively handing approval to them on a plate- with no strings attached and all the costs. It's a lose/lose situation for both Council and the Community, Joe. We effectively sign away all hope of placing *any* constraints on the thing."

Christabel was barely concealing the disappointment in her own voice. But her elegant, expressive hands and the hands of her fellow Green Councillors, were tied.

"Whereas…if we approve the development with certain rigorous conditions, we may actually be able to knock it down from ninety four townhouses to something more digestible like, say…seventy five."

Joe and Barbara both looked shocked. That was still way too many.

"I'd go for sixty personally, but that may be reaching for the sky. If you want to stop it what you've really got to find is some knock-out legal punch. Something that will stand up in court. And quite frankly, that's pretty unlikely. Because Mondeigo is a master manipulator of the rules. His homework's always impeccable. And if everything else fails, he's still got that winebar full of tax-deductible QCs lined up, ready to stall and obfuscate."

"Liars ,Guns and Money," added Barbara descriptively.

"But all this is clearly unsustainable." Joe was gesturing towards the DA, calling down what he thought were popular buzz words. "It destroys the very thing most people came here for in the first place. A bit of peace and quiet. A relatively empty beach. Some of our natural capital left standing."

"So define 'sustainable'," retorted Christabel, playing devil's advocate and putting her expert, slender finger on the nub of the matter. Joe noticed the wedding ring for the first time and for some unaccountable reason felt doubly down cast.

"I mean, I agree with you one hundred percent, Joe; but that's your problem in a nutshell. What's sustainable and what isn't, is- like everything else- subject to legal interpretation. And as we all know that's about as consistent as a town planner's guidelines. Get two lawyers in a room together and you've got five opinions."

"Well, it's not sustainable to simply truck in hundreds more residents when Heaven already has the highest unemployment rate in the country," Joe argued. "How are the school, the hospital, the water supply, the fire brigade, the life counselors at *Seventh Heven* going to cope?"

It gave them all pause for thought.

"Okay, *Dreamtime Beach Estate* is private property," he conceded. "But so is my little shack. Surely, I have a right *not* to be overwhelmed by sixty or seventy five new dwellings right up against my back fence, forcing property values down, creating noise, destroying privacy, adding to the pollution impact on Limbo Creek. Since when does land zoned 'Freehold Residential' convey the right to open slather?"

Nobody had an answer to that either. And maybe there wasn't one.

But, sensitive to their frustration and disappointment, Christabel tried to moderate the blow with: "My best guess is that Council will split 4-4 down the middle, and the mayor, as usual, will use his casting vote to side with the developers." She ran quickly on, anticipating Joe's objections. "We all thought Bruce Phelan was a Greenie too- until he got elected. Now he's obviously rolled over to the dark side. It always happens. How the developers get to every mayor, or what blackmail they hold over them, nobody knows. There's a remote chance our fearless leader may still have some spunk left and a residual grasp of what constitutes ethical behaviour- but I wouldn't put next week's pay cheque on it."

Joe resigned himself to this slim hope. Not having a pay cheque to look forward to himself. Democracy! Always a numbers game.

"It's not just Carlos Mondeigo and Lech Da Groot that you're up against here either," she added. "Apparently there's a mysterious, sinister character behind even them who *really* calls the shots. My best guess is, 'Mr. Big' would have to be someone connected to that weird cult Mondeigo ripped off on Ibiza."

"The Pathsandras?" queried Barbara, suddenly curious. Being a tour guide for modern pilgrims, she had a thing about all religious sects and spiritual aberrations.

Christabel nodded. "As soon as the Smiling Swami died (allegedly from food poisoning) a whole lot of money went missing from the Pathsandras' Swiss Bank accounts- along with most of the precious temple decorations from their ashram in Barcelona. Two weeks later, funnily enough, Carlos Mondeigo pawned two diamond encrusted gold chalices and an ivory elephant in Sydney. When I first saw him arrive in Heaven shortly after that, all he seemed to have was a broken down Holden station wagon and ten dollars in his back pocket. But a few land deals later he was showing prime bits of undeveloped coast to potential investors from the deck of his luxury catamaran."

Christabel leaned in close, lowering her voice, drawing even keener attention from the eavesdropping A list spread all around. "What we *do* know is that Carlos José Mondeigo (alias Bhagwashanti, alias Shaftinundra, alias Sheik Rattle'n'Roll) put a cash deposit on a block of radiotoxic wasteland out near Heaven's industrial estate, got it rezoned residential, and copped a 500% profit in eight months. The rest, as they say, is history… Unfortunately."

"How did Mondeigo get it rezoned?"- Barbara as concerned as Joe now, at this new twist on their opponent's sordid past.

"Same way he got south Heaven's Development Control Plan 'fixed'. Same way any developer gets what s/he wants in this town. You grease the right palms and you make sure your friends are looked after- preferably via the monthly poker game on Bryce Keitel's back deck. It's the only gamble people like Mondeigo and Da Groot are happy to lose. It's common knowledge that Bruce Phelan and Wal Piper always come home winners."

"That's completely corrupt!" stammered Joe. Aware that it also vaguely matched what Ronnie Rainbows had told him.

"Try and prove it," Christabel countered. "It's rotten as hell but nothing is ever written down. No official inquiry or Royal Commission will ever find anything wrong- so long as Mondeigo and his developer mates don't break ranks and start dobbing each other in. Which is always on the cards by the way, given their inherent self-interest and greed."

There must be *some*thing we can do to stop it." Barbara was glancing down, idly twirling the spoon in her skinnycap.

Joe could guess she was already half a world away on a fully armed and missile protected El Al jumbo to Israel. Her ticket out of here. (After she was sure Julie and her baby were okay.) Joe also knew that without Barbara at his side, fighting this hideous development would be next to impossible.

Still sensitive to the general depression, Christabel wanted to throw her constituents a lifeline. "These 'projects' tend to fall over when you look closely at the engineering aspects- the potential for flooding perhaps, or landslip factors. Mondeigo is going to have to fill an awful lot of wetland to put nearly 100 townhouses down there, and that's something even the Property With Little Amenity Tribunal might have to sit up and take objection to."

"We'll need to hire an engineer," Barbara realised, "as well as a lawyer."

"Perhaps the Nullumbah Shire Protection Society can help?" offered Christabel. But Joe wasn't optimistic. NSPS numbers were down at recent meetings. People had basically stopped going. In fact, numbers only ever went up when someone- some national park or native fauna lobby group- threatened to remove dogs from the beach. On the other hand, it *was* the only community organization they had. Christabel pushed her mobile towards him. "Borrow my phone if you want to get an extraordinary meeting organised."

"Every meeting of the Nullumbah Shire Protection Society is extraordinary," Joe boasted hollowly, while staring at her mobile with a certain dread. Mostly he worried about getting brain cancer from the microwave radiation.

Impatient and disappointed with him, Barbara picked up the phone to dial Mrs. Geogharty's number. For the next 10 minutes she got the octogenarian's adventures of the past few months, including being nearly run over by a car in *Canonisation Court* (again). After which, Barbara finally managed to get her to fire up the NSPS telephone tree for an emergency meeting- before handing the phone back to Christabel, conscious of the cost of the call.

"Not to worry," offered Christabel. "All in a good cause. I can leave the plans with you for a few days, but I'll need them back next week- before it all comes to the vote."

They thanked her, and as soon as she moved off Barbara turned back to Joe, casually asking: "So, what did the live blood analysis show?"

Joe was floored by this spectacular change of subject. In all the confusion that had followed his dental appointment, he'd completely forgotten to pick up the results of his annual medical check. The live blood analysis could only be bad news. He hadn't moderated any aspect of his ruinous lifestyle since last year's doomed resolutions.

"Come on Joe, Beanland told you to stop drinking I hope."

"How much did you bribe him to say that?"

"What was your cholesterol reading?"

"Normal," he lied.

"Bullshit."

"It is."

"And triglycerides?"

"Fine." Another (probable) lie. He wasn't fooling anyone. Least of all Barbara.

"Come on, Joe, the truth."

"All right, you want the truth…" Joe paused for dramatic effect, before letting her have it. "Gail Divine reckons I've probably got a terminal heart condition."

Now Barbara could worry about something *real* for a change.

But she just looked at him and broke into a broad smile.

"Really? I should be back just in time for the funeral."

"I'm serious."

"So am I. Gail's only stating the obvious."

Joe took a deep breath. This was their oldest and, in effect, their only real argument.

"You have no self-discipline, Joe."

"I intend to make it to 120," he boasted without any viable proof.

"120 kilos," she mocked back.

And right on cue, a cholesterol depth charge in the form of his double strength, full cream, full-caff mugachino arrived. Max, beautiful man, had read the scriptwriter's mind- well almost read his mind, Joe was thinking latté but a mugachino would be fine. He took the mug, savoured the chocolate topping, and gave the Café proprietor thanks for that which he was about to receive: his daily sacrament.

Barbara, however, was not being diverted. "What did Beanland *really* say?"

"What did the clairvoyant say?"

Now Barbara was thrown.

"How did you know I'd been to a clairvoyant?"

He shrugged modestly, hiding his smile behind another sip of chocolate flavoured froth. "Oh…I just have these premonitions…"

Joe was finally enjoying himself. He had Barbara on the back foot for a change. Not giving anything away. It was a good guess. He'd figured she would want to know something about her future on the cusp of going away to a war zone again. Then he pressed his advantage, amused at how easy it was.

"Come on, what did the Archangel Gabriel say? 'Fess up, Barbara."

"Nothing much…"

For a moment Joe frowned. It wasn't like Barbara to be so low key about a session with Heaven's favourite psychic and channeller.

"That sounds a bit ominous."

"Nothing I didn't already suspect."

"Now who's avoiding the issue?"

Why was she being evasive? Joe's lover usually cut straight to the chase. Advantage Barbara.

"I'm not avoiding the issue," she evaded skillfully.

"Yes you are. I can tell."

"You don't really want to know," was all his life partner would commit herself to.

"Tell me."

"I asked you first."

Instead of answering her directly Joe felt a small but weird desire to lean across the table and kiss Barbara fully on the mouth. In fact, it being his birthday, this is exactly what he did do- to her slight, but not unpleasant surprise.

"What's that in aid of?"

"In aid of the fact that I can't live without you."

"Joe, don't…please."

"You're my soul mate, Barbara. I just don't understand why we've spent so much of our lives apart."

CRASH CUT TO:

SOMEBODY'S GOTTA BE EVERYWHERE

Homes on the run—just another one of the many colourful
holiday accommodation options for the budget-conscious
traveler in **HEAVEN US**traylia. ('Slide-on' pictured fits any
Holden Ute made before 1967.) Treehouses, teepees,
tarpaulin shelters, old Kombi shells, plus a wide range of
back sheds and cow bails also available.

#16 of 33 Postcards from Heaven

16
SOMEBODY'S
GOTTA BE EVERYWHERE

"How can Justice be seen to be done
when she also has to be blind?"
(Gra'eme *Today's News = Tomorrow's Fish and Chip Wrapper*)

Café Celestial, Two seconds later ...

Barbara was really embarrassed now, not that spontaneous kissing in public would move heads in Heaven any more than it would say, in Paris or Rome- or even Kabul where kissing in public once tended to see heads *re*moved in fact. Fortunately, nobody in the Mecca of cool that was the Café Celestial paid the slightest attention to bodily contact in any of its many inventive and distended local forms.

No. Barbara was embarrassed because it put her on the spot again. Just where she didn't want to be, with less than 10 hours remaining before the *Aurora* took her south to Sydney, and ultimately out of Joe's life again for possibly half a year- given the time she'd now have to spend with Julie before being released to move on to her beloved, Muddled East. Joe and Barbara were facing one of their longest sabbaticals ever.

"I want to take you home and make wild passionate love to you on the kitchen table," he declared playfully.

It seemed worth going for broke. The guilt factor alone should have been enough to get him over the line. Barbara owed him. Bigtime.

"It's too hard on my knees," she avoided.

"Not girls on top again!"

"Always."

They were both laughing. At last. Joe sipped his mugachino and gave himself permission to slow down and finally marvel at the classic, autumn afternoon it was turning into. Heaven at its best. The air so crisp and clear, the clouds so high in a breathtakingly blue sky. The colour of sunlight itself waning to a kind of luminous ochre as the earth tilted once more and tugged the summer north again. The unsettling westerlies of August were still four months away, and the humidity of February receding to a warm inner glow as you just sat there- anywhere- and let a divine sun do its healing, vitamin D, thing.

And so and thus, despite the hassles and a pretty rough start, Joe found himself inside yet another reasonably good, still potentially fabulous day. Even if it marked the start of a new war to keep Heaven sane and beautiful.

Barbara, however, was glancing groundwards, as if staring at something under the table. Or affecting a sudden, unlikely moment of doubt. In fact she was fiddling with a business card which read:

Gabriel
Professional Archangel
Guidance, Healing, Protection
-Private Sessions Available-
(please: no red or black clothing)
www.gabriel@heaven.cosmos.com

"Don't get your hopes up," she warned him. "Julie's terribly depressed. I have to distract her."

"Distract her!" Joe couldn't believe he was still forced to defer his conjugal rights to Barbara's oldest, dearest friend. On his birthday!

"Plus, she put her name down on Raiina Virago's waiting list. I promised to drive her over there on the off chance of a cancellation."

All of which could take most of the rest of the afternoon, Joe realised as he sighed rather ungenerously and gave up. Wondering if he could risk a slice of chocolate mudcake- as a consolation prize. Barbara still owed him.

"They say people eat chocolate to displace feelings of loneliness and abandonment," he hinted vaguely, testing the waters. "Plus the flavinoids in chocolate are actually cardio-protective, according to a new study…"

"Later."

"What?" Joe looked at her with dawning hope. Would she allow him the mudcake after all? Or was she hinting at greater things?

"We'll have a joint and make love later. Julie can take a walk on the beach. A long one. She needs it."

Barbara smiled and Joe fell in love with her all over again as his heart skipped a beat. He was both enormously and amorously grateful, pushing the mud cake completely from his mind.

"You know I'm still the best tantric partner you ever had," he gloated, not without a sense of Welsh security about the claim.

"You'll be making love to a menopausal woman."

Barbara playfully coy. "Will that rate as a first for you, Joe?"- meekly asked for a change. Almost self-effacing.

It was so uncharacteristic for her to be this shy and retiring that Joe was genuinely *gob-stopped* and *hung there, slack jawed,* like a *stunned mullet*…to borrow most of the reaction phrases he'd just removed from his working corkboard.

Barbara was rummaging in her bag-that-had-everything for the lab report she'd just collected from Sister Carmody. "It's official. I'm an old maid."

"Oh darling …" was all he could manage.

The association of 'old' with Barbara was of course an oxymoron. She had too much energy. Age may largely be a state of mind, but the remorseless, merciless body clock just kept on ticking whether we liked it or not. Until finally, one of its major alarm bells rang loud and clear. As it did for Barbara now.

"This is even more important than my birthday," Joe generously conceded. "Now we've got a double celebration."

"Who's celebrating?"- Barbara disliked birthdays. Especially her own. Partly because it fell on Xmas Day. A blight on any childhood (even a Jewish one). Effectively robbing her of one of its few excuses for unencumbered self-indulgence. Proving once again that mothers could lovingly damage their children simply by virtue of *when* they gave birth.

"You're still gorgeous. You know that," he genuinely flattered. "How come you only seem to get more radiantly beautiful with each passing day?"

"Stop it."

She smiled back at him though, embarrassed at the compliment, but not about to be distracted from her main theme.

"So what did Dr. Beanland say!?"

He looked at her and slowly shook his head, casting a weary, avoiding-the-issue sort of glance back out at Angel Avenue with its steady stream of tourists and ferals, mystics and misfits, bakpakahs and talented locals dawdling by, 'killing' (sic) Time. Out to look and be seen… Joe squinted up towards the town clock at the far end of the main street, trying to read its closest face. The really slow one.

"How many hours have I still got you for? Eight? Eight and a half? Nine?"

Without a watch in Heaven, it was always hard to be sure.

"Joe …don't…please."

"How many hours have any of us got? Really?" he sighed.

She could sense a morbid phase coming on. "You're only making it harder for both of us."

"Barbara, I've just privately thrown away a well paid job, you're leaving me, our tiny home is about to be swamped by a colossal over development, virtually everything I ever came to this place for is walking out the door- before I do…"

"Joe- "

"How am I going to take on Mondeigo and Da Groot and whoever pulls their strings if you're not here to help me?" he queried selfishly. His voice descending to a rasping, pathetic quality.

"You'll have lots of people helping you. Everyone's been expecting something like this for months," she reminded him. "Half of Heaven will be on the barricades, you'll see."

All Joe could see was the enormous expenditure of time needed to rescue his backyard and secure some permanent, personal peace of mind. The two were intimately linked. 'Time' and 'Peace Of Mind'. Another coda to Joe Deegan's 'Theory of Relatively Everything'.

"Look, Joe. You said yourself: 'everybody's gotta be somewhere'. And sometimes *this* everybody's…" (touching her heart) "just got to be…in, you know…over there." She pointed off vaguely to the north. Across half a planet. "Israel is a place I *have* to be."

"But *is* Israel real?" he punned badly, mixing letters. Hoping to put her off it a little. When it was clear that he couldn't, he relented with: "I can't compete with a whole country, can I? A state of mind. And what a country! What a mind!" he conceded. "But in crises like this, somebody's gotta be everywhere too, Barbara, and that somebody looks like being yours sincerely. Unless *I* take Mondeigo on as a personal crusade *nothing* will happen, you know that."

"Why do you underestimate the Nullum Protection Society?"

"That's exactly what I mean: Mrs. Gaa Gaa, Normal Bob, Lynton O'Flannery, Alistair Piggot, Old Frank, Ronnie Rainbows…my comrades in arms? I rest my case!"

"Don't forget Cassandra Virtue, the Waif, Benny the Process Server…you'll have women warriors and legal hatchet men on either side of you."

But Joe was too wound up now to listen to reason, and deftly using his spoon, scooped the last creamy brown froth from the bottom and sides of his mug. A clearly neo-suicidal act for someone with his sluggish metabolism and double figures cholesterol reading. This should normally be a spiritual high point of his average Beautiful Day- savouring the dregs of one of Max's aromatic mugachinos.

Joe anticipated her disapproval: "It's okay, Beanland tested for diabetes- and gout. Both negative. I'm as fit as a mallee bull half my age," he alleged.

"You got the bull part right."

Joe glanced at the Café Celestial's specials' board and (having dumped Ronnie's luke warm tofu pie in a bin at the Pearly Gates Hotel) remembered that he still hadn't eaten a proper lunch yet. He was tempted to go for a macrobiotic zenburger but didn't want to incite another argument about his weight. Greater problems loomed.

"How many times have we actually gone through this ritual of saying 'good-bye' to each other?"

She made an old point: "Look, Joe, if we didn't have a break every now and then we'd be at each other's throats. You know that. This time it's been nearly four months together. And already things are getting a bit dodgy."

"No they aren't."

"Yes they *are*! Just remember how great it is when I come back." She touched him gently on the cheek and they held each other's eyes for a moment longer than necessary as Joe felt his heart skip a beat. Again. It was just a silly romantic thing, but he didn't like it when his heart skipped beats. Especially now- in the wake (perhaps literally?) of Gail Divine's warning.

Barbara noticed Julie lugging shopping bags back towards their table and quickly withdrew her hand from Joe's cheek. Joe noticed Barbara notice and didn't like what he saw. Julie too had seen the gesture and it's rescission, and it made her even more irritable. Here was another happy relationship. Something she didn't have.

"I might go home." Julie pointedly didn't sit down, even though Christabel's ex-chair was available.

"Joe can take your stuff back while I give Raiina Virgo's clinic another ring." Barbara was groping in her bag-that-had-everything for the car keys.

"No I can't," protested Joe.

"Why not?"

"I've got to do the party shopping." (Still completely forgetting about Gra'eme, and now more than an hour late!)

"But I have to stay in town and say good-bye to the choir. They're rehearsing in Hallelujah Hall," stalled Barbara.

Julie intervened, ending the argument. "Thanks anyway, but I feel a walk back along the beach might get me tired for the train. I'll never sleep otherwise. Call my mobile if you have any luck." She was trying to make it sound happy and upbeat. But it wasn't working. Although Joe thought it was good to see the personal pronouns back in place… Her old selfish self slowly re-emerging from its grubby chrysalis.

Barbara accurately read all the warning signs and reached for Julie's last minute purchases. "Let me at least put your bags in the car."

"Yeah okay, thanks." Julie gratefully handed Barbara the extra junk she'd just bought for all her 'friends' in Newtown: bach flower remedies, handmade soap, some posters of the light house with dolphins… Then she shimmied away on the verge of tears, sort of hunched over, trembling.

"What's all that about?" asked Joe, turning back to Barbara. Tears always unnerved him. Especially his own.

"Uh, oh! She's sucking in her bottom lip again."

"Is that bad?"

It was a warning sign with which Barbara was only too familiar. "Yes," was all she offered.

"What does it mean?"

"Don't ask."

Joe struggled to understand Julie's problem. "It's not still the baby thing is it?"

The topic was a reminder that Barbara and Joe had failed to produce their own offspring. Not for want of trying. Their lovemaking had been frequent, vigorous and passionate (guests permitting). But fruitful it wasn't. And now with Barbara officially menopausal, even that remote possibility was gone.

"She's just depressed that's all."

Joe threw up his hands in an overly histrionic gesture of despair. What else was new? Then he said something he was later to regret- and probably for the rest of his life:

"Sometimes I think depression is just an excuse for some people not to take responsibility for themselves."

Barbara rounded on him. "That's as cruel as it's inaccurate and unnecessary!"

Too wound up, he ploughed recklessly on, inviting disdain. "I mean, really…if she didn't know where her next meal was coming from, or she had some genuine problem, or real illness…try living in the horn of Africa for example, or Canberra in winter. Then you'd have something to get depressed about. I mean she's got a job, she owns a tiny flat in Sydney forcrissake! How artificially wealthy can you get?"

"This is why you need Personality Realignment Joe, you have absolutely no idea."

"Barbara, if you weren't around to wipe her nose and tie her shoelaces she'd *have* to cope."

The last great love of Joe's life just stared at him with renewed disappointment. His lack of feeling deserved a real blast. But her shoulders slumped. What was the point? All that came out was:

"It's always a bad sign when she sucks her bottom lip." Barbara was following Julie's progress up Angel Avenue until she turned right at the Pearly Gates Hotel and disappeared into Salvation Strand, heading for the beach and the long walk home. Alone.

"You still haven't told me what Gabriel said." Joe was keen to throw the ball back into Barbara's court. Distract her from her best friend's problems. "Come on, I told you about my blood tests," he lied.

"No you didn't. You've hardly said anything," she accurately pointed out.

They were interrupted by Helen Strongfeather gliding past, holding her eight month old daughter, looking for a table. Barbara was immediately drawn to the baby, "Hi Moonshadow!" she chimed, eager for a chance to fondle any infant.

"Can you hold her for me?" Helen offered.

Barbara swelled with willing anticipation. But Helen bestowed Moonshadow upon Joe's lap. "I've got to change a nappy," she explained.

Joe smelt the reason why, and held the baby away from him a little, jiggling her up and down, making silly faces- much to Moonshadow's delight. Barbara hid her disappointment and waited for Joe to mismanage it so she could pounce to the rescue.

"Would you like a 'bristle pudding', Moonshadow?" Joe goofed, looking for an excuse to keep holding the baby at arms length- feeling nostalgic for his own damaged childhood. Moonshadow giggled as he buried his face in her small, flabby tummy, quickly scraping his stubble from side to side, blowing raspberries. Just like Brother Carol used to do with those unfortunate sub-juniors invited up to his bedroom for a one on one anatomy tutorial.

The baby shrieked with delight. "Would you like another one?" Joe looned, pulling more faces. Which even Barbara and Helen found amusing. Moonshadow too, produced a lovely smile for her mother and turned back to Joe, clawing her little fist with its writhing fingers into his mouth and nostrils- setting off a new round of bleeding.

Ignoring the dubious hygienics now in play, Joe kept hamming it up, poking his face into her tummy for a second 'bristle pudding'. This time the baby's squeal of delight came out more heavily laden as she projectile vomited the contents of her morning breast feed straight onto the top of Joe's mattered curls. Barbara seized her moment and scooped Moonshadow up as the former playwright, partly blinded, leapt to feet, reeling back.

Mortified, Helen plunged into her New Guinea string bag for a fresh nappy. "Sorry, Joe. She's got a bit of colic at the moment."

"Hope it's not contagious,"- Joe, forcing out a grim smile, trying to look on the bright side (dentist's orders). In fact, trying to look per se, as he struggled to scrape most of the milky ooze out of his eyes with the second nappy.

Moonshadow was crying now. So Helen took the baby back from Barbara and, slipping off the thonging on her tasseled, suede-leather halter top, quickly silenced her daughter with a quick top up from the right breast. Barbara looked disappointed. Joe couldn't help noticing the large 'Tezza' tattooed through a big red heart that covered Helen's nipple.

"Moonshadow loves Joe," smiled Helen, revealing a row of teeth yellowed from smoking.

Joe and Barbara exchanged a raised eyebrow. The news was a surprise to both of them. He would've liked to explain to Barbara (privately) that the connection wasn't all *that* close. But was too busy wiping as much of the vomit off as he could manage. And in any case Joe couldn't so easily disperse the odour. The bad smell that started here for Barbara would linger a lot longer. There now seemed to be something definitely missing between them. The old zing of their bi-annual farewell wasn't quite as fond or as electric with longing as it used to be. They were changing. Their relationship evolving. As relationships do, as they must…

Helen went on breastfeeding and when Barbara realised she wasn't going to get another chance at a free cuddle she handed Joe the list for the Stupormarket and stood up.

"I'll leave you to it then,"- uttered not without a subtext (Joe realised) as she gathered up Julie's plastic bags, and turned to leave.

He stalled her with: "You still haven't told me about the clairvoyant…"

On her feet, standing over him, Barbara took a deep breath and let Joe have it with both barrels, suddenly irritable: "Gabriel predicted someone close to me was going to die soon, *very* soon," adding a look that said: 'Satisfied?'

He threw a look back that said: 'Oh kerrist!' And felt like a carpet snake suddenly deformed by the outline of a rat it had swallowed. Of course he took that 'someone close to Barbara' as himself. As did she. Now she was definitely being cruel (but only in order to be kind). Perhaps it was the German in her that made it so easy.

"The first throw of the cards…it looked too awful," she happily elaborated. "Neither of us could quite believe it. So Gabriel reshuffled the pack, but the 'Hanged Man' came up trumps a second time. There was no mistake."

"Well the Archangel's timing's a bit out- I nearly died this morning. Julie too,"- Joe conceding that Julie was close to Barbara. Glad he had remembered to throw her best friend into the awful mix of likely candidates for the local funeral parlour.

But Barbara was already moving away- offering to meet him outside the Stupormarket after she'd seen the choir.

"You don't believe Gabriel do you?" challenged Helen, with a twinkle in her eye, once Barbara was out of earshot.

"Of course not. What's one clairvoyant among dozens around here," Joe swaggered, reassuring himself as much as anybody. "I'll get a second opinion from Vasuda Devi," he fibbed, having already decided never to go near the cranial rebalancer again.

"Although Gabriel has been remarkably accurate in the past," chipped in Max unnecessarily, as he brought Helen's immune boosting, celery and wheatgrass juice up to their table.

"Thanks, Max, I think I really needed to know that."

"By the way, no take-aways at the table thanks," the Café proprietor joked, admiring Helen's exposed breast.

Her laughter was like a deep, penetrating gurgle. Stronger than you might expect from someone so normally shy and self effacing. Her happy expression wrinkling the deep scar above her right eye. Joe had always meant to ask Helen how she got it. Beaten up no doubt. By Tezza perhaps? Or any one of the many boyfriends who staggered drunkenly along the concrete path to her caravan, carton of stubbies in hand…

Studying her face as she glanced Madonna-like, down at her offspring, Joe realised that Helen was actually quite plain. A kind of twisted, washed-out/worked-out look. almost grey and ashen (like his own?). As if she'd spent too much time pulling beers in some smoky bar, or cleaning motel rooms. But cheerful still, despite all that. Open to giving one more hopeless drongo another chance in the great partnership lottery. As you do, as you have to, when you bump along life's pot-holed autobahn.

Max tore his eyes away from Moonshadow's top-up and turned back to Joe. "Raiina Virago will give you a second opinion, mate- if you're really worried. We're thinking of putting some of her potions on our beverages menu. I'll save you a toadstool smoothie."

"Never one to miss a business opportunity," Joe sarcasted back, still conscious of Helen listening. "Thanks Max, but I think I'll pass on the fungal cure. Call me fussy, but I'm afraid I'm allergic to anything that grows in bullshit."

Max laughed with him, generously, and began collecting empty cups, giving their table a once over with his cloth, wiping away the last flecks of Moonshadow's liquid breakfast- including the spot where the soiled nappy had been changed, spreading gossip and bacteria in equal measure.

"By the way, comrade, word's out that you're having a spot of bother with Carlos Mondeigo."

"News travels fast, Max."

"It's been the talk of the town all morning."

Joe was relieved to hear it. In the real politik of the Enchanted Triangle, winning was all about rumour mongering (sometimes called mobilising public opinion)- or so the ex TV hack thought, in his crazy, romantic, child of- the-sixties sort of way.

"Don't worry, mate , everyone's right behind you on this one." Max assured him, grinning broadly.

Joe blanched. Why was he suddenly leading the charge of the anti-Mondeigo brigade?

"I was kind of hoping, Max, a few point scouts might be out the front and round the sides, you know- sort of a collective effort?"

Max looked both ways (somewhat overdramatically Joe thought) and leaned in close, lowering his voice. "Listen Joe, I'd be *very* careful of any dealings relating to Lech Da Groot or Carlos José Mondeigo- alias the 'ant man'."

There was a pause as Max enjoyed Joe's alarm. "You *do* know how he got the nickname don't you?"

"I've got a sinking feeling you're going to tell me," Joe slumped, while trying to remain cool and composed in front of Helen.

"Any house Mondeigo wants to buy where there's a recalcitrant vendor he quietly sneaks white ants into the stumps and walls. It takes only a few months for all the wooden frames to fall apart. It's even said he once used a colony of bull ants to torture a journalist who tried to ring alarm bells over some shonky development Mondeigo and Co built in Surface Paradox. Except that, Carlos baby went too far and the journo died of toxic shock. This guy you're up against Joe, is the crim de la crim."

Joe looked at Max absolutely stunned. His host did another quick, fearful sweep in both directions- looking for potential eavesdroppers and maximum effect: "It's said that if you drilled into the concrete foundations of one of the Cold Coast's tallest block of units you will find the poor bastard's skeleton..." Max touched his nose with the tip of an index finger. "No names no jackhammers."

The blood drained from Joe's face. Why him? Why did the developer over his back fence have to be so palpably awful?

Café Celestial's owner hung there, studying Joe keenly for signs of pre-emptive buckle. "It's basically why no one has been game to take him on...until now. Thank god we've got people like you, Joe, prepared to put your neck on the anthill."

Max thumped Joe on the shoulder, and took the money for everyone's coffee, cake and biscuits from his outstretched palm. Leaving the reluctant local hero kind of marooned in public, already grappling with some deeply troubling thoughts. Not the least of which was: that he had just paid for Julie's brunch as well!

At this point in the average Beautiful Day, Joe should be coasting into the banana lounge for a postprandial lie down (usually with a chilled Chardy or two to hasten those drowsy eyelids). Yet here he was, a party to horror stories about the cruel killing machine he had supposedly, 'personally' taken on in a clearly life-threatening, anti-development crusade! And what's worse- Joe hadn't even *had* lunch yet! So there wasn't even any 'prandial' to be 'post' of.

On the upside, Max's news had suddenly robbed Joe of his appetite.

Before he could escape however, the master conspiracy theorist came back with Joe's change and took the opportunity to impart one last bit of scurrilous gossip:

"These developers will stop at *nothing* to get what they want, Joe. They have access to unlimited funds..." Max dropped a few silver coins into Joe's top pocket and spread his hands wide before joining them in a kind of blessing- or perhaps: last rites. Either way, anointing the small TV hack as a martyr to the Common Good. Someone brave (or silly) enough to actually take on Carlos Mondeigo, Lech Da Groot and the so called 'Mr. Big' who stood so implacably and so devastatingly cashed-up behind them.

As Max happily sauntered off to concoct more coffee and mischief from behind his espresso machine, Joe was left wondering how you could ever believe anyone in this town. About anything. Heaven seemed to thrive on malicious rumour mongering. There were just too many bright people with too little to do.

While the newly unemployed scriptwriter debated whether to leave the change as a tip or pocket the 35 cents whole, he suddenly became aware of Helen staring back up at him with those big, wounded, wistful eyes. Certainly the skin around them was wounded. He could count at least seven stitches on the major scar alone. Yet the shy yearning behind her look was almost flattering. She knew Joe was no great catch really, with his raggy clothes and his weight problem. But he almost owned his own house (even if it was a dump). And was gentle and sensitive- in a Piscean sort of way. Possibly kind, certainly reasonably intelligent- if not that great in bed.

Little did she know! surmised Joe- about the last bit. That is, if he could read her mind (and she could read his)-which was quite impossible when you considered it…sort of. Except in some cases… When there's this incredible synchronicity between two virtual strangers… Such as there seemed to be now, between the lifelong scribbler-for-a-living and this no longer, quite so young single mother of numberless children to nameless fathers.

What Helen understood, instinctively, was that Joe would be a good surrogate 'uncle' for somebody's kid. It was important for any boy or girl to have at least one male role model around (no matter how dilapidated). Someone to explain the mysteries of footy and fishing.

Indeed Joe, for his part, was actually toying with the idea of shouting himself a birthday massage from Helen- after the BBQ shopping. Again demonstrating his complete blank-out about the appointment with Gra'eme- the whole reason for his trip to town in the first place. But before he could ask, Helen got in first with:

"You know, I'm always there if you want me, Joe."- volunteered with that imploring, fetching look she produced so effortlessly.

He just stood there, staring back down at her, utterly taken by surprise. Again. (And probably not for the last time.) Was Helen talking about a massage now or something more life altering?

"You don't have to be by yourself all the time, you know…" she offered, faintly, her voice trailing off to a husky murmur.

He was searching her eyes for some subtext, trying to work out exactly what this actually meant. Too shy himself to ask directly. That (he didn't realise) was also part of his charm.

"I must book another massage with you soon, Helen," was all the word merchant could manage. Still feeling pretty disappointed with his social ineptitude generally.

"Sure Joe, anytime. You've got my number…" Her words remained loaded, hanging there like ripe passionfruit. It was as if she'd be expecting his call tonight. Straight after Barbara's train left. Counting on it. Even hoping for it. Her gaze back at him was flushed with a certain vestigial longing. Which he found hard to handle, if not fondle, almost impossible to resist…

"Helen, you know I think you're… wonderful." Joe was looking at her wounded eye and tanned, healthy body, with lips as full as cherries that even a man much stronger than Joe could trip over and fall face down into. And that wasn't ruling many blokes out. But, before he could consummate his feelings into words, or at least try to express how he truly felt, Moonshadow was off the breast again and crying.

"It's the colic," Helen apologised, as the baby noise increased and soon neutered any further adult interaction. It was probably just as well.

With an equally wistful and ambiguous smile/nod good-bye, Joe finally wrenched himself away and walked as if floating, out of Café Celestial back into the heady swirl of Angel Avenue, back towards the intersection with Saint Street, heading for the monlithic brick tissue box of Kingdom Come Inc...

BLEACH OUT TO:

STUPORMARKET SYNDROME

Creatively designed by a 'qualified' civil engineer and inspired by a Great Wall of China theme in brown and ochre, colourful **KINGDOM COME INC** is **HEAVEN US**traylia's premier shopping destination. With everything for the compulsive buyer arranged along rows of unending plenty. Fill a trolley today! You'll never need to patronise a locally owned business again.

#17 of 33 Postcards from Heaven

No animal or dolphin suffered in the making of this card
(apart from, of course, its author)

17
STUPORMARKET SYNDROME
"Platitudes are only little rations of wisdom
dressed up to look familiar."
(Gra'eme *Having Your Life And Living It Too*)

1.01pm, Kingdom Come Inc, Friday 13th March

It could have been the strips of fluoro lighting- colour shifted to make vegies look greener. It may have been the dummy security cameras with their flashing blue lights almost daring you to shoplift. Perhaps it was the strange alien voice that constantly broke through the muzac: announcing a discount on some product you didn't need and couldn't afford. Or it might even have been the harassed mums with their hugely over packed trolleys. Perhaps it was the fact that Kingdom Come Inc had somehow turned it's back on Saint Street with a windowless brick wall where real shops used to be, providing neither view nor sunlight nor breeze, and thereby shutting out anything that might distract customers from the business of an extremely large, globally franchised duopoly removing hard won douleurs from their pockets. Or was it just the ghosts of the former butchers, bakers and candle stick makers driven mad and out of business by kilometres of shelves that never emptied and always had something to tempt you with, even if you'd never use it…?

The only things Joe had come to Kingdom Come for were the balloons, streamers and party toys needed to 'send up' his birthday celebration- to have fun with his few acquaintances and get them to lighten up a bit by wearing silly hats and blowing silly whistles. However, without quite knowing how or why, he soon found himself pushing shit up hill (literally): a trolley-full of dips and chips, nuts and lollies, olives and biscuits, tins and toothpicks- up and down and round and round, going nowhere in circles. Again.

When he couldn't find the party shelf he realised he was supposed to be doing the normal grocery shopping anyway. This was Heaven's only stupormarket- which by definition made it the most expensive place to buy anything. Still, Kingdom Come had certain goods that other shops lacked (like tacky party crap). But one limited one's visits there to the barest minimum.

Joe tried to remember the list he'd forgotten. The one Barbara had just re-given him after he'd neglected to take it from under the fridge magnet in the first place. Some days, preparing a shopping list was the only actual writing Joe achieved. He could remember putting it in his wallet at the Café Celestial after taking it from Barbara and noticing it still there when he pocketed the small change from Max after paying for everyone's cake and coffee. But now it had vanished again. Like it usually did.

Then, as if by some miracle, he found himself in front of the party shelf proper. And died a little at how pathetic and awful the choice really was. This is how people had fun now? Without thinking rationally, Joe rifled through bags of balloons, hats, streamers and candles (three packets of 24 this year for the first time) and bolted for any sort of break in the dense queues of bakpakahs constantly forming behind the one or two checkouts that were actually open.

He quickly surveyed the trolleys in each queue, and couldn't help notice how incredibly full some were- marvelling at people's ability to consume such huge packets of chips, or vast, distended bottles of unnaturally coloured soft drink. The stupormarket trolley as a window onto the average punter's lifestyle. Their little habits and addictions. Whether they bothered about real food, had grannies or kids to support, or had even heard of atherosclerosis. Mostly they hadn't.

Realising he'd missed the mid-day lull and every queue was already too long, Joe toyed with the idea of fudging his way through the '8 items-or-less' checkout, but there was an argument breaking out over there about whether a bag of oranges constituted one item or six. Some 'A' types just never let go. Why the great rush of blood to get ahead of everyone else when they'd just shortened their life span with all the stress involved?

147

It was tempting to trick fate by going for the obvious. But the shortest queue was never a good bet. Joe would always find people who had arrived after him in the adjacent, longer one, getting through well before he did. Sometimes, he would make a feint for the shortest, then pull away swiftly at the last moment, and go for a longer option… Only to find, on that rare occasion, that the shortest *was* the best bet after all. Of course.

Today, being his birthday and feeling lucky, Joe attempted a radical new tactic and went for a medium sized queue with a reasonably competent looking checkout girl…and immediately became bogged down behind the woman who seemed to have chosen every product in the store without a bar code. This required some underpaid young lad in a cheerful bow tie, to wander listlessly up and down the aisles, looking for the original shelf they came from, and soon overcome by Stupormarket Syndrome himself. Often lost in the maze of aisles never to be seen or heard from again.

So Joe cut his losses and moved to a longish queue- just as the pimply faced kid returned and the birthday boy watched the line he had so foolishly just abandoned, quickly diminish. If any gambler was as bad at picking horses as Joe was at choosing stupormarket checkouts, they would soon find their family home the subject of a bank enforced auction and their kids trading drugs on the street, just to keep a bit of fruit on the sideboard.

After what seemed like half a day, Joe finally arrived at his (badly) chosen cash register and was loading all the crap onto its adjacent conveyor belt- just as Ronnie Rainbows appeared from out of nowhere asking:

"Having a party, mate?"

Joe swung round, flustered. Ronnie was casting a sour eye over the conical hats, streamers and balloons, wondering why Joe couldn't have bought most of these things second hand at the *Alternative Everything*- especially since Ronnie had so graciously and recently dropped him there. And given him a free lunch.

The subject of this generosity took a pre-emptive defence with: "What are you doing here, Ronnie? Shopping with the enemy?"

Then he noticed his friend was holding a crisp new pair of thongs. The holes in Ronnie's old ones had at last become too big, even for Ronnie.

Recoiling visibly from the whiff of vomit congealing on Joe's splattered curls and parts of his Hawaiian shirt, Ronnie couldn't hide the hurt and betrayal he felt as he took in all the junk Joe was about to pay real money for.

But how could the ex-*Golden Sands* writer (so practiced in verbal deceit) honestly explain that the absence of an invite was a Barbara thing? That Ronnie's dress code and generally slovenly habits really got to her. Of which the old thongs were a pretty classic example. (Even if he was about to buy new ones.)

"It's not a birthday party is it?" Ronnie asked as if he couldn't guess. "Must be someone pretty old… "- noticing the three boxes of candles.

"No, no, no," lied Joe shamelessly, "just a…a sort of going away bash for Barbara."

This got Joe off the hook- marginally- since Ronnie would've realised that Barbara didn't exactly warm to him.

"She just wanted to put the candles in paper cups to light the back deck. It's a Jewish thing," Joe fumbled.

"So she's off again, is she?"- Ronnie stalling for maximum embarrassment. Determined to milk the opportunity and make Joe really squirm. "You didn't mention it this morning." ("When I gave you the lift," going unstated.)

"Didn't I? Oh, well…yes she, ah…she leaves tonight in fact. It's no big deal, Ronnie. Just a quick bite before the train."- Joe, trying to down play the significance. This much was true. It *was* partly a bon voyage for Barbara (and Julie), and most of the guests would be Barbara's friends anyway. Joe not having many of his own. Ronnie being one of them- or used to be, as it could now turn out.

But before Joe managed to safely change the subject, Helen Strongfeather glided past on her way into Kingdom Come carrying Moonshadow and, quickly glancing at the absurd contents of Joe's trolley, also sensed her exclusion.

This was now cripplingly embarrassing since Helen hadn't been invited either. And here Joe was, standing in a going-nowhere queue, totally exposed as a bit of a snob. Not having the generosity to invite certain moderately close friends to his party.

"Hi Joe."- Helen's disappointment beaming out through her discomfort. She'd caught him at an awkward moment- for both of them. The not-so-young mother flushed deep crimson. Making Joe feel even worse. If such a thing was possible. Which it was.

"Helen, we can't go on meeting like this," he joked, completely failing to make light of their collective embarrassment.

She was hiding hers by rummaging in the New Guinea string bag for a small package; which Ronnie had to pass over to Joe on account of the chubby writer being hemmed in between his trolley and the trash magazine stand.

"Happy birthday, Joe," was all Helen could manage, her throat catching, her voice going all dry and husky with dismay. Giving the lie to Joe's earlier lie to Ronnie. Joe felt his own face now go a deep redish-purplish-orange from the mixture of egg and subcutaneous blood gathering there.

He swung back to the check-out girl, seeking to deflect his guilt, but she was still waiting for the price on a packet of unbarcoded 'Iced Vo Vos'. Joe wished he could just slide onto her conveyor belt and disappear into a waiting plastic bag- like all the other dumb things he had bought. Sliding towards some kind of exit, like a coffin at a crematorium. Like Kate...

Joe caught himself struggling for breath again. As if overcome by too much demand on his heart. He hoped it wasn't connected to symptoms he need worry about. Either way, he'd lost it again momentarily- for neither the first nor the last time that day. What the fuck was happening to him? Then he heard a voice calling. It dragged him out of a deep hole.

"You can open it now if you like."

When Joe turned back to her, Helen was staring at the ground. Unable to camouflage the fact she was mildly unimpressed he hadn't already done so. Embarrassment compounded by bad etiquette.

Ronnie savoured the moment as they all waited for Joe- including the young girl behind the cash register, now effectively on a short tea break.

"Look, Ronnie, why don't you pop around anyway, we're just having a few drinks- and you too, Helen, of course," Joe muttered pathetically as he quickly cast aside Helen's expensive wrapping paper to discover an anthology of love poems. He flicked open a random page. It was 'The Dream'- one of John Donne's.

Joe glanced down at a couple of random lines and read:

But when I saw thou sawest my heart
And knewest my thoughts, beyond an Angel's art...

...before quickly snapping the book shut.

She was looking at him as if the words had come from her personally. About the situation right now. And Joe knew it, and Helen knew it, and she knew he knew she knew he knew it.

"Thanks Helen- that's great. John Donne. One of my favourite metaphysicals..." was all the former Master of English Literature could manage, before the cheerful young bloke with the bow tie finally shouted back from three aisles away:

"Iced Vo Vos- two, ninety nine."

With the transaction in front of him concluded, Joe's balloons, paper hats and synthetic food finally began making their halting journey towards the laser reader, an electronic bip legitimising their passage out of here.

With Ronnie hovering behind him, holding the new thongs, Joe paid for his stuff and avoided Helen's (wounded) eyes as he took his change. It was obvious she expected something more from him. But all Joe could manage was a mumbled farewell and brief nod in her general direction as he gathered his shopping and slinked away. He could hear Moonshadow's crying and felt Helen's gaze following him- like a stab in the back.

Nearly one thirty already and he still hadn't eaten anything! Joe was now officially starving.

Emerging from Kingdom Come, he almost tripped over a dirty, lost-looking blue heeler, sleeping on the footpath. The dog whimpered a bit and moved away from him- like everybody else seemed to.

Yet, while Joe waited for Barbara and Rusty, he was relieved to see a still perfectly cloudless blue sky and was able to turn his thoughts to higher things. It seemed, even this early in the afternoon, that the Curse of the BBQ Hot Plate might finally be lifting. If it did, no rain would fall on the party for his big 5-Oh! (assuming that's what it was).

So far so good. Despite the traumatic start, and the setbacks along the way, it was always possible to get a Beautiful Day back on track. Especially a Beautiful Birthday. The relief at beholding that huge, wonderful, bright blue sky slewed for Joe into a sort of halting, overall pleasure about things generally. A kind of relaxed feeling even took hold as he saw Barbara drive up, on time, in their smoking Datsun. His life partner come to rescue him. To take him home.

But, as Joe dumped the party stuff on Rusty's back seat, the sight of the overdue reggo papers lying right beneath the widening crack in the windscreen drew Joe's attention back to his underlying financial crisis. In all the hullabaloo of this chaotic morning, he'd completely forgotten the impromptu career workshop with Gra'eme!- whose pet hate was unpunctuality.

Apologising to Barbara for the change of plan, Joe had to pass up a lift home with her and race back down Saint Street towards *Seventh Heven* at the corner of Angel Avenue. Guilt and blood pressure rising. He looked up at a couple of the town clock's colourfully unreliable faces and realised he was around about, somewhere in the vicinity of, between eighty five minutes and nearly two hours late! The Apostle of Time would be furious.

JUMP CUT TO:

No visible means of support

Fear of Flying? Try 'Falling From Aeroplanes'—just another
one of the many colourful, death-defying attractions
awaiting the high-sensation thrillseeker in **HEAVEN US**traylia.
(See also Swimming In Rips, Skin Diving With Sharks, Sharing
Bongs With Foreigners and Public Showering Without
Thongs.)

*Affix
stamp
here*

#18 of 33 Postcards from Heaven

printed on gently mulched, plantation-grown, organic bamboo fibre using
recycled greywater and bound with a biodegradable non-toxic glue

No animal or dolphin suffered in the making of this card
(apart from, of course, its author)

18

NO VISIBLE MEANS OF SUPPORT

"A cat may have nine lives but it only dies once."
(Gra'eme *Watching A Cloud Go By- Very Fast*)

1.28pm, *Seventh Heven*, Friday 13th March

Gra'eme was.

"Unpunctuality is so selfish it's almost a form of fascism," he fumed, lying like some hairy island in the molded plastic sarcophagus of a *Seventh Heven* float tank. They had the Ghandi Room to themselves, Gra'eme's favourite place, and always a highlight of *his* Beautiful Day. The disgraced former corporate auditor had already consoled himself with the fact that the extra two hours would go onto Joe's next monthly invoice. Due in eleven days.

The disciple mumbled an apology, stripped down to a pair of black speedos, and clambered into the adjacent tub, thick with salts. The mood was set by faint whale song from underwater speakers. This afternoon's masterpiece: a duet between what sounded like laughing monkeys and a series of clicks (as if someone in stiletto heels was dancing the *flamenco* on a cement/brutalist driveway).

Gra'eme kept his lid open so they could talk- or rather, so he could chastise and his client could feel suitably humiliated.

"It would seem," he began sternly, "that the revenue-neutral tax arrangement I designed for you (at some considerable expense) is now officially revenue negative…"

"But Gra'eme," Joe protested, anticipating the scorn to come. "I can't write *On Golden Sands* anymore. I've lost the spark. What's the point when they completely ruin everything I give them? I mean, where are my moral rights?"- throwing it back at his financial adviser while not being terribly coherent. But still angry, still stewing over what Carmel Savage had done to his 'original' (sic) version of Craig's silly plotline for episode 1113.

"Yes, well, you see, 'moral' rights now…you must understand, Joseph, anything remotely to do with morality has most pliers of the legal trade reaching for the sick bucket. Speaking of which…" Gra'eme sniffed the steamy air above his bergamot scented water. "…what's that dreadful pong? Is that coming from your pile of rags?"- throwing a disapproving eye over the lip of his tank at them.

Joe didn't need another lecture right now on personal hygiene. "Gra'eme, I'm 50 years old. It's time I did my own thing."

"Are you ? I thought you said you were only 49?"

"No. I'm 50," insisted Joe uncertainly.

"Oh well, I'll have to change the card…"

"The point is…all my life I've written other people's stories, other people's ideas, to a given set of characters, following a certain 'in-house' style. Everything I've ever done has been answerable to some dreaded 'visionary' director or worse- a committee of Men In Suits flanked by police advisers and frustrated script editors. After all these years, slaving away in commercial television, churning out stuff I feel embarrassed to read now…what the hell have I really got to show for it? Look at it from my point of view," he challenged selfishly. "I want *finally* to write something I'll be able to read again in say, five minutes- let alone five months or five years, time."

"If you live that long…"

That was a bit below the belt, Joe thought. Or about chest level- as the case may be. But the tiger/artist in him stuck to his guns. Sometimes even an infallible prophet can fail to see the point.

"Gra'eme- I'm sick to death of prostituting my talent in the service of some demented story editor's corny plotline. I want finally to claim my *own* narrative for a change. What's wrong with that?"

"Nothing."

Joe was so surprised at the lack of objection that, for a moment, he wasn't quite sure where to go next. "You're saying…"

"Go right ahead if that's what bugs you. *Tell* your own story. It's called the 'narrative cure', Joseph. Find out you're terminally ill on the day your girlfriend leaves you- great! Fashion it into a screenplay and you'll not only clean up, you'll overcome the heartbreak. You mightn't survive to enjoy royalties, but at least you'll know you've achieved something. Venting your spleen on paper is the best self-medication money can't buy." (see *One Small Stagger Forward For Wo/man, One Hopeless Shamble For Wo/mankind*)

"No more bullshit, Gra'eme. That's my line in the sandwich from now on."

"Writers must be fighters and should always lie the truth."

The observation gave Joe pause for thought.

"Yes, I suppose we do. Except of course, when you're writing something like *On Golden Sands.* Then we lie the lies."

"True."

Gra'eme seemed to be in an unusually tolerant mood- despite Joe's belated arrival. It was all very unsettling.

"Trouble is… I'm tired, Gra'eme. I suddenly feel old."

"You're only as old as the person you're feeling… " (see *How Not To Blow A Kiss*)

But the joke went right over Joe's head. Which wasn't hard. He felt about as low as he could go- even discounting the fact he was lying flat out in a tank full of dense, salty water. Feeling any lower didn't seem either hydrologically or psychologically possible.

"There's this…lethargy I have, almost every day now. Do you think it could be late-onset diabetes?"

Gra'eme closed his eyes, hardly listening to his client/friend's familiar hypochondria, conscious only of the whale song and a sense of detachment from the real world that the float tank always seemed to bring on- so readily and without effort.

Joe had expected more opposition than this, and was pleasantly surprised to find the supportive Mentor instead. However, it *was* merely the calm before the scorn…which arrived in the form of a question, throwing the wordsmith completely off guard:

"So just how did you plan to finance this 'doing your own thing'?" (enunciated distastefully) "How will finding your *'voice'* be revenue streamed do you think?"

Joe figured it was time to go for broke (literally): "I rather wondered Gra'eme, whether I mightn't *invest in myself for a change?* In some *intellectual property?*"

The italics were Joe's, choosing his words carefully, letting them hang in the incense between the tanks, half-fearing the explosion they were likely to cause. But it didn't come. (Not yet.)

"Mmm …" murmured Gra'eme dreamily, "meaning…?"

"Well- *invest* in my own copyright. You know?- actually *control* the work I produce for once in my life…" Joe was still using what he thought were financial buzz words, hoping to tread on Gra'eme's ground a little (while avoiding his toes and corns).

"You've actually *got* copyright in something? Dressed up and ready to flog?"

"No, of course not."

This was trick questioning from his accountant, fraught with danger. Joe could smell a trap but ploughed on- like the lone, disabled zebra, cut out from its herd and stalked by nearby lions.

"How could I? I've squandered most of my talent and a fair bit of my eyesight in bondage to the mainstream. I'll have to knuckle down now and churn out some really crash hot ideas. Perhaps work as much as two hours a day." Joe thought that was offering quite a lot, but could sense the ritual humiliation building behind Gra'eme's reasonable tone. Like a beautiful wave.

"And live on *what* exactly, until this copyright becomes a 'trade-able' commodity?" Again, the invisible quotation marks were put around the 'trade-able' part, inviting suspicion, threatening derision.

"I don't suppose we could sell some of those ethical investments of mine?"

Gra'eme laughed out loud. "My dear boy, they're barely worth the paper they're not written on. Owning 'ethical investments' is like inheriting an exhausted banana farm: too steep to build on, and so riddled with toxins as to make the soil lost to agriculture for the next 1500 years. What you've got in those green futures contracts you *forced* me to buy is an asset about as popular as a share in a Multiple Occupancy- on a property infested with groundsel. You couldn't *give* them away."

"You let me buy them!"

"I tried to warn you!" Gra'eme scolded. "I told you, over an over again, Joseph: 'never let your conscience guide your financial planning'. But no, you knew best…"

Joe couldn't deny it. That was the last time he had put his foot down and over-ruled Gra'eme's always, pretty well, spot-on, financial advice. Now he was paying for it. And not just in hard currency.

"Joe, you know you're more than just a client to me. In fact, I feel privileged to say you're one of my most valued friends."

(Or 'valuable' to put it more arithmetically, thought Joe, somewhat ungenerously.)

"But I have to tell you, mate, if you don't suck your way back onto the *Golden Sands* active writer's list you will be swiftly, officially and very spectacularly downwardly mobile- as in mobile home. That's what you can expect to be living in once the bailiffs come for Casa del Fibro."

"I just can't see the point in wasting any more time on things that aren't going to generate some sort of future royalty stream." Joe persisted. It was his best strategic position. Making it sound fiscally responsible. When of course, it was always a risk, like anything. It was all a gamble. Even this line of argument.

"Absolutely right. No point at all. So long as you realise your lifestyle will have to undergo a cashflow bypass."

Joe sighed. "I suppose…I could limit myself to twelve dollar bottles of wine. Or second mortgage the house…(?)" It was half a question.

"Then be prepared to kiss it good-bye. That's exactly what I'm talking about. Banks are crazy, ruthless unconscionable monsters, but I doubt even they will lend you anything more on #13 Redemption Road without a viable income. To be brutally frank, Joseph, your house is what's euphemistically called in the trade a 'renovator's opportunity'. About the only thing valuable in the actual dwelling itself is the concrete slab underneath it- as the garage floor for some new house that's likely to capitally appreciate for a change. The only solution I can see for you personally would be to round up some old school chums from St. Patrick's reformatory-for-wayward-youth and start a class action.

Joe was shocked. "Sue the Brothers!?"

"Why not? If they ruined your life as much as you claim. Sequester the soutanes off them."

Joe's hopes sank. His body even dropped a little in the thick salt water- which again didn't seem physically possible. How could he sue Brother Carol, Father Murphy and that strange nameless Brother they kept moving from school to school whenever allegations of improper conduct came up? Seek justice against the tormentors of his tender years? The ones who crippled the young Joe Deegan with his painful shyness, ignorance of women, and unshakeable guilt complex? The incompetent teachers who had beaten an education into him and his schoolmates even if it killed them- or severely maimed them- whichever came first. It was all so long ago. And no amount of litigation could repair the damage- visible or otherwise. What had been inflicted was over and done with. The necessary surgery and trauma counselling had or hadn't taken place; and the whole episode could now be written off as all part of a colossal systemic mistake- caused largely by the vow of Chastity (at the age of puberty, but not alas, in an Age of Probity).

Nor did Joe bear his childhood torturers any real grudge- if there were any of them still alive or out of gaol (let alone wearing soutanes).

As Gra'eme himself said: "Anger is too debilitating, it produces bad enzymes" (see *'Minding' The Body Temple*). Some poor Brothers actually thought they were making sacrifices on their pupils' behalf. The order itself had started as an organised attempt to rescue poor Irish street kids. It ended as a failure over a century later. And for all these reasons Joe felt it was better to let the shameful past remain buried in the confessional where it had (or hadn't) been hidden.

"I don't think so, Gra'eme…"

"Aren't there any scars you can point to?"

"Only the ones in my soul…"

Gra'eme snorted, unimpressed (from both the legal and cosmological point of view).

"How could you build a case on the fears I still have of leather straps, or men in long black frocks?" Joe protested, standing his ground for a change.

"Listen, Joseph, never underestimate the depths to which a plaintiff's lawyer will stoop. My old chums at Slawter and Pryce are extremely good at finding liabilities where there aren't any."

Gra'eme's predictable scepticism brought their conversation straight back to the problem at hand- from which it had wandered like the undisciplined rogue that it was.

"I'd really rather solve my fiscal needs using my own craft skills, you know…*as a writer*? I'm mean, geezus, Gra'eme, I'm…" Joe hesitated only momentarily, "…fifty years old fercrissake, isn't it high time I wrote something I can honestly claim is mine!"

"Do you actually *have* any ideas?" Gra'eme was being rhetorical, even a trifle sarcastic, but Joe took the invitation literally.

"I've got a fantastic starting point," he boasted modestly.

"Think of me as your next producer. Give me 'the pitch'."

Gra'eme settled back into his tank for a little lite snooze- the best part of any Afternoon Meditation.

Fortunately Joe, sunk below the lip of his tank, couldn't actually see his adviser's eyes glazing over. He blindly regarded Gra'eme's willingness to listen as some sort of personal breakthrough. This was exactly what the scribbler-for-a-living was hoping for. He required less of the master/guide thing from Gra'eme now and more of the producer/partner. He needed to explore his ideas, bounce them around a little- much like his body right now, in the tank. Mind and body in sync in a sink at last.

"I'm just not sure how real to make it," Joe tested.

"If the author is fictional the characters can be real," opined Gra'eme drowsily, but spot on as usual.

"Or where to start exactly…"

"Never start at the beginning, never finish at the end."

It was on hearing little pearls like this that Joe realised why Gra'eme's monthly retainer was such a great investment.

"It's called *One Day The Earth Stopped.*"

"Is that the title?" Gra'eme opened a heavy eyelid. It wasn't going to be as easy to sleep through this as he thought. The Master realised he'd have to actually pay attention to the some of the early bits. He'd ask questions later.

"Could be. Working title anyway."

"So what's the hook?"

"Well- it's 2020 and a huge asteroid is detected, hurtling straight for our dearly beloved home planet…"

"…And in a bid to stave off global annihilation all the world's nuclear powers mobilise to blow it apart…I think that's already been done, Joseph."

"There's a twist." Joe's patience was waning. "They don't blow it apart, they only manage to nudge it off course. But the near miss causes Earth's spin to drastically slow down…"

"What an imagination you've got!" It was genuine surprise from Gra'eme.

But Joe again mistook it for a compliment, and pitched on.

"As the earth slows the world's weather goes completely insane. Even worse than now. Cataclysmic storms wash floods across entire continents, the rush of air from hot side to cold creates devastating electrical interferences. Time itself starts to warp."

"Well, Time is relative, look at the Rainbow Coast."

"Yes, exactly. So just like here- what used to be a 'day' stretches out to 30, 40…100 hours. Then a week, a month…until eventually, it takes a whole year for the sun to rise and set. Strange flora and fauna appear as parts of planet Urth become alternately roasted dry during the long noon and later frozen during the months-long midnight. Mosquitoes will grow as large as pterodactyls, horses will become small again- the size of cats. Camels and cacti will overpopulate on the daylight side, owls and giant bats on the night half. As the spin gets slower and slower, people rush from one hemisphere to the other, avoiding the ultra violet rays from a depleted ozone layer- desperately searching for the best place to be when it *does* stop: the two strips of twilight zone where the temperature evens out and agriculture is still possible. There'll be wars and pestilence, and land grabs that in turn will become worthless as these long, thin habitable zones shift slowly round the globe- now effectively turning like a planet-sized roulette wheel. The entire human race constantly, irritably on the move. In fact it will be the last human race…" Joe quipped, discovering puns in his plotline even as he articulated it- out loud and for the first time.

"What- so the Urth ends, not with a bang, but a sort of…grinding-to-a-halt?"

"Precisely."

"Pretty gloomy stuff."

"Not necessarily." Joe was uncharacteristically defensive- and rightly so, he figured. He was going to fight like a lion for this idea.

While Gra'eme, despite his better instincts, actually found he was becoming a trifle intrigued.

"There would have to be a final, massive war, wouldn't there?" he prophesied, "-if the rich countries missed out on getting the best bits of any stationary earth? Operation 'Inalienable Right' or 'Noble Purpose'? Something of that nature?"

"Exactly. Yes, of course, Gra'eme. Everyone would want to live in Patagonia or Western UStraylia- wherever it stops- inside the two permanent twilights: sunrise and sunset. The only places where any kind of normal life would be possible.

"And what if those habitable strips just happened to be in the middle of the Pacific and Atlantic oceans?"

With characteristic brilliance Gra'eme had put his chubby, hairy finger on the story's structural earthquake.

"Then we're all doomed," Joe concluded glumly. Not just talking about himself…

Again the whale song took over- sounding like a chorus now of belching frogs stuck down a drain pipe. And for a while they just lay there listening, coincidentally reflecting on the many down-sides to globalisation. Realising how quickly it was wrecking everything precious and valuable.

"Tell me something Joseph, what do you *really* want to write?"

"This…this cataclysmic story. Gaia's revenge."

"Are you sure?"

The inference was so riveting that for a moment, Joe actually had to pause again and think about it.

As he floundered (literally) for a fuller response, Gra'eme cut to the chase: "Isn't it more some kind of wish fulfillment you're peddling here? I can see it quite clearly, Joseph. It's *you*. Again! You just want to stop the world so you can get off…"

Joe took this mild, but accurate rebuke in silence. What *did* he want to write? Deep down? From the heart? From some cavernous inner truth? His operating mantra had always been that a great writer needed great feelings. Well, that sort of thing was a little thin on the ground in Joe's life right now. In fact meeting up with Barbara was the last, best, most truly positive experience he could point to. And now her passion for everything and her energetic lifestyle was nearly killing him. He simply couldn't keep up anymore. He knew that. Barbara was gradually outstripping him in the 'keep-up-with-me stakes'. Running gradually away from him. Always out in front. Lengthening the distance between them. And him just barely able to keep her in view…

Joe wanted to write a film because he was old enough to remember a time when people looked to the cinema as the role model for some kind of higher, nobler way of carrying on. Where heroes and heroines achieved great things and treated each other with respect. Once upon a time, in the dark of a cheaply built, barn-like building in the main street of every country town (not just Nullumbah), silver dreams were fulfilled and evil punished.

But Joe also knew that life wasn't really like that. Evil quite often got away with it and dreams so easily morphed into nightmares. On the cusp of the third millennium since humanity took a Christian, monotheistic turn, existence seemed mainly to consist of a hopeless chasing after improbable fantasies. If Joe was to ignore the mainstream and write works of great integrity, let alone lasting importance…who the hell would be interested? Most of his potential audience had been brainwashed by television and was long gone as a source of support for something genuinely new.

It was a shock to realise that he'd have to find another way…

WOOZE IN AND OUT TO:

15

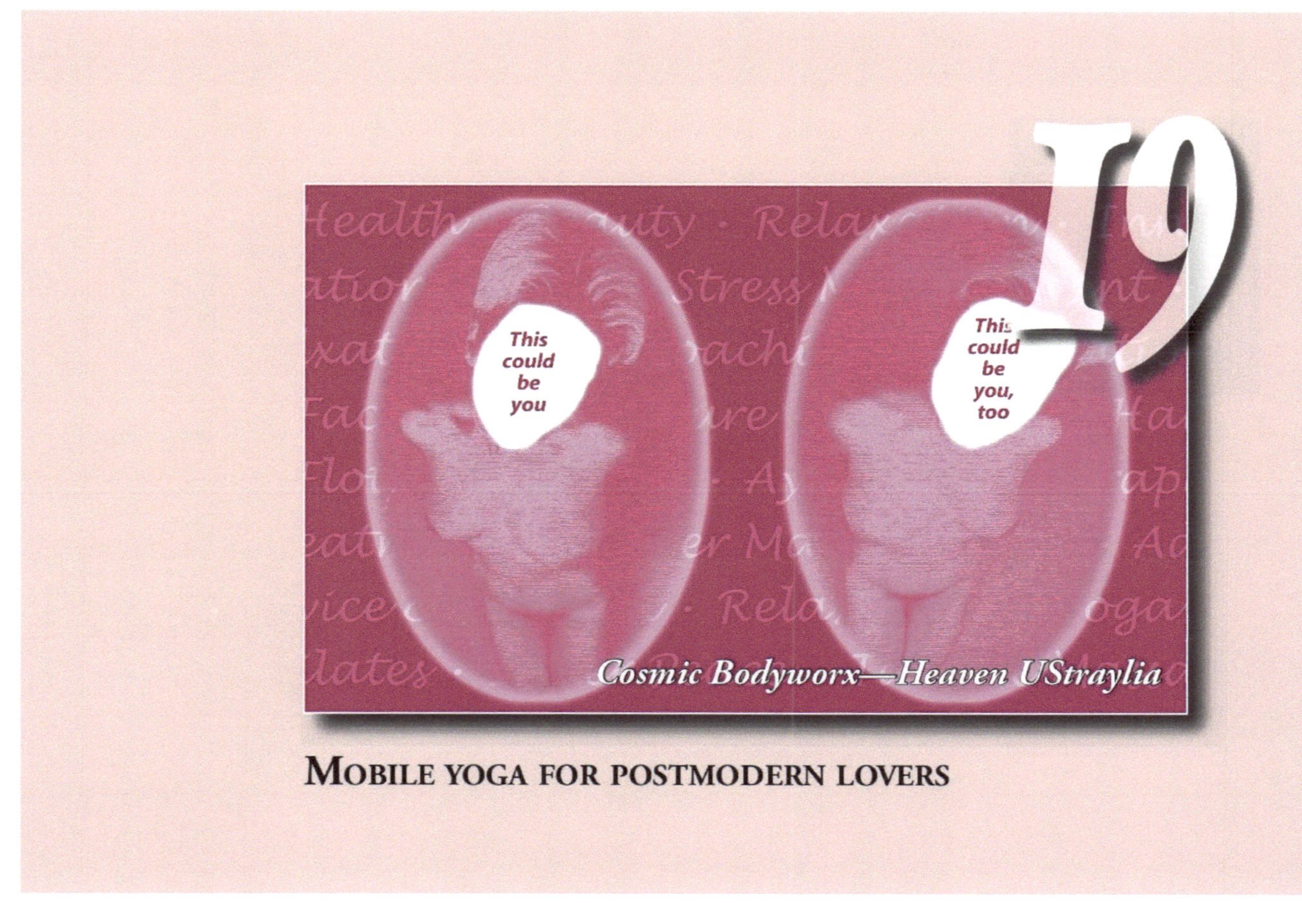

MOBILE YOGA FOR POSTMODERN LOVERS

Fed up with those tired old bones creaking morning, noon and night? Personal plumbing in need of attention? Already onto to your third prescription for reading glasses? Book the failing life vehicle into **HEAVEN US**traylia's colourful Cosmic Bodyworx for an introductory float/massage and full makeover. Discover how life can begin at 50. (Special rates for Pensioners. Arthritics welcome.)

#19 of 33 Postcards from Heaven

printed on gently mulched, plantation-grown, organic bamboo fibre using recycled greywater and bound with a biodegradable non-toxic glue

No animal or dolphin suffered in the making of this card
(apart from, of course, its author)

19

MOBILE YOGA FOR POST MODERN LOVERS

"Never worry about avoiding temptation.
The older you get, it avoids you."
(Gra'eme *Ageing Disgracefully*)

2.09 pm, The Ghandi Room, Friday 13th March

And so, for several precious birthday minutes, Joe just lay there in his float tank enveloped by a fog of depression- feeling even more stressed and anxious than when he came in. As a counselling exercise this appointment with Gra'eme was a long way short of some of the remarkable guru's more successful sessions. Joe knew he had to stop striving to be popular; and that applied to his ideas as much as himself. Not everyone is going to like you.

"Or you them," Barbara added once, pointing out the obvious.

"Or what you produce," Joe now realised (without Gra'eme's help). Not everything was *his* fault. He had to shake off the worst inheritance of his childhood: this terrible, Catholic Welsh/Irish sense of inadequacy and unworthiness. Besides which, some people are inherently nasty and nobody could do anything about that either. Joe didn't even have to get his ideas right- just written. As his working corkboard used to urge him. He eased off his speedos and flicked them aside, feeling a certain need to be stripped bare.

Eventually, Gra'eme woke up and climbed out of the adjacent tank to shower off. On account of now being late himself for one of his *Prophecy For Dummies* workshops, he offered Joe his mid-afternoon massage- as a kind of, off-the-cuff birthday present.

Curious, and a little perplexed, Joe tried to sit up in the dense salt bath. It wasn't easy. He bobbed hopelessly around, struggling to regain his balance- just as Helen Strongfeather entered the Ghandi room, bearing towels and aromatic oils.

After explaining the slight change of plan, Gra'eme's parting words to her were: "Poor lad needs a full chakra cleanse, my dear. His girlfriend's leaving him tonight..." before smirking quietly and making himself dangerously absent.

Joe and Helen's eyes locked for a tantalising nano-second as he strove to regain both some balance and thereby a little dignity- neither of which the clumsy Piscean could quite manage as he continued to bounce inanely around in the dense salt water, bumping into the sides of the tank, his togs way out of reach.

"Do you mind?" She asked shyly, as soon as Gra'eme left. Head bent as usual. Looking down. Blushing a little. Again.

Joe assumed Helen was talking about this humiliating idea of her being some sort of present. (Or was she perhaps making a sympathetic reference to Barbara's imminent departure?)

However, Heaven's most talented masseuse was actually referring to her baby daughter; and taking Joe's silence for assent, reached around behind the door to bring Moonshadow in, all re-nappied and tucked up neatly in her little leather papoose.

Helen placed the child on a bouncinette in a quiet corner of the room before striding across (with that wonderful predatory lope she had) to the massage table. Here she laid out her tiger patterned towels, and for several heartbeats neither of them spoke. There was unresolved (and perhaps unresolvable) sexual tension in the Ghandi Room. As hot and steamy as its tiled walls.

"Would you like the 'Scentual' or the 'Ylang Ylang'?" she asked, idly toying with several small bottles. Still looking towards a patch of floor in front of her sun browned bare feet.

Joe was too flustered to properly answer, preoccupied as he was with trying to regain his balance. Unable to stop bobbing up and down in the dense, salty water. This time Helen read his hesitation incorrectly and assumed he didn't want the massage (like her book earlier). The disappointment glaring through again. In fact building on from their embarrassing encounter in Kingdom Come (and probably going as far back as Moonshadow unloading her milky breakfast onto Joe's head at Café Celestial). In a spasm of depravity Joe glimpsed the oedipal eroticism of that primitive mammalian moment, and immediately wished he hadn't. The idea was too Dali-esque. What the hell was happening to him? He seemed to be losing all sense of moral self control.

Yet Helen remained with her head bent so fetchingly to one side, still regarding the floor submissively, offering her services unencumbered. The slave and her Roman/Welsh master, awaiting his daily anointment. Another 3 or 4 gyrations of the light house passed, three or four little eternities, when empires collapse and destinies come and go…

Of course Joe wanted the massage. It was fear that held him back. Fear and the anxiety that naturally occurs in any situation where body contact occurs between a man and a woman, (or a man and a man, or a woman and a woman)- whether 'married' or not. And not just because one, or both of them, happens to be naked. But that was silly too. Because Helen Strongfeather was as pure and wholesome as bio-dynamic, organically certified whole grain rice. (And about the same colour.) There was no question. Joe was a willing masseusee.

Willing, because Helen was not only fabulous at her job (and justly celebrated as one of Heaven's best flesh pleasurers- in a town packed with them); but her body, while no longer arithmetically 'young', was nevertheless tanned and svelte, her tummy ridiculously flat. Despite the recent pregnancy. Or pregnancies? (Joe had lost count of her many offspring.)

Either way, Ms. Strongfeather exuded health and vigour. Indeed, there was much about the woman warrior in her that reminded Joe of Kate. And it was strange that he should feel the Kateness in Helen because he had first met the forty something single mother shortly after Kate's death. As if he was going round and round between two sets of soulmates- Kate look-alikes, and women who resembled Barbara. (All of them Capricorns.) Like those solar systems that have two suns, with planet Joe forever wobbling in some erratic course in between. It confirmed his wider theory (of 'Relatively Everything') that there was a sort of gravitational inevitability about the way people are drawn together. Sometimes (often) to crash into each other and bring ruin and catastrophe, leaving ugly craters behind (not that Helen's acne put him off at all). At other times, the unified bodies orbited in perfect harmony with each other- to the music of the spheres.

Indeed, despite her quite plain facial features and damaged eye, Helen Strongfeather could still turn heads in any street she cared to walk down- moving as she did, high on the balls of her feet, with the supple athleticism of the huntress. It was almost a sort of stalking, swaggering forward, the energy coiled within. In everything she did (the way she held her baby, the fetching pose she now adopted with one statuesque knee bent slightly forward, her right arm perched on one hip, her hair falling forward and covering her shy blushing face)…it all manifested a Chi, a certain life force that men like Joe found irresistible and quite often women too.

Yet Helen was so bad at picking 'boyfriends' that they never lasted more than a few months. And it always ended in tears…or scars- or both. It could only have been a craving for the 'limerance' thing: that rush of blood to the head at the start of any new relationship. The feel-good factor when the object of one's desire can't do anything wrong. When attitudes that will later become insufferable, nagging character traits, are still regarded as cute little foibles. Foetal Attraction. Failing in love again. Helen was obviously hooked on the necessity of always having a bloke around; yet she failed spectacularly to form any 'normal' relationship, to find (and hold onto) one of nature's gentlemen.

So was Helen the ghost of Kate? A living vessel for Kate's soul to return and haunt Joe with? Like the tormented, dis-embodied spirits who hung around massacre sites waiting for some stray mortal to stagger through and be taken over…

Or was he just seriously cracking up again? After the day had finally seemed to settle down.

There may have been a time, long ago, when Joe could have been mistaken for good looking, if not actually 'handsome'. But why on earth someone as radiantly beautiful as Helen, would now be attracted to somebody as functionally shambolic as Joe, the TV hack, for the life of him, could not remotely imagine. Unless again it was the Tom Jones/Richard Burton/Dylan Thomas factor kicking in. (Probably, thought Joe, in retrospect.)

BLUR OUT TO:

The Ghandi Room, one minute 11 seconds later...

It felt like an eternity since she had asked the question, and in a sense it was. So long ago in fact, that Joe had virtually forgotten it's content. Today's woozy index creeping up the scale again.

"I'm sorry?" he mumbled pathetically, emerging from his reverie. If nothing else it was proving to be a day of reflection and disappointment, a classic example of Gra'eme's idea that: "We live constantly in the gap between remembering and imagining" (see *Stop Me If You've Heard This One Before*).

"Do you want the Ylang Ylang' or the 'Scentual' ?" she repeated patiently, holding up two small bottles- one blue, one red.

"What would you like?" he fumbled.

"It's your choice," she extrapolated.

"I only want to pleasure you, Helen."

What!? What had he said !? *Pleasure* her? Then quickly, turning a bright shade of beetroot: "I mean *please*- please you."

This was pitiful. She blushed again too. His one chance to impress her with some bright, clever, writerly quip, some witty *bon mot,* some pithy insight, and he'd blown it- badly. He was reduced to corruptions of old Beatles lyrics. She was embarrassed for both of them and rightly so.

"Can I have both?" Joe struggled for a way out of this ridiculous verbal foreplay. "Would that work?"

"You can have whatever you like," she murmured without a subtext.

"I've got my speedos here somewhere... " he looked clumsily round for those, oh-so-recklessly, cast away budgie smugglers.

"It's better if you're naked.".- said so causal and offhandedly that Joe almost believed her.

The massage was going to be difficult enough. To get through it without even the flimsy protection afforded by nylon togs was to invite disaster. To open the door and just let it walk in. Nevertheless, he clambered, clumsy and dripping, out of the tank and dropped naked as the day he was born onto her warmed tiger patterned towels spread over the Ghandi Room's massage table. Lying face down, tucking his tackle away, wondering why there wasn't a hole for them too. Like that special chair in the Vatican they use for testing each new Pope, just to make sure, in fact, that he *is* a bloke with testes intact. A clever ploy designed to avoid the debacle of another Pope Joan. But then, again, on that second thought, Joe was glad that there wasn't.

Without hesitation or making any big deal out of it, she removed her suede leather miniskirt and halter top. "I prefer to work naked myself- if that's okay? It's more comfortable don't you think?"

'Comfortable' wasn't exactly how Joe would have described his current emotional or physical state. After towelling his back dry she rubbed Ylang Ylang in her hands to warm them up, then puckered her lips and blew her angel's breath up and down his spine- before standing at the head of the table and gently pressing both palms onto his shoulder blades- holding them there in a kind of inaugural, prayer moment. As if bracing herself, saying grace for that which Joe was so gratefully about to receive.

Immediately the touch of her soft, but firm hands filled him with a warm, inner glow. Hands that also reminded him of Kate: the stocky peasant fingers, the tough, slightly hairy knuckles. He already felt healed and really comforted. A sort of natural, reiki energy radiated through him like a bolt of electricity. Then her fists played into his back like magick wands pressing into playdough, punching him hard, kneading tired and underused muscles everywhere.

All Joe could do was groan quietly as she worked her tactile genius up and down his spine, adumbrating individual disks in his backbone with quick staccato whacks from her knuckles. Sometimes concentrating on the base of the neck, then on the edges of the shoulders. Slapping out a rhythm like a feral child with a set of bongos.

He could feel all the tension and anxiety lifting as effortlessly as mist from a valley floor. Like columns of ghosts at dawn on the summit of Mt. Lookout!. It was erotic without being sexual- if such a thing is possible (which it probably wasn't). Then, for a while, she pulled and tugged his right shoulder- pummelling in under the 'angel's wing'.

Finally she said: "You're blocked, Joe."

"Mmm… " was as much as the dazed word-merchant could manage. Eventually, something in his shoulder seemed to give- like a rotten old tarp suddenly torn apart.

"Did you feel that?"

"Feel what?"

How could she expect him to discriminate? Joe was lost in a haze of deliciousness.

"There, that blockage in your right shoulder. I just worked on this lump- it was like a big ball of puss."

"Oh thanks, Helen- thanks for putting it so…clinically," he moaned.

"I worked on it 'til it just went 'phhut' and sort of broke up and started moving again."

He marvelled at how she seemed to know more about his body than he did. Obviously capable of 'reading' a person through her fingertips.

"Your chakras are like cement."

"So you keep saying- every time I get a massage."

"It's not healthy, Joe."

"Tell me about it…"

Which of course was a deeply rhetorical question, being merely the prelude to his launching off into a litany of complaint. That torrent of woes and ailments any decent rub down seemed to evoke in people. So much so that professional masseuses now got workcover for the counselling and Personality Realignment they themselves required after being forced to listen to so much angst, drivel and disappointment.

"Most people aren't aware of their bodies, Joe. We ignore the signals," she'd once warned him. "Like traffic noise on a busy highway. We block it out, and so the muscles go into spasm around some damage that you're hardly even aware of. Massage is like…letting your consciousness seep back into your body. Where it belongs. I'm only making you aware of the damage. The healing part you do yourself."

Helen (like Barbara, like Kate), was in touch with a certain basic physiological wisdom about the world, a mother instinct for common sense and how the body functioned. The traffic analogy was so apt. It explained…everything.

"There are worse jobs that being a writer, you know," she assured him. "Tenosynovitis is a small price to pay. At least you don't have to deal with members of the public all the time. Try being a waitress for example, or a barmaid."

"I suppose…we're all members of somebody else's public," he mused dreamily- the witty word weaver almost showing off. Then wished he hadn't. Why was he cursed with this alienating articulateness? The gift of the gab? A way with words? *Away* with words!- he mutely urged himself.

Joe knew he had to stop this ceaseless, if well-phrased brooding. Cut the wisecracking schmiel act already and stop sounding like Graeme- or the dialogue in a bad novel. Fortunately, Helen was intent only on slapping chakras and freeing his Chi.

"Of course, I know I should detox and get healthy …" he was almost fainting with pleasure now.

Then she found something…

"What's this?"

He frowned at the question. By now she was astride his back and working her way around his scalp, scattering dandruff and tugging playfully on his unruly locks (one of Joe's many favourite bits). She had lifted his head backwards off the table- pulling his face straight out of the nose hole- and was now rubbing her aromatic hands round the subcutaneous cyst in the middle of his forehead. Curiously, she'd never noticed this mound of hard gristle before.

"That's the lump I got when my mother dropped me out of a pram."

"It's like a third eye," she speculated, intrigued by its crude, volcanic shape.

"You think so?"

It was a dazzling insight. How amazing and appropriate that Helen was the first healing professional to put a finger on it- literally. The answer to a question Joe had been asking himself most of his life.

"Our third eye is like a coming together of the other two," she explained. "As Jesus himself said: 'Let your eyes become one and allow the light in'."

"Like an in-built, surefire, bullshit detector."- Joe was quoting Hemingway and thinking of writing generally. Showing off again. But he was also thinking of the cyclops view any lover had of their partner when up close. Like this morning in bed with Barbara. Her two eyes coalescing into one…letting *her* light shine.

"It's incredible, but now that you're actually massaging it, Helen, I can *see* what you're talking about. There's this kind of…overflow of amazing feelings."

"We've all got a third eye, Joe" she assured him. "But I've never actually, *touched* one before." Helen seemed lost as to how best to describe it, recoiling a little as she poured more Ylang Ylang onto it, then continued working her amazing thumb and forefinger around the cyst, sort of mesmerised by it.

"It also helps to keep my hat on- like a little clip," he quipped, before regretting it again. This stupid tendency to play the clown. Why wasn't his bullshit detector switched on now!?

"I've got a pretty large head, you see, it's not easy to find a hat that fits," he tried to make it sound like he wasn't boasting. Claw his way back to some credibility- having drawn attention to another one of his many deformities.

"I noticed."

"Despite my small stature."

"That doesn't matter."

He was glad to hear it.

While she kept massaging his 'third eye' Joe almost passed out again from the sheer physical pleasure of it. This was definitely going down as a highlight of his birthday. Her glorious strong, stocky peasant fingers kneaded their tactile brilliance into the little carbuncle of gristle- right in the middle of his forehead- circling and soothing it, seducing his consciousness into a state of total bliss: an overload of pure unadulterated and (thus far at least) unadulterous delight.

"Oh, Helen, what you're doing is so…divine. You're hitting a spot that…I dunno… I'd never thought about it like a third eye; but as you're rubbing my cyst now…it's like an Aladdin's lamp. I suddenly *see*- again it's the only way of describing it- I suddenly see *inwardly*, what I *have* to do!"

"To do?" she kept weaving her rhythmic, ineluctable spell, drawing him on, siren-like. He could feel her breath caressing the back of his neck in short bursts of exertion.

"To end my mid-life cri…"

He broke off talking again. Their bodies harmonically united by the kneading and circling of her thumb and forefinger round his lump- like the turning of the lighthouse, round and round, sweeping out the measure of their common heartbeat, synchronizing two separate pulses to a single, primeval rhythm.

"The solution is really very simple. Why couldn't I *see* it before? Why didn't Gra'eme see it for me? Oh thank you, Helen, thank you for showing me just exactly what it was."

She looked surprised. All she'd done was point out the obvious. Nominate the site (sight?) of his third eye. A simple matter really.

"It occurs to me now…that this mid-life thing I've been afflicted with…has actually been a kind of interminable writer's block. A creative illness after all! And only now- thanks to you- I can *see* that I've been stuck because I'd lost my muse. And when a writer loses access to the dream, s/he is finished. It follows absolutely that I had no zest for life. Everything looked too difficult and impossible. In fact I'd cut myself off from the world. Because the thing is- we really only know ourselves *in relation* to others! An artist has to connect absolutely to the rest of society, not just to him/herself. That's always been my big mistake."

Then the defining insight: "All you need is love…"

"All you need is toilet paper…"

There was a shocked pause as Helen looked towards the door and Joe tried to swivel round under her.

"…but you won't hear many songs written about it."

It was His Master's Voice calling, and it wrenched Joe rudely from Helen's spell as Gra'eme poked his smirk back into the Ghandi Room, all showered and redressed in his denim overalls. Joe suspected a set-up: his guru's mischievous return timed to cause maximum embarrassment- perhaps, to catch them at a point of no return? If so, the Apostle of Time had miscued it badly. Score one to Joe. Finally!

" 'Just popped back to say: we haven't finished with your revenue negative predicament yet." (A likely excuse.) "You'll need at least two more workshops, Joe. Which I'll try and squeeze into some cancellations next week. But I'll outline the main steps at your BBQ…"

And was gone almost as quickly as he had appeared, having shattered Joe and Helen's beautiful spirituo/physical tandem. Joe was annoyed; but Helen, ignoring Gra'eme, continued to work on Joe's 'third eye' seducing the couldabeen minor playwright back to a state of pure goluptiousness.

"Self knowledge begins with self criticism."- It was as if Joe was speaking to Gra'eme directly, in absentia, as much as he was to Helen. "Ten years after Kate and I'm still unable to let go. I want to write something that rings bells for people, Helen. That touches them at some really deep, almost visceral level. And so what if I'm just an old unreconstructed hippie romantic who happens to believe that most people are basically decent creatures; and if left to themselves, things will always turn out for the better. My generation was brought up with too much hope. With a strategic belief that we could change the world. Of course we were bound to be disappointed."

Mercifully, his rave trailed off again and there were several more heartbeats in which their bodies throbbed as one and Joe felt about as close to another human being as he figured it was possible to get without being genetically or legally related. Yet the only thing he could manage to utter was: "Oh Helen, that's just so…wonderful, what you're doing is…amazing…" -platitudes followed again by a sort of incoherent moaning.

Eventually, softly- so as not to break the spell- she asked him to roll over and when he did so, he lay there looking up at her, physically and psychically at her mercy. An open book, a feeling machine, 'a patient etherised upon a table'.

Joe was quoting TS Eliot now (in his mind's eye). She was wondering what he'd look like if he lost fifteen kilos.

And as she started working on those long dormant tummy muscles Helen's perspiration, springing from the dark tufts of her underarms, was soon coursing along a contour of rippling biceps down to the plump beating fists of her hands, and falling as light drizzle onto Joe's scented chest. He willed his eyes to close and could feel the saline drops gather in a little depression just below his sternum, where they pooled briefly before draining off to the tiny lake of his belly button: the umbilical full stop, the direct mother-connection.

He wallowed in a sudden bizarre, uncontrollable urge to bend forward and drain the gift of her moisture with his parched tongue (if his pot belly would allow him to bend that far- which it probably wouldn't). Again, it was insane and more than a trifle mentally unhinged, but he wanted to tell her this, to muster his feeble courage and announce his desire…

However, as soon as the word: "Helen …" left his lips, she whispered:

"Shh, Joe… don't speak. Just let it go…"

He was putty- or at best, warm squishy jelly- in her hands.

"Helen, you're just the most marvelous…"

"Shh …" she hissed softly, the physical dance of her powerful hands slowing without ever breaking contact or coming to a halt. They worked round his neck in a mock choking gesture, then up to his scalp and through his hair again, pulling at the damaged curls like an expert wool classer handling drought afflicted stock (or the fleece on some poor lamb, stigmatised with disease and abandoned on a stranded live transport in the middle of the Indian Ocean).

Nor would today's massage end there- as it usually did. It went straight back to Joe's third eye, where it trailed off to a bare minimal rotation of fingers on forehead. Skin on skin. Nerve endings on depleted adrenalin triggers. Now, the less pressure she used, the greater the effect- like many things today: a paradox.

"Helen, you're so…wonderful," he swooned.

"No I'm not."

"Yes you are. You're beautiful, intelligent, shy- perhaps a little too shy…like me," he conceded, risking a comparison.

"Stop it, Joe, Please."

She was close to tears. It surprised him. Why would she be so suddenly upset?

"It's true, Helen, you are incredibly beautiful."

"No I'm not," she pleaded.

"I knew you'd say that."

"My face has fifteen stitches in it."

"Scars turn me on."

Actually he was surprised- he thought he could only count about a dozen.

"You're just feeling good because of the massage," she proclaimed.

"I'd say it anytime, anywhere, you're the most extraordinary, wonderful person…it's the absolute truth."

"There's no such thing as an absolute truth," she tensed, self-defensively, all her many muscles flexing visibly.

"Yes there is."

"Like what?"

"There is," he repeated, running out of argument before he'd hardly started.

"Name one absolute truth," she challenged, standing her ground. Firmly. Like a Spartan.

He had to think about it, raiding his own personal experience. Wanting to be completely honest with her.

"Well - there's the undeniable fact that we're all going to die, for example."

"Ah, but how do you know that for sure?"

Joe couldn't believe anyone would doubt it.

"No human being has ever made it beyond 136- so far as it can be documented," he asserted.

"What if I told you that there are a dozen people living on the Rainbow Coast today who are convinced they're going to be around forever?"

"You're joking! " he spluttered, half chuckling, not sure if she was pulling his leg, but not wanting to put her off- if she wasn't. Actually, she was pulling his head, almost out of his shoulders. It hurt, but it felt good.

"They call themselves the "Nullumbah Immortalists'."

"Immortalists?" Joe scoffed, openly sceptical. He'd done enough cult analysis with Gra'eme to resist most of Heaven's more loony beliefs and sillinesses.

"There were thirteen of them originally, but..." she hesitated, blushing slightly, "one of them died."

"I rest my case," Joe laughed out loud, convinced (and relieved to find) she was a fellow sceptic after all.

"He was expelled- posthumously." She hastened to add. And she wasn't smiling.

"Well, obviously. I hate to say it, Helen, but the other twelve are in for a big shock too- eventually."

"But there *are* things that happen which we can't explain," she persisted, a trifle desperately. "There must be more to it than this little life that we get in the here and now."

"I doubt it."

"We *are* spiritual beings, Joe. You can feel it. Deep down. It's an intuitive thing...to do with the soul." She was trapped in clichés and he felt sorry for her. No. Stronger than 'sorry'. Make that 'compassion'. Because she did have a point.

Joe was reminded of his strange tendency (like an electromagnetic vandal) to blow out street lights by simply walking under them in a highly charged mental state; and of those times when you knew an old sponger was going to ask you for money- only moments before they did so. Not to mention the intense longing he was feeling right now to be united at some deeper 'spiritual' level with Helen. Something he knew he already had with Barbara. Something he had had with Kate...

But he who professed to write for a living, and be honest about feelings, neglected to mention it. And because why? He asked himself. Because the condition known as 'being in love' with somebody was where humans most closely approached the divine. That *was* as good as it got. However, all these things- mind, spirit, conscience, aura, morale- were only feasible when you had a body to start with. And as everyone knew, and even 'Immortalists' discovered: bodies don't last. Not even cloned ones. (In fact they wore out faster.)

Sometimes, when he could bear to look in the mirror, Joe felt his own life vehicle visibly deteriorate in the time it took to have a shave or wrench his hair into something approaching a respectable shape.

Or was that all just an illusion too, produced by his own deteriorating eyesight?

Helen was moving inexorably, reluctantly, towards the climax of the massage as she finally worked on his cheek bones then around the thick jowls and, up through the damaged curls again, towards the thin layer of skin covering his skull- signalling it was virtually concluded. Or perhaps she was just moving her hands randomly now. All over his face and body in no particular order, waiting...as we all waited...for something to happen?

"We *do* have a spiritual side," Helen whispered. "We know we're powerful in certain ways- in many different ways, Joe. Like the two of us here, now. We feel connected, right? There's a current between us that's not measurable. Because you can only *feel* it."

It was as much a challenge as a question.

What Joe did feel was: Helen's strength, especially as she lifted his head again, twisting the neck in a kind of penultimate wrestling manoeuvre, a reverse-venus-fly-trap-with-suplex designed to guarantee submission.

"You *are* beautiful, Helen." he croaked from within her headlock, his nose snuggled against her gamey armpit, her smoky body odour swamped by Ylang Ylang, her moist hair tickling him slightly, threatening to bring on an embarrassing and probably bloody sneeze.

Then she sighed...

And suddenly stopped.

Letting his head fall back onto the table with a light 'phumpt'. The massage was over and it had ended both badly and early. Premature eventuation. The finish had come before anything else had had time to. Including Joe. Fortunately.

However, even an ordinary massage should never end that abruptly. Something was wrong. It was presumptuous of him to have drawn attention to her inner and outer radiance. To pay tribute before the altar of her Venus-like divinity. Normally Helen's fingers would linger for one final delirious moment as they gently frolicked over his follicles in a kind of parting, tactile caress.

Frowning, he sat up, calling upon all of those under used tummy muscles (the one's submerged in the wobbly goitre where his stomach used to be, hiding the washboard tummy that hadn't been glimpsed since his Rugby playing days three and a half decades ago). Joe Deegan faced Helen Strongfeather and reached out for her hands, a gesture of thanks, but also of reassurance. Certainly fondness, compassion and respect were also in there somewhere.

She stood naked and adorable before him. He sat naked and fairly ordinary on her massage table.

"You know that don't you, Helen? You're one of the most gorgeous women I've ever met and what's more, you're good- you're a *good* person."

There was a pause. It needed more. A final flourish, some apt metaphor.

"And I like you very much."

(*'Like!?'*- that was truly pathetic. Plumbing the depths of embarrassment now. Again.)

"I'm not good. I'm a very bad person," she argued, playing devil's advocate, teasing out his case for the defence.

"Crap. Look at you: single mum, struggling to bring up your child- children- making sacrifices, working at whatever wretched job you can find. Full of a simple, physical wisdom. You're an inspiration, Helen, an angel."

There was no need to lay it on quite that thick and Helen rightly dissolved in the tears that now welled up out of her as if from some deep, hidden aquifer. She stood facing him and dropped her head on his shoulder as he hugged her back, comrade-like, partners in misery together; feeling her sobs break like a glorious plunging cascade through an endangered national park as her shapely body convulsed into his. So violently that the leather thonging holding her pony tail shook loose and her soft, silken hair tangled round his naked shoulders, flecking him slightly like a whip as she hugged him back and shook her head (still denying her worth)- discharging in waves of emotion as perfect as the glassy cylinders produced by light north westerlies as they rustled across Purgatory Beach.

On an impulse and unable any longer to resist, Joe rose and folded her into him, their bodies meeting as one. It was scary. Like hovering on the edge of an abyss. Like standing between a shopaholic and a bargain somewhere. Anything could happen and probably would. A sensation similar to falling overcame him. He let go and felt himself drop…

…just as a door squeaked open behind them, and the entwined couple both heard another woman's voice say:

"Joe ?"

Barbara was silhouetted in the frame of the Ghandi Room's doorway. Exactly where Gra'eme had stood when he'd set the current, devastating train of events in motion. For a moment the last great love of Joe's life actually believed she had stumbled into the wrong place by mistake. All Barbara could see was the flabby back of an obese sleazebag clutching a naked prostitute.

"I'm sorry, I was looking for someone else," she apologised, about to turn away again, embarrassed at having surprised two strangers so manifestly in the act; disappointed to discover that *Seventh Heven* had also become a brothel.

At which point Joe swung round as his eyes locked (horns) with Barbara's and for a moment he wondered whether he would ever breathe in again- overwhelmed by guilt, self disgust and the urgent need to explain this perfectly innocent but superficially compromised situation. It was the second time today he'd found himself wrapped in the arms of a third party to his primary relationship, and neither of these events had turned out terribly well.

Barbara remained heroically calm, almost impassive; as if at first she refused to accept the evidence of her own eyes. (Which she shouldn't have.) Then she slowly folded her arms and hung there, allowing herself another morally superior moment. Just to let him know, unequivocally, that she had seen everything- looking as though she might have expected this kind of betrayal- before slamming out again, banging the door like the gates of hell. She was too stunned to even bother abusing him. That could all come later. And endure for some time.

It took another stunned second or two before Joe was able to gather one of Helen's tiger towels around his wet, flabby body and race after Barbara- effectively causing a second small plaque of congealed matter to break off in the circumflex artery, thus doubly ensuring the heart attack his dentist had already predicted.

"Barbara !" he croaked, his voice thick with emotion "darling, it's not what you think..."

Alarmed by all the slamming and shouting, Moonshadow woke up and began crying. Adding to the collective embarrassment and general confusion.

"Barbara Please..." Joe staggered on after her, past *Seventh Heven's* meditation chapel, disturbing several patrons and putting excess strain on his heart.

CUT TO:

2.54pm, Saint Street, Friday 13th March

Joe ran so fast he almost fell down *Seventh Heven's* front staircase and finally caught up with his (ex?) lover/life-partner out on Saint Street, managing to hold a stubborn shoulder and swing her around to face him; demanding her attention for his simple explanation and failing that, his grovelling apology.

But Barbara couldn't bring herself to look at him directly. The confusion of emotions she herself felt was wildly out of sync with the passing circus of startled tourists, gaily costumed locals, and bemused bakpakahs.

She tried to contain her voice to an aggravated whisper but it wasn't easy. "I can't believe what I saw just now!"

"It was nothing, nothing!" he pleaded unconvincingly. He would never live this down. It was finished and over between them.

All the angst of her going, all the frustration and loneliness just ballooned up in Joe (displacing his guilt- but unfortunately not his vascular plaque) as he exploded out with:

"I just don't know if I can take this going away all the time, Barbara. I've got to have some sort of physical contact with another human being! God, it was only a massage forkerrisake! Helen always does it naked."

"Massage!" she spat back. The outburst drew stunned reactions from a passing family down from Brisbane. They'd come to Heaven for a quiet jeer at the hippies (not realising hippies had become ferals and were jeering back).

"Barbara, I need to *feel* the touch of another human being. While you're away."

"I haven't gone yet!" she hurled back at him, abandoning all decorum, ramming home the obvious.

The Brisbane family stared at the ground and moved on. A couple of the older kids actually giggled- more out of embarrassment than genuine amusement- already pretty unimpressed by the complete absence of theme parks and waterslides in Heaven.

"There was nothing, *nothing* unfaithful to you in any of that just now. I'm just...(his voice cracking a little)...just so sick of being alone all the time."

He was bordering on tears. Again. The fact that this had never happened before. With any woman. Ever. The fact that *nothing* had happened. And Barbara had seen it! It was all too ludicrous and crazy. He'd never been unfaithful to her and never would.

"I mean, here we are, with you leaving again- tonight! And we can't even have sex because your bloody girlfriend- that dopey, hopeless egomaniac- is hanging around all the time, like a wet blanket. You know, if it's a relationship with a woman you want, Barbara, then bloody well go for it! See if I care. Although, why you'd waste your time on anyone so in love with herself, is completely beyond me."

Joe was glad, at least, to have found an outlet for the grief and anger *he* was feeling.

"Julie just attempted to take her own life."

Barbara let the words do their own wounding.

At first Joe was calm. (Like Barbara had been on busting him just now with Helen.) Only Moonshadow's distant wailing from deep inside the Temple of Sin intruded into the gap of silence between them. Giving voice to the discontent and discomfort they all shared. Calling out like the shameful product of some sordid act. The sick thought now assailed Barbara that Moonshadow may indeed be Joe's love child. He sensed her sensing this too, and was about to categorically deny it- offer a DNA test even; but un/fortunately, Julie's tragedy intruded.

Barbara gave it to him matter of factly, brilliantly playing against the emotion for maximum guilt effect. "After Julie walked home along the beach she went straight into the garage (guestroom/archive/study/library) and took an overdose."

Joe closed his eyes. Now he felt really monstrous.

"I'll be staying with her at the hospital till we leave tonight."- uttered in a way that said 'nothing-I-ever-do-from-now-on-will-ever-include-you-ever-again'.

Deep down, Joe felt real concern for Julie. Despite his natural dislike of her and the fact that her attempted suicide had just killed off his last great relationship. There was shock as well, that it could happen, so out of the blue. In his house. To someone he knew. Someone who's life he'd saved only this morning! And here she was proposing to simply throw it away again a few hours later! Geezus. Part of him wondered why the other part of him had even bothered. Julie might have mentioned something as he was trying to keep them both afloat, swallowing gallons of seawater, preferring to cut and run. But of course, Joe could voice none of this now. Especially not to Barbara.

"It's over between us," was all Joe's life partner could manage before swinging round and striding off towards Rusty- with as much moral high ground as she could reasonably muster. Which in Barbara's case was always pretty alpine.

…Leaving Joe to slink back into the Ghandi Room, find his filthy, stinking clothes, apologise to Helen, and rescue from this ridiculous disaster whatever shreds of dignity he may still have left (which weren't many).

SLOW DISSOLVE THROUGH TO:

20

STAIRWAYS TO HEAVEN

Just another colourful, rainbow-clad, blue-sky day at busy Nullumbah International Airport—the modern gateway to **HEAVEN U**straylia, now capable of landing some of the world's smallest aircraft. A transport hub only several million Loyal Traveler Miles™ from virtually anywhere else on the planet.

Affix stamp here

#20 of 33 Postcards from Heaven

printed on gently mulched, plantation-grown, organic bamboo fibre using recycled greywater and bound with a biodegradable non-toxic glue

No animal or dolphin suffered in the making of this card
(apart from, of course, its author)

20
STAIRWAYS TO HEAVEN
"The Goddess is not dancing. She's dead.
Like all the others. So get over it and move on, forgodsake!"
(Gra'eme *Cemeteries Are For The Living*)

3.08pm, All Hallows Hospital, Friday 13th March

An old man wearing a pink smock and attached to several bags of clear fluid (hanging like Xmas decorations from a mobile frame) shuffles past Joe and Barbara who are sitting on a long grey bench, in the colourless, but unfortunately not odourless main corridor of Heaven's small, chronically underfunded rural hospital. The once were lovers are locked in their own separate worlds, looking sadder even than someone playing frisbee with themselves.

The mix of emotions in Joe and Barbara right now probably includes confusion, guilt, grief and incredulity. But grief comes with loss and Julie hadn't gone- yet. Despite the alarm bells Barbara had heard ringing loud and clear for weeks now, and should have done something about- she chastises herself. But only with the wisdom of hindsight. Suicide is a sneaky business. It surprises everyone except the victim.

Although there were clues. Julie had once told Barbara that the birdsong which woke her each morning was so irritating she wanted to scream back at them to 'shut-the-fuck-up!'. Julie even feared that if she did manage to kill herself she might be reincarnated with her bipolar disorder intact and thus be forced to endure the roller coaster of manic depression all over again- in another body but with the same old mental baggage, still malfunctioning...

A bright afternoon sunlight vaults from somewhere vaguely outside and bounces off the polished lino floor; but otherwise doesn't penetrate as sunlight, only as glare- with that rosy/golden hint of autumn in it. There was something about the smell of drugs and bad food and cleaning fluid in hospitals that always made Joe want to escape them as quickly as possible. But you couldn't, could you? Because you had to wait, he realised patiently. Like we all waited.

Barbara is thinking about how her plans will have to change again, postponing Israel altogether- staying on in Sydney until Julie's child is born and her shrink can put her back on lithium. (Fortunately the overdose was mild enough and treated sufficiently early for it to have had little effect on the baby.) Either way, Julie will need lots of support until the medication kicks in, and for some months afterwards.

Joe is thinking of the things he wanted to say to Julie but couldn't, and now probably never would. Like: 'thanks for saying good-bye'. But Joe's need for emotional closure would have been the least of Julie's concerns. And he realised, deep down, that if Julie could do it- we all can, and do. And maybe will. Because the real hero/ine is one who can stare down this awful fate we all have, this depressing mortality thing, and despite the pain, still hang in there. Life is only ever so many precious heartbeats, anyway. And to limit that in any way just didn't make sense. "Because in killing yourself Julie, you're killing all of us," he wanted to declare out loud. "You're cutting *us* off too...from *you*. And deep down, we all seek love and fail to find it. All look up to people who will eventually disappoint us. All place our trust in others only to have it betrayed. And despite all that, it *is* worth going on because we *can* only know ourselves in *relation* to others (having just had this insight with Helen). So we aren't finally alone, Julie. We exist because others do. The brother/sisterhood of man. And irrespective of all that, why the bloody hell did I risk my life this morning trying to save yours (and your unborn baby's) when here you are, barely six hours later, throwing both of them away!"

But of course, Joe never said these things- to Julie or anyone else. Not even to Barbara. And in any case (as Barbara could tell him) it was easy for Joe with his buoyant, if chemically sustained, optimism and self-administered altered states, to take the moral high ground when he knew nothing of the dreadful stabbing paralysis, the mind numbing depression that had (almost) brought Julie unstuck...

The old man shuffled back, his drip bags fluttering, exercise regime still on track. The lymphoma puffing up his legs like collapsing sacks of fluid reminded Joe of Kate's last few weeks and how her body also became distended in odd places. He suddenly realised- to his surprise- that this was the first time he had actually been in a hospital since her final (futile) operation. The one just before they left Melbourne, heading north- looking for the miracle cure.

Kate, who had clung to life with such desperation and blind hope, and held onto it for all she was worth; and Julie, who had found hers so unbearable as to want to discard it altogether. It just didn't make sense.

Thirty seven seemed an absurdly young age for Kate to get cancer. Yet most people died *with* cancer, if not *of* it. Like everything else: it was a 'natural' process. Cells that reproduced too much and were not technically 'foreign'. Cancer looks like us. It feels like us. It fools our defence system. We fool ourselves.

RIPPLE DISSOLVE BACK TO:

A Melbourne Hospital, 10 years before…

Joe and Kate are sitting on a long grey bench, in the colourless, but unfortunately not odourless main corridor of a large Melbourne hospital feeling as if they've just been hit by a sledgehammer and flung into a waking nightmare. She was diagnosed with cancer, stage 2A. And it seemed as if you needed a medical degree to know where to go to find the books to ask the right questions about what to do. Doctors themselves pooled their knowledge, working out the best strategy. Radio or chemo first? And operate when? In the final analysis though, and when the dust had settled, for Kate there really wasn't much choice at all…

Joe remembered, to his shame, almost coming to blows with her after the radical hysterectomy. He couldn't recall why. (Did they need an excuse?) Kate was barely conscious from the anaesthetic and already lashing out at him- like it was all his fault- having to take out her anger on someone. And him lashing back. Having to take out his too. They were each other's favourite, softest target.

He let her rage roll on over. He could see the pain. He was feeling it with her. Later, during another battle at home, in a tantrum of abject frustration, he slammed the door on a kitchen cupboard so hard that it came off its hinges. Instead of replacing it, Kate thumb tacked a tea towel over the gap. It consisted of the word 'Peace' in twelve different languages. Something everybody wanted: pax, frieden, mir, shalom, salaam, paz, pace…

Joe lost count of how many hospital visits they had made all up, how many anonymous beds he had settled Kate into, how many side lockers he had placed her books on and her stuff underneath, how many cheerful nurses they had met and come to know almost as friends. How many scans, ultrasounds, and x-rays? How many hours waiting in a corridor during another operation? Waiting for news. Waiting Kate's turn on the big, radiotherapy machine. Waiting for a nurse who was better than any doctor at finding a vein to put the drip in…Waiting like we all waited. Most of the time.

Joe and Kate quickly became hapless adjuncts of the medical industrial complex. Instead of going to work each day they went to hospital. Partners in a virtual tango with healing professionals and all their latest cutting edge cures. It was almost as if it had become Joe's disease as well. There was so much to do and catch up on that he had to abandon all prospect of any other occupation. A bad habit that later became almost impossible to shake off; and certainly triggered the life crisis he subsequently slumped into. There was little time to accomplish anything else outside this totalising dilemma about statistics and procedures and therapies. It seemed as if they'd become bogged down in a unending series of tests and small rations of hope. Much like an overheated property market, the disease was 'progressing', but Kate's prospects were not.

It started to put a pall over everything. It was the unanswered question. How long have I got? How long has anyone got?

CUT TO:

A Melbourne Hospital Carpark, one year later…

It was just after the cancer had come back a second time and Kate's legs are starting to swell around the ankles. A symptom like no other that her lymph system had broken down. The original surgery and radiotherapy obviously hadn't been enough. The cancer just too advanced.

She is carrying the results of her latest catscan to an appointment with yet another oncologist who would offer a second (or third) opinion. There was always the last ditch hope of chemotherapy. But the doctors were becoming less optimistic.

Halfway across the hospital car park Kate stops.

"I'm going to die," she says.

In the whole eighteen months of her search for a cure, this was the one time Kate seemed to stare unflinchingly at what it all meant. Where it was heading. It suddenly hit her in a way that she could give voice to. With him there listening.

So she plonks herself straight down on the hot bitumen- in the middle of the carpark, in the middle of a baking Melbourne summer. Stubborn as a Capricorn. Refusing to endure any more tests, or pain or procedures. As if she wanted no more of this doctoring (especially from ones who couldn't find a vein to put the drip in). So she sits down on a roadway and rejects the idea of going on- until someone (Joe for example) admitted it was true: that she was going to die.

Or did she want him to deny it? To offer some alternative where others couldn't?

He looks around. The car park is ringed by hospital buildings, yet the whole place seems curiously empty. As if they are alone in some city where everyone has left town or gone underground- fearing an attack with weapons of mass distraction.

So he sits beside her as she remains focussed on the ground just beyond her sensible shoes. Hugging her knees with both arms. Unable to say anything more. As if there *was* nothing else you could say. And is she expecting anything from him, really? A denial? A re-affirmation of her chances?

But he only stares with her, at a loss. What hope could he offer? All Joe knew was that we get through the daily humdrum by shunting the blindingly obvious off to one side. Of course we're all going to die. As to when? -is the only thing that keeps us on our toes. Our existence could end today, tomorrow or next century. Life's a miracle, the universe is unfolding perfectly, and there's not a damn thing anyone can do about it. Mercifully, a butterfly fluttering its wings in China generally does not cause a cyclone in Peru...

In this Melbourne carpark, in the midst of a week of dry, desert northerlies, Kate already belonged to a club to which we are all potential, if not actual members: people who can see a world in which they will soon play no part. The swelling in her legs meant it could only be a matter of months at most. Even her dreams offer no escape. Kate will wake up each morning and know it's still there. One day less. Not another day gained. Cancer forced you to ask the only question that's ever relevant: what the hell *is* it all about? Anybody's life. This little ration of time...and which day will be the one that doesn't end for me?

"We're all going to die," he offers pathetically.

And knows it isn't much, even as the words come out. Unfortunately, it's all he can think of. Not the sort of thing she needed to hear right now. Or the sort of idea he wanted to convey. But at least, and at last, it is out in the open. In this hot empty space, between deserted hospital buildings. A certain weight had lifted- for both of them.

"I'm going to die," she repeats, hugging her now fatal, mortal coil. All she had. The gesture excludes everything outside herself, even Joe. He takes a deep breath and wonders if this is the exact heartbeat in which she finally gives up her unreal but not unreasonable hopes.

Being clever with words was a skill that now utterly deserted him, as it so often did at moments of real crisis. He could surely have come up with some better formulation than the bleeding obvious. Something that might have encouraged her more. Perhaps some lines of an appropriate poem. Some piece of ancestral wisdom. What would a Buddhist say? Why hadn't Joe been more optimistic, loving and sensitive? Was this also the moment of his greatest failure? If he had loved Kate more could he have saved her? Could love be measured and found wanting? He often asked himself later, weighing up the guilt he felt: that he might have saved Kate with a greater effort of loving...

Joe could have (should he have?) put his arms around her at that moment, sitting on the bitumen, in the car park, and held her and said: "No" emphatically. "NO, Kate. You're not going to die. Because..." (why ?) "Because I love you and I won't let you die. Because we're moving to the Rainbow Coast and you're going to get well up there. We'll heal ourselves, de-stress and become whole again. Nothing but salads, fresh juice, macrobiotic rice- and old Marx Brothers movies. Miracles are as natural as sunlight and as necessary as oxygen. Anything is possible if you believe it strongly enough. And one day- soon- you're going to be so fit and healthy we'll climb Mt. Lookout! and watch the ghosts rise in columns from the Limbo Valley floor..."

But instead of saying all that, instead of reaching out across the fatal, mortal gap, Joe fails as many do. He searches for words of lesser comfort. And in fact, all he said was:

"You're not going to die, Kate."

And she didn't believe it any more than he did. He couldn't even put an arm around her. It had gone beyond that. Kate seemed already apart from him, hunched in on herself, outside a world in which someone like Joe could still plan a future. (One day without her.) His heart is breaking and he wanted to offer *some*thing, but Joe Deegan scrapes to the bottom of his soul and finds that there is no hope he can offer. At least none that a character like him could find.

Yet hope gives us both the reason and the means to go on. Hope is what binds us to our fates as willing participants. She was sitting down in the middle of a carpark because she had just faced the reality of her own cancellation and she is virtually saying: 'Now nothing matters. Nothing at all. Not even this relationship.'

Which was true (kind of). From which point her eyes took on the thousand mile stare, that blank, penetrating look only people who are somehow already out of themselves seem to have. Their eyes are open, but the view is inside, or outside, or both at the same time...

CUT TO:

Tullamarine Freeway, 9 years ago...

The letter Joe carries from Kate's Melbourne oncologist to the doctor she would have to find in Heaven reads:

"Dear Dr. Beanland,

Thank you for agreeing to assist this unfortunate patient..."

Was 'unfortunate' doctorspeak for 'terminal'? Joe wondered as he read the letter in a taxi to the airport. How many 'unfortunate' letters did a cancer specialist have to write in an average career? For them also a lose/lose situation.

CUT TO:

Tullamarine Airport, twenty nine minutes later...

Unable to walk by that stage, Kate is loaded onto the Nullumbah flight in a special, narrow wheelchair designed to fit down the aisles of a plane. For some reason (some strike or other, or perhaps another airline collapse?), the ground staff weren't operating the automatic ramps that swing out from the departure lounges and all the ordinary (able bodied) passengers are forced to go down onto the tarmac and climb aboard each flight via a set of mobile stairs. Like in the old days when planes still had propellers and before airports became 'terminals'. But this flight was terminal for both of them, since it also included the death of Joe's other, former self. That old hero who thought he was capable of anything.

What both selfs had in common however, was that they both hated flying. For Joe it was way too synthetic and artificial. Being above the clouds didn't seem our natural province either as fallen angels or risen apes. It was unnecessary to travel this fast, or that high, he calculated.

And as he looked up at the silver steps leading to the door of the medium sized jetliner into which Kate had already been conveyed (via a kind of large fork lift): he marvelled at the insane manipulation of physics that enabled such a heavy object to defy gravity and actually fly. It may have been a (statistically) safer way to travel than the cab they'd just caught to the airport, but- quite apart from the magnetic detectors and x-ray machines you had to pass through- there was also the severe ionising radiation penetrating the plane's thin aluminium tube at an altitude of ten kilometres. Kate had already been subjected to enough gamma rays and Joe didn't want any more himself.

For all these reasons, his foot hesitates at the bottom of a set of strike-breaking silver steps leading up to the plane. And suddenly, an old song comes unstuck from the rusted-on hard drive of his memory: *Stairway to Heaven*. Which this plane journey was for Kate, in more ways than one. And would be for Joe too, if it were to crash- as he always assumed likely (given his pessimism about things generally).

But right now, Joe was so buried in Kate's nightmare that he couldn't care less if the capton wiring did fail, or the plane plunged into fog-shrouded Mt. Lookout! prior to landing. Better to go quickly, he figured, like his old man with his heart attack. Better to go in the fireball of a plunging commercial jetliner with its payload of avgas- than slowly, and in pain, like his mother, or like Kate…

And so, propelled (appropriately enough) by a certain reckless indifference, and the sudden memory of an old song, Joe unfreezes from his panic at the bottom of the airline's mobile stairway and lurches on up, not just towards a small community on a quiet bit of coastline; but to life 'Up North' generally. To 'The Beach' and the great, summoning beacon of the lighthouse on Cape Surprise! Calling him back again to the region where he had been born, and back to where he would, he hoped, spend the rest of his days (however many he may have left). To Casa del Fibro, and Rusty and Larry. The place they'd settled on for Kate's 'convalescence'- which in the end only became the site of her final struggle and letting-go.

But at last! And finally! Joe was waking up! to the second half of his life. Rousing himself from the long slumber of Melbourne, to a more fulfilling experience. To Time in Heaven, where he would look after Kate and plan the Beautiful Day and make an easy writer's living from bad television.

And despite everything, it felt good. He had to go forward- with Kate. He had to climb that metal staircase to whatever cut rate, troubled paradise their new home offered, for however long he still had her…which in the end was only a few weeks.

JUMP CUT TO:

THE SYMPATHY ORCHESTRA

Just another last surviving example of the colourful Pandanus forest that once covered the sand dunes of Purgatory Beach—until wiped out by sandmining in the late 1960s. Visit beautiful, endangered **HEAVEN** UStraylia and glimpse some of the world's rarest flora and fauna hurtling towards extinction as they make way for hundreds of modern pink-and-lilac cement bungalows.

Affix stamp here

#21 of 33 Postcards from Heaven

printed on gently mulched, plantation-grown, organic bamboo fibre using recycled greywater and bound with a biodegradable non-toxic glue

No animal or dolphin suffered in the making of this card
(apart from, of course, its author)

21
THE SYMPATHY ORCHESTRA

"If you don't stand for something, you'll fall for anything."
(Gra'eme *A Towering Work Of Incomparable Genius*)

Nullumbah Shire, Two hours later, nine years ago...

As soon as their plane touched down on Nullumbah airport's tiny runway, Joe realised how inappropriate the warm Melbourne clothes were. It was good to know he and Kate would never need a jumper again. He hailed a maxi-taxi (for the wheelchair) and it delivered him and Kate to the bus that carried them south along the Rainbow Coast towards Heaven, then up over the foothills behind Mt. Lookout! and down into the leafy green, forest glades of its lower caldera (already a world away from the concrete glare of the megalopolis left behind).

They passed through tiny villages clustered around crumbling sugar mills and derelict dairy co-ops. A landscape shaped by rolling green paddocks that were edged by rows of camphor laurel and crowned by old wooden houses overlooking rivers as broad as their cool, breezy verandahs.

Then on towards that bend in the road, just past the little shop with its chocolate coated mangoes- where you got this sudden stab of panorama, south-east towards Cape Surprise!. It was the same thrill- that dazzling glimpse of Pacific Ocean- Joe got as a kid on day release from boarding school, out for a trip to the Cold Coast and riding in the back of his dad's big Chrysler Royal as it crested the last hill before Surface Paradox- revealing the glinting of a thousand diamonds sparkling on waves- holding all the promise of a morning surf. Here was a view of that same ocean again (40 years later and a bit further south), calling Joe home at last, calling him back with Kate to be reborn and to know the place for a second (last) time...

He felt a leap of hope at that view of the lighthouse, so white and immutable, the crystal lenses turning endlessly. And falling into their rhythm Joe felt again the immediacy and relief of living only for the moment. Realising how close to laughter crying is, and hearing the creak of a larger wheel turning- colliding events and forces and people, reshuffling the deck of fate...and bringing forth change.

Joe knew then that he and Kate had made the right decision and taken the necessary step. Because all she had left was Heaven Time, and as Gra'eme so beautifully pointed out, "we all know that can go on forever..." (*Time, Space And The Whole Damn Thing*)

CUT TO:

Casa del Fibro, One month after that ...

During the final weeks of Kate's struggle, Casa del Fibro became a single bed, palliative care ward, stocked with oxygen tanks, a fridge full of liquid morphine, strange machines in the bathroom, and friends and relatives ('the sympathy orchestra') come to help Joe and keep Kate company. To 'be' there for them both. Dr. Beanland also dropped by when he could. He was assisting in the struggle to keep Kate at home and away from All Hallows Hospital as long as possible. It was her wish and Joe's command. He understood why. She'd had enough of hospitals. And so had he.

CUT TO:

Casa del Fibro, Monday 17th May, 9 years ago...

Throughout her last night everything moved in kind of eerie slow motion. Unable to lie horizontally because of the fluid in her lungs, Kate was slumped in a padded chair with the oxygen mask on, breathing heavily. A kind of rasping sound as her body shut down and her life ebbed out. At 3 am it had been impossible for her to swallow the oral morphine. Another notch down the ladder of disability. The drug would now have to be injected. And Joe wasn't sure he could stick the needle in and find the vein so many doctors had failed to. This was crunch time. The battle to keep her at home effectively over. He experienced complete defeat. Not cut out to be a nurse after all.

CROSS FADE TO:

Casa del Fibro, Two and a half hours later...

As dawn broke and the sky started to lighten, Kate jerked awake and attempted to rise up out of her chair, her stick-like legs kicking out wildly as she tugged at the gas mask, leaning forward onto her frail arms. She seemed to be surging out of the coma she had lapsed into several days before, and she kicked and flayed about like an infant straight after it's born, thirsting for air. Our lives bracketed by this strange body spasm. Entering and leaving…

Joe just stood there, a hapless voyeur. Watching as if spellbound. She stood up, took one step forward, intending to rise out of the chair…but of course, it was fantasy to imagine she could stand, let alone walk. He caught her in his arms and lowered her back down onto the bed. The one they had brought up from Melbourne.

Then he sat close and watched while her breathing became even slower and more laboured. The harsh rasping tapering off a little as each intake lasted longer than a sweep of the lighthouse. There were times when she would expel some air and he would remain breathless with her, his heart pounding as he wondered if she would ever breath in again. When she did so he could hear her lungs gurgling at the effort, full of fluid. Her vital organs shutting down, her body giving up (the 'ghost'?). A final letting go. Her eyes were open but she was not awake. At least, not in any sense that Joe could understand.

Yet he remained transfixed and at the same time strangely detached. Watching himself watch, but unable to move or help in any way. He hovered with each breath she took as if his own life was slowly fading…until finally, it did stop. There was one long, slow, rattling breath in…and then a long, slow, sigh out…and then nothing. Only silence.

The moment where the light went out in her eyes would stay with him forever. It seemed both mysterious and inexorable. A sense of something leaving as her pupils dilated and her head arched back, her mouth frozen open. Joe watched as if hypnotised. Seeking clues in Kate's eyes as to what it was all about. What life meant as it hovered on the brink. Here was that seminal moment. The one between being and not being. He saw in her moment of dying the proof of his own mortality; and also the presence of something other- the spirit that left when Kate's inner light switched off, and her pupils irised-out to their full extent, signifying: something gone, something over. Her body 21 grams lighter as the 'soul' escaped.

But the grief of actually losing Kate would come later, the grief now was for the pity of a life as it flutters out. Like a candle extinguished- flinging off that long, thin wisp of smoke from where the flame had been. This gave the lie to Gra'eme's heresy about our sweet, little consciousness being all we get. Here was clear evidence Joe felt, in Kate's slow, visible passing, of the spirit that animated us all. That connecting thing again. The force that keeps the heart pumping, moment to moment. Glimpsed so briefly, but convincingly, as it left.

He was suddenly flooded with a sense of gut-churning loss- as if his own body had been torn apart. As if that half of him which belonged to Kate went away with her. Sailed out and upwards into the sky just as the first slash of red cut across some clouds to the east, heralding a new day in Heaven. The first of the rest of his life without her.

It was only then that great sobs exploded from deep within, almost choking him on their way to the surface. As if he too, might stop breathing- like a diver with the bends, or a baby some midwife needs to slap hard to kick start into life. Kate was dying just as Joe was being reborn- or at least being allowed to continue, even though he was being cracked apart. What drives the heart he wondered? (Not for the first or last time.) What divine spark plug keeps it firing? What propels that impulse to breath in and then…out.

He covered Kate's face with a sheet. (In how many thousand movies had he seen that done?) And almost unconsciously flicked over to automatic pilot. Acting out some innate, primeval reflex hardwired to the collective unconscious, he went and gathered flowers- whatever bits of colour he could find in the garden outside. Then, still like a robot, he came back and scattered them over the sheet that covered Kate's body- released at last from all that suffering and false hope. He felt relief for her, and relief for the end of everything that had gone wrong…

And as he sat quietly with her for a few more moments, the sky gradually lightened through their window and that bird that seems to wake all the others up started its irritating loud chirp (the feathered world's alarm clock). Soon the kookaburras joined in- setting off more birds, including the flock of lorikeets who had come to settle on the banksias in the front yard. Here was the new day, the other life now calling him. Time without Kate. So be it. Let it all go, he coaxed himself. The dark cloud had passed. For her, and him. She was free, gone, asleep, ascended…

Joe felt weak and drained as he moved over to the cylinder and, still on cruise control, turned off the oxygen, put the morphine bottle back in the fridge, and wandered as if floating, down Redemption Road and through the rainforest to the beach and his favourite titree. Where he sat and howled out loud again. Confidant that it wouldn't disturb Old Frank or the neighbours on the other side; grateful at last to have a huge empty beach on which to unload the pent up grief and anger and frustration of that whole dreadful eighteen months of her illness, and shoo them all off into the great soak of the Ocean. Salt tears to salt water…

Finally, Joe tore off his clothes and wandered into the surf to let the sea do its purifying/baptismal/mikva thing. And for a moment he thought he might perhaps just dogpaddle out and go on swimming until the mermaids took him…

But he let that idea pass, thank Gaia (and Neptune).

And as he came back to Casa del Fibro the flock of lorikeets reared up out of the large banksia that stood beside Casa del Fibro's front door. Joe knew, without them volunteering it, that the birds were taking Kate's soul away. Her spirit dispersed up amongst the chattering pack. Not in any one creature, but in the whole mad gang of them. So birds were angels afterall. And Gra'eme was wrong about that too. Because birds (as angels) were there to look after us. To usher us into life (as storks?) and to carry us away again as these lorikeets were doing for Kate.

Later that day the van came from the funeral parlour, and her body was wheeled out on a gurney. And after that, a small truck arrived from All Hallows to take back their padded water chair and the half litre of unused morphine- so that Joe was free at last to go for his second surf that day, only to find a large sea eagle hovering over his 'weeping spot'- the titree under which you could let it all hang out. Joe knew this sublime creature also carried a message from Kate. As much as to say: "It's all right, my dear, it's over and I'm gone- but not very far…"

CUT TO:

Casa del Fibro, 20th May, 9 years ago…

After the funeral, when he was putting her things away, separating out the clothes to go to St Vincent's and the stuff to pass on to the sympathy orchestra, Joe came across Kate's diary- something she started keeping just after the first diagnosis. An early entry read: "Joe loves me and I love him."

Written there as an insurance. A little mantra of stability. A recognition that in the sudden chaotic whirlpool into which she'd been thrown there was this one constant. A bond that can be held onto- like a five foot ten *Aloha* when you're going under for the last time. A friendship, mateship, through-thick-and-thin-ship sort of thing. What it's always- ever- all about.

And if Joe (thanks to Gra'eme) couldn't quite accept the idea of God, he did nevertheless still have two bob each way on angels. And if ever he needed proof of *that* he only had to look to Barbara.

But before Barbara could rescue Joe there was a year-long black hole in which the shapely narrative he thought his semi-talented life had been, suddenly came brutally unstuck…

HAZE OUT TO:

The Happy Hunting Ground Teepee

EXERCISING YOUR INNER DEMON

Just another couple of satisfied customers outside **HEAVEN** ustraylia's colourful, healing, Happy Hunting Ground Teepee. Feeling out of whack? A little detached, suddenly, from the main game? With scars no one else can see? Give Vasuda Devi a call today. (Specialising in Cranial Rebalancing, Aura Cleansing, Esogesic Colourpuncture and Colonic Irrigation.)

Affix stamp here

#22 of 33 Postcards from Heaven

printed on gently mulched, plantation-grown, organic bamboo fibre using recycled greywater and bound with a biodegradable non-toxic glue

No animal or dolphin suffered in the making of this card
(apart from, of course, its author)

22
EXERCISING YOUR INNER DEMON
"Whatever doesn't kill you generally makes you weaker."
(Gra'eme *Getting Real And How To Stay There*)

Casa del Fibro, 8 years ago…

It was almost as if Kate hadn't quite left yet, and was still making her presence felt- just as she often did whilst still an earthling. Prepared to overstay her welcome if the situation demanded.

Joe could 'feel' her in their bedroom. A low squeak in the door sounded like someone calling his name- particularly spooky when the wind suddenly blew it shut. Once, in the middle of the night, he woke in a sweat and heard a deep moan: like someone close by taking their last breath, in the spot where Kate had done so.

Then, in a dream, she appeared to him and said quite clearly: "Remember me." Or, another time: "Don't worry, Joe. It's all right. I'm okay."

But why couldn't he quite accept that it was okay?

The flock of lorikeets that came every autumn to chatter and squawk in Casa del Fibro's banksias still carried some hint of her, fading a little admittedly, as the months and years rolled by. Sometimes Joe would be drawn by the shape of a cloud suddenly fringed with sunlight, reminding him of how she curled her hair once for the play they did on a riverboat- giving her face a whole other look. Like a halo.

When street lights started popping off as soon as he walked under them, or when Joe picked up cosmic static on his ear plugs in the surf (such as when a cloud cut across a rainbow) he did start to wonder, quite reasonably, about his own sanity. In fact, he realised he needed help, and some years after Kate's death sought healing from his Master's voice. But Gra'eme only referred Joe to a book on the 'slaves' who built the pyramids. They heard voices too. They thought their kings were gods. And willingly went to the task. Somebody had to live forever. If only to offer a faint hope that it was possible. Hearing voices was really nothing new, as far as anyone could tell. It's what Joe did for a living in fact. Or used to, as the case may now be…

From a distance, and as seen from the back, certain strangers began to remind Joe of Kate. So much so that he was often tempted to catch up with them in the street and pass in front- just to see their face- to convince himself that he wasn't hallucinating. Once, he actually spotted Kate's rain coat ahead of him in Salvation Strand. It had a unique pattern, in green camouflage colours, with a hood- making the wearer look even more eerie and ghost-like. As soon as Joe saw it he almost stopped breathing (again)…until he realised he had taken the coat to St Vinnie's with all her other stuff (for recycling to the poor and the fashion conscious). And there it was, on someone else. As it was meant to be. That was the whole point.

The wasted months drifted by as idly as clouds on his beloved Purgatory beach. The other shrubs and wattles that he planted grew up and passed on; flourished, flowered, fell over and started to rot. In all that grieving time Joe did very little he could point to and allege as constructive or useful. He accomplished even less. Mournings in Heaven achieved without effort. And quite often afternoons too.

It was as if he had been overtaken by a kind of fatal lethargy. Creating something new and vibrant and unique by drawing on all his old energies became impossible. Joe no longer felt funny, so how could he convey a sense of humour to anyone else? And if the act of writing had to involve a jollying of oneself up, as if going to a party- just to get the words flowing- then clearly, the effort was beyond him. His modest talents to amuse were buffeted aside by a cruel fate. With his parents and Kate all gone in a short couple of years how could he be anything but passive and unconfident? Again, not lazy so much, as pretty majorly lacking in the 'will' department.

And so, and thus, Joe Deegan tumbled into a self-constructed, womb-like black hole. And for a whole year and then part of another one, absolutely nothing happened. His existence in what's called the real world (always a fragile thing) had slipped into some kind of soporific catatonia.

Joe procrastinated for ages about actually taking Kate's clothes down to St. Vincent's. They were just occupying space after all. It was time to let other people make use of them before the moths took over. But there's no way he could part with the singlet which he never washed because it still had the scent of her body on it (all sweaty from tennis). It surprised Joe just how little there was to give away: a suitcase full of clothes, a box of scripts, a portfolio of characters she'd brought to life in her short but brilliant career- work that would live on only in the memory of those who saw it. The most permanent record of anything.

There were also a few treasured books from her school days, an album of photographs, the guitar someone had given her which she never played, a make-up case and a folder stuffed with published reviews of the plays she had been in. The small baggage of an actor. Travelling light (like Barbara), and prepared to drop everything or go anywhere for the next gig. Not much really. No superannuation. A dud car. Half a share in a fibro beach shack mortgaged to the hilt. Just enough in the bank to cover funeral expenses...

It was in the box of play scripts that Joe found Kate's little notebook of 'affirmations'. Lists of things to sustain her through the final drama. This is where he found the note which read: "Joe loves me and I love him."

Did she mean it? Really? Was he that lucky? He read it again. And again. Over and over. And for a while it haunted him like a mantra. And tweaked at his sense of guilt- like a tropical sore that won't heal and you hope isn't itself some kind of melanoma.

He allowed himself the luxury of believing that she must have meant it and wasn't just committing it to paper to hold the allegation up for scrutiny, or to exorcise some demon of doubt. Because it was, after all, true. Kate did love him and he did so most profoundly love her. And in the end, or the beginning of the end of his grieving, it became the one thing that kept him going. That simple jotting- despite his conviction that he could have (should he have?) loved her more. And thus maybe saved her? Because 'love' conquers all? Because he'd faced his life's greatest challenge and been found wanting...?

Gra'eme decided (when the ex-playwright finally turned to the Great Man for help), that what Joe needed was a proper wake. A genuine letting go. A 'Wake UP!' call for himself and others. Something that could even be produced- like a play. Not the bereft, empty ceremony that had taken place at the crematorium with Father Hanlon in Nullumbah.

But the only sense of 'letting go' Joe could conjure was the image of the light going out in Kate's eyes at the exact moment of her dying. He dwelt on it like a film sequence, replayed endlessly before his inner 'I'. This moving image was as fresh as yesterday, but stuck on a loop in the projector, unable to progress forward to the next scene- towards any kind of resolution. As if Joe was held in thrall inside a suite of moments from which there was no real progression...

In short, Joe was cracking up, and had nothing to offer the cancer fund when they routinely pounced on him for a cash donation a week after Kate's funeral notice was published in the *Valhalla Times*. The fact that he was now pretty well flat broke himself made it a little easier to crunch up the bulk letter and consign it to the compost bin. A last straw (after the call from Bryce Keitel asking if he wanted to sell the house) was junk mail from a lonely hearts club. Obviously they raided the death notices too. Joe got as far as reading "Single again?" before angrily tearing their blurb to shreds and burning it. Here at least were the beginnings of a ritual letting go. A bonfire of the impertinent.

But the mail kept coming for Kate too. People who still hadn't heard. The tax department informing her they were doing a desk audit. (Struggling thespians were being picked on that year while UStraylia's rich and powerful continued to pay almost no tax at all.) Joe smiled as he chucked that particular letter away. Let them squander their time and money trying to find her he grumped. Obviously you can escape taxes- but you've got to be dead first...

One day dissolved seamlessly into another.

Joe had come to Heaven for the healing, yet it had failed Kate and was patently damaging him too. Tearing him apart along fracture lines already inherent in the Deegan body (in)corporate. He even thought of faking his own death and taking on a new identity. That at least would seem like an adventure. Several friends quietly pushed forward the phone numbers of their favourite shrink. Unfortunately, Joe had lost faith in all the healing arts. He repeated his old excuse: there was nothing a psychiatrist, therapist, mind reader, channeller or clairvoyant could tell him about himself that he didn't already know. The narrative cure would have to come later. But at a cost. Always at a cost.

Why then couldn't he just get over it ferkerrisake? People lose loved ones to cancer all the time. In much worse circumstances. And of course, the great lesson of Kate's dying was *not* to give up. To fight it all the way. Never to take 'No' for an answer. But Joe preferred to stand back from the main event. He opted to reflect rather than do. He indulged all his worst habits and became almost permanently stoned. Knowing full well that if this continued he was staring at serious dysfunction- if not terminal illness himself.

And so, and thus, Joe Deegan, flawed romantic idealist and failed husband, drifted into an almost endless mid-life crisis. The dark night of the soul. His excuse for bailing out of everything. A crippling failure of the will. But was 'crisis' even the right word? Crisis implied some kind of climax, some panic, some building up of momentum. It presumed an initiating drama, an *activity* of sorts. But *nothing* was happening. That *was* the problem.

Standing above all this, overlooking both the town and Joe's tiny life crisis, was the great 'clock' of the lighthouse. Still marking out each fifteen seconds of Heaven Time. Round and round, day and night, into an infinity of time. Four times a minute, two hundred and forty times an hour.

During that first year without Kate Joe could feel his life ooze out like toothpaste. It went on and on, day after day, days drifting into weeks and weeks into months without hardly noticing. Then a whole year was gone and a new one had turned up in its place. Once, just before the first Xmas without her, Joe was shocked to realise that Kate's birthday had already passed and he hadn't remembered.

It was a jolting reminder that the sweep of the lighthouse, like squares on a calendar, notches on a clock, or the pages of a diary, aren't the only ways of measuring time. When it was all said and done, these mechanical approximations were irrelevant. Heaven Time could only truly be measured by the spasms of your own heart muscle. Each beat of the body-pump coaxing Time into being by the same force that powers the hypothalamus, that little inner spark plug- an organ as dependable only as your will to go on. That one something that tricks, or prompts the heart into beating, minute after minute, hour after hour, night after night, decade after decade in the depths of your sleep and the marine trenches of all our depressions. Kick starting your life over and over again, causing another breathe in and another breathe out...

The heart was a muscle/pump that only stopped when you did, Joe now realised. And it hardly ever missed a beat as it pushed us all forward, urging us on from moment to moment, leading us into new territories of time, allowing us to colonise what lies ahead. Opening up the little backyards of days into the paddocks of weeks, and onto the broad plains of months before ranging out over vast regions of years and continents of decades. Measuring out our blood like a laundry sponge, soaking it up, cupful by muddy cupful, and pushing it on into arteries and capillaries alike. Sixty thousand miles of them in every one of us, delivering vital oxygen to the hundred trillion cells that run the body, beating a hundred thousand times a day, three quarters of a million times a week! Towards the total, finite number of heartbeats that we know, deep down, we are all allotted. And which pass so agonisingly quickly. Or slowly. Depending on your circumstances. Depending on whether you're in paradise or in hell. Heaven or Surface Paradox. Whether you're waiting, or have arrived...

Because Time wasn't 'out there' happening to someone else; it was always here, deep within us, coursing through our ravaged blood vessels. Through us and out of us as we blazed our way from our shameless pasts headlong into the grand night of our own personal futures. Neither sure about where we have come from, and not quite certain sometimes, or even terribly keen about just where we might be heading... Let alone how we could end up. But forging on nevertheless, sometimes blindly, frequently without hope. Each one of us granted our own little eternity called an ordinary lifespan. Alpha and Omega. Amen and Awomen. Thanks be to Gaia.

That Kate was gone and could be taken so easily away, that time no longer coursed through her body, convinced Joe absolutely that there *was* no justice in the world and that the idea of a fair go for all had to be just another human fantasy. Ultimately as futile as the fictions about God and the afterlife and all our other many comforting illusions. (As Gra'eme so rightly pointed out in *Life's A Bastard Then You Discover Your Real Dad.*)

Joe sought some sort of solace in a series of fumbled, personal encounters. Not reaching the status of relationships as such, in fact barely more than one (or two) night stands. Embarrassing in retrospect. These shy gropings he attempted with various women towards something- sometimes each other. Often in the dark. Understated, unsure, undressed and up in the air. Nice people. Women Joe could pour his heart and soul out to. But who wanted to hear all that blighted stuff about losing your partner? It was hardly an auspicious start to anything...

Mercifully, both worms and worlds do turn. Almost inevitably there was a spring coming in Joe's life. And almost without realising it (certainly without planning it or doing anything positive to bring it about), things started to pick up. A certain, faint hope returned that not all was lost. That he could go forward and was allowed a second chance. There was still time to write and something to say (despite his residual, underlying depression). A new day was dawning for him after all.

Because by then there was Barbara...

JUMP FORWARD TO:

23

VIRTUAL JERUSALEMS

The Old City of Jerusalem with its colourful Dome Of The Rock—just another golden 'nuclear reactor' channeling straight to **HEAVEN US**traylia via Gaia's cosmic modem. Fly there in person from busy Nullumbah International Airport and discover one of the globe's most precious historic icons completely at the mercy of bulldozers and grossly inappropriate overdevelopment.

Affix stamp here

#23 of 33 Postcards from Heaven

printed on gently mulched, plantation-grown, organic bamboo fibre using recycled greywater and bound with a biodegradable non-toxic glue

No animal or dolphin suffered in the making of this card
(apart from, of course, its author)

23
VIRTUAL JERUSALEMS
"Make peace, not love."
(Gra'eme *Alien Dialogues*)

Melbourne, January 17th, 1991…

Joe and Barbara's lives collided at an 'Armageddon' party in the suburb of Caulfield. It was the night that Gulf War I erupted. The prospect of another major conflict in the Muddled East had pretty comprehensively ruined Barbara's tour guiding job, so she came 'home' to Melbourne while people waited to see if Saddam's scuds would bring about the end of the world. Confidant of course, that they weren't nuclear tipped, and therefore wouldn't. The 'Armageddon' bit was meant to be a joke. But Joe, true to his mood at the time, and always expecting the worst, stubbornly refused to get it.

He was on one of his aimless wanderings back to Melbourne, looking for something to fill the gap that had opened where his sense of fun used to be. He became aware of Barbara on the other side of the gathering through a haze of smoke. There was a certain glance from her making it clear she'd noticed that he'd noticed her fish net stockings. His eyes lit up like a pub's till on Friday night. It was lust at first sight. And- given Joe's romantic talent- for quite some considerable time afterwards…

Barbara taught him the tango. It changed his life.

Because she also made Joe realise that grief was a kind of shutting down. He knew she knew he knew that if he didn't rouse himself out of this slough of despond he would probably, simply… just fade to black. And pretty soon.

Which seemed kind of a waste, really.

As soon as the skies above Jerusalem cleared of rockets and a sort of peace settled over the Muddled East once more, Barbara took him back with her. To her promised land…

CUT TO:

Jerusalem, Four months later …

They are strolling through the strangely monochrome streets of Mea She'arim, the ultra-orthodox precinct of Jerusalem, north west of the Old City.

"Ask anyone in Jerusalem today if they're the Messiah and there's always a teeny pause before they try to deny it…"

Joe waited, smiling.

"That's bullshit." Barbara rejected out of hand (after a pause).

He laughed. "There's even a name for it: 'Jerusalem Syndrome': an 'inexplicable intoxication with a place'. They all had it: King David, Jesus, The Crusaders, Father Murphy…a lot of the prophets, most of your settlers. It's like a virus."

"I'm not infected."

"I rest my case," he teased, "you're not affected, yet you can't stay away from the joint."

"Because it *is* special. You feel it here. People are more alive, Joe."

"Jerusalem is a state of mind," he concluded.

And Barbara let it pass.

He had come to find out what this other part of her life was all about. But he's defensive, obviously. She wants him to enjoy the experience as much as she does. Competing lovers with their competing heavens-on-earth. They wander on, heading for Mahaneh Yehuda, the Jewish market. Joe's Hawaiian shirt is something of an affront to the pious men in Hevrat Shas Street who hurry past, sweating profusely in hot black coats and big black hats like baddies in a Hollywood western. On Shabbat the hats are ringed with fur and the coats made of padded silk- costumes transplanted from frosty, snow-bound Poland a hundred years ago. Which made a lot of sense in a sweltering desert climate.

Signs all around warned people to 'dress modestly', 'stop talking', and 'keep moving'! Nothing could be allowed to distract from the crucial business of praying to God and studying His holy texts.

Yet in Mea She'arim the streets are blest with an absence of cars most of the time. On Shabbat not even a taxi would dare go there. Which, in a city as polluted as modern Jerusalem, was as close to paradise as it seemed possible to get. Joe gave thanks for the idea of Saturday, and the gift of the weekend.

"Look, Barbara, I agree with you," he placated. "If religion keeps young men busy pouring over books and going slowly blind in large rooms together, that's fine. If it gives them respect for older people generally and keeps cars off the streets, where's the problem?" he shrugged Jewishly, lifting and dropping his shoulders, holding his palms up like a prayer- or a plea.

Joe knew that Barbara's favourite city, this strange dystopia, hung on the idea of a book- in two volumes. The people of Mea She'arim spent their lives on the first one, endlessly arguing over it, and hurrying from session to session to discuss the nano details. It was a picture-free version, however. No graven images there. The illustrations came with the second volume, the continuing story: the New Testament. Where every scene, every event, every miracle in the great drama of the Christian story had its own church: The Flagellation, The Garden Agony, The Ten Lepers, The Nativity, The Ascension, The Annunciation, Ecce Homo, The Holy Sepulchre… Jerusalem was a living (and dying) museum that retold and re-pictured these same events over and over, binding them together like a codex.

And inside every church the same events could be found recorded and imaged, with slightly different inflections: Franciscan, Benedictine, Orthodox, Armenian, Coptic, Luthern, Anglican… An account of a man who thought he was on a mission, apparently cured people, and even talked to somebody who wasn't there- all long before the advent of mobile phones.

The whole of Jerusalem, ancient and modern, was a theatre, a stage for an endlessly repeated drama. A place built on a book and like a book, consisting of page upon page, and layer upon layer of critical happenings. Every 10 metres of earth under the Old City encapsulated another 2000 years. And pilgrims (fortunately for guides like Barbara) fell over themselves to get there and read it for themselves (war permitting).

"I've finally understood what it is that you do," Joe revealed to her once. "You're an agent of history, Barbara. A purveyor of things past. And even if He didn't exist He would've had to have been invented because above all, people in this part of the world needed to learn something about turning the other cheek and making love instead of war."

Joe added the capital 'H's just to show there were no hard feelings. It was the old St. Pat's boy speaking, the Christian Gentleman still buried deep inside, where his scruples should've been.

Coming from the antipodes, Joe saw Jerusalem as a high desert oasis town pretending to be European. You could be in Mea She'arim one minute; then cross over a road to Al Quds (Arab East Jerusalem) and find yourself inside another world altogether. You could even drive an hour to the coast and have a surf at Bat Yam, Israel's answer to Surface Paradox- with its monolithic hotels and windswept, denuded beaches. Joe imagined an archaeological dig of the future turning up rusting iron rods inside broken slabs of concrete. Remnants of a civilisation here now, but long gone one day. Eventually to be part of someone else's history…

"That's what I love about the place," Barbara declared. "The contrasts, the energy, the sense of standing on hallowed ground…"

They were sitting now, sharing a mango juice in Ben Yehuda Mall, surrounded by not so hallowed dust and very loud noise. No conversation within their hearing is pitched at a normal level if it can be shouted from six feet away- like a character in *On Golden Sands.* Israeli police cars even had mega-megaphones. Louder-than-life voices. In a place where voices were important. And 'hearing' voices created problems.

The only surprise about modern Jerusalem was how a place so triumphantly holy could end up becoming so grimy and kitsch. It offended the ex-altar boy in Joe when he saw tourists photographing themselves on top of 'Calvary' in the Church of the Holy Sepulchre. As if it was the Sydney Opera House or the Eiffel Tower and you needed the slides to prove you'd been there. Shrines had become things to be gawked at. Like the ferals in Arcadia Park. At least the Muslim guards at the Dome of Rock had the good sense to throw all foreigners out every few hours. Driving them off the temple mount like Jesus with the money lenders, back to their hotels and restaurants for lunch. Leaving the place at peace for locals to pray in, and the nearby felafel cafés both counting profits and thanking prophets. If only the wisecracking girls behind the counter at Heaven's small Post Office would do the same to the growing numbers of bakpakahs (leaving the queues open for the locals to get through) Joe grumbled-thinking of the curse of tourism generally.

Since before Abraham, pilgrims had come to Jerusalem to find the cosmic modem connecting Heaven to Urth. The place where time began and where it would surely end. The Dome of the Rock was a line-in socket straight to God's website. The Holy of Holies. The spot where Abraham almost barbequed his son Isaac, and where Mahomet rode his horse, Baraka, up to Paradise. But the Heaven sought in Jerusalem so passionately by so many over thousands of years belonged essentially to another world. People came to Heaven UStraylia, knowing that paradise was already in place, on the ground, so to speak. Ready and waiting. Essentially natural, and therefore free of dogma, thanks be to Gaia…or so Joe would argue.

"It's just too crowded," he rankled to Barbara when they were stuck for half an hour in the Arab souk, jammed together like crayons in a box, while an endless stream of Polish Catholics in yellow caps crushed past. They were all carrying pine crosses and singing hymns.

"You'll have to build a replica of the place somewhere else. A Virtual Jerusalem. Something to divert the tourist hordes from the real one, and give the lovely old place a chance to breathe."

But the noise in the streets was music to Barbara's ears. Hearing Hebrew spoken, people arguing, bargaining, flinging their hands about. She drank it all in. A cultural alcoholic. Happy, addicted and serene. A Melbourne girl come home at last.

Once, she took him to the steps that lead up to Herod's temple. Where Jesus *must* have walked. If he existed. She told him that Neil Armstrong had stood there too, and declared this was 'more important' for him than 'standing on the moon'.

"I rest my case," laughed Gra'eme when Joe told him about it later. "Religion- it's outa this world!"

RIPPLE DISSOLVE FORWARD TO:

3.17pm, All Hallows Hospital, Friday 13th March

Joe and Barbara are still sitting on a bench in the main corridor of Heaven's small, chronically underfunded rural hospital- turned slightly away from each other

"What's it all about, Joe?" she finally asks.

Barbara meant their relationship. He knew she meant it. And she knew he knew she knew he knew she meant it.

Because there was now the distinct possibility she would leave him. As she had every right so to do. There was nothing holding her back. It wasn't just about Helen Strongfeather specifically, or the fact that Joe had declined to join Barbara in adopting a child some years earlier. Of which this whole saga with Julie was a jolting, painful reminder.

"But Barbara, I love you," he explained, reduced again to cliché.

And it sounded fake even as it came out. Why shouldn't he let Barbara adopt a kid when he would have given anything to have seen some image of her recreated and mixed up with his own hopeless genes. And they had tried, all those years ago. But something was wrong- which even IVF couldn't fix. Or maybe they didn't pursue it far enough. And now it was too late. He was too tired, too old and too grumpy. And he lacked, to his shame, enough generosity of spirit to let a third person come between them. (If there was now anything 'between them' at all.)

"What does that mean? 'You love me?'" She spits it back. The eternal question. The one that's always impossible to answer.

"It means…I…care for you," came his fitful, inadequate reply. "I want to give you something…" quoting Father Murphy's one and only sex talk to the combined sub-junior classes. "You're my soul mate, Barbara. Some essential element of who *I* am." Again, looking at it from his own selfish point of view.

"Love…" she said, "is caused by a hormone called 'oxytocin'- they've done study, Joe: that 'loving feeling'? It's just a biochemical reaction."

WIPE BACK TO:

24

POWER OF ÆTERNITY

Egypt's sensational Mt Sinai, scene of divine intervention in human affairs (for the purposes of moral improvement)—just like its antipodean counter-chakra point: colourful **HEAVEN** ustraylia. Visit the Rainbow Coast and discover a place where the first commandment is: 'Thou shalt always have a good time'.

Affix stamp here

PRETTE TAIZE PONTOAIE

#24 of 33 Postcards from Heaven

printed on gently mulched plantation-grown, organic bamboo fibre using recycled greywater and bound with a biodegradable non toxic glue

No animal or dolphin suffered in the making of this card
(apart from, of course, its author)

24
POWER OF AETERNITY

"The only place for holy wars is either Heaven or Hell."
(Gra'eme *The War On Horrorism*)

The Cemetery House, East Jerusalem, 8 years ago …

It's Joe's first trip to Israel and Barbara brings him out onto the patio of the house she shares with her friends Amnon and Dinah, halfway up Mt. Scopus. The Old City and its epicentre, the Dome of the Rock, panoramas before them- like a golden nuclear reactor dropped inside an ancient stone town. Beyond it are the high rise towers of modern West Jerusalem, silhouetted against a sunset skyline gone an extra deep red this evening on account of the dust from an exploding volcano in Indonesia half a planet away. The Arab boys minding sheep among the olive trees in the wadi below are showing off by galloping around, standing on the backs of donkeys- much like they would have done fifty or a hundred generations ago.

Joe marvels at the view, thinking of all that history. Twenty seven conquests or occupations in three thousand years, and still counting.

"My eyes are focused but my head's in orbit." He turns and regards her fondly for a moment, amazed at the good luck that's brought them together. Imagining he might have been a Roman governor or Crusader knight (from Wales) and she his local concubine.

"You're quite unusual, aren't you?" he flatters.

"No I'm not."

"Unusual people always say that."

He's smiling, wanting her to like his Heaven-on-Earth as much as she wants him to like hers. It was subtext for where they might end up living- if they lived together.

"You noticed Amnon's gun?" She looks at him. A twinkle in her eye.

"Yes."

Joe had spotted it the moment they walked in the door- left lying so casually in its holster on the kitchen table, like some rogue piece of cutlery.

"Any guide can carry a gun if they want."

"But you don't?"

"No."

"You sure there isn't something about living in the Cemetery House I need to know?" He's still smiling, prepared to believe the worst, but not take it too seriously.

The limestone cottage they're living in was built by a 'colony' of American Christians in the 1870s. Most of whom lay buried in the small cemetery beside it. Hence the name. Paradoxically, Barbara felt protected by the graves. The superstitions connected to places of burial in this part of the world provided an invisible, but tangible barrier. No one would dare cross it. Although there was always the risk of getting stoned as they drove through the Arab suburb of Sheik Jarrah on their way up Mt. Scopus. Technically, the Cemetery House straddled a kind of no-man's-land: the 'green line' between Israel and Palestine. That bit on the map where a general's chinagraph pencil had smudged out during the peace negotiations after the Six Day War, and blurred the exact point at which the West Bank became Israel proper.

"We've had a couple of windows broken, my car radio stolen…the government picks up the bill." Barbara shrugged. Like it was the price you paid for such a fabulous view.

When Joe still looks dubious she pre-empts him with: "There *is* a war going on."

"I noticed."

He thinks about the differences between Israel and the Rainbow Coast. It feels stranger than paradise. Barbara steps forward and kisses him. Their embrace becomes more passionate- almost blasphemous when you consider the holy backdrop…until Joe breaks off a little and stands back. Regarding her fondly.

"But I've never been in a kitchen with a pistol before."

Downtown West Jerusalem, a few days later ...

Joe and Barbara are sitting, flirting with coffees, watching the passing cavalcade in Ben Yehuda Mall: a gathering place that is packed with seekers and mystics, misfits and buskers, tourists and bakpakahs, pilgrims and poseurs- just like Heaven really, Joe realised, struck by the many similarities.

"Israel is a drug for you isn't it? You're intoxicated."

"I'm happy here."

"You actually get some sort of charge from the danger." And it always amazed him.

"You'll feel it too- eventually - the attraction."

"You wish."

"You'll cast off your pagan doubts, Joe Deegan."

"I can't live here, Barbara," he confessed, disappointed in himself. "I mean, it's fascinating, granted. All this history…amazing. But, I…I guess I just have an allergic reaction to mindless violence."

"There's only ever a handful of extremists- on both sides. Eventually it will all settle down again. Like it always does." She lifted her shoulders and dropped them again- an acceptance of things as they are, like it hardly needed saying.

"Israel is the land bridge between three continents," she explained. "It will always be a battleground- today it's about oil, tomorrow it will be water, in times past it was spices or textiles. It's the economy, stupid. That's why someone will always want to control it.

"Yesterday, when we got stuck in traffic near the Damascus gate," Joe recalled, "a young Arab kid glared at me with such hatred…I thought: if looks could kill he would have sliced out my heart on the spot."

"Well, you do look a bit Jewish with your broken nose and curly hair."

"But *I'm* not oppressing him! I'm an atheist, forgodsake!"

"For him that's probably worse!"

"I don't like seeing civilians wearing guns in the street," he disgruntled. "Or getting stuck behind a column of tanks every time we go for drive in the country. I just want to look up and see stars at night instead of military satellites. I want to wake up in the morning and hear birds singing, not some call to prayer, or an attack helicopter rattling the windows."

"I don't like it either," she insisted.

"Then Israelis and Palestinians have got to come to an amicable divorce. You've got to end the poverty on the other side, sort out the dispossession and restore some honour. It's called reconciliation. A lot of UStraylians still don't get it either."

"Of course we have to end the occupation," she retorted. Both Israelis and Palestinians have a right to feel safe. There's two sides to everything, Joe. That *is* the point."

Jaffa Road, The Next Day...

Joe and Barbara are on a bus (the #9 from Mt. Scopus), stuck in traffic gridlock caused by a 'suspicious object' somewhere. Joe can see small robots, like extras from *Dr. Who*, hovering around a rubbish bin half a block away. A wide area has been cordoned off. All of central West Jerusalem remains at a standstill while the bomb disposal squad goes about its curious work. In his worst moments Joe imagined this was how life might become for most cities in the future- as the War on Horrorism failed, and the planet's urban concentrations hurtled towards social dysfunction- becoming impossible to live in, with frequent power blackouts and all movement brought to a standstill…while we waited for robots to clear the way ahead…

"Look, if it's not safe to take my group into Jericho or Nablus, I won't go. If the army has just been through hassling people, or there's a strike on and somebody tells me it's not safe- fine. I don't deliberately take risks," she insisted, quite sensibly.

"But just living here is a risk."

"Israel is one of the safest countries in the world."

He shakes his head at her familiar mantra. "This bus we're sitting in has already been bombed. Twice!"

"You could be taken by a rip in Heaven any day of the week, yet you still swim there all the time."

She had a valid point. (Even years before the saga with Julie). In fact, Purgatory Beach was so dangerous it was surprising how many bakpakahs actually survived its treacherous waters- despite the example of the Three Sisters staring them in the face.

"In any case the rest of the world doesn't need Israel," he deflected somewhat ignorantly.

"Oh yes it does. You'll see."

It was both a threat and a warning.

JUMP CUT TO:

The Cemetery House, Jerusalem 4 years later …

Joe is packing for a dawn flight home to UStraylia. His second trip to Israel, and it's still dark outside. Although a loud call to prayer is booming up the wadi from a minaret in Sheik Jarrah.

Something is wrong. There's an awkwardness between them. This particular visit has not gone well.

"Barbara, I can't live in a place where people don't smile back at you in the street."

"There's not a lot to smile about."

"Where there's no peace there's no sovereignty," he quoted (from Gra'eme's *The War On Horrorism*). "Like the Crusaders, Israel's occupation will fail," Joe predicted- again fairly inexpertly. And somewhat ungenerously, given all that she had done for him to make his visit as eventful and interesting as possible.

"It's not about occupation. It's about survival. As long as there's anti-semitism in the world, Israel *has* to exist."

"But nobody owns the land, the land owns us."

It was the most important thing Joe had learnt since moving to Heaven. And he was grateful to the Nullumbah Nation for their insight. Impressed by how appropriate aboriginal understanding was- to any land grab, in any country, at any time.

JUMP BACK TO:

Be'er Ada, Negev Desert, 4 years earlier…

Joe's first trip to Israel and it's Yom Kippur in the desert. A full moon for the holiest day of the Jewish year… And nothing moves. Not even the Israeli tanks parked nearby, their crews gone home for the special day of prayer and atonement.

Barbara, Joe, and her Welsh choir (from Felinheli) are camped near the historic well of Be'er Ada in the Negev desert. It's sleeping bags only. No need for a tent.

The lovers are lying on top of theirs, gazing up at the stars, enjoying the fabulous clarity of a night sky in the desert- except for the smudge of hundreds of satellites zipping all over the place and capable of deciphering the logo on a t-shirt. Joe wanted one that said: 'No More Satellites!'.

"That's the thing about cities," he observed. "There's too much light pollution. You lose sight of the sky at night. That sense of wonder at finding ourselves apparently alone in this amazing, enormous universe…"

"Perhaps that's why things get done in the city- because it's easier to turn your nose to the grindstone- when there's never any sense of the big picture," Barbara theorizes.

And Joe had to agree.

Eventually, she props herself up on one elbow and turns to him. "Come with me. I want to show you something…"

Curious, Joe gets up and follows her away from the camp. The moonlight bouncing off the silicon in the sand is now so bright you could read a book. But it's an eerie kind of, lunar powered, pseudo-illumination. Reflected. Not quite real.

Barbara leads him to the summit of a nearby hill. Here she surveys the surrounding landscape, eyes widening. Joe frowns, wondering what this is all about. He feels like a ghost in an enchanted landscape.

"What ?" he asks.

"Listen…"

There's dead silence.

"Listen to what?"

"Shh. Just listen."

Again the silence. Joe listens.

After another moment she declares: "Isn't that amazing? No birds or leaves rustling, no water…Nothing at all to disturb the absolute silence."

Joe is overcome by a vague, dislocating feeling- almost like vertigo. "My ears are ringing."

"That's the tinnitus that's always there. Only now you really hear it."

Joe reacts. It's absolutely the quietest place he's ever been. "Like on the moon."

"Yes."

"It's amazing."

"Yes." She's delighted for him to be sharing it.

"You're amazing."

"Please, Joe, don't…" she hated anyone drawing this sort of attention to herself.

He just laughs and glances back over the shimmering, mystical landscape, struck by another idea: "No wonder they heard voices out here. All those mad old prophets. The desert sort of overwhelms you."

"Because you feel so small. And humbled by it."

"Totally."

"And it's clean," she added, being partly German.

"And there's wonder. You just stand in awe of it. That ancient impulse to bow down before something that's so big and bright and empty."

"Yes."

There's a pause as they continue to stare at the surrounding hills and valley, drinking it all in. Then she adds, pointing: "That mountain to the right…"

Joe looks. The immense, dry plain of an ancient valley shimmers below them, irradiating moonlight.

"At the Y junction of the two wadis…"

"Yes, I see it," he was excited now, sharing it with her.

"That's also another candidate for Mt. Sinai."

"If it existed."

He stared hard at the sharp angles of a barren mountain to the west, standing like a vast natural pyramid. The point where two ancient riverbeds came together. Dry now. Perhaps for decades at a time. Easy to imagine as the place were commandments might be handed down. Just seeing it in this surreal, dream-like luminescence stimulated higher, bolder thoughts. Something 'other' than the puny self. You could feel eternity in the shape of it. As permanent as rock.

Or was it just Joe's own godspot kicking in? he wondered, afterwards. When the excitement settled.

"It's not surprising is it, that religion starts in places like this?" he mused. "It feels…kinda creepy and exhilarating at the same time. Like you're on display, standing in the centre of this huge arena. On stage in the middle of nowhere…and everywhere. Yet spotlighted by the moon. As if given a certain tiny prominence in the vast, cosmic panorama of it all."

And so for quite a while, perhaps even half an hour, they hung in the silence while eternity blazed around them. There was something about a sense of place that always excited Joe. Something primordial in the attachment of humans to a given area. A tribal thing. Eventually, he turns to Barbara. She becomes aware of him staring.

"What ?" But she's smiling. Curious.

"You *are* amazing." He's smiling too.

"You're only looking at the world through rose coloured glasses, Joe. Oxytocin, remember? This attraction you feel- it's just a biochemical reaction."

"How am I ever going to contain you?"

"You can't."

"Or understand you? Let alone keep up with you…"

"It's not possible."

Why couldn't he just say: 'Bugger it, let's get married' and have done with it? Why was it always so hard to commit to the best thing that had happened to him in a long, long time.

CUT TO:

The Cemetery House, Jerusalem, a few nights later …

Amnon and Dinah have taken a group of Mormons to Nazareth, leaving Joe and Barbara with the place to themselves.

It's midnight and there's a trail of sheets from their small bedroom to the kitchen. Moonlight filters through large, circular windows. Their security bars throw a prison-cell silhouette on the stone floor. The lovers are lying naked on it to keep cool, feet resting up against the kitchen table, as if they had just tumbled off it. (Which they had.) Suddenly Joe remembers something funny.

"What?"

He turns to her. "Look at us…we said we were going to have a quiet night."

They laugh.

"You were flying then, did you feel it?" she asks.

"Yes."

"You were riding my magic carpet."

"Another flight on that airline and I *am* going to have a heart attack."

When she actually looks a bit worried he adds: "I couldn't think of a better way to go." He's grinning broadly. Pretty sure of himself and genuinely happy for the first time since he can remember.

But Barbara remains thoughtful, doubtful. "I'm afraid, Joe."

"Afraid of what ?"

"Of the intensity of what's happening.

"What is happening ?"

"You tell me."

"I asked first," he insists, still grinning. Turning the prize winning fangs to their full advantage. Drawing on all his positives. When she looks away again (as she sometimes does), he realises he really is being called upon to respond.

"There has to be something more, Barbara. Something deeper than a bio-chemical reaction. It can't just be the thrill of passing on our DNA (an upfront bit of pleasure for all the heartache of parenthood to follow). It's got to be a feeling that, I dunno…no matter what happens, we'll always be connected. You know?"

"It doesn't seem natural…" she concludes.

"How much more natural can it get?"

They embrace again and floor drops away…

CUT TO:

Another night, Same place, same trip, 8 years ago…

There's a trail of sheets from their small bedroom to the kitchen floor. Joe and Barbara are lying side by side, their naked backs on the cool stones, feet resting up against a table, as if they'd just tumbled off it. (Which they had.) Joe is sweating, exhausted. He suddenly thinks of something funny:

"Look at us…we said we were going to have a quiet night."

"We can't keep making love on the kitchen table."

"Why not ?"

205

"Too hard on my knees."

"It's not always going to be girls on top!"

They laugh. It will be the beginning of an old joke between them.

Then a slight pause. Sharing the moment. A couple alone in a house together. This time Dinah and Amnon are away with a busload of Anglicans in the Galilee.

"You picked me up, dusted me off, and put me back together. Only angels do that sort of thing," he declared, half meaning it.

"I'm not an angel. I'm a devil in disguise…" she sang. Acting the whore again. One of her many roles in the little games they played.

He just stares back at her, grateful and amazed at how his life has turned around, a slow smile evolving, curling the corners of his mouth…heavenwards.

CUT TO:

The Cemetery House, Mount Scopus, 4 years later…

It's early morning and Joe is packing for a dawn flight home to UStraylia. It's his second trip to Israel- the one that didn't go so well.

There is intermittent gunfire below them in Sheik Jarrah. Occasionally, a helicopter gunship swoops low overhead, shaking the walls. Seen from below, the chopper resembles the pale green underbelly of a huge turtle, bristling with barrels and rocket launchers. A mega-megaphone is heard off in the distance, shouting threats and warnings in Arabic and Hebrew. Sirens wail. Smoke rises in severe columns from clash points dotted around the village. Not like ghosts at all. More like funeral pyres.

Once again Jeru-shalom, city of peace and angels, is on the brink. Soon seventy six people who woke up that morning will not see the sunset. For them this day will never end. Sanity, trust, honour, truth, respect and hope- all casualties with them.

Barbara watches Joe pack, then says: "I'm bad."

"Who says you're bad?"

"I know I am."

"What do you do that's bad?" he asks, seriously doubting it.

"You'll see."

"All I've seen is your St. Barbara act- always putting yourself out for somebody else."

"Not always."

"The only thing you can't help is…you can't help not helping people. Especially when there's a single mother in trouble. You're too giving, Barbara."

She attempts to deny it. Failing badly.

"It's true. Accept the facts. You're a *good* person, Barbara. There aren't many of you left. Especially around here."

"That's bullshit."

"You're only saying that because you can't stand flattery," he surmises.

"There are lot's of good people in Israel- and Palestine. We've just got to find better ways of bringing them together," she concludes

Joe finishes packing and closes his suitcase. Another ritual parting in a relationship full of them. He comes towards her but she holds him at arms length for what seems like an unnecessarily long time. Then asks:

"Who *are* you?"

Joe doesn't even have to think about it. "How the hell would I know ?"

CRASH CUT FORWARD TO:

HEAVEN
ustraylia
LAKE LETHE
RAPTURE ROCKS
PACIFIC OCEAN
BEACH
STRAND
PURGATORY
SALVATION
SAINT
ANGEL AVENUE
DEVIL'S LANE
EVERLASTING LANE
HEAVEN
TO SYDNEY
N
FLOOD PLAIN
PRIVATE GOLF COURSE

Last opportunity to buy off the plan! Colourful, proposed Dreamtime Beach Estate—just another one of **HEAVEN**'s latest modern subdivisions. Put your deposit on 99 square metres of paradise today! (Golf memberships included, floating houses a specialty, radiation counts available on request—no responsibility accepted for mosquito-borne viruses.)

Affix
stamp
here

#25 of 33 Postcards from Heaven

printed on gently mulched, plantation-grown, organic bamboo fibre using recycled greywater and bound with a biodegradable non-toxic glue

No animal or dolphin suffered in the making of this card
(apart from, of course, its author)

NODDY PLANNING TOYLAND
"Just because you're paranoid
doesn't mean the bastards aren't out to get you."
(Gra'eme *The Rat In History*)

3.26pm, All Hallows Hospital, Friday 13th March

Four years later, Joe and Barbara are standing on either side of Julie's bed. At a loss. Realising how little they know.

Soon the resident psychiatrist will come from Nullumbah to sign Julie's release and then Barbara will be able to take her home to Newtown on tonight's *Nullumbah-Sydney Aurora*. Having saved both Julie's life and her child's, there was little more a hospital like Heaven's could do for her. And Sister Carmody always needed the bed.

She comes to give Julie a wash, pulling the curtain around, forcing Joe and Barbara back to their bench in the corridor. Joe realises to his dismay, that he's already spent more time on this article of furniture than a average day's quota in the hammock.

Jerusalem, the Cemetery House, and nights in the Negev with their enchanted moonlight and absolute silence seem to have occurred in another lifetime on some other planet. Or was it just that Joe and Barbara were getting too used to each other? Seeing more of the faults than the upside now. He'd been mocked, vomited on, had foregone a well paid, if meaningless job, nearly been taken by a rip, seen his mailbox decapitated and had now lost Barbara's respect- thanks to her grotesque misreading of that ridiculously innocent physical and emotional stretching session with Helen Strongfeather. A farcical case of catastrophic bad timing brought about by his accountant's impromptu generosity and their house guest's attempted suicide. Nothing was turning out well.

On any normal Beautiful Day Joe would, by now, have showered off after the second body surf and be thoroughly enjoying a mid-afternoon dose of gossip and rumour mongering at Shangri La La Land- Heaven's coolest bar. A ritual, 3 pm-ish gathering of local wannabes, potters, glass blowers, pulp novelists and other scribblers-for-a-living known as the 'Poet's Breakfast'. An opportunity, on a daily basis, for Joe to connect up with some troubled fellow souls round a blueberry friand and a glass or three of chilled Verdelho, prior to his cycle home along Blessed Boulevard and a quiet smoke at Point Paradise. Instead, he now had to get to an emergency meeting of the Nullumbah Shire Protection Society. And Barbara still wasn't letting him have Rusty.

"Aren't you coming?" he urged, despondent.

"No."

"Barbara, you're far and away our best organiser."

"And my best friend just attempted to take her own life!"

Of course she had a point, and Joe could see that Barbara's fabulous energy would now be lost to The Cause. He understood why. But still felt helpless.

"We're talking about the peace and quiet of our backyard for possibly the next twelve years," was all he could manage, trying to include her in its ownership. But it wasn't even an issue for Barbara.

"We finally got a cancellation at Raiina Virago's. I'm taking Julie over there as soon as she's discharged."

"Right…"- Joe still toying with the idea of seeing the young white witch himself, glancing over at All Hallows broken public phone, frustrated that he couldn't ring her immediately and inquire about any cancellations tomorrow.

"After that, I'll have to drive her back to the house to collect our bags."

No longer 'home,' or 'go back to our place'- just the indifferent 'house'. A machine for living in.

"So that's it then?"

Barbara shrugged, too angry and disappointed with him generally to offer anything more. Categorically the worst 'good-bye' they'd ever had. In a relationship full of them. It may well be the last. It already felt like it…

JUMP CUT TO:

3.35pm, Old Bogwater Road, Friday 13th March

Minutes later, walking back from All Hallows to the centre of town, Joe caught sight of himself in a convex traffic mirror set beside the railway crossing- looking even more pathetic and mis-shapen than he could have imagined. How insignificant everything that used to stir his interest now seemed- almost without trying. Could the struggle to protect a small patch of untouched littoral rainforest with its half dozen endangered species be worth it? He asked himself rhetorically and failed to get an adequate answer.

CRASH CUT TO:

3.44pm, Hallelujah Hall, Friday 13th March

Joe had taken his sandshoes off at the door and was staring up at the ceiling fans in Hallelujah Hall, with faint hope of their achieving anything in the cooling/refreshment department…staring and wondering whether it mightn't be easier just to chuck the towel in, admit defeat, and let Mondeigo's bulldozers do their worst. Nothing was more important than his relationship with Barbara. Why had he even bothered to call this emergency meeting of the Nullumbah Shire Protection Society? Once a property developer set his/her mind and considerable fortune on achieving some dreadful outcome it was virtually impossible to stop him/her. All Joe could see, in addition to the havoc that had already been wrecked, was further damage to his own health and sanity. With the same end result: medium density, pink and lilac cluster townhouses in the cement/brutalist style glaring down at him like nazi bunkers. No more showering off *au naturel* after a swim. No more naked gardening by torchlight…or daylight for that matter. He'd even have to build a greenhouse to hide his dope plants.

The eleven people sitting in today's circle were the sum total of the troops ready for battle. A near record for any Protection Society meeting. Let alone one called at such short notice. It underscored the depth of feeling. This was an encouraging start Joe figured, even though, as residents, they were all facing the same prospect of a blitzkrieg of large earthmoving machines, cement mixers, quarry trucks and tradesmen's utes, blaring out racist talkback on Redneck FM- for however long it would take to build those 94 appalling townhouses.

It was time to stop the insanity dead in its tracks. That's what this call to arms had to be all about. And it would have been great to feel energetic and raring to go, but it was so hot! The afternoon having evolved into a classic Heavenly scorcher, turning normally well drafted rooms into de facto saunas. A cooling body surf right now would have been delightful. And Joe could hear the waves calling, siren-like, a mere 25 metres from where Hallelujah Hall stood, at the south end of Salvation Strand.

But the waves would have to wait. Like we all waited. While Joe did 'his duty', stuck under ceiling fans that did little more than swirl warm air around overheated human bodies, causing waterfalls of perspiration to trickle down the moist wadi of a man's back- drenching the top of his tattered shorts. Joe swiped at a mossie and missed! Third one he'd missed today. It set him worrying that either mosquitos were getting faster or he was getting slower. As you do when you're about to notch up your first half century…

Everyone could feel the thunderstorm building up throughout the afternoon. The north westerly- so useful for wave and beach formation had, on the downside, been concentrating all those irritating, misleadingly named, positive ions in the atmosphere. Sending even normal people a bit sub-troppo. A thunderstorm held out the promise of rain and a drop in temperature, swinging the wind round to the south. A payoff for putting up with so many days of howling winds and such unbearable heat. But for weeks now, no storm had actually broken.

It was as if the climate itself was failing to reach its own climax- as Joe had failed so to do with Barbara since waking this morning- realising now (especially after the shameful imbroglio with Helen), that his ritual birthday treat was categorically off the menu of their last day together. He would be lucky even to glimpse Barbara again before she left. Unless he put in an unscheduled appearance at the station, dragging himself away from his BBQ- or she came to the party, as he was still hoping she might do…

The NSPS secretary, Cassandra Virtue, handed out the attendance book for people to sign and started reading the minutes from their last meeting- listing all the things that were supposed to have been done since; but which nobody had actually followed up on, sending a tidal wave of guilt crashing through the meeting and getting everyone off to a really demoralising start.

To compound the situation, their president, Alistair Piggot, had become hopelessly trapped in a side conversation with Mrs. Geogharty as the animated octogenarian regaled him with the colourful story of how she'd nearly been run over by a car yesterday in Mother Theresa Terrace and had to hold on to a tree for support after it zoomed past- almost causing a near death experience on two fronts: from the shock *and* the potential collision between her frail body and the high-set, four wheel drive full of screaming primary schoolers.

While most of those present might have wished the car had found its mark and relieved them of Mrs. Gaa Gaa's tedious time wasting, Alistair unfortunately, was nodding and smiling indulgently- as he usually did, trying to deflect her stream of consciousness back to the agenda at hand with comments like: "Yes, the footpaths are in a terrible condition, Mrs. G.," and "We have been lobbying council about it now for years, but the developers have virtually bankrupted the Shire with all their appeals to the Property With Little Amenity Tribunal. So there's no money left to spend on the vital infrastructure that all this extra development requires…"

Lynton O'Flannery made a brave attempt to cut in on Mrs. Gaa Gaa with: "You'll remember last year we submitted a plan for a footpath upgrade in South Heaven to Council's Works Committee, Mrs. Geogharty…"

Lynton was the Protection Society's 'honorary' solicitor, but the ink stain at the bottom right hand corner of all his shirt pockets didn't exactly inspire confidence in any of his abilities- given that he couldn't seem to manage to put the top back on a biro. Joe was convinced that if they paid a competent lawyer, the NSPS might actually *win* a case occasionally and get costs awarded *to* the community for a change (and thus be in a position to fund a proper professional in the first place).

Unfortunately, this didn't wash with Alistair who reminded Joe of how generous Lynton was with his time. The fact that he had a lot of time to be generous with because nobody in the real world would ever use him as their solicitor (honorary or otherwise), always seemed to elude the argument. It had also quite naturally occurred to Joe (as it had to Old Frank and Cassandra Virtue) that Lynton was some kind of developers' time bomb ticking away inside the only organization the citizens of Heaven had with which to fight back against the tidal wave of overdevelopment about to engulf the town. But Lynton was too unskilled even to manage that kind of gross betrayal.

In fact, the eyes and ears of the developers at this meeting were carried by the 'Stranger'. Their identity kept changing, but there was always this, often tall, usually bearded person (sometimes with a neat pony tail), and dressed like they'd come expecting Northern California with a warmer climate and less pollution. The 'Stranger' would mingle with the locals before any meeting, spinning the usual yarn about how he had just bought into the area and how concerned he was to know what was going on, wanting to get involved, and expressing mild distaste at the way things were turning out.

Almost everyone in the NSPS recognised this character for who he was, and tried to feed him as much disinformation as they possibly could, without sounding implausible- always a risk with people who lived in Heaven.

But the mere fact of the 'Stranger' sitting there looking so smug and in control was enough to propel Joe into action. So that finally! he broke across Mrs. Geogharty's incessant, self-centred whinging with: "Forgodsake! Forget the bloody footpaths, Mrs. Geogharty!"

There was silence. Joe had the focus. And time was running out.

"We're only here to talk about *one* thing: i.e., what the hell we're going to do about Carlos Mondeigo, Lech Da Groot, and the massive development they want to plonk down in the middle of our pristine coastal rainforest! This is an emergency meeting, okay? Called specifically to deal with one thing. Our survival as a viable community."

"Joe's right," declared Cassandra, asserting her considerable authority. "The time for lodging objections to Mondeigo's latest Destruction Application lapses in two days would you believe. He's really snuck this one under the back door, hoping we'd all be asleep, or on holidays obviously."

"As usual," added Ronnie Rainbows.

Joe felt enormous gratitude for Cassandra's energy and determination. If only Barbara was there to back her up Mondeigo and Da Groot wouldn't stand a chance. No matter who or how actually 'big' their Mr. Big really was.

"Well, we all knew it was coming and sure enough it's a whole lot worse than we imagined," Cassandra started depressingly as she blu-taked the scale drawings of *Dreamtime Beach Estate* onto a white board facing the circle. There was an audible gasp like the sound of disbelief and consternation that ripples through any plane from Queensland when the pilot reads out the weather report prior to landing in Melbourne.

"I've never seen a proposed sub-division so crass in its use of every available square metre of land," Cassandra declared. "They even want to pipe Limbo Creek underground and turn parts of it into a canal."

But before anyone could react to this new catastrophe she barrelled on. "What's more, the 'architects',"- wriggling two index fingers to put dubious quotation marks around their qualifications- "have tried to vary the plans with a verandah here and a garage there, instead of a living room here and a patio there; but essentially it's the same basic template for every single house. All 119 of them."

This had been what Joe noticed about the architecture too when Christabel Eaton first showed them her copy of Mondeigo's DA. How mass produced it looked. It was such a relief to realise Cassandra had put her very capable finger on one of the key problems.

"Take away the odd cosmetic touch and what you've got is basically the same housing design in a densely packed complex that will virtually *double* the population of south Heaven in one foul swoop."

"Hang on a sec..." Joe did a quick recalculation of the numbers. "I thought it was only 94 townhouses?" He felt a kind of chill run down his body like a dull thud.

"It was," Cassandra replied grimly. "But a late amendment to the DA went in to Council at lunchtime. Mondeigo and Da Groot have obviously stitched up a deal with Bruce Phelan and Wal Piper to add another twenty five townhouses right up against your back fence, Joe- where the bike path was supposed to go. That makes 119 separate dwellings altogether."

Joe felt his world kind of unhinge itself a little, creak open, and slam shut again. It meant this additional 'cluster' would directly overlook his whole backyard!

"Why the dickens should these men profit from the destruction of one of the last remaining areas of untouched rainforest on the entire coast?" Normal Bob demanded to sustained applause.

An intensely reasonable and cheery man, Bob was married to an ordinary wife, dressed sensibly, went fishing, had 2.7 children, watched 14 hours of television a week, loved selling raffle tickets for any worthy cause, and looked forward to washing his car on Saturday afternoons while listening to the footy in winter or the cricket in summer. Bob, in short, was so severely unremarkable and average that he was quite possibly one of the strangest people ever to have set foot in Heaven.

Nobody could quite understand what the hell he was doing there, or why he wouldn't' prefer living in some place like Caboolture or Brisbane. But Bob would never swap his tree-less brick veneer, with its colourful cement pathways and little windmill out the front, for any place anywhere. And kept his back lawn mowed to bowling green perfection just to prove it.

"Not only that," shouted Cassandra over this encouraging response, "but- wait for it- each one of these 119 'townhouses' has *two* bathrooms and *two* kitchens- which means that at some future date they can all be strata titled and internally sub-divided into *two* units each."

"That's clever," chuckled Old Frank, who seemed to be treating the whole thing with insufficient seriousness. Had Joe's neighbour, in some way, given up? Again? Because of Filthy Mick and the Utta Bastards cruel occupation of his house? Old Frank lost so heavily to two SP bookies from Heaven's own, home grown Motor Psychle Club that he now had to let four of them live in his house rent free. (It was either that or lose several toes.) The noise from the Endless Bikie Party next door and the half hour warming up of Harley Davidsons each morning prior to the hunt for bakpakah chicks was already beginning to loom large as Joe's next Major Problem. He knew it would soon be time either for a serious talk to Old Frank, or that final admission of defeat- a drive with the front door keys back to Bryce Keitel's unReal Estate office- offering him an exclusive contract to sell. Should Joe do it anyway (and take Kate's poinsettia with him)? If Mondeigo's horror 'got up'? It was a depressing option that could no longer be ruled out.

"All of which means, we're now looking at a potential total of 238 separate dwellings further down the track," contributed Lynton O'Flannery trying to make it sound like he was adding something, but proving merely that he could multiply large numbers by small ones.

"Geezuskerrist !" exploded Joe. "This is totally outrageous!"

"Yeah, fully…" added the 'Waif'- Cassandra's girlfriend who sat at her lover's feet in more ways than one. The young feral activist's matted dreadlocks dangled above a small pair of pink angel wings (again the angel/fairy motif today). These were glued somehow to the back of her one-piece bathing suit. Below the swimmers the Waif wore ripped, fish-net stockings which ended in a pair of Doc Martens- a quite fetching, if somewhat inarticulate fashion statement. Nevertheless, this young woman warrior was extremely adept at doing 'her bit' for the environment. Unafraid for example, of chaining her neck or ring pierced lips to a railway line in order to hold up some ghastly trainload of toxic waste.

"This isn't development, this is Noddy Planning Toyland," quipped Gra'eme as he arrived (late) from his Prophecy workshop. Despite the catastrophe staring them all in the face Joe appreciated his oracle's familiar gallows' humour. Others were smiling too. Old Frank laughing openly, so openly it was becoming frankly disturbing.

Having formed the perfect dozen for the meeting, everybody now expected Gra'eme to say something insightful and he didn't disappoint as he added above the general amusement: "Mondeigo's development is really about the whole future of our community and whether we've got any say in it at all. A clean, green environment with a lot of trees and a few endangered species is everyone's inalienable *right*- not a privilege. It should be obvious. It's why we all came to the Rainbow Coast in the first place. And if we lose this battle we can basically kiss our gorgeous little town good-bye. *Dreamland Beach Estate* will simply open the flood gates."

Which certainly gave everyone pause for thought.

Except Lynton, who further dashed morale with: "Well, it's going to be virtually impossible to stop them. Mondeigo and Da Groot have planned this thing for years. They've amassed an enormous war chest to fund the best legal brains money can buy."

"Not necessarily an advantage, right?" quipped Gra'eme again, clawing the mood back from the black hole into which Lynton had plunged it. But few got the joke- only those with any personal experience of the destructive power of barristers and solicitors generally.

"…plus they've got virtually every planning requirement covered as far as I can see," added Lynton- which wasn't very far as far as anyone could tell.

Nor was anybody in the NSPS going to offer Lynton O'Flannery fees on a par with some posh-modern Sydney silk, competent or not. Nevertheless, he ploughed ineptly on.

"If you factor in the actual material cost of each unit at about 83 thousand to lockup stage- including labour; and multiply that by 119 twice over and take it away from a conservative selling price of three to three fifty grand apiece, less the cost of the land- which was negligible…Mondeigo and Da Groot are looking at a rough profit of between forty and fifty mill," concluded Lynton crunching the numbers on his pocket calculator (and still getting it wrong). "What we obviously need is a *killer legal punch*…"

"What we need is a new lawyer," muttered Old Frank with a low chuckle.

Which Lynton chose not to hear as he added: "In my experience these things usually fall over on the engineering detail."

"What about endangered species in that forest?" challenged Normal Bob.

General murmurings of "yes" and "spot on, Bob" and much nodding in support of Bob's point- including from the Waif who, of course, had put most of them there in the first place- just before Council's environmental impact study was carried out.

"Not to mention the probability of acid sulphate contamination, stormwater runoff, increased traffic…" but Normal Bob was only reeling off points that were depressingly familiar.

"You need something more than that," Lynton cut in, shaking his head like a magistrate who didn't believe you'd gone on the detox programme. "These are all valid items *for consideration,* but they're not fatal to the enterprise." Lynton checked his notes. "Council's fauna survey identified at least half a dozen endangered species in that forest including…" he paused to turn to another page in his ink stained note book, "Mitchell's Snail, the Spotted Quoll, the Nullumbah Red-Wing Butterfly, a couple of small reptiles and the Common Stuttering Frog- now becoming distinctly uncommon. But you see, Mondeigo's already proposing to 'ameliorate the impact' on these endangered species by banning all cats and dogs over 10 kilograms. The developers have got an escape clause on every objection you can think of."

"'Ameliorate the impact'!" thundered Cassandra. "Forgodsake, the world is losing seventy three species every week! Half of them in Queensland. *All* domestic pets should be humanely gassed and put into mass graves as soon as possible."

Which really set the cat among the pigeons as far as the dog lovers present were concerned.

"Ban all developers over 10 kilograms!" roared Old Frank, effectively laughing off a fatal split as everyone enjoyed the joke. At least morale was rising, even if the odds were stacked against them.

"The point is- he can get around the endangered species thing- it's not enough to stop him," persisted Lynton, depressingly.

"But dogs and cats *under* 10 kilograms are much more likely to threaten the frogs and the spotted quoll than bigger animals," pointed out Alistair correctly. "They're designed to burrow into small nests in the forest understory.

"What the hell *is* a quoll ?" asked Normal Bob genuinely puzzled (and pro-dog himself).

"It's a kind of a carnivorous marsupial," informed Ronnie Rainbows.

"*All* dogs and cats should be banned everywhere," repeated Cassandra. "And that goes for dogs on the beach too," returning to her original point.

It was starting to happen. Here was the archilles heel of any NSPS meeting. The subject of 'cats and dogs' and what to do about them was a ballistic missile designed to fissure the group into hopelessly opposed factions within seconds.

"I do worry about toddlers picking up some dog poo by mistake and eating it," chimed in Benny the Process Server thinking of his own three year old. "Who knows what pathogens they'd be exposed to."

"Responsible dog owners collect their poo," insisted Mrs. Geogharty, herself the proud mistress of three pretty ugly chihuahuas.

Joe just held his head in this hands, almost giving up. He had come to Heaven, among other things, for a rest. (In fact, some days he spent so much time on his back he worried that he might have contracted some mild form of narcolepsy). But here he was, fighting this crazy battle just to preserve a little nature, a little peace and quiet. And now, in the depths of his guilt and despair about Barbara leaving, Joe wondered why the hell he even bothered. What, after all, did he think he was going to achieve here? Between Mrs. Gaa Gaa's verbal diarrhoea, Lynton's morale destroying incompetence, the 'Stranger' reporting their every move back to the camps of the enemy, and the NSPS itself now splintering into hopelessly opposed factions on the dog issue, the campaign to save Heaven was looking like a lost cause even before it started. Cassandra sensed this too, and realising her strategic error in letting the dog out of the bag so to speak, tried to gather up the flag and put down the demon of 'pets' vs 'pests' once and for all.

As she harangued and corralled people back to the only item on the agenda, her gestures carried a hint of Kate, Joe thought. The way she had of propping her elbows on the table, joining her hands and resting her chin on them as if onto a kind of platform- from which she would occasionally flick one hand forward, rotating it out, chopping the air in front of her to make a point, just as Kate would have done at some group meeting or rehearsal. Authoritative, across the material, in control, karate power.

But Lynton's requirement of the killer legal punch still eluded them.

Always ready with his notebook, Joe stood up and took centre circle, clawing the focus back to the key issues, working on pure adrenalin (he'd been responsible for calling the meeting afterall).

"I suggest we draft a letter to Council outlining our official objections. "In fact, I've already sketched out a motion to be put to the meeting."- writing, his strong point. The one real skill Joe could offer The Cause.

"Yes, but even if we *can* convince Council to knock it back," chipped in Lynton, "Mondeigo will just go straight to the Property With Little Amenity Tribunal and get the decision overturned."

"What about aboriginal sites? There must be dozens of middens in there," prompted the Waif, cantering on over Lynton's pessimism, and already scheming to plunder the wheely bins of Heaven's two seafood restaurants for oyster shells and crab claws prior to burying them in some appropriate hole on Mondeigo's land- to cheat the truth. To reinforce the point that the Nullumbah nation had occupied the land millennia before anyone else. And had never been paid a cent for it by its current occupiers. And in any case owning the land was irrelevant. Because it owned us.

"That's already on my list," indicated Joe, impatient to read it out.

"Aboriginal relics won't stop him either. Mondeigo and Da Groot will just pay someone to do an archaeological survey and make sure they get the intended result," objected Lynton.

"Then what *will* stop him!?" demanded Gra'eme, "You're our solicitor."

Unfortunately Lynton, true to form, really had no idea.

"Look- what I've got so far," interrupted Joe, ticking them off on his note book, "is: endangered species, traffic overload, the need for an impartial archaeological survey…"

"Is there enough sewerage to cope?" asked Benny the Process Server, still taking the health angle.

"Probably not," realised Alistair. "The local Treatment Works has been pushing shit up hill- literally- for years."

"Add that to the list," ordered Cassandra as Joe scribbled hard, her willing clerk.

"The residents of south Heaven demand a full and open EPA audit on the town's STW." She demanded, displaying acronyms. Council simply can't approve any more development in Heaven until the town's sewerage system catches up."

"But developers could just put in their own private systems, have them break down in a few years time and leave the unfortunate new residents to discover that there's no one left to take responsibility for fixing them. Then we all watch helplessly as these failing private sewerage systems slowly pollute everything in Limbo Creek upstream of our vital fish breeding grounds," pointed out Gra'eme truthfully, but unhelpfully.

"In any case you're still wide of the mark. There's no killer punch in any of this." Lynton was beginning to sound like a broken record- something from the fifties with straw hats, sequins, a lot of pink on the cover, and the word 'Party' somewhere in the title.

"What about Acid Sulphate?" prompted Cassandra.

"What about it?" demanded Lynton, folding his arms, enjoying his devil's advocate role, feeling confidant about being across all the legal jargon and bursting with negatives.

"Well, he's going to be putting great bloody roads through untouched wetlands for a start!" declared the Waif, as if it was obvious.

"Digging out swimming pools, laying foundations, putting down slabs," illustrated Cassandra.

"We all know there's high humic content in that soil," agreed Ronnie Rainbows, who among other things, had a degree in Botany.

"Mondeigo got Council's soil officer to say there's zilch possibility of any acid contamination," countered Lynton flicking through to the relevant page in the DA which nobody except him and Christabel Eaton had actually read.

"Why should we trust the Council or any of their officers?" Ronnie challenged. "The bastards privatised our Golf Course, sold off the Caravan Park, then they just gave away the land set aside for the school, and even threatened to close our Library down. I mean, where are the parks in Heaven? Where is our public open space? Why aren't there any proper footpaths? What has this bloody Council actually given back to the community from all the development revenues they were supposed to have collected in the first place?"

There was a general rumble of agreement, with people hoping that the mention of footpaths wouldn't set Mrs. Geogharty off again. Mercifully, (and incredibly, given the energy of the debate) she'd fallen asleep. *Her* afternoon nap wasn't going to be put off for anything.

"There's also the question of soil structure," Ronnie added, getting very nuts and boltsy. "It's quite peaty down there. You'd have to wonder about the land's ability to take construction in the first place. I mean, foundations could just topple over."

"Write that down!" Cassandra commanded Joe again. He was delighted to comply, clarifying on paper just how really awful it was going to be.

"Plus more unemployment," continued Alistair, consulting his own list. "Negative Social Impact. There's hardly enough work for the people who *already* live here"- thinking of himself mainly. "Where are all the extra jobs going to come from to service these 119 or 238 single parent and welfare dependent families?"

Joe was writing furiously in his notebook. This was more like it. This is what he had been hoping for. A genuine think-tank, everyone contributing. United at last. And here he was, standing up, doing his bit. How could anyone achieve anything unless they tried? There was hope. People were wonderful. And a people united can never be defeated. 'Negative Social Impact' even had a nice, sound-bitey ring to it. Things were looking up. The potential damage from *Dreamtime Beach Estate* was colossal.

"Not to mention the extra pressure on hospital services, road maintenance, garbage collection and so on," added Benny the Process Server who was not so put off by the lucrative (for him) social chaos of all those extra down-market living rooms with their shattered lives, torn lounge suites and deeply unhappy people. Parents without hope, children without a future, girlfriends taking out Apprehended Violence Orders- all the social dysfunction that a servant of the legal system like Benny thrived on. But he also wanted a truck-free road for his kids to play on (since there were no parks).

"We know there's been some pretty dodgy tree removal on that block," put in Normal Bob. "We should push for a full restoration order. Da Groot's been quietly nibbling into that forest for years now without permission."

"I'll put that as a motion at the end," decided Cassandra.

"All Mondeigo and Da Groot want is bucks- fast." surmised Gra'eme. "It's maximum profits in the minimal amount of time, with no responsibility whatsoever for the mess they leave behind."

"Which all of us will have to live with," agreed Alistair.

Joe was scribbling madly, trying to capture the detail of Gra'eme's excellent phraseology- 'maximum profits, minimum time…'- this was very, *very* good now.

"What about flooding?" It was Mrs. Geogharty again, putting in her two bob's worth as she snapped awake from her power nap.

"We've already got 'flooding', Mrs. Geogharty, we're just trying to frame a motion here- something to send Joe off with." Cassandra was keen to wind the meeting up and get herself and the Waif over to their Ecstatic Dance Workshop.

However, Mrs. Gaa Gaa was not going to be deflected. "That whole block," (pointing to the proposed *Dreamtime Beach Estate* on the map) "was under 6 foot of water in the '74 cyclone."

The meeting turned to her as one. None of the younger, more affluent residents had been in Heaven for more than a couple of years. This startling information meant that a lot of their houses would be six feet under too- if a cyclone ever came again (as it would, as it had to). Some visibly blanched. All were quiet. Awaiting a punchline. Mrs. Geogharty had their full attention and her inner egomaniac was going to milk it for all she was worth.

"I remember waves coming straight through from the beach and crashing into the sewerage ponds at the Treatment Works. I have an excellent memory," she lied, happily caught up in the nostalgia of a simpler time, long gone- one when people made their own entertainment round a piano, and SARS was still a kiddie's soft drink.

"Well there it is!" hooted Lynton triumphantly, mercifully cutting her off and regaining centre stage. "There's your killer legal punch! If the land is *that* flood prone there's *no way* Council could *ever* let anyone build there. Even the Property With Little Amenity Tribunal would have to knock it back."

Joe suppressed rising elation. He would have kissed Mrs. Geogharty- if he'd been closer in the circle and didn't feel the headache that'd been building up all day might be the herald of another cold sore.

"Given that the 1-in-100 year flood is due sometime in the next decade, Council could be sued from here to kingdom come by anybody and everybody who buys one of these godforsaken lots," Lynton concluded, relishing the 'flood' of legal work this would bring- should the NSPS still lose. Which they probably would, if he represented them.

Cassandra already had Council's official maps out and was studying them keenly, trying to get the overlap with where Mondeigo's land lay. "It doesn't say anything here about a flood prone area," she revealed, double checking the DA, her voice also containing a certain sense of victory mixed with outrage. "Mondeigo's hydrological report actually claims everything's hunky dory- all 'perfectly within council requirements' quote, unquote- at 2.8 metres above the high tide mark."

"That's bullshit!" exclaimed the Waif overlooking her lover's shoulder and taking the opportunity to rest her chin fondly upon it. It was quite fetching really, Joe thought.

"On top of everything else, Mondeigo's folly constitutes a major public health hazard," pointed out Ronnie. "Not just flooding problems, but flooded *sewerage* problems."

The shit was hitting the fan beautifully.

"Somebody has altered these maps," concluded Cassandra, sniffing real evidence of a bureaucratic smoking gun. Corruption that could be proved at last.

"And if Mondeigo has colluded with someone inside Council to do so, then it's actually a form of criminal fraud." Lynton was sounding like a solicitor in charge of a winning case at last. "Which could actually put him and Da Groot and whoever's behind them, behind bars."

"Where all developers should be!" shouted Ronnie, encouraged like everyone else at the way things were turning out.

Joe was on his feet again, terribly excited. "Look, I move that we delegate someone to go straight to Mondeigo and simply put it to him directly that we've got them by the short and curlies on this, and their whole project hasn't got a snowball's chance in hell."

"Unless it's a Viking hell," chuckled Gra'eme irrelevantly.

Joe cast a slightly irritated glance at his accountant/mentor and proclaimed: "Either Mondeigo pulls the plug on *Dreamtime Beach Estate* or we drop all the details of their map-altering scandal right in the lap of the Criminal Prosecutor's Office."

Which forced Gra'eme to explain himself: "I don't think that's a particularly bright idea."

"Why not?" demanded Cassandra.

"Well…we'd show our hand," shrugged Gra'eme, always the master tactician. But curiously ignoring the fact that the Stranger would simply pass on this info anyway.

"Think of the money we'd save," calculated Alistair. If we could stop it now- without going to court."

Lynton tried to hide his disappointment.

"I agree with Joe," Cassandra was putting her final seal on the discussion. "Let's confront Mondeigo with the facts and point out that the flooding aspect alone shoots his development dead in the water- literally. How many times have we seen these bastards get away with murder when *finally* we've got something concrete that *will* nail them at the tribunal."

"How many mango seeds have sprouted in vain under municipal garbage tips?" retorted Gra'eme, huffing his shoulders, offering one of his irritatingly vague aphorisms. If they weren't going to take his advice, then let it be on their own heads.

And this left the gap for Alistair to jump in with: "I nominate Joe."

Joe froze. He'd agreed to draft the official objection. Writing a letter, a nice turn of phrase- that was the one thing he was good at. But he'd assumed the actual personal confrontation bit would be taken on by somebody more official and battle hardened, like- Cassandra, preferably. Especially when thrown up against anyone as ruthless, as litigious and outright dangerous as the fraudulent evil mastermind, and probably homicidal, Carlos José Mondeigo.

"Seconded," seconded Ronnie and Normal Bob simultaneously.

"All those in favour?" Cassandra was already counting the forest of raised hands. Joe was trying to concoct a plausible excuse: he had a script deadline to meet (sadly no longer true), it was his birthday and their house guest had just tried to kill herself (true but hardly relevant), Barbara was leaving, he had to find another mail box, there was a mid-life crisis to resolve…

But the hands went up like a regiment of spears in some Elizabethan tragedy- the army urging its puny emissary forward, hoping he'd save them from having to actually kill people (assuming he himself survived).

"It's unanimous. Thank you, Joe." Cassandra declared, formally writing it down in the minutes book. Committing Joe's fate to the public record as easily as he'd done himself to so many characters in too many soap operas.

Joe quickly dropped his hand. It had been raised only to make a point of order- he wasn't voting for himself! Shit! It wasn't unanimous at all! This was both unfair and inaccurate. And how could Mrs. Gaa Gaa's vote be counted? She was barely more than *compos mentis* at the best of times. And what about the 'Stranger's' vote? He was part of the problem. Joe hung there in the middle of the disintegrating meeting, as if struck by lightning…

"We're right behind you mate," chuckled Ronnie, slapping the ex-hack on the back (a little too hard Joe thought)- as the low sensation thrill seeker continued to mentally scroll through a list of possible excuses: he had a cold coming on, Barbara wouldn't lend him the car, he was hopeless at personal confrontation, he'd already done his bit…

"Any other business?" queried Alistair as he stacked his papers, ready to close the meeting and hurry off to chair a gathering of the Rainbow Coast UFO Committee- of which he was also president. There was a comet approaching and it was exhibiting strange anomalies. This could be the one they'd been waiting for- with the alien spaceship hiding behind it.

"I'll double check the flood maps held by the Library," offered Cassandra. "Maybe we can get Christabel Eaton to raise the discrepancy as a matter of urgency at Monday's Council meeting. That gives us only three days to spread the word…"

And so, without anybody officially declaring anything, the NSPS gathering was effectively over.

Joe felt like someone who had just broken wind after a particularly murky curry. His friends and neighbours rushing off in all directions, like galaxies from our solar system, leaving him feeling about as hopeful and effective as a filter on a cigarette. Yet there he was, still clutching at straws:

"Ah…are we sure it's such a great idea…that *I* go ?" he pleaded to no one in particular.

"What have we got to lose?" chuckled Old Frank. "Except you?"

"Don't worry, mate," reassured Ronnie, stacking chairs, "if no one has seen you by early next week I'll get Sgt. Doreen to put out a Missing Person's Alert. By the way, I've got an old flack jacket in the shop if you want. Ex-Vietnam, only two bullet holes, nowhere near the heart."

"We're also losing the element of surprise," Gra'eme was throwing his friend and client a life-line, hanging back near the door. "I just don't think it's such a brilliant tactic to show our hand like this, draw attention to the flood maps…"

"Neither do I!" stammered Joe, to anyone who would still listen- in the vain hope of a quorum for a rescission motion.

But only Lynton seemed to be paying any attention: "That's why you've got to convince Mondeigo the game is up, Joe. Like- immediately. While the injunction against the chainsawing still holds. If that runs out there'll be nothing left in that forest worth saving."

"Good luck, mate," Benny actually hugged Joe, comrade-like, around the shoulders (mercifully, only for a short moment- not being a Pathsandra himself). Then quietly whispered in Joe's ear: "I've got a gun too, if you need it, point three two calibre. As much ammo as you want, just let me know. I'm not serving papers on any farmers this week so I won't be needing it…" before hurrying out. Leaving Joe all wobbly on his feet. Again. A gun was the last thing he needed! Geezus. He hung there like a man condemned, if not factually abandoned.

How could any single day continue to go so badly? Joe wondered, as he shuffled out into the inferno of Heaven's cruel afternoon sun. With still no time for that oh-so-necessary cooling swim, let alone a proper lunch or any hope of a Serious Lie Down!

Even without Lynton's point about the urgency of the case, Joe was determined to put this kamikaze act quickly behind him and get on with the rest of his life (assuming he survived). But, with Rusty still pressed into service by Barbara to ferry Julie around, he had to power-walk back to Casa del Fibro and fetch his equally rusty Malvern Star. Joe didn't even have a proper set of wheels to get him up that incredibly steep escarpment to Mondeigo's palatial enclave.

Overall, the Birthday From Hell, had just taken a wrong turn for the worse…in a downward spiral.

WIPE ACROSS TO:

26

Bearing a striking resemblance to the Three Sisters off Point
Paradise, and directly connected to **HEAVEN U**straylia through
one of the global quadrangle's 11 main chakra lines, the
colourful pyramids at Giza, Egypt, are only a gagamillion
Loyal Traveler Miles™ from busy Nullumbah International
Airport. Call <terminal_travel.com.ust> today and put
yourself in this picture.

*Affix
stamp
here*

#26 of 33 Postcards from Heaven

printed on gently mulched, plantation-grown, organic bamboo fibre using
recycled greywater and bound with a biodegradable non-toxic glue

No animal or dolphin suffered in the making of this card
(apart from, of course, its author)

26
GULLIBLE'S TRAVELS

"It's not what you eat.
It's how you swallow."
(Gra'eme *Recovery Recipes For Diet Victims*)

4.07pm, Casa del Fibro, Friday 13th March

Joe's clothes were drenched by the time he had managed the two kilometre shamble home from Hallelujah Hell Hall- a pitiless afternoon sun beating down all the way, causing a revival of the slight migraine that had been threatening since his near drowning this morning and which he still thought might be the herald of a particularly nasty cold sore. He realised immediately that he needed to change (in more ways than one!). But how to power dress for such an important, if impossible mission?

After rummaging through the plastic milk crates that served as his wardrobe, it was a choice of either shorts and t-shirts- or…t-shirts and shorts. One pale cotton blouse with double pockets was about as formal as Joe could get. There wasn't a single item of clothing with which to impress a businessman- even if he was only a developer. Joe's mother would have been ashamed of him. (As she frequently was during her short lifetime.)

He hung the Hawaiian shirt and tattered khaki shorts out to dry, put on a (semi-clean) Ho Chi Minh t-shirt under the blouse (loosely opened), found a spare pair of tattered shorts, added his notebook, cracked raybans (held at their broken hinges by small safety pins), and- as a small concession to going upmarket- slipped into his best pair of dunlop volley sandshoes. These were the last ones bought and kept in near pristine condition by virtue of being worn only inside the house as de facto slippers. Joe thought about socks but decided against them, it being so hot. What Mondeigo saw was what Mondeigo would get. Stuff him.

Plus, Joe was now officially starving! After 4 o'clock already, and Joe still hadn't eaten a proper lunch. It was when he opened the fridge, scavenging for food, that he noticed a new line of 'magnetic poetry' had been added to its door.

Below: 'my flesh burns with the flavour of your eyes'
 and: 'lips sparkle like cedar wine in summer cups'
had been added: 'this relationship is fucked'

Barbara must have called 'home' (sic) en route to Raiina Virago. And Joe was angry- not so much with the sentiment and its depressing, probably accurate prognosis (which was fair enough, given the circumstances)- but with the fact that Barbara had used up the last of the spare 'c's and 'k's to make 'fucked'.

Nor was there any indication as to what was now happening exactly, re his BBQ- or even whether Julie and Barbara were attending. Though they would still have plenty of time to do so before the *Aurora* left Nullumbah for Sydney at 10 pm. What could be more socially embarrassing than having to throw a birthday party all by yourself?

CUT TO:

4.16pm, Skypilot Drive, Friday 13th March

Mondeigo's mansion had been erected on the very edge of the Xaviour's Shoot escarpment. Thus contravening at least half a dozen local by-laws prohibiting development along ridge-lines. The ride up there was an unfit cyclist's nightmare. Especially given the Malvern Star's failing spokes, spongy tyres, and stretched chain wheel. In fact, Joe frequently had to stop and walk, with only the increasingly fabulous view providing any compensation. By the time he arrived at the gates of the enemy his fresh clothes were drenched again (as anticipated), right down to the near-pristine dunlop volleys.

CUT TO:

4.25pm, *Eden*, Friday 13th March

Too bad, Joe thought as he jabbed an intercom button next to the large, bright red, solid steel, British post box. (No bunch of juvenile delinquents could decapitate that!) An ornate wrought iron sign arched across the top of the main security gate announcing, simply: *Eden*.

After a couple more presses on the buzzer an irritated voice came on and said:
"Piss off."

With sinking heart Joe recognised Lech Da Groot's primitive growl and struggled to bury the slight tremble in his voice. "I'm here to see Carlos Mondeigo," the short writer declared. And for a bit of extra leverage added: "...from the Nullumbah Protection Society."

"Nullumbah Retards Society," Da Groot hooted, mocking Joe with that chimp-like screeching laughter he had, further proof of an IQ plummeting towards the lower register on Gaia's genetic wheel of fortune.

Joe was contemplating actually giving up on the spot, having at least turned up and made the attempt... until some residual anger from this morning's chainsaw humiliation made him stand his ground. He certainly wasn't going to be intimidated by a gormless thug like Lech Da Groot. After all Joe was a 'Representative of the People'. And everyone was behind him...a long way away...on the coastal plain far below.

"It's about *Dreamtime Beach Estate*. We've got new information that is critical to the project's future," Joe persisted, standing his ground.

Encouraged by the silence this produced, he ploughed on. "Tell Mondeigo we've found the missing flood plain maps..."

The anger of a quiet man is the only weapon Joe had. *Nobody* was going to fob him off. Especially not someone like Da Groot.

"... the documents someone stole from Council and tried to bury..." he added, knowing that this alone could sink their project.

Again no response.

"Luckily, for all parties concerned, the NSPS has unearthed an old copy from the Nullumbah Library archives."

Pause, more silence.

"I'm sure none of us would like to see any shortcomings in the hydrology of such an important development, Lech. Especially given the *awesome* legal consequences..." Joe threatened, sarcastically, feeling the power of words. And his ability over them.

But again Da Groot made no response. Was he checking with someone? Perhaps Mondeigo was there too, listening in?

"Who wants to give the lawyers a free picnic?" Joe added as he loitered with intent now, glancing up at the gates of *Eden*, which appeared to have been looted from an ancient Hindu temple or Balinese shrine. A moment later these elaborately carved, massive wooden doors creaked open and a different, almost gentle voice said:
"Come on in..."

As Joe entered Eden he found himself staring into some kind of private botanical gardens. In fact, there was such a range of endangered flora in there that the ex-fashioner of cop-shows began to wonder if Mondeigo's real estate interests might actually be a front for some kind of exotic plant and fauna smuggling operation (now rivalling arms dealing and drugs as the world's largest criminal enterprise). He dumped his bike helmet in a milk crate on the back of the Malvern Star and pushed forward along a narrow driveway made from ancient Mayan cobblestones, feeling like he should be using the servant's entrance- just as the huge iron gates closed automatically behind him with an unnerving, echoing clang.

After roughly fifty metres, the driveway opened out to reveal a breathtakingly huge mansion whose verandah poles were carved with the totems of some long vanished Polynesian tribe. It's slate roof diverted pure rainwater into a large ornamental fish pond sitting in the middle of the front courtyard. Joe got an overall impression of something imitating something that was copied from an idea that had once been stolen from a book and plagiarised as an article on the 'Japanese Look' or 'The Oriental House and Garden'.

The temple/palace/mansion and it's zen-like landscape all looked far too Feng Shui and civilised for a man who had defrauded elderly widows and stashed bodies inside the concrete foundations of some of the Cold Coast's highest high rise buildings. How peaceful and serene it all seemed. So unlike the explosion of noise and building activity about to overwhelm Joe's own humble handkerchief of paradise.

Mercifully, Da Groot was nowhere to be seen. In fact, apart from one tragically shy kookal bird trying to hide behind the giant crystal embedded at the far end of the fish pond, the place looked completely deserted. Although burning incense filled the air and soft, sitar music was coming from speakers deployed inside ornamental rocks.

Suddenly, a figure detached itself from the overall stillness and got up from a lotus pose directly in front of the giant crystal. To his slight surprise, Joe realised this person had been 'hidden in plain view' all the time and immediately recognised Carlos José Mondeigo from a rare photo published a few years back in some brave Sydney broadsheet (since driven out of business). The wealthy developer was wearing a kind of elongated shirt (an Arabian jabilyah) that almost covered…dunlop volley sandshoes!

Joe found it hard to fault his adversary thus far on matters of taste relating to either architecture or footwear- despite the pot-pourri of styles and pirated cultural influences surrounding them.

Oddly, the shy millionaire didn't seem surprised to see Joe. His handshake was soft and unassertive, like his voice.

"Carlos Mondeigo, pleased to meet you."

"Joe - Joe Deegan."

Joe thought the man seemed vague and almost sleepy, having just come out of his afternoon meditation, obviously.

The Portuguese aristocrat had a tanned, finely chiselled face, almost gaunt. With just a hint of grey at the temples- indicating he was also probably on the cusp of fifty? Perhaps? Yet, unlike Joe, in much better physical shape. Party to the kind of healthy lifestyle that a hack scribbler-for-a-living could only dream about. Or write about as the case may be.

Mondeigo was smiling at Joe as if there was some joke about him that he'd heard somewhere and everything Joe said or did, continually reminded him of it- only the object of such derision would never discover what it was. It was like that smirk Christopher Plummer seemed to have all the way through *The Sound Of Music*.

"I've come from the local Protection Society," Joe began, getting down to business.

"Yes, Lech tells me you're concerned about some aspects of *Dreamtime Beach*."

"Well, apart from the fact that it's going to be smack bang in the middle of a flood plain, and that you're going to have to destroy an old growth rainforest just to get in there- yes there are a few concerns. A fairly long list in fact."

Joe was reaching for his notebook. Determined to cut to the chase. Enough bullshit had marred the way. At last he had a mission to fulfill on behalf of the Common Good. Something that might shake him out of his interminable mid-life crisis (dentist's orders). The points he'd summarised on paper were a script to be performed, amounting to an irresistible argument. Joe was going for real outcomes here.

Curiously, Mondeigo was not at all troubled by Joe's assertive tone- or the notebook. "Let's get comfortable," was all Joe's host offered as he gestured vaguely towards somewhere inside his lavish enclave, leading the way…

Joe followed him up the short marble staircase to a broad verandah made from local hoop pine. Expensive kilims dotted the spaces between comfortable cane furniture, and behind it all billowed bright, Thai silk curtains. Mondeigo led Joe on into his spacious 'office'. Here the view out over the Xaviour's Shoot escarpment was absolutely sensational. Vast glass doors, costing more than Joe could make in a single year, took full advantage of the spectacular panorama that included the light house and the coast in both directions: from Point Paradise all the way past Cape Surprise! north to Goanna Head. Twice as much coast as Gra'eme, Joe calculated, as he glanced out at the ocean and saw some beautifully shaped waves going to waste…

Mondeigo stood beside Joe and politely took in the view himself. Still smiling.

"I've always been excited by a sense of place: the way rocks tumble down a high mountain creek, a stand of trees, or the view from the top of a waterfall. The coastline near my family estate in Portugal never fails to stir something really basic in me- whenever I get a chance to go back there."

Mondeigo's eyes drifted off over the landscape spread out before them. As if seeing the real comparison for the first time- between where he had come from and where he was now. And maybe there was a growing sense of doubt about whether he chosen the right place to end up in afterall.

"We do live in a very special part of the world," Joe conceded, without diverting from the underlying transaction at hand. "Pristine, endowed with great natural beauty, wilderness in need of protection." (Just to rub it in.)

"Ah- but if it needs protecting, how can it be a true wilderness?" Joe's host countered brilliantly.

Good point. Mondeigo one, Joe unable to score.

"Yet, I agree with you," the developer also conceded. "There *is* a Magick inside the Enchanted Triangle, isn't there? We all feel it surely- the spirit dreaming contained within the landscape. I mean, the aboriginal idea of songlines…what a fantastic concept. Knowledge as a map. Music as the key to that map. Clearly this place holds us in thrall- as if we are the 'victims' of some kind of spell. Don't you think?"

If nothing else, the bloke seemed keen to be politically correct. Joe had read somewhere that Mondeigo was also a dedicated tantric. Very well, he would pitch his appeal, body surfer to body surfi.

"That's why we can't afford to stuff it up, Carlos. We must be responsible custodians,"- Joe going for whatever 'spiritual' feelings Mondeigo may profess to have about landscapes. Certainly, a fair bit of sensitivity in that regard was obvious from the sort of palace he had filched from various Third World countries and then reassembled jig-saw style around himself.

Mondeigo took a carved, ivory mulling bowl from between two African masks on his mahogany desk. "I'm just going to twist up a couple of bush heads if you're interested," he said as he lead Joe through a hallway of Brett Whiteleys out onto a wide terrace overlooking the very rim of the escarpment- with no protective handrail!

Joe almost subconsciously stood back from the edge. If this criminal developer was as ruthless as the rumours implied there was little to stop him from nudging the chubby writer headlong onto the rooftops of *Canonisation Court* (his hideous former sub-division on the old public golf course) three hundred metres below.

Nor was Joe in any position to say 'no' to this kind offer. It had been one of those days when a late afternoon spliff was sorely needed. The one this morning (that Onecoat Kev almost stumbled upon) had long since worn off. And while he may have missed a second swim at Point Paradise, here at least, Joe could catch up on some remnant of his Beautiful Day.

"My idea of a 'smart drug' is one that gets you high, while remaining technically legal,"- Mondeigo lighting up.

"Oh?"- Joe immediately curious, hoping for elaboration.

"Like corkwood, for example, or ganga cloned tomatoes. Of course, it's all bound to be legal one day. The health benefits of dope are there for all to see- as the ayurvedic yogis so well knew. And I'm not just talking about marijuana's ability to cure cancer by inducing accelerated cell death. There are real benefits for people with glaucoma, arthritis, migraine, epilepsy, multiple sclerosis… It's even been used to treat bi-polar disorder- now the most common illness in the developed world. And apart from the high tar content, plus the slight possibility of schizophrenia, what's wrong with it?

Joe shook his head, at a loss. Carlos was, of course, preaching to the converted.

"In any case, schizophrenia is what any artist must suffer through, and finally conquer- inorder to create. Am I right, Joe?"

Again his guest had to agree. Nodding politely, gesturing vaguely.

"It's the price we pay to see a way forward," theorised Mondeigo, including himself in the artist category, obviously. "Plus the damage caused by nicotine and alcohol- the mindless violence, disease, social malfunction, *car*nage and death- is phenomenally greater. We'd be much better off if we banned alcohol and legalised dope."

Joe wasn't quite prepared to go that far. But before he could object his nemesis added, sealing the argument with: "Nobody I know ever died from smoking pot."

"I wonder though…"- the ex-playwright seized his chance to interrupt the flow, hoping the joint might come his way if he could just get his host to stop raving, "…doesn't dope addle the brain a teeny bit? Sap the will to achieve?"- hinting at a negativity. Anything to put subliminal pressure on Mondeigo to get the smoke moving in Joe's direction.

"Does it?" snapped the wealthy businessman. "Are you sure? I wouldn't describe myself as a failure exactly. Are you a failure, Joe?"

That was a pretty loaded question on a man's 49th…or 50th birthday. The subject of the question hesitated…weighing it up.

"I don't think so, from what I hear."- Mondeigo supplying his own answer. (Which was rather nice of him.) "What, with your work in television…I dare say dope even helps the scripting process a little, no?"

Joe shrugged a non-committal 'yes' to that. It would be hard to think of a line he had written in the last twenty years where he wasn't under the influence.

"In any case, the world- humanity generally- could do with a little moderation in its aggressive, out-there, conquer-everything attitude," Mondeigo continued. "Imagine how much more pleasant the twentieth century might have been if only Hitler or Stalin had taken the odd bong or two. No, damnit, we all need a little lack of incentive and a slight failure of the will every now and then. In fact, if we don't slow down, Gaia will force us to. Don't you think?"- throwing the question back to his would-be adversary, along, finally! with the joint.

The people's emissary had to agree as he took it all on board (smoke and ideas) and finally relaxed, feeling a bit like Alice in Wonderland as he sank into a very comfortable squatter's chair- again not unlike his own back home. A home that now seemed a trillion light years away; although, from this gods-eye view of Heaven, Joe thought he could just make out the banksias and sheokes bordering his troubled back fence- along with the adjacent thin green line of rainforest: all that was holding back Mondeigo's bulldozers from accessing the clear, sub-dividable patch left by sandmining in the centre. It must be hard not to feel unstoppable Joe realised, when you had a back deck as commanding as this one.

And it suddenly occurred to the soapie hack that, whereas Jerusalem had it's Dome of the Rock, it's Holy of Holies, Heaven had its (en)Light(enment)House, glinting now in a hazy, late afternoon sun that twinkled sparks off the row upon row of crystals in its giant lenses.

Heaven and Jerusalem. Two towns obsessed with the spiritual- the 'Other', the invisible side of things. High energy places on different sides of the globe, yet both at the mercy of large earthmoving machines and both increasingly clogged with traffic and weirdos, prophets and ponces, channellers and choristers, angels and acrobats, shamans and charlatans- who were either predicting the end of something dreadful, or the beginning of something wonderful, and vice versa and either way, offering to help you understand the change for a mere gold coin donation. Heaven and Jerusalem. Key chakra points on the body of our mother planet. Both in urgent need of cosmic acupuncture. One, the desert mountain crucible of many religions for thousands of years; the other, a temporary human settlement upon a pagan coastline where healing and insight came without dogma or divine intervention. Thanks be to Gaia.

"It's practically an island isn't it?" offered Mondeigo, taking his joint back.

"Heaven?"

The developer sucked deep and nodded, speaking and holding the smoke down- giving his voice that slightly higher pitch of the truly greedy dope addict.

"You can see from up here how our little village is almost completely surrounded by the Limbo Creek Wetlands- including Lake Lethe. Which is what makes it so desirable of course." Then exhaling, long and slow, voice returning to normal. "Because there's only so much land on an 'island' that can be bought and sold, Joe. Terror Firma- the one asset they're not making any more of."

"That's why we must protect it. What's left of it," Joe pointed out. Again trying to drag both the agenda and the joint back to the point at hand. Preferably his hand. And failing. But did it matter? If nothing mattered? In any case they were both over familiar with the arguments.

"My business Joe, is to give people what they want. Ordinary, everyday UStraylians. All our projects allow for large, open-plan living/dining rooms, white walls, polished floorboards, slate bathrooms and stainless steel kitchens. My clients want clean lines and low maintenance, plus a street their kids can play in without getting molested by some psychopath."

-Like, for example, one Lech Absalom Da Groot, thought Joe. Although, again out of courtesy, he refrained from saying so.

But the former Network slave felt he knew what 'ordinary UStraylians' wanted too. He had been churning out entertainments for them for the best part of his working life and he felt he understood the average mug punter just as well as Mondeigo did. They weren't all idiots.

"Supply and demand. It's as simple as that," declared Carlos Mondeigo as he graciously handed his guest a second puff.

But Joe was already finding it hard to believe that either a) a second toke was necessary or b) that such an urbane and apparently gentle man was capable of the grasping evil with which he'd been tagged. Were the rumours themselves not to be trusted?

Indeed, seeing Mondeigo now- in the flesh so to speak, you tended to doubt the horror stories. The accusations of murder, deceit and mayhem must be well wide of the mark. Were they simply typical, misguided gossip after all? As Gra'eme often said: 'Word of mouth is the least reliable source of anything. Because we all like to show off and embellish. The writer and the defamer both lie the truth.' (see *Never Trust Anyone Under Forty*).

In any case, the bush heads had just started playing notes that set off neurological catherine wheels in Joe's frontal lobes. "Look, Mr. Mondeigo ..." he attempted to say.

"'Carlos'- please," Mondeigo insisted, holding up a ringed hand and taking the joint back for a third time. It was lucky for Joe he didn't have to drive home. Nobody was going to need terribly much of this stuff he realised as he suddenly felt an intense desire to cut to the chase- whilst still capable of doing so.

"Carlos, as you know, I've come straight from an NP- SPS, NP…SS…" Joe was losing it. His motor neurone system gnashing gears and forcing his jaw to operate as if submerged in playdough.

Mondeigo seized on Joe's inability to speak properly: "*SS* is right! The Nullumbah *Green* SS if you ask me,"- causing Joe to lose another point in their verbal foreplay.

He even found the developer's defamatory joke amusing, obviously abandoning all sense of balance and possibly control. The view started to spin a little. (Again.) As Joe wondered how his opponent could stand so impossibly upright- on the edge of such a sickening drop.

"Carlos, even apart from the flooding issue which blows it right out of the water all by itself- if you'll excuse a mixed metaphor. There are just too many things wrong with *Dreamtime Beach Estate*… far too many," Joe was fumbling for his notebook and already it sounded pathetic. He'd lost his flow, a certain rhetorical flourish was missing.

In the pregnant pause that followed the writer and lover again forgot where he was and even *who* he was (let alone *how* he was, where he had come from, or what he was meant to be doing)…

Then he remembered. Thanks to his notebook. And, although his sweaty shirt pocket had made the text virtually indecipherable, Joe began counting off the sins of Mondeigo's 'dream' project on his fingers- as much to jog his failing memory as to sound serious and organised.

"It's also the trees you want to cut down, Carlos. It's the traffic overload. The sewerage system that can't cope. The potential for acid sulphate runoff. The architectural design- which, if you'll pardon me for saying so…"

Mondeigo politely waved him on, encouraging frankness.

"Well it's…the plans for the townhouses are so uniform and mass produced, they're completely out of kilter with what already exists in our part of Heaven. I mean, pink and lilac cluster townhouses, forgodsake, Carlos. In the cement box/brutalist style. What were you thinking!? "

Joe was running out of fingers. He started using some of them twice. "There's no Social Impact Statement, no Archaeological Survey, no rain tanks, no proper soil structure analysis… Plus we're talking at least *six* endangered species- which Council's own EIS clearly identifies."

It was getting technical- down to acronyms. Joe could've said 'Environmental Impact Statement' but wanted to sound across the data, and in any case the surf was calling. In any Beautiful Day- no matter how flawed- Time was always of the essence.

However, Mondeigo merely saw another opening and pounced again: "Ah- there's a new amendment to our habitat control measures: we're now going to ban *all* cats and dogs," he protested mildly. "Especially those *under* 10 kilos."

It was pretty clear that this intelligence was coming straight from the 'Stranger' who must've been on his mobile to Mondeigo and Da Groot immediately after the NSPS meeting broke up. While Joe was staggering 'home' (sic) on foot.

"Even so, how can you possibly ban cats and dogs in the middle of a suburb? Of any size!" Joe demanded, also probing for weak spots. But with decorum, still managing to be the Christian Gentleman about it.

Mondeigo sighed as if he had heard all this before. And he had, it was what fuelled most of the complaints in the extensive letters pages of both local papers- as well as the hundreds of written objections to his developments.

"Look Joe, the whole of Heaven was sandmined 30 years ago. Every cubic inch of 'Bogwater Creek' was flooded, drained and sifted through. After which, the miners left the place a virtual desert. There's nothing particularly environmentally unique or pristine about that bare patch in the middle of our *Dreamtime Beach* block- or *any* of the rest of Heaven for that matter. And I'm not just talking about the radiotoxic dumps and dip sites left all around town that have since been built on. If Heaven hadn't changed and moved on there'd still be rivers of blood flowing from the meatworks out to the packs of sharks off Purgatory Beach. You'd still see whale carcasses rotting in the sun over by Limbo Creek…"

Joe waved all this unfortunate industrial history aside. "But there *is* something pristine about that rainforest," he insisted, "the one you're trying to chainsaw your access road through. Sandmining never disturbed that area."

"Cross my heart and hope to die, Joe, there will be minimal impact as a result of that road. Not only will we replant 38,000 trees, we're going to ameliorate the fauna damage by gathering up all the endangered species personally- every surviving, individual example- and take first class care of them in a private veterinary hospital. At least until they can be permanently relocated under strict zoological supervision in our reconstituted rainforest."

Joe thought about coming straight out with it and saying: "No way José." But felt enough bad jokes had already been uttered for one day.

And there was that phrase again: 'ameliorate the impact'. A euphemism, dressed up as a threat that said: 'I can spend a fortune on lawyers if I have to, and I'll see you in bankruptcy court along the way.'

"The point is, Carlos, this *Dreamtime Beach* thing you're proposing- by any criteria you care to name- is not sustainable. It's *too* big, there's *too* much of the same type of architecture, and it's in *completely* the wrong area!"

Joe was pleased to think he had remembered the rhythm of his favourite sound bite- despite his otherwise rapidly declining mental shape. "Can I be frank about this?" he challenged.

Mondeigo laughed and urged him on. "Be bold. Be 'Joe' even."- but like so many today, the pun was lost on it's target.

"You basically want to dump an intolerable burden of people and social problems onto my community, wreck our environment, rape our natural capital, and degrade Heaven's social amenity. All for a quick profit of what…forty or fifty mill? Aren't you already extremely rich, Carlos? Haven't you done *enough*? How much money can any human being *spend* in a lifetime? The pleasure of all this must be exhausting."

Joe gestured theatrically at the palatial enclave that surrounded them. "I mean, how many creature comforts can any individual body temple sustain?" -All uttered without a hint of envy. Joe had his (modest) slice of paradise, Carlos Mondeigo had his. It was more than enough for either of them. Joe wanted for nothing else but to live at #13 Redemption Road in the manner to which he'd become accustomed. That, unfortunately, was directly threatened by the developer who still stood so impossibly upright and implacable before him.

…A man who now sighed and slumped a little. For his part, Mondeigo also felt he was being eminently reasonable. And of course, money wasn't just about spending power. It was about power, full stop. (see Gra'eme's *Power Is The Only Drug- All The Rest Are Flowers*)

"Look, *Dreamtime Beach Estate* is zoned Freehold Residential, Joe. Our Council, in its wisdom, has already decided that this is land suitable for building on. The State Government *expects* new subdivisions to occur in precisely these areas- especially a disused mining wasteland. Everyone can see there's a population shift to the Rainbow Coast. Not just retiring baby boomers like you and me, but anyone who has the foresight or good fortune to get in on the ground floor of a Property Skyrocket. And who can blame them? Why even your own house had an impact on the environment when it was originally built. And will eventually be worth a fortune."

Joe looked doubtful. The idea of Casa del Fibro actually appreciating in value any time soon seemed ridiculous. Despite it being a classic example of fishing and drinking class architecture. He could feel a 'buttering-up' phase looming and braced himself.

"Even though it's got asbestos in its roof and walls and will cost an absolute mint to demolish."

"Well, it's a mint condition example of the classic fibro beach cottage." Joe boasted. "I imagine the National Trust will put a preservation order on it well before that could happen."

Joe felt both cocky and troubled. Mondeigo seemed to know an awful lot about him personally and Casa del Fibro technically. Had the intelligence gathering been going on for some time? Or was Joe just being paranoid- always a danger with dope. No matter how psychologically well adjusted one can outwardly seem.

"Okay, you got here first, Joe. You're ahead of the queue. Lucky you. But you're still *in* the queue, aren't you? You still have an impact. You produce sewerage and garbage like everyone else."

That was hitting a little below the belt Heaven's newest green hero thought. He did in fact maintain a compost bin and scrupulously put his newspapers, cartons and wine bottles into Otto's recycling compartment (where it remained until re-mixed with all the other landfill again at the municipal tip behind Mt. Lookout!).

"Why shouldn't the people who come after you also have their little slice of paradise?"

Mondeigo paused, letting it sink in, then added:

"And there'll always be somebody coming after you, Joe."

The not very well known writer was shocked. The idea of somebody 'coming after' him predicted a time when Joe would be absent somehow. Was this a not-so-veiled threat? Were Joseph Michael Deegan and Carlos José Mondeigo, ex-altar boys and committed tantric body surfers and sufis, finally reaching the end of some sort of threshold of politeness that would now disintegrate and pour over into honest, animal aggression?

Apparently not. Because the developer continued in a rather resigned tone.

"Of course it's a depressing, historical fact that the whole mad chronicle of white settlement in this part of UStraylia has been one rapacious land grab after another, with callous disregard for previous ownership *or* the environment. Nature existed only in order to be conquered. It was a barrier that had to be fought against in the stampede for arable land. The squatters and early timber cutters obliterated an entire sub-tropical ecosystem using only steel axes. They cut down a rainforest the size of Belgium in less than a decade. And sure, it provided a few good seasons for the dairy herds that followed…until the fertility of the ancient rainforest soil (not used to monoculture) was quickly worn out. Some farmers even ring-barked huge, ancient eucalypts- the most massive life forms on our planet- simply for the water that would fall out. And all they got was a season's worth of grass around the dead base: a small patch of fodder for their beef cattle. An animal whose cultivation represents the most wasteful, inefficient and prodigal way to produce protein known to man- or woman. In place of those huge gums, figs and cedars, we now have forests of camphor laurel from China, lantana from England, as well as groundsel and bitu bush from South Africa. Lacking any local predators these infestations currently run riot across the denuded farmlands and still continue to colonise this whole region in ways as predatory and destructive as any conquistador."

Joe was getting a lecture with which he was entirely in sympathy, unfortunately.

"And along with that environmental holocaust comes a form of defacto genocide." Mondeigo continued. "Was it the same mindset that ringbarked trees as ringbarked whole tribes of people? An ethnic cleansing from which today's inhabitants of Nullumbah Shire still benefit, however vicariously. And therefore are still liable. Land title then, as now, Joe, was always based on the shabby fictions of the real politik. The British regarded the continent as 'empty': 'terra nullius'. And took it for themselves without any compensation to anyone- let alone its native custodians. These brilliant nomads knew that land title can no more be eternal than people can. And anyway, the land owns *us*!"

It was a speech Joe could have written himself (if he'd been that talented). He listened in complete agreement with his host. Not bothering to point out to the Portuguese venture capitalist that his homeland's shabby maltreatment of its own native peoples (in Timor as much as Brazil) was just as bad as the UStraylian colonial example. But Joe hadn't come to score broad historico-political points. Just to stop Da Groot's chainsaw.

It was doubly depressing to realise that, with the general thrust of Mondeigo's spiel Joe could find no counter argument. He felt, despite his initial reservations, that he was actually growing to like the guy; even- dare Joe admit it- admire this natural asset destroyer in some peculiar way. Carlos José Mondeigo said what he thought, thought about what he said, and not all of it was bad…

JUMP CUT TO:

INFINITY LTD

More waves going to waste at the exact point where lovely Limbo Creek meets the Pacific Ocean on pristine Purgatory Beach. Just another one of the many colourful delights awaiting any visitor to **HEAVEN US**traylia. Capital of the Rainbow Coast. Gateway to the eternal moment.

#27 of 33 Postcards from Heaven

No animal or dolphin suffered in the making of this card
(apart from, of course, its author)

INFINITY LTD.

"There used to be only one law of Supply and Demand:
basically, create a Demand by cutting off Supply.
But that was before jungles became rainforests , swamps wetlands,
and pirates, captains of industry."
(Gra'eme *Money Doesn't Talk, It Swears*)

Eden, a few seconds later...

Joe's gaze flicked back to the view from *Eden's* elegant and intimidating terrace. A light but cooling sea breeze finally began to assert some authority over the sultry afternoon- obviously a bonus for ostentatious mansions built illegally on ridge lines. Even at this distance, Joe could see he was missing the best of the low tide with that gentle, almost minimal, north westerly still lifting the swell up into perfect, glassy cylinders. More waves going to waste! Such sacrifices he made in the cause of human (and natural) progress. There would be some fantastic dumpers down there right now, lovely curling walls of water you could throw yourself at and become lost in.

Joe Deegan and Carlos Mondeigo. Ex-altar boys of the same age, with priests for mentors, brothers for tormentors, and holding apparently identical attitudes on nature and local history. Yet Joe had no desire for grandiose, overblown palatial enclaves. Or million dollar views. He could get all that just by strolling a mere one hundred metres down Redemption Road to Purgatory Beach. No, Joe knew (because he was forced to write about it for a living) that great fortunes only made great slaves of their owners. Happiness was generally inversely proportional to the size of one's share portfolio. What the failed minor playwright craved was unadorned peace and quiet in a clutter-free house with a few good ideas to get him through each (usually) Beautiful Day. And all this he had already. He didn't want private wealth anymore than private health insurance. He just wanted *privacy*. (And good health.)

Mondeigo followed Joe's look out to that perfect curving horizon, where the different shades of blue met. He seemed to understand instinctively his guest's vague longing.

"No two waves are the same...you ever noticed that?"

"Yeah," said Joe. "Yes I have, as a matter of fact."

"It's really quite incredible, don't you think? Given all the possible combinations of wind, tide, current, swell, seabed underneath..."

Joe nodded and sighed. This sort of day with its clammy heat and mild, listless wind was as good as body surfing got on Purgatory Beach. And here he was, *missing out again*! He should be frolicking down there right now, having a fantastic sunset swim. Yet here he remained, locked in an impossible argument with an admittedly, pretty charming bloke. Was Joe really doing 'his bit for the community' in the cause of the great goal of Sustainability? Or was he just protecting his own backyard after all? As Ronnie Rainbows so pointedly pointed out.

Carlos Mondeigo seemed too reasonable and accommodating, with his infuriating smile and air of complete confidence. It either charmed you or drove you mad. Was this why Joe still faintly distrusted the man? Or was it perhaps the association with Da Groot? A creature so transparently hostile and boorish that he almost single handedly justified Gra'eme's idea of involuntary euthanasia.

Joe knew he had to bring their discussion back to some sort of critical mass.

"Carlos, what I'm trying to say is...in cutting down that forest for your access road, you're destroying part of the reason why people want to come here in the first place- even, potentially, why they would want to buy one of your townhouses. How are you any different really, from the timber cutters, whale catchers, and dairy farmers you rail against?"

"I must protest." Mondeigo held up both hands in the 'stop' position, palms facing Joe, ringed fingers spread wide and innocent, smile broadening, opals gleaming. "Every single dwelling in *Dreamtime Beach Estate* will have solar hot water, twelve volt renewable power, *and* a composting toilet."

"Putting all that aside, there just aren't enough jobs in Heaven for all the extra residents this development will seduce into the place. The Rainbow Coast already has the highest unemployment rate in the country."

"Highest unemployed and highest educated,' Mondeigo corrected.

"True," conceded Joe, proud to feel part of a community that was recognised as being smart, even if it was also somewhat wasted.

"Statistics prove that an expanding population brings jobs and skills with it," the developer predicted. "More people equates directly with increasing demand- for services, restaurants, cinemas, great coffee, mobile phone shops, internet cafes, adventure tourism, anything and everything a full, fee-paying visitor requires. It's the oldest law in the book, Joe: Demand guarantees Supply will happen. Okay, so there's a bit more traffic on Angel Avenue. So what? You can always cycle around it on your trusty Malvern Star. Thumbing your nose at the stranded automobiles. I actually like the fact that there's life on our streets at night. Somewhere to go. Always a good cover band at the Pearly Gates... You wouldn't get that sort of amenity in a town ten times the size. I can't imagine a more depressing prospect than trying to find an exciting night out in someplace like say, Rockhampton or Albury. 'Soon as the shops close you could shoot a cruise missile down their main streets and hit nobody! Is that the kind of town you want to live in? Change is good, Joe. Change is Life. Nothing stays the same."

Joe slumped. Again.

And again Mondeigo tried to be reasonable. "Look, it's natural for human beings to act out of some sort of tribal impulse and gather together in smallish communities. It satisfies that need we all have to feel part of one big, extended family. Where people care about each other and each others' misfortunes. Where partner swapping can happen at dangerous levels. It fills the hole in modern life where the clan used to be, or the plains-wandering horde group. That's why people like you and me are attracted to places like Heaven, Joe. Not just because we all want to maintain its pristine natural beauty. But because we feel at 'home' with all the other eccentrics drawn here too. Like moths to an aromatic oil burner."

Joe was about to point out that the wonderful, crazy mix of people living in Heaven was already being diluted and priced out of their rental accommodation by the surge of bakpakahs and overdevelopment which people like Mondeigo had already inflicted on it. But he just didn't have the energy. Or the inclination.

Their argument was clearly going nowhere. And speaking of which, neither was the joint. It seemed to have permanently parked itself between the platinum and opal encrustations on the middle fingers of the wealthy criminal's left hand. Not that Joe needed any more THC. How high can you get? he wondered rhetorically. The point was: Mondeigo himself seemed momentarily to have forgotten it. A sign like no other that it was having an effect on him too. Although little else about his behaviour gave the slightest indication of this.

"You see, what I'm trying to build here Joe, with *Dreamtime Beach,* is an 'intentional community'. Something that embraces architecture, landscaping and social demography. I always strive to see the potential in a block of land. I look at it like a kind of raw diamond. Then I cut and polish it to bring out the sparkle, that special, inner glow. Our property- that bare patch left by sandmining in the middle of the forest- *has* to be developed one way or the other. That's already been decided by people in corporations and governments far, far away. Virtually half the population of UStraylia desperately wants to relocate itself to the climatically perfect, mid-eastern and far south western coasts. A nation for a continent and all that nation does is plonk itself down on a few beaches at the extreme outer edge. I'm only making it easy for them and doing it in an environmentally conscious way. The fact is Joe, Heaven is lucky it's got sensitive developers like me and Lech doing it for you."

That's drawing a pretty long bow Joe thought- the idea of Da Groot holding anything as complex and evolved as actual human feelings; but he let his host blather on as Mondeigo's stoned rave drifted away with the breeze…

He argued that the world was becoming one vast ghetto; and agreed with Joe that over-population, pollution and the 'Third World' War that was now spreading and linking up all the little wars from Chechnya through Bosnia to the Muddled East, India, Pakistan and Indonesia- would soon transform most of the planet's larger urban concentrations into crime infested, horrorist filled, toxic slums. He was also pretty convinced (as a result of digital technology making the need for cities a thing of the past), that within a few short years, the international glitterati would soon be clamouring for a clean, green and peaceful enclave from which to pursue their fabulously lucrative on-line businesses. That island of purity and inter-connectedness was already here on the Rainbow Coast. And there was no way he, Carlos José Mondeigo, would tolerate the destruction of what attracted his customers in the first place. Especially when he intended staying on himself. So okay, he and his investors were set to make a bundle. (Since they had bought the land so cheaply.) The only real problem was the capital gains tax involved, but thanks to their brilliant financial genius, the *Dreamtime Beach* consortium was going into serial bankruptcy. All things in good time and everything for a purpose…

It was hard to put a finger on it, but the phrase 'all things in good time everything for a purpose'…sounded awfully like a Gra'emism. For some reason it also triggered a dim memory in Joe of the old rumour about Mondeigo and houses mysteriously burning down. Why Joe should suddenly think of this though, was hard to say. It was surely the dope speaking. Paranoia writ large. Joe knew he had to quit smoking. This 49th…or 50th birthday was the perfect, 'Heaven' sent opportunity. Time for Mr. Reality Check to come knocking and break down the door.

"Think of it this way," continued his host, "if it wasn't people like me reshaping Heaven with some flair and sense of style, you'd be stuck with one of those unconscionable white shoe brigade idiots from Surface Paradox. It all comes down to *'how'* it's done, Joe, not 'whether'; and quite frankly- not to put too fine a point on it- I'm as good as you'll get."

Joe conceded that, despite the architectural uniformity, *Dreamtime Beach Estate* did have some bikepaths (if not actual footpaths- as Mrs. Geogharty so self-interestedly pointed out). There was also the massive tree re-planting programme. And if all dogs and cats were going to be banned, this too, had to be a positive. Even though such a move was impossible to police. He glanced down at his own best pair of Dunlop Volleys (still grubbier than Mondeigo's) with some slight self-embarrassment. White shoes, no matter how scruffy, were a fact of life in the subtropics. They kept the feet cool. Clearly, insults based on the colour of one's footwear were gross over simplifications. Was it also symptomatic of a larger myopia on the part of Heaven's green brigade?

As this very peculiar day wore on things kept getting more and more complicated.

"My other projects on the Rainbow Coast are held up as models of sustainable development by Shire Councils all over UStraylia," Mondeigo crowed, referring to a gated community right on Purgatory Beach, just under the lighthouse, on what used to be the public caravan park. You needed a 'smart' card to get past the electrified brushwood fence; and, with direct access to the beach, land values in there had already quadrupled in the last six months.

"At *Messiah Meadows*, for example, we put in *five times* as many trees as we took out."

"But it will take them a hundred years to catch up with the ones you should never have been allowed to touch in the first place," insisted Joe. And he wasn't just speaking for himself, but as the voice of a whole community.

"How the fuck can you build inside a forest without removing trees?" Mondeigo swore- growing a little uncouth (finally). "Unless you build tree houses…"

The faint smile twitched back at the corners of his lips, turning them upwards again, spiking the sudden flare of impatience. "I thought we had enough of them in Nullumbah Shire already."

Fortunately, Joe was alert enough not to be diverted by an argument about ferals and their strange habitation choices. He was sticking to his main theme:

"Carlos, when I see gated 'communities' (sic) springing up everywhere, I always think of the wagon train slowly drawing a circle round the cowboys to fend off the Indians. My own house has no front fence." (Although, since OneCoat Kev's rude invasion this morning Joe had resolved to get himself one as soon and as high as possible).

"All I'm saying," resisted Mondeigo politely, sensing the hostility, "is that some so-called 'green' politicians in this town ran a very successful election campaign last year on the back of opposition to my previous developments. The lies and disinformation was staggering. People even said I defrauded old ladies out of their estates or buried bodies inside concrete foundations. I won't even dignify the 'ant rumour' by trying to deny it. Or the one about drugs inside bodies shipped back from the Vietnam War. I mean, is there anything *less* reliable than word of mouth? Don't tell *me* about Heaven's vicious libel factory! I'm its chief whipping boy. The place is open slather on anybody trying to make a difference."

For the first time Mondeigo actually showed signs of real anger. And while it shocked Joe out of his complacency about the man, it also made him realise that their argument, like the joint, was *still* going nowhere. The people's emissary had clearly failed in this naive and obviously doomed attempt to get a property developer to change his/her plans, let alone her/his mind. But before Joe attempted to rise out of his squatter's chair, Mondeigo stopped him with a question guaranteed to give any scriptwriter hunting for a new feature idea, pause for thought:

"You want to know how I made my fortune?"

Joe shrugged, not wanting to give anything away. "You got lucky with real estate."

It seemed an innocent enough guess.

But Mondeigo shook his head. "Before that. The thing that got me *into* real estate-while I was still the penniless second son of a bankrupt Portuguese count."

Joe waited.

"I saved an old German guy from a rip down there many years ago…"

Mondeigo was nodding towards an area of golden sand where Purgatory beach met the Three Sisters at Point Paradise. "The tourists just don't get it do they?- how treacherous our beaches really are. Anyway, the poor fellow died of a heart attack just a few months later. Probably as result of the aftershock. And it turns out he left me a castle in Tuscany and a house on Ibiza. I had no idea he'd changed his will until some lawyer emailed my mother from Düsseldorf. How was I to know the man didn't have any family? Apparently he'd written a codicil to the will saying 'I'd given him something priceless- his life'."

"What made you want to do that?" Joe asked, genuinely curious, having just survived a rip himself, and not even thinking about the heart attack part. "Why risk your whole existence for a total stranger? Someone you mightn't even like." (Again the parallel with Joe saving Julie this morning was uncanny.)

"I've often asked myself the exact same question." Mondeigo remained thoughtful for a moment frowning at the drop in front of him, all the way down to the uniform rooftops of *Canonisation Court.*

"I suppose, I assumed I could always swim out of trouble- if I couldn't actually manage to save him- if I had to cut and run, so to speak. Drift parallel to the shore…and get out further down."

"Nevertheless, you did risk your life…?" prompted/congratulated/queried the writer.

"Yes. And to level with you Joe, I don't think there is any simple, logical, explanation," Mondeigo confessed, genuinely puzzled at his own inability to find one. "Truly, I'm no hero normally- ask any greenie round here," he smiled again. "Nor am I a particularly generous person by nature, to be brutally honest,"- rubbing his chin, still intrigued by Joe's question.

It had him hooked. Indeed had the developer ever really thought about it? Really? Deep down? Why he had risked his greedy, comfortable life to save someone who he didn't owe a thing to?

"I guess..." Mondeigo speculated, "it's about...seeing someone in trouble and feeling this instinct that you're *bound* to them in a...I dunno- some really basic way..."

"Like- we're all alive together? At this moment. On this planet. For all we know, alone in the universe...?"

"Yes."

"And you save them, Carlos, because you *have* to, because their death would somehow kind of limit who *you* were- diminish you as well?"

"Yes, I suppose that's it. I saved him because...in a way, I was saving *myself*...?"

Mondeigo turned to Joe amazed at what he'd just come out with. Yet it made sense. It was logical from a greedy point of view. As if it was a totally new insight for him. And he half framed it as a question because it was Joe who had been responsible for producing the answer- by asking in the first place.

"Exactly!" Joe seized his moment perfectly, punching a fist into his palm. "You felt *connected* to them at some deep, almost visceral, even scatological level."

Mondeigo was nodding, he wasn't thinking scatological exactly, but visceral was close enough. And the more he thought about it, the more quizzical he became, frowning openly. Like Joe was teaching him something he didn't already know.

"Not in your heart or your head even, Carlos, but in your guts somehow. A place so deep we don't even know it's there..."

"You're absolutely right! It must've been...a really deep, profoundly deep connection..."

Joe sensed a defining moment, in both this conversation and their relationship. "Then can't you *see*, Carlos, that somehow, the idea of an 'ecology' is *precisely* that we're *all* connected. That what affects me, affects you. What effects one, affects the rest of us- plants *and* animals, and humans *as* animals. And so what you're proposing to do with this *Dreamtime Beach* fiasco is a fatal fracturing of that interdependence and mutuality- by pushing ahead with something that *nobody* wants. That damages a pristine environment. That violates some bond we all have with the way our wonderful, beautiful, precious little slice of Heaven is *now*! I mean *238* separate dwellings, forcrissake!!"

Significantly, Mondeigo didn't deny the doubled figure. Despite Joe leaving a pause for him to do so.

"I'm sorry Carlos, it's too big, it's too much of the same thing, it's squeezed into too small a space, and it's in completely the *wrong area*!"

Joe felt he'd finally got the rhythm of his sound bite just about right. And it was a great moment to do so. "You're breaking faith with this community as custodian of a large parcel of its land."

At which point Joe's mind returned to where this whole struggle began six hours ago and stood to attention for a minute, even if it was a little shaky on its feet. And thus re-energized, Joe's inner poet seized the moral high ground now opening up before him, throwing in his main reserves of argument:

"Nothing gives anyone *carte blanche* to blast a road through a pristine forest, mate. Besides which, medium density cluster townhouses are meant to go in the middle of cities where the environment is already fucked. And it's not just about cats and dogs. It's blokes on Saturday morning washing the four wheel drive with detergents and draining brake fluid straight into our stormwater system- and therefore ultimately into the underground streams that percolate towards Limbo Creek beneath the forest. You're not developing here, Carlos, you're *destroying*. And if you're not part of the solution you're part of the problem."

"Ho Ho..." Mondeigo responded hollowly, quoting Joe's t-shirt with its picture of the grandfatherly leader. Like Joe, he was old enough to have been affected by the Vietnam imbroglio too (whether or not he smuggled drugs inside dead soldiers bodies). Like Joe he could still remember all the hope for real change that came out of that catastrophic war- only to be cruelly dashed again a decade later, by the same old forces of darkness.

"Irrefutable engineering facts, Carlos, okay? One:" Joe counted them off, "the South Heaven Sewerage Treatment Works is polluting Limbo Creek and therefore Purgatory Beach, at levels that are already way off the dial. The Environmental Protection Authority is bending over backwards just to allow the Treatment Works to keep operating- at *present* population levels. And that's not counting the peak loads at Xmas and Easter. Two: the land is clearly flood prone. It's a wetlands forkerrisake. Three:…"

"Okay," Mondeigo held up his hands in a kind of surrender gesture. He looked keenly into Joe's bloodshot eyes and came straight to the point: "How much do you want?"

Joe frowned, not quite sure of the sense of the question. And not trusting his failing hearing all that much. "What I want is for this development not to happen."

"I mean how much do you want for your house?"

"My house is not for sale."

"If you sold it to the *Dreamtime Beach* consortium we could push our access through from Redemption Road- straight across your block. We wouldn't need to touch any more of that rainforest."

Of course this was true. Technically speaking. From a topographical/civil engineering point of view. If you looked at the map.

But Joe was shaking his head. Even if he could afford to buy another house somewhere else (which seemed unlikely, the way things were going), he still had no intention of seeing Kate's hallowed site buried under tonnes of bitumen.

"Carlos, you just don't get it do you?"

Mondeigo finally ashed the joint and reached into his jabilyah, extracting a rhino hide chequebook. "I'm formally offering you a million dollars for your property. I hope a personal check is okay? I'll make it out to 'Joe Deegan' shall I? Is that the name on Casa del Fibro's title? Or would you prefer cash? Gold? Diamonds? Cocaine…?"

He said it like that- like an American. Not 'cheque' as it was supposed to be spelt, but 'check' now as in *check mate*! thought Joe, his mind reeling. During the 3.77 seconds it took Mondeigo to write six zeros after the 'one' in the amount section, Joe realised that, not only was this a serious offer, but he could now both save a forest (his original mission) and make a fortune. On the downside it would also remove any lingering doubts Council might have about the whole project and thus ensure *Dreamtime Beach's* speedy approval- effectively selling out all of his friends and most of his neighbours.

On the upside, if Mondeigo bought Casa del Fibro Joe wouldn't have to live next door to the Utta Bastards Motor Psychle Club because he could then afford to build anywhere he liked- with enough room to store his entire paper archive in a properly humidified, dry space. Probably on an untouched block of land with ocean views and enough acreage to see peace and quiet guaranteed. (He could always take Kate's Poinsettia with him, especially if he dug deep enough to take out what remained of her ashes.) It was as if the failed playwright and hack television dramatist stood on the edge of a dizzying crossroads. What he was being offered was nearly eleven times the true value of his humble, asbestos-riddled shack. He'd never have to work for any Network ever again.

A million dollars. As simple and as complicated as that.

"You know Joe, there's nothing wrong with being comfortable."- Mondeigo, now playing on all the writer's weaknesses like the virtuoso manipulator that he was. "Why shouldn't you have a car that won't break down? A thirty dollar bottle of red every now and then?"

Joe's mind remained in a state approximating that storm on Jupiter that's been roiling around its equator for 60 million years. Mondeigo had presented him with the worst dilemma imaginable: to sell out his most cherished basic principles, his integrity and all that the NSPS stood for- in order to achieve his greatest personal dream (true independence as a writer with a house that would capitally appreciate for a change)… Or remain morally pure and utterly destitute in a health-threatening hovel for all of his remaining, probably cardiologically circumscribed days.

"It's not for sale," Joe heard some person resembling himself say, feeling sick to the pit of his soul. Assuming he had one.

Mondeigo just stared at him, unable to believe he stood before someone this disreputable looking who couldn't be corrupted, bought off, cajoled or black mailed.

"You can't put anything there, Carlos, because your entire building envelope is within a gazetted flood plain. And no matter how corrupt or pliable Council's town planners may be, even they would have to baulk at that. Once we point it out to them. The huge amount of fill required would just push the whole flooding problem downstream."

"We don't have to fill, we can build pole houses. Above the flood line." Mondeigo was clutching at straws- or stumps as the case may be. "I've actually got a very exciting research project underway into houses that will float," he dithered.

But for the first time the superior smile waned slightly, and he started to look a trifle desperate.

"What- like Noah's Ark ?" Joe scoffed. At last. Encouraged by the fear he saw. "Carlos, the NSPS has found the missing flood plain maps that Council's tame engineer- the one you bribed- tried to hide when he did his snow job on your development application. The hydrology of *Dreamtime Beach Estate* is totally fucked- if you'll excuse my Flemish. We also did a check with the Environmental Protection Authority, and it's now almost certain that the South Heaven Sewerage Treatment Works is barely cutting the mustard- if you'll also forgive another fairly colourfully mixed metaphor. In fact the EPA are about to cancel its licence. The shit isn't just hitting the fan, mate, it's blocking up all the way to the bottom of this escarpment. Heaven's entire sewerage system faces a terminal case of global constipation."

"But I already told you, we're putting in composting toilets. *Dreamtime Beach* will be effluent neutral." There was an encouraging desperation behind Mondeigo's protest now.

Joe just laughed. Composting toilets were always the last refuge of the truly desperate.

"Mate, you haven't got a legal leg to stand on. *Dreamtime Beach* breaches at least 27 specific provisions of the local Development Control Plan- from the size of building footprints to setbacks from fence lines. And the our lawyer is still counting." (Which they both knew Lynton was capable of.)

Joe could see that Mondeigo looked beaten, and somewhat ungenerously began to rub salt in the wound, scenting complete victory. Why give a developer an even break- even if they were so personally likable?

"You see Carlos…you and your 'partners' thought you'd sneak in a quick DA before Easter, grease a few palms, and wring a lazy, what?- forty or fifty mill out of the whole shebang in the minimum amount of time it takes to turn the profits round. Then, like every other developer in every other poor benighted 'paradise', you planned to piss off with the profits and leave my community struggling to cope with a crippling legacy of population overload, social dysfunction, infrastructure breakdown and a fucked environment."

Mondeigo finally looked beaten and Joe figured it was time to sink the boot in.

"What you're proposing is wanton ecological vandalism barely hidden under a cloak of pseudo-environmental concern. And basically Carlos, my community can see right through it. Because, finally here, in this humble backwater, this somewhat ego-driven little town, you have a bunch of ordinary/extraordinary people, a rag tag collection of colourful eccentrics and under-utilized intellectuals, who are prepared, through me, to stand up and say: 'No!' Loud and clear. 'We're united, we're powerful, we're mad as hell and we're not going to take it anymore!'"

Realising that the recently resurfaced flood plain maps would sink the project all by itself, Mondeigo finally closed his cheque/check book and dropped into the squatter's chair opposite Joe. The objections raised were demonstrably insurmountable. Mondeigo knew it, Joe knew it, and soon, thanks to Mrs. Gaa Gaa and her verbal disorder, all of Heaven would know it too.

Even the Property With Little Amenity Tribunal would find out about it in due course. The only alternative for Mondeigo's 'architects' would be to go back to their drawing boards and come up with a hugely scaled down, more environmentally sensitive proposal- or better still just sell the land and cut their losses. Leaving it all as some kind of communal nature reserve in perpetuity…

Or so Joe fantasised.

"You see, Carlos, we all breathe the same air, drink the same water, swim in the same gene pool, and we have to stand up and say it- now and forever: 'Enough is enough'. Your lifestyle affects me, and mine yours, and ours everybody else's. Sorry, cobber, but if *Dreamtime Beach Estate* was your big retirement plan then you'd better get another one. Because a community united can never be defeated."

At which point Mondeigo slumped forward, his head dropping towards his chest. And for a slightly alarming moment Joe thought his opponent might have fainted- or gone into some deep trance. Perhaps even had a quiet sort of, epileptic fit. His breathing slowed and Joe almost felt sorry for the man, separating him personally for a moment, from the Natural Asset Destroying class to which he belonged.

Eventually, Mondeigo pinched the bridge of his nose, and held his head still for a moment longer, as if pushing out a migraine or looking at a cool forty million lazy dollars slipping from his grasp. Right now, Carlos José Mondeigo wore the appearance of someone who was about to lose a lot more than money.

"I suppose we could always go for the simple, sub-division option. Forget the 238 townhouses."

"Like *Missionary Meadows*- no medium density clusters?" Joe had to be sure on this point.

"Yes. Build only a few, very beautiful mansions, surrounded by trees, designed by the best local architects available."

"And charge a fortune for them?" Joe prodded, teasing almost. Sensing the value of Casa del Fibro going up with them. Finally!

"We'd still be copping a pretty staggering loss," the developer declared- although not in any way that was actuarially or forensically auditable.

"Not if you make those half dozen mansions really exclusive, accessible only to the hyper wealthy."

Mondeigo shrugged, accepting Joe's point as valid financially, if not arithmetically. Certainly none of this was going to help those looking for affordable accommodation on the Rainbow Coast.

"Pole houses?" double-checked Joe. They weren't so much questions now- more in the nature of demands. Obviously, he didn't treat the floating house option terribly seriously.

Mondeigo nodded to the view again, as if making this pledge to the whole of Nullumbah Shire direct: "Pole houses, minimum impact, above the gazetted flood line. Which doesn't leave much. But…whatever the NSPS say is allowable. There will be no more damage to the hydrology of the Limbo Creek estuarine system, or its pristine coastal rainforest. That I can assure you."

Joe was trying to contain his elation. He stood on the brink of a very considerable, if unlikely, personal victory. The sort of thing that might well evoke a 21 cappuccino salute next time he fronted Café Celestial as Heaven's newest green hero.

"And you'd have to insist on at least a fifty metre buffer zone right around the remaining forest?"

Joe was going for broke now. Pushing Mondeigo's building footprint back as far as he could squeeze it- mixing even more metaphors and acting out of an unfamiliar, no-bullshit, frame of mind. Mondeigo knew this meant foregoing the use of an additional two thirds of his block. And if the rainforest was to remain intact, then future residents would have to be given access to their blocks through a narrow, leafy bikepath. Leaving their vehicles parked in Redemption Road. This car prevention measure could downscale *Dream Beach's* value, or (like Venice) make the place even more ravenously sought after. Probably the latter, thought Joe.

Either way, the developer nodded his acceptance of the scriptwriter's terms; then buried his head in his hands again, shaking violently, his shoulders trembling. Joe thought he might actually be crying and satisfied anyway, on this log of claims, and that all the 'logs' in the claim were safe from more predation (there was no need to prolong the agony or the puns)- the people's emissary made ready to go… Assuming that a) he could stand, and b) then walk.

"I don't think anyone will object to the proposed bike path," he offered (as a dedicated cyclist)- trying to leave Mondeigo with at least a few ticks. And having won just about everything he'd come for, Joe almost felt a kind of sympathy for his defeated opponent.

"…So long as there was a bit more public open space offered?" The NSPS emissary couldn't believe how bold he was becoming, closing the deal with a little sting in the tail like that. 'Extra public space'. Amazing! Chutzpah on a par with Barbara's astonishing front.

"Fair enough." Mondeigo looked broken now, in a humbling kind of way.

And Joe felt so happy he almost wanted to make amends. Here it was in black and white: you pointed out the obvious, face to face, and the ground shifted. Force of argument *does* work. Moral authority still had a purchase on things. Thanks be to Gaia.

"Of course, if you didn't want to go ahead with any of this you could still sue Council for letting you buy a block they've zoned Freehold Residential- which just happens to sit in the middle of a flood plain," Joe suggested, wanting to sound generous in return. "You'd make a handsome profit on the court case alone- at the ratepayers expense of course. Assuming Council gets costs awarded against it. Which they usually do in the Property With Little Amenity Tribunal. At the very least, you'll get back what the land cost you- plus a little fruit on the sideboard for your efforts."

There was a significant pause. Joe noticed that this morning's north westerly had now definitely turned to the east and was fluttering the edges of Mondeigo's long Bedouin shirt. The gentle zephyr carried with it a certain salty aftertaste, bringing the smell of the beach (a heady mix of salt, rotting seaweed, dog poo and sunburnt thong)- summoning reminders of the fabulous swim Joe had been missing out on since his near drowning nine hours earlier. There was just enough time to wind up this extraordinarily successful negotiation ('confrontation' seemed too strong a word) and get down there and wet. Enough of the community champion stuff already. It was an afternoon profitably spent (for once!) and a job well done. Albeit at some considerable personal sacrifice (for both Joe and Mondeigo). Besides, the people's champion had a birthday party to attend and it was finally starting to look like a celebration. The entire membership of the NSPS were invited anyway (including Ronnie) and there'd be plenty for them to feel quietly proud about.

"All right," Mondeigo declared as he glanced up with his cloying smile back in place. He wasn't crying after all! The shuddering shoulders had merely been suppressed laughter. First Old Frank and now Mondeigo? Had an outbreak of some dreaded humour virus overtaken the shire- seeing only the funny side to every bad situation? Like an Irishman, or a person with nothing left to lose. What could be so amusing from Mondeigo's point of view? About any of this?

"I'll arrange for our legal team to give Alistair and Cassandra a call and they can all put their heads together with Lynton O'Flannery over the fine detail. But basically, you've got what you wanted,"-said without looking at Joe directly anymore.

Mondeigo seemed suddenly irritable and a little bit grim. As if he too, had missed his afternoon massage as well as a tantric body surf. A man obviously not used to losing and already hankering to be some place else.

"And congratulations by the way, I've never come up against a community that was so well organised, informed and represented. The NSPS has had a big win here. I hope the residents of Heaven realise how well looked after they are."

Joe couldn't resist blushing a little. He'd basically achieved everything he'd come for. It all seemed too easy (and it was).

"Well Carlos, funnily enough, the more you oppress a community the more united they become. That's the use-by date on any dictatorial process,"- not wanting to make it sound too personal, or triumphal.

Mondeigo nodded. "Of course, I'll have to run all this past an extraordinary board meeting. I can't guarantee every detail absolutely, but I can assure you they'll accept the nuts and bolts of it- certainly the main points. The luxury-mansion option, with community title (but without the gates and high wall), was always our fall back position- if we weren't able to bribe the relevant Council staff…or keep the flood maps hidden." He hesitated as if trying to swallow the enormity of what he was losing "… and push through the 119 sub-dividable beach units."

"Townhouses," corrected Joe- calling a spade a bloody hideously ugly implement for moving dirt.

Mondeigo waved the distinction away. "Whatever…"

But that wasn't quite good enough: having to refer matters already agreed upon to a third party. Joe wanted it all. And he wanted it now!

"What Board?" he snapped, still looking down from the moral high ground. Even though Mondeigo was the one actually standing- Joe remaining deeply sunk in the squatters chair- uncertain as to the operation of his legs when thrust into a vertical position and called upon to propel an uneasy writer forward. The biomechanical practicality of his actual physical departure remaining a moot point, why couldn't Joe just accept all that he'd achieved and go!? Allowing Mondeigo's board (whoever they were) to sign off on the nitty gritty and have done with it. Why couldn't Joe just rest on his considerable laurels and savour the delicious and unfamiliar sense of personal achievement. Fercrissake, the surf was calling!

However, Mondeigo remained surprised at Joe's question and for a few moments he glanced quickly around him as if he'd lost something- a slip of paper with an important email address, or a crate of vintage champagne. Finally, he turned back to Joe, like here was this unnecessary stranger. An outlander from the peasant class.

"No, of course not. How could you know about the 'Board'? Despite what the Green Police think, I'm not the only person involved in *Dreamtime Beach Estate* you know."

Joe nodded. This was always assumed. "You're talking about Lech Da Groot."

I'm talking about an outfit called *Infinity Ltd…*"

Joe waited. He knew what was coming. Here at last was the admission of the mystery backer. The 'Mr. Big' who everyone suspected was behind most of what Mondeigo and Da Groot did. The brainy evil bastard with access to an endless line of credit.

"I always form partnerships for my work- not just to spread the financial exposure, but because well, I like working with people; and lately you see, this particular association has stabilised across a number of projects, and frankly I'm bound by what's decided by… "

"Yes, I know," Joe cut in. "You answer to someone else"- demeaning Mondeigo's role a little.

"Well *two* other people, to be precise." *Infinity Ltd.* is our shared, high-risk, investment vehicle."

"Right- so there's you, Da Groot and Bryce Keitel…" Joe prompted/speculated.

"Lech's not a 'partner' as such, in the full fiduciary sense. More a…subcontractor. "

Joe was glad to hear the complete dingbat relegated to his proper low status in the overall scheme of things.

"Bryce handles the fine detail. He knows who can be bribed and who needs blackmailing. He also makes sure we're sufficiently cashed up when some real bargain is coming onto the market."

"Oh? Such as?" queried Joe, off hand and neutral. Exploiting this rare opportunity to get some priceless inside information.

"Such as when a vendor say, has little- or preferably, no- idea of the true value of their property."

"How can that be? Are people so stupid?" Joe scoffed. Still fishing for potentially useful financial intelligence. This wasn't giving him much.

"Well for example, because it lies right across the access point to some larger development- like your own property."

Joe looked suitably put back in his place.

"…or they reside interstate, or are quite simply mentally challenged. And let's face it, there's no shortage of *them* around here."

"Isn't that just a teeny bit corrupt, though?" alleged Joe- hardly surprised by anything Bryce Keitel would get up to.

"Oh, all the agents have their favourite investors. It's a win, win situation all round. The vendor sells, Bryce takes his commission *plus* his cut of the profits, and we all get a property at a rock bottom, fire-sale price. In fact, sometimes it's literally that. Our Mr. Keitel has been present at more than one house fire around town recently. A 'guilty bystander' watching the fire brigade do their courageous thing. Alas, too late in most cases- for the residents concerned. And believe me, there's nothing more effective than a blazing dwelling to help steel a wavering vendor's decision to sell. Although, this tactic is only ever attempted on the most recalcitrant home owner," Mondeigo hastened to add. "Certainly, no one with a large family to support."

Joe was glad to hear there were still some ethical constraints in play- while inwardly staggered to think that Mondeigo would hand him such potentially incriminating information on a plate. Then again, none of this was written down or being recorded. Mondeigo was hardly giving Joe proof of anything.

"So who really cuts the deal? We all know there's a Mr. Big somewhere…" Joe coaxed, wanting to wind up the discussion and go celebrate.

Mondeigo looked at Joe like the short scriptwriter was really slow (which he was).

"Why, Gra'eme of course. Who else could've designed Infinity Ltd.'s tax-free currency transfer arrangements? The profits we never make are mind blowing."

Joe looked blank. "But Gra'eme's a member of the NSPS. He's on *our* side."

"Of course he is. The more successful your little Protection Society became at stopping development in Nullumbah Shire the more incredibly valuable *Dreamtime Beach* and every other property we owned on the Rainbow Coast became."

It was as if someone had just scalded Joe's brain with a sackfull of pool chemicals. His trusted Mentor, the man to whom he had quite frequently hung his soul out to dry (along with some substantial fees)- hand in glove with Bryce Keitel, Carlos Mondeigo and Lech Da Groot!? Geezus! Gra'eme! The architect of all the chaos that was tearing Joe's house and the wellbeing of his entire community apart? The unscrupulous bastard was even at the meeting designed to stop this monstrous rip-off! It seemed unthinkable.

But as Joe processed all the permutations and recent hints and logical conclusions through his materially deteriorating central nervous system, two and two was starting to equal: 'pretty massive total betrayal'; and he realised with a shudder that it was only *too* thinkable, indeed.

In fact it was rapidly becoming pretty clear that in the flawed and poisonous example of Gra'eme, Joe was staring at a man whose pamphlets asked the deepest questions and provided some of the shallowest answers. The disgraced former corporate auditor was clearly all things to all people and nothing to nobody.

IRIS OUT TO:

CERTAIN FAILURES IN ANGER MANAGEMENT

Blind King David of Angel Avenue. Just another one of the many colourful monarchs, leprechauns, fairies, channelers, sadhus, shamans and charlatans wandering the cosmopolitan streets of **HEAVEN** ustraylia. Visit the Rainbow Coast and discover the stress-relieving properties of lyre playing. (Gold and silver coin donations accepted in all currencies including Euros, Shekels, Francs, Yen and Pounds Sterling.)

Affix stamp here

#28 of 33 Postcards from Heaven

printed on gently mulched, plantation-grown, organic bamboo fibre using recycled greywater and bound with a biodegradable non-toxic glue

No animal or dolphin suffered in the making of this card
(apart from, of course, its author)

28
CERTAIN FAILURES IN ANGER MANAGEMENT

"There 's always a middle way.
It's straight, so it's easy to follow;
but narrow also, and sometimes hard to find."
(Gra'eme *Success Is A Journey, Never A Destination*)

5.42pm, Skypilot Drive, Friday 13th March

Much like his mood, Joe's deteriorating Malvern Star took an erratic turn for the worse all the way downhill from Mondeigo's palatial enclave- partly because of the uncontrollable wobble in its front wheel, partly on account of the failing brakes. In fact, he almost skittled a lost looking blue heeler attempting suicide by hanging about in the middle of Skypilot Drive. In more ways than one it was a total come down. Everything about Casa del Fibro had now lost its warm, inner glow- not including the radiotoxicity left under its slab floor from the debacle of sandmining.

Joe should have gone straight over to *Utopia* and had it out with Gra'eme, man to arsehole. Or at least write a letter to the *Nirvana News* outlining the bastard's deception for all Heaven to see. Perhaps even drop a few hints about the guru's sordid past in Sydney- matters relating to his disgraceful behaviour as a corporate auditor. Throwing a bit of betrayal back. Kerrist, Joe didn't even know Gra'eme's surname. Nobody did. How weird was that?

The reticent whistle blower knew he should at least confront Gra'eme and dispense with his 'services' formally and forever. Let him know that loyalty cuts both ways…(see *Pleasure Is A Two-Way Street*)

But he wouldn't, would he? Joe couldn't bear scenes like that with everyone waving their hands about and shouting. Like a character in *On Golden Sands.* No matter how necessary such anger might be, Joe bottled it up. Like everything else. He let the idea of direct confrontation slide; but decided there and then that he would never see, or have anything to do with Gra'eme ever again. Or (as with Vasuda Devi), part with any more hard won funds in his/her direction.

Why, why couldn't Joe get really pissed off with him? With Mondeigo, Da Groot, Perry Huxtable, even Brother Carol and Carmel Savage? Why this palpable failure of backbone when called upon to rail against the very people who were so clearly wearing him down? Because he'd been too *nice*, because he wanted everyone to *like* him. But that was neither feasible nor necessarily desirable. Joe had a problem with anger management alright, but it was a failure to *get* thoroughly furious when called upon to do so. Not so much containing his rage as firing it up in the first place. Amotivational Syndrome writ large. He was shakin' but he couldn't be stirred.

In the absence of real anger therefore, Joe formed a new resolve: he wasn't going to be *nice* anymore. If Da Groot or Mondeigo or any of their army of exploited casual labourers touched so much as another leaf in that rainforest they would be dead meat…

And if Gra'eme dared show his ugly dial at Joe's birthday party he could piss right off again!

JUMP CUT TO:

5.51pm, Casa del Fibro, Friday 13th March

Feeling like shit warmed up on a plate, Joe parked his bike in the shed and, as he walked towards the front door, caught sight of a letter sitting on Larry's shortened neck (where the head used to be). A birthday card! At least somebody had remembered. Onecoat Kev must've gotten the streets mixed up again and some thoughtful neighbour had obviously passed the card on- hoping Joe would do the same for their mis-directed mail.

However, it was only a photocopied letter from Perry Huxtable informing the 'active' (sic) writer's list that all episodes of *On Golden Sands* would be written from now on by an inhouse committee who'd have to live in Surface Paradox because they'd be required to turn up at the CinemaWorld studio complex every day, eight to six.

Joe scrunched up what was effectively a retrenchment notice and flung it into the compost bin. If he hadn't privately, internally, resigned this morning they would've booted him out anyway! He'd made an honourable, if invisible escape just in time. And given that *On Golden Sands* was now going to be fashioned by a gang of indentured hacks under Perry's incompetent narrative direction, then there was no hope for the show. Such a pathetic strategy would bland it out even more and drive away the diminishing audience faster than you could say 'Network Axe'. Joe was safely clear of that particular Titanic. And only just in time…

With not even eleven minutes left to squeeze in a twilight body surf before the first guests were due, Joe lit the fire under his cursed BBQ hotplate and rifled through the party food, virtually starving. As he scoffed down half a dozen cold frankfurts he switched on the fairy lights strung through the hills hoist, then went back inside and got the prawns and dips out of the fridge, chopped some garlic and opened a bottle of Chateau d'Migrainé- the cheap bubbly he'd bought for the freeloaders. It was his party and he could become severely inebriated if he wanted to. Fortunately/unfortunately there was no Barbara to hold him back…

… Although, there was still the faint hope she might put in a surprise appearance- if only to say 'good-bye'. It seemed unthinkable Barbara would leave for Israel (via several months in Sydney) without a proper farewell. Even though she had every right to be totally annoyed with him and quite justified in making a big deal out of it.

Joe returned with the cheap plonk back out to the BBQ and squatted on a milk crate to stoke the fire- his inner sanctum, this holy of holies within the temple precinct of his backyard. Playing with the flames like a naughty altar boy. All his life in the presence of fumes. Still the same basic pyromaniac. And why not? When a fire was more interesting to watch than most UStraylian television.

And while he waited for the first guests to show (headed by Ronnie Rainbows, ravenous as ever), Joe knew he had to stop this obsession with his own mortality and death generally- the feelings of gloom and despondency that seemed to have overwhelmed him today. It was too depressing, too isolating. He had to get out more. He was becoming a recluse. Barbara was right, time to re-engage with the world. Or go mad!

Should he even follow her to Israel as soon as Julie was sorted? Like Barbara always urged him to? After he'd made his grovelling apology? Joe was unencumbered by children or pets or a car that needed proper storage, or even a particularly horrendous mortgage. He could rent Casa del Fibro for a while and this would not only cash-flow his travel plans but also allow him to avoid the blitzkrieg of bulldozers that would inevitably now descend- whether it was going to be townhouses or an expensive sub-division for the exclusive few. Absolutely no one could be trusted.

The main thing was: that all important tree-line remained intact, and while it stayed unchainsawed no further damage to Heaven's last remaining coastal rainforest could take place. Joe was determined to defend those trees now more than ever- no matter what the cost or how many others he'd have to rope in. It would become a symbolic line in the sand for the whole shire. A defining battle in which the Common Good would finally triumph over vested Self Interest- despite the Property With Little Amenity Tribunal.

Gra'eme was exposed for the facile, scheming, supercilious rip-off merchant that he was. Their relationship was over and Joe could employ the considerable sums thus saved on something that might actually help him for a change. Probably Wicca Craft. Things between Joe and his ex-accountant would never be the same, ever again. Thank Gaia. Whatever devious game plan 'Mr. Big' might now resort to, the Nullumbah Shire Protection Society had at last rid itself of its one major white ant. In fact, Joe was determined to ensure that the NSPS lobbied Council to apply a full restoration order for the trees already cut down and thereby spike *Infinity Ltd's* village-destroying plans for good.

Joe almost felt happy in himself again as he stirred the fire and glanced into it. The dead wattle burning nicely. Stars were becoming visible in a sky blissfully empty of both clouds and satellites. Dare he hope? Was it conceivable (after all that had gone wrong with today) that the Curse of the BBQ hotplate- like his association with Gra'eme- was something Joe might finally be able to put behind him? The occasion of his first half-century had apparently broken the spell. After all, the hotplate had known about this party for some time and here it was, a full thirteen minutes after lighting the fire, and the moon was still shining, night birds were chirping, frogs stuttering, even the wind had dropped.

Joe relaxed, expelled a sigh and gave thanks to his guardian angel…just as the first few drops hit the hot plate- where they hissed and spluttered for a bit, before sizzling into oblivion. A moment later more clouds snuck up from the south-west without warning, followed by a huge crash of thunder as it came bucketing down. This is what the unbearable humidity of the afternoon had been all about. The fire underneath the cursed hotplate was soon reduced down to a grey, lifeless sludge. As cold and damp as a Viking hell.

Joe threw a tarp (always on hand for this sad, recurring inevitability) over the hills hoist, and improvised a sort of giant umbrella with it, which he shuffled his milk crate under. The fairy lights soon shorted and fizzled out, and the tacky paper streamers that Barbara had threaded through the Cyprus pines went all soggy as their colours bled onto the lawn.

The boil of the day's heat may have been lanced, but the timing couldn't have been worse. All the bowls of chips, nuts and biscuits spread around on other milkcrates soon became so soggy they were fit only for the compost heap- if the worms would have them (which they probably wouldn't). The raw chops and sausages for the carnivores stacked next to the BBQ, looked like nothing so much as the cold dark matter that was supposed to fill most of the universe.

Perhaps now Joe would finally accept defeat and bury the damned hotplate over the fence on Mondeigo's land- where it would hopefully blunt the blade of some hideous earthmoving machine. Alternatively, he could purchase a curse-removal from Raiina Virago that would deconstruct the terrible spell someone had placed on this infuriating slab of mild steel.

JUMP CUT TO:

6.32pm, Casa del Fibro, Friday 13th March

Joe checked the clock in the guestroom/study/library/archive and returned to his milk crate. Six thirty-ish already. Late enough for any social event in Heaven and here he sat, drenched and miserable, still the only one partying.

Where *was* everybody? He could accept that Ronnie Rainbows might be cheesed off enough not to come (despite the free food); but all Old Frank had to do was walk through the gap in their shared fibro fence. Barbara's absence was expected, and Gra'eme's positively longed for. But what of the NSPS crowd? And Helen Stongfeather?- despite Joe's embarrassingly impromptu invite.

Already today he'd been humiliated, betrayed by, and had betrayed others. He'd failed at several key moments of moral reckoning, and was now being stood up (it was becoming pretty obvious) by all of his friends and most of his neighbours. What more could go wrong, Joe wondered, just as bolt of lightning struck so close by it knocked over the plastic cat he had glued to the top of the hills hoist to stop the currawongs and magpies from fertilising the washing.

This lifeless feline- as it landed with a plop onto an expanding lake of water in the middle of the backyard- reminded Joe that, in sheltering under the hills hoist (with its metal pole and radiating wires), he was in fact, putting himself right next to a rather large lightning rod. Or possibly a cosmic radar dish that would hotwire his aura to some strange planet on the other side of the galaxy where it would be marvelled at and held as evidence of semi-intelligent life elsewhere.

So he moved back out into the torrential downpour, re-placed his milk crate next to the dead embers of the fire, and let the heavens wash away his despair.

RIPPLE DISSOLVE TO:

By half past seven-ish he'd finally abandoned all hope of anybody coming, and opened a third volume of Chateau d'Migrainé, swigging straight from the bottle. Resolved that there would be no cleansing of glasses to worry about from this 'party'(sic).

PULL FOCUS AND BLUR OUT TO:

29

EVENTUALLY NOBODY WAS ANYWHERE

Just another one of the many colourful sunsets on **HEAVEN**'s popular Purgatory Beach—a 5KM arc of pure golden sand (apart from the dog droppings) and washed by one of the best tantric bodysurfs in the world. (Swimming alone not recommended during rips or shark feeding times.)

Affix stamp here

#29 of 33 Postcards from Heaven

printed on gently mulched, plantation-grown, organic bamboo fibre using recycled greywater and bound with a biodegradable non-toxic glue

No animal or dolphin suffered in the making of this card
(apart from, of course, its author)

29
EVENTUALLY NOBODY WAS ANYWHERE
"Shit may happen, but arseholes are always involved."
(Gra'eme *An Irishman's Fear Of Vikings*)

8.03pm, Casa del Fibro, Friday 13th March

Joe stood back from the scene (metaphorically speaking, since it was becoming difficult for him to remain vertical again), and took a cold hard look at the cold hard food, along with his current circumstances- the state to which he'd sunk: squatting on a stolen milk crate, in the middle of a near cyclonic downpour, watching his backyard fill up with so much water that even his precious paper archives in the guestroom/study/library/archive were starting to go under- only serving to highlight yet again, that hardly anything lasts and therefore nothing matters. Not even this party that never happened, a birthday which didn't seem quite real, and whose actual arithmetical quantity Joe still couldn't be totally exact about. Although things were so bad now he was pretty convinced he must be 50 after all.

Nobody came. Not one of his friends. He could imagine a few of them actually forgetting (that went with the territory), and several others having second thoughts (as he would with their birthday parties). But no one? Not one of them could manage to make it? And no smoked scampi from Julie's repertoire of culinary delights? A promise made only thirteen hours earlier that was clearly about as probable as it was sincere. His own golden anniversary amounting to absolutely the lowest point of a fairly altitudinally challenged life. Joseph Michael Deegan's personal narrative gone in increasingly bizarre cycles and now spinning wildly out of control. Again.

Just when he thought it was okay to feel happy in himself here he was again- the social outcast par excellence. About as alone as he felt that time sitting next to a blind stranger in the cinema, watching the film through the man's ears, seeing him laugh at all the wrong things. If word got out about this non-event birthday humiliation Joe would even have trouble showing his face in Café Celestial for some time to come- despite his recently acquired local hero status. He'd have to lie about who actually came. It would make idle chit chat really tricky.

His mood was echoed by a long mournful cry from 'Mandi' next door, Old Frank's thoroughbred greyhound. Bred a little bit too thoroughly in fact and therefore a touch underdone in the intelligence stakes. Frank was no doubt stuck at the TAB losing this week's pension cheque. The dog's plaintive wail about the saddest sound you could hear. A fitting epitaph to a categorically unFabulous day. One which now saw Joe staring down the growing evidence of his own imminent indigence with a nonchalance only a child of the carefree fifties could understand (or want to emulate). The closure of the last day of another year of his not so great life's journey- one less in the allotted time span. And he would soon be single, probably terminally ill, destitute, and surrounded by inappropriate development. Great.

Joe knew he had to stop being so self-centred and inward looking. To stop living so much in his godamned head! He also knew that he had to forgive and forget. He would do so straight after he got really angry with Gra'eme and told the bastard just exactly what he thought of his blatant manipulation of the Nullumbah Shire Protection Society. Joe was determined to do that now. If not in the letter pages of the *Nirvana News* then certainly in public (probably at a Poet's Breakfast). And thus get rid of this great knot of revulsion and distaste that had twisted up his stomach since getting the full story from Mondeigo barely two and a half hours ago. Otherwise these feelings of bitter resentment would probably incubate the near perfect pre-conditions for some horrible bowel cancer- with which most of his mother's side seemed to have been afflicted.

Joe knew he had to forgive his parents too, for that day when they'd left him on the steps of St Patrick's junior boarding college. A bewildered seven year old suddenly abandoned to the tender mercies of big men in black frocks with hairy nostrils and smelly, nicotine stained, constantly wandering fingers.

He might even, one day, find it possible to forgive Gra'eme for the apparent environmental holocaust he had unleashed- not to mention the honey trap the bastard had set for Joe with Helen Strongfeather. Leading to that cripplingly embarrassing scene with Barbara outside *Seventh Heven*. Gra'eme had even destroyed Joe's most precious former possession: the last great love of his life.

The couldabeen minor playwright felt so good about being so pissed off at last, that he decided to open a fourth bottle of cardio protective fermented grape juice, naively hoping Barbara might forgive him too, just as he now forgave everybody else. Barbara was like that, thank Gaia.

Joe sighed and took another swig of Chateau d'Migrainé. Glad that nobody had come because it meant he could at least get to bed early. The Big 5-Oh! had been one long, humiliating, debilitating and exhausting experience- something he never wanted to see repeated in his lifetime (and it wouldn't). Getting finally horizontal just after eight o'clock in these circumstances would be no disgrace. If Barbara bothered to turn up now, as a sort of reconciliation gesture, before the train left, that's where she would find him- in the sack. Alone.

… But available of course. (Should, by an act of cosmic serendipity, Julie not be with her.)

Joe felt his head droop and his eyelids assume the weight of lead curtains. He yawned and realised he was actually too weary even to stagger back into the house, to the comfortable womb-like cocoon of his doona.

Anyway he was too filthy for that. He'd have to shower off first, or he couldn't live with himself. Certainly, he couldn't sleep with himself. Nor would Barbara…if she did turn up.

His head sank a little further and he bent forward to crouch over his cold BBQ hotplate- just to snatch a quick, micro-snooze before heading inside to a decent soak in the bath (if there was any solar hot water left after Julie's Guinness-Book-of-Records busting shower). He yawned so hard he almost dislocated his jaw and just felt so very…very tired…

Supporting his head on folded arms (like they did in grade two at St Mary's - for an afternoon nap on the desk) Joe decided to take just twenty winks, a quiet power nap on the cold hotplate…before cleaning up and heading inside…

SPIRAL ZOOM IN TO:

The Cyst On Joe's Forehead
With the sound of Joe snorning over…

SPIRAL ZOOM OUT
AND RIPPLE DISSOLVE TO:

8.30pm, Casa del Fibro, Friday 13th March
Pull back from Joe, asleep on his knees, hunched over the BBQ hotplate…

Suddenly…is he dreaming? It seems as if his whole backyard is trembling- which couldn't be an earthquake, Joe reasons. Not in the oldest, most geologically stable continent on earth…

The newly unemployed writer frowns and shambles uncertainly to his feet, head spinning. True, he has drunk more than twice his daily quota, but feels he really must be getting old if three and a half bottles of an unremarkable sparkling chardonnay could make him this unsteady on his feet. He suspects some sort of delayed exhaustion from the near drowning this morning. Or any of the many aftershocks that followed… Surely this isn't the beginning of delirium tremens? He reasons. At his age? He's only fifty years old!

However, as the ground continues to shake, Joe focuses his mind long enough to realise (to his immense relief) that the source of the trembling is actually *outside* his body. But if not an earthquake, then what?

With the downpour trailing off to a light drizzle, then a kind of early winter's mist, Joe hears a sound not unlike that of a panzer: the ominous, high-pitched shriek of metal tracks on steel rollers. He jumps up on the cold BBQ hotplate and gapes in bleak astonishment at the spectacle of a massive D9 bulldozer charging headlong into defenceless banksias and lovely drooping sheokes.

Joe can just make out the prone shapes of giant trees already pushed over- as the steel monster virtually obliterates everything in its path. A last remnant of coastal rainforest is being totally destroyed! The dozer's flashing amber light- like an evil little lighthouse- throws horrified melaleucas and brush box into stark relief. Or despair as the case may be (from the trees' point of view, the few left standing).

How could this be happening? Joe wonders. In the dead of night?! There's a Council injunction in place. Yet precious old growth is crashing down everywhere as the pitiless juggernaut simply gouges huge root balls sideways- up out of the ground. Small furry creatures, never to walk the earth again, are squished to a bloody pulp beneath its remorseless tracks. From now on this part of the Rainbow Coast would be a habitat only for mosquitos and sandflies. It was War on Nature. Mutually Assured Destruction. Enough to propel Joe Deegan, reluctant local hero and born-again greenie, into action.

As soon as he jumps over the fence Joe can see Da Groot's ugly face inside the dozer's cabin. The dim idiot had obviously run amok! It is time finally, to disarm the malicious. But with what?

Looking round quickly for something blunt and heavy, Joe grabs an old shovel used to stoke his dysfunctional BBQ and leaps over the fibro fence like a man possessed, truly angry. At last! But feeling about as optimistic as the Polish cavalry charging Hitler's panzers in 1939.

In fact his legs are wobbling so badly Joe thinks his knees might crack. Yet roused to action by some supernatural energy (and sobering remarkably), the small indignant writer strides on. Too shaken up and driven half insane by all that has happened to destroy this unhappy birthday. What should have been just another fabulous day, capped off at its conclusion by such a vicious, criminal act.

Joe yells at the thing to stop. And amazingly, it does come to a halt…slowly lurching round…until its spotlight locates the lonely protestor standing before it, and temporarily blinds him. The would-be tree hugger feels like that guy in Tienamin Square in 1988, standing before a People's Army tank with two bags of shopping. (As if he'd suddenly decided to assert his democratic rights on the way home from the stupormarket.) But instead of holding firm, Joe sinks to his ankles in some sort of quicksand- just as the bulldozer guns its motor and charges forward full throttle, straight towards him!

What follows is like the nightmare where your body's trying to escape something horrible but you're going nowhere. Except that Joe's legs aren't even pretending to move. His feverish attempts to wriggle free are just miring him further into the mud. He is rooted to the spot, and rooted, full stop. In a few seconds the dozer's enormous blade will plunge straight through him (about torso level) and Joseph Michael Deegan will be sliced neatly in half, then ground into compost. A sackfull of blood and bone to sprinkle on the future gardens of *Dreamtime Beach Estate*. Is it courage, stupidity or simple physical paralysis that keeps him there?

At least the ooze rising around him stops his knees from wobbling. If this grotesque machine doesn't kill him in the next few seconds Joe feels pretty sure he'll drown in the quagmire anyway. With nothing left to lose, and in a sort of penultimate defiance he screams out:

"You're a criminal environmental vandal, Da Groot, you knuckle-headed nazi, and you're going to gaol!"- anger management no longer a problem.

But the steel giant just keeps on coming- like a bull charging its tiny matador. The fucking bastard is actually going to run straight over him…!

At the last second, Joe somehow manages to shuck his feet from the slime and hurl himself out of the way- just as the beast trundles past, carried forward by its own unstoppable momentum, shrieking tracks missing Joe's feet by inches- crashing into more trees and knocking them over like pins in a bowling alley. Striking out. A blind giant dancing.

Joe is so furious now that he picks up his shovel and, abandoning all common sense, begins to chase after the thing, eventually leaping up onto the narrow platform beside the cabin door. There is hardly enough time to enjoy the shock on Da Groot's face as he tries to lock himself in, because the dozer suddenly lurches wildly up on one side as its left track strikes a huge root ball- tipping the machine sideways and knocking its driver off balance.

Seizing the moment, Joe smashes his way into the cabin with the shovel and plunges straight for Da Groot's throat in a fit of homicidal rage so uncharacteristic of any Piscean. Reeling back, and caught off guard, the dim moron struggles for a moment, but eventually slips to the floor. Joe goes down on top of him, holding on to developers' red neck, easily avoiding his hands as they lash out in a futile attempt to break free. The ecovandal's thin, tarantula like fingers claw fresh air and finally stiffen.

Amazingly, Joe has clamped on with a viciousness and energy that surprises both of them. (Until one realises that strong fingers from decades of typing are the only physical asset a failed writer has.)

All Joe can think of doing with it right now is squeezing hard and shouting: "You're going to die you fucking fascist nutcase!"- shaking Da Groot's dense head so furiously that it lolls about on his shoulders like a deranged, lank haired teddy bear. Then bangs into the accelerator pedal before dropping even more unconscious than usual, onto the floor. One arm flays out to the side, knocking a gear stick and sending the enviro-panzer into reverse- away from the rainforest and directly, at speed, up towards Old Frank's house!

Joe struggles to his feet, stumbling over Da Groot's lifeless legs. It's a cabin built for one with no room to manoeuvre. The People's Hero is shocked to think he might have seriously injured someone; but is even more preoccupied by the fact that he's now fairly drunk and in charge of a vast, destructive machine he knows nothing about- one which doesn't even seem to have a steering wheel!

Yet it's still moving. Fast. Less than fifty metres from Old Frank's …

Just to be sure, Joe gives Da Groot's limp head a whack with the shovel and, satisfied with the hollow ringing sound, turns to take stock of the 'situation'. It doesn't look terribly promising. He desperately searches for a key or switch that might shut the thing down. But on failing to find one, begins- not unreasonably- to panic. A condition in which the worst aspects of his dyslexia always kick in- just as the dozer is about to slam through Old Frank's back fence…

Nothing on the dashboard looks remotely like a car. Joe pulls a lever and the cabin swings wildly in a sickening, 360 degree spin- worse even than the Gravitron Ride at Luna Park. But with the same effect: causing Joe to review (in the abstract so to speak) most of the recently consumed cold frankfurts (decomposed in cheap plonk) as they unload onto the unfortunate (though fortunately still unconscious) developer beneath him. Joe hardly has time to enjoy the relief and satisfaction this brings because his hand/eye co-ordination is disintegrating at a moment when he most needs it; and at a rate faster than shares in a genetically modified seed company.

He tugs another lever with all his might and endures the same disorienting turn (in the opposite direction)- only this time it swings the cabin door open and Da Groot's comatose body is flung straight out into the dark. Joe is grateful for the extra room (both internally and externally). But to do what?

He pulls a third lever and the dozer's giant blade goes straight up over the cabin- in imitation of an over enthusiastic St.Kilda cheerleader with pom poms. This is hopeless! Joe yanks at another lever and one track freezes…so that finally, the dreadful beast turns away from Old Frank's house…but towards Joe's! At which point the giant blade drops down again, just in time to crash through Casa del Fibro's corrugated fence, exploding asbestos dust everywhere and knocking aside the brick BBQ like a stack of puny leggo blocks.

In one final effort Joe wraps his arms around all the levers he can mange and pulls hard, hoping to stall the thing somehow, perhaps conk its engine out. But this merely causes the machine to lurch wildly one way, then another- completely wrecking the back wall of his house- before moving on to demolish the guestroom/study/library/archive with all its precious manuscripts, photos, tapes, films and books. Virtually destroying everything Joe has produced or valued- apart from his fast vanishing relationship with Barbara (which was probably effectively terminated hours ago anyway).

The steel beast now seems to have a mind of its own (one in sore need of Personality Realignment). But the task of controlling it is simply, congenitally, beyond Joe. The dozer surges disobediently through Casa del Fibro's thin bedroom wall (the one that has ruined the writer's sex life whenever guests were present)- smashing its way towards the middle of the tiny living/dining room- taking most of the roof off as it goes.

Wardrobes, shelves, sinks, chairs, crockery and light fittings spark and crash onto the concrete slab as clothes, television, video, stereo, fridge and furniture are blasted about and pulverised beneath those relentless, unstoppable, squealing tracks. Cupboards pop off walls while plates and glasses crash to the floor. The toilet is sheared off its pedestal and sends up a geyser-like fountain of backed up raw sewerage. (Heaven's case of global constipation temporarily relieved.) The stove slides sideways, pulling itself free from the last remaining internal wall and immediately flays thick electrical cables out across the gathering puddles of muddy toilet water, short-circuiting themselves as they snake and spark this way and that.

Joe's tears of rage and helplessness inside the cabin fail to save every scrap of paper he'd ever owned or written upon (including the overdue notice for the house insurance)- going as far back as some early school essays and mediocre one-act plays. Precious negatives and browny/grey videotape spools out of broken cassettes. Computer disks, and tapes of workshops, and the video record of Joe's 100-odd episodes of TV drama, all disappear somewhere between the cruel tracks of the dozer and the house's intractable concrete slab. Crushed to a millimetre thick ooze. Pulp fiction at last and literally.

The dozer's blade swings wildly up and down in a final, all conquering death-spasm, effectively slicing off Casa del Fibro's fuse board. And apart from giving Joe a pretty nasty electric shock inside the cabin, this also causes more wires to spark around the small tin of fuel for the whipper-snipper that he had neglected to put back inside the front shed two days ago. It promptly explodes and spurts a blazing torrent of napalm all over the scattered and pulverised, archive/library. (The books that have nurtured him, the photographs a snapshot biography of a life that is still unfolding- albeit not for very long). And, whatever hasn't been crushed or drenched, flares up into the long predicted bonfire of the inanities. Joe's fatal clumsiness finally striking in devastating fashion.

The last thing he remembers seeing is the dozer (itself now in flames) as it lurches out through the inferno carrying Casa del Fibro's blazing front wall with it, before trundling on towards Redemption Road- shrieking to a halt just inches from Larry's headless body. Along the way a hook on the side of the dozer has somehow latched itself onto Otto, and (in a lovely touch), drags the wheely bin back out to the edge of the footpath. Where Joe had failed to place it that very morning. Here, as the 'Magick Happens' sticker posted onto Otto's left side slowly blisters in the heat and melts into the bin's thick, toxic plastic body, Joe's house and everything else he has owned, accomplished or treasured, burns to a crisp in the general holocaust.

But at least the rubbish had been put out. Albeit fourteen hours late (or six days early).

The couldabeen minor playwright somehow manages to clamber out of the flaming cabin of the big D9 just before the fire reaches the dozer's fuel tank. He staggers away from the ensuing explosion and sinks to his knees on the footpath overcome by an uncontrollable sobbing. This in turn fetches up a certain breathlessness followed by a crushing pain in his chest which seems to travel down his left arm. When it suddenly occurs to Joe that he has failed to pay the home and contents insurance on time, he merely rests his head on the cool grass beside the gutter and proceeds to have a pretty serious (and long overdue) myocardial infarct. Literally pouring his heart out. There on the street where he used to live...

THERE'S NOTHING TO BE AFRAID OF
THAT CAN'T BE UNDERSTOOD

The Santa of Saint Street. Just another one of the many colourful buskers, tarot readers, spruikers and didgeridoo players clogging the streets of HEAVEN USTraylia—where every day is Xmas Day and even gratuitous charity is nothing to get terribly worried about.

Affix stamp here

#30 of 33 Postcards from Heaven

printed on gently mulched, plantation-grown, organic bamboo fibre using recycled greywater and bound with a biodegradable non-toxic glue

No animal or dolphin suffered in the making of this card
(apart from, of course, its author)

THERE'S NOTHING
TO BE AFRAID OF
THAT CAN'T BE UNDERSTOOD

"Prophecy is simple. You only have to look at the facts now-
because the present always contains what will follow."
(Gra'eme *Everything You Need To Know You've Already Been Told*)

9.02pm, Travelling Ambulance, Friday 13th March (to the sound of a siren wailing)

In the delirium that overtakes Joe after everything he possesses has been destroyed and the walls of both his house and part of his heart have collapsed, he 'imagines' he has the following conversation with Barbara…

'Imagines' because the heart has a memory too, so that when part of it dies (as in a heart 'attack') then something is forgotten. Some passion or emotion erased. This was blindingly clear from the moment Joe's cardio vascular system first got smashed by the great, wrenching, rabbit chop of seeing Kate die. In consequence of which a lot of his desire to go on was effectively extinguished- the trigger for that complex syndrome of inertia called, somewhat inadequately, his mid-life crisis. Because once again, and not for the first or last time, he's forgotten what he's supposed to be doing, why he's here, and what it's all about…

What Joe *does* recall of the rest of that near fatal, 50th birthday is: lying on his back, staring up at a shimmering, pearly white ceiling. It could have been the roof of an ambulance, or an intensive care ward somewhere- it might even be the view from a gurney as he's about to be admitted to All Hallows hospital. Or some ante room attached to the gates of 'Heaven' proper, perhaps? Proving Gra'eme wrong. Again.

Either way, Barbara is standing or sitting beside him. She looks tired and a little bit uninterested. For once, her batteries are flat, the fabulous energy missing. It unnerves him to see her so drained. First Julie and Joe in the surf, then Julie, then Joe and Helen, now Joe again…

She is saying: "Unless you change I'm leaving you."

"Barbara, you're leaving anyway."

Ignoring that cheap shot, she continues: "I can't be with you when we have meals, anymore, Joe. It's too stressful to watch the over-eating."

"Then…if we can't eat, and we can't sleep together…what's left?"

Slight pause.

"Do we even have a relationship?"

She doesn't contradict the negative implications of his question.

Even though he wasn't really asking. And didn't require an answer.

PULL FOCUS AND BLUR OUT TO:

9.11pm, All Hallows Hospital, Friday 13th March

Joe remains on a gurney, waiting in the corridor to be admitted to Heaven's chronically underfunded rural hospital. His heart running out on him in more ways than one.

Yet Barbara remains beside him. She is saying: "You don't respect me as a woman."

"That's not true."

"You don't, Joe."

She fiddles with something. Looking down again, like she did in Café Celestial around lunchtime- the car keys maybe, or her train ticket out of here. Wondering about the ties that bind, the lies that undermine. She addresses mainly the floor. Weary beyond caring:

"Your attitude to women is fucked, Joe, You know that. It's like you're still at boarding school. And I'm just your 'mate' aren't I? Someone to pass the time with…"

"Barbara, the question's academic. I'm dying here."- Joe, as always, bringing it back to his own selfish point of view.

He feels intense pain. Not unlike all his worst hangovers revisiting en masse. Trashing his neurones like out-of-town revellers on New Years Eve. In fact, Joe isn't actually, technically dying quite yet, because the emergency shot of Glyceryl Trinitrate that Dr. Beanland has just given him finally loosens the vice in his chest. But the price of *that* is a crushing headache from the blood vessels now expanding inside his brain. The ones similarly expanding around his heart are what is keeping him alive. The downside is that this now gives him a false, and fairly dangerous sense of security about things generally.

"I need to give my life a structure, Joe. I need to *do something.* Otherwise what's it all about?" Then rounding on him like an afterthought, "You ?"

It doesn't sound like a lot.

"Twice a year I schlep halfway round the world to come back here. And for what?"

"Okay, there's a problem, Barbara. I'm sorry. You want to live in Jerusalem, I can't leave Heaven.'

"Our relationship is over, Joe."

"It's just going through a rough patch." He's lifting his shoulders, acting nonchalant, behaving Jewishly again.

"Bullshit. I'm leaving you."

"No you're not, you're just going away for a very long time. Like you always do."

"This time I'm not coming back."

BLUR OUT AND RIPPLE DISSOLVE TO:

9.20 pm, All Hallows Hospital, Friday 13th March

Joe surveys the world from the cage of a bed with stainless steel railings all around it like a baby's cot (or a small, mobile prison). He realises he must have been unconscious when they wheeled him in here and notices a local clock on the wall opposite that seems to suggest it might probably be around about some time in the vicinity of the post 9 pm part of the evening. Chemicals dissolved in clear fluid drip into one arm via a big needle with plastic taps and tubes attached. It looks like a small, alien spaceship has landed on his left wrist- probably the one Alistair and his UFO Committee have been expecting. Only much smaller and sneakier than anyone could have predicted. Amazingly, Barbara is still there. It seems like a good opportunity for Joe to set the record straight.

"Barbara, I do understand you- as a woman. Your need for a child. It's just that…we tried IVF and it didn't work. Now it's too late. We're too old and I'm too cranky and selfish. I mean geezus, the whole of today's been…just about…absolutely the worst day of my life." Joe is hovering on the verge of tears. Again. "Fifty years old, and nobody even bothered to come to my party."

"Oh, no. Everyone came." She doesn't contradict the fifty bit.

"Barbara, I lit the BBQ, I drank half a bottle of cheap champagne," he lies shamelessly. "It started to rain. *Nobody* came. Not even Ronnie Rainbows and he never misses a free meal. I may have had a heart attack, but I haven't lost my marbles."

Barbara looks at him like he's really slow. Which he is. "I'm talking about the surprise party Gra'eme bankrolled for you at Shangri La La Land."

"Surprise party?"

"Everyone was sick to death of your boring old, stock standard BBQs. I'm sorry Joe, but it always rains, and it's always so…uneventful. Gra'eme decided we'd let you pretend to stage one, then I'd come back with Julie, discover no one had turned up, commiserate with you, and suggest a quiet, farewell dinner for three at St. Peter's Pizza. Then we'd pop into La La Land for a nightcap before the train- where everyone would be waiting, holding balloons and singing old Pink Floyd numbers."

Joe is genuinely gob stopped. He'd been writing about the condition long enough as a soapie hack, now he really understood what it felt like. Gra'eme honouring Joe's love of Pink Floyd was a stunning touch. And it was generous of the accomplished tax dodger to pay for it all. Although this wouldn't soften Joe's new anti-Gra'eme crusade one bit. Besides, there is a larger problem to worry about:

"So…what you're saying is…my birthday party went ahead without me?"

Barbara shrugs a 'so what' to that.

"Because you didn't come home!?" For the second time that day Joe is experiencing real anger. And it feels good but depressing.

And if Barbara holds any guilt about any of this she's hiding it well.

"I was really pissed off with you, Joe. You could've at least had the decency to wait until I'd left."

He doesn't want to go into all that right now- fixated as he is on the party he's just missed.

"Who came?"

"*Le tout* Heaven was there."

Joe is dangerously elated. "Everyone? Even the 'A list'?"

"Freeloading as usual. They all had a great time."

"What- the glass blowers? potters? poseurs? pulp novelists?

Barbara sighs. "Architects, jewellers, restaurateurs, seachangers- both the wannabes, the has-beens and will-never-bes. Most of the Protection Society, my yogalates class, your dentist, the choir, Old Frank, Dr. Beanland…"

"And you never told me!"

Joe was reeling. He didn't know whether to laugh or cry. It was difficult, and possibly not a good idea to mange both at the same time. While Barbara declines to feel any guilt about any of this.

"And nobody even asked where I was?" he demands.

"Not really."

"Who did they sing happy birthday to?"

"I think we sort of forgot. You know how it is- the rumour mongering and exchange of local gossip just sort of takes over when that mob gets together. In any case, the 'A list' are only ever interested in the party itself and the consumables provided. Who or what it's for is totally irrelevant."

"Where are my presents?"

Barbara looks blank, unsure if there were any. Then remembers: "Gra'eme bought you a dozen pretty drinkable Hunter River chardonnays. They lasted about ten minutes. Sorry, I meant to save you one, but the poseurs just surrounded the bar table and froze everyone out till it was all gone."

Joe was hardly going to be impressed by anything Gra'eme did, ever again.

"Oh great. No one even asked where I was? No one *cared*?" he challenges egocentrically.

"I said you were sick. Which, as it turns out, was more spectacularly spot-on than I could've imagined. Anyway, when they did finally remember what they were supposed to be celebrating, people then had too much fun slagging you off. Virtually everyone had a humiliating story to tell: about one of your many hopeless moments or cringingly embarrassing faux pas. Your party was a big hit. In fact, people were still running you down when Dr. Beanland got the emergency call from Sister Carmody."

"So I finally make it onto Heaven's 'A list'- just as I'm about to die !" he whinges.

"Forgoodness sake Joe! They'll put a stent in and you'll be fine. It's a simple angiogram. You don't even need an anaesthetic. It's all done via a small hole in your groin while you're awake on the operating table. There's only a 21.3% chance it will block up again and cause a secondary (usually fatal) heart attack. They'll probably even kick you out of here in a couple of days."

"Then who'll look after me?" He had to try, even if it was a lost cause.

"I'm sure one of your many female admirers will be delighted to empty the bedpan and bleach the sheets."

"Barbara, Helen Strongfeather is just a friend okay? What I feel for her…is a mature, yet caring, if not actually physically loving friendship. Loving…in a certain friendly, sharing, caring, adult sort of way…"

There are far too many 'lovings', 'carings' and 'sharings' in all of that for Barbara.

"It *is* possible for a man and a woman to have a friendship, Barbara. A truly platonic thing. It doesn't have to be about sex. It doesn't have to be anything that comes between what *we* have," he insists, blindly and without admissible proof. Certainly nothing that would stand up in the Marriage Breakdown Court.

"We *can* love more than one person. You know that, Barbara. I'm not jealous of all your many girlfriends."

Why couldn't he just say it in plain English? She is the only thing that matters in his whole life (especially now that virtually everything else has been eliminated, and the thing itself was running out on him- prematurely and without warning).

But this conversation is going nowhere and neither is Barbara, she realises, as she risks another glance at her watch. Julie is waiting outside. On the same bench Barbara and Joe sat on while they waited for Julie earlier. And on which Barbara had waited for Joe until Sister Carmody let her in to All Hallows' single bed intensive care ward. For some absurd reason Joe now wants to hurt his most significant other.

"You'd better go. You'll miss your good deed for the day."- dismissing her, wanting to appear unaffected, playing the martyr. It was a pathetic gesture. And he knew it. And Barbara knew it. And he knew she knew he knew she knew it.

Fercrissake, why couldn't he be more generous? He reasons with himself. He's in no position to bargain for Barbara's affections. Or anybody else's right now. This was selfishness's end game. Where putting yourself first always got you: alone and without friends.

She is searching for the best exit line. A simple, old 'good-bye, Joe' seems a touch callous, even melodramatic in the circumstances.

"St Barbara of Jerusalem. Helping her best friend in need." He taunts, one last time.

"I'm leaving you Joe, get used to it."

"But who'll nag me about my weight? All my addictions? The fact that I don't exercise enough. That I don't go anywhere... I'll have no pain or humiliation to look forward to."

If this is meant to be a joke it falls flat on its face, picks itself up off the floor, and promptly falls over again.

"The way you're going that may not be such a terribly long time." She points out accurately.

Joe can't help smiling. Barbara always seems to find the funny/tragic/stupid/funny side. That's what he loves about her. He seizes the strategic moment now opening up before them and fires off his best salvo:

"You're leaving because you're afraid of this relationship."

She rolls her eyes. "Not afraid Joe, just tired."

"But Barbara, you want me to stop this and give up that, and accept the fact that you want a child. But when I ask *you* to do something for *me*- something I really want, you won't give an inch."

"To do what !?"

"To stay! And *not* go back to Jerusalem!"

Barbara finally explodes, letting all her pent up frustration and disappointment with him volcano out: "I'm talking about your survival!"

"And I'm talking about yours! Israel is bad for you."

"You can't use that argument."

"You could be killed over there just waiting for the bus, or having a coffee."

"You can be killed anywhere, anytime, Joe. Look at this morning- here on your precious Purgatory beach!"

Joe senses, for the first time, that she is floundering a little. Not just because she has stooped to criticise his passion for body surfing. (He hasn't even touched on her obsession with tango yet.)

"You're just shifting the goal posts," he claims.

"It's not the same argument," she repeats. Running out of them herself.

"Yes it is. You just don't like it because it's one you can't win. What's more, you're afraid of commitment, Barbara. That's why you have to go traipsing off all the time. You can't settle down anywhere because you're too deeply afraid of having to stick something out for a change. To *stay* and see it through. That's your biggest problem. You have no staying power. You always cut and run."

"Look! Look at you!" She spits back. "Look where you've finally ended up as a result of your *beautiful* lifestyle!"

She is really annoyed with him now. As she has every right so to be.

"You think I like being negative all the time? Trying to get you to do something that might actually *save* you for a change?!"

He guesses the answer is probably 'No'. And it's precisely at this point that Joe's brain takes a peek at the great sump of unconsciousness pressing in from all sides and decides to dip a toe in as…

…the fluoros above him produce a certain white-out effect, not unlike snowblindness….

BLEACH OUT TO:

9.22 pm, All Hallows Hospital, Friday 13th March

Two minutes later colours slowly return to the field of Joe's vision as familiar shapes reassert themselves and he finds his troubled chest at the end of Dr. Beanland's equally troubled stethoscope. The good doctor, Joe's main hope, is not looking terribly sure about what it is he's come to measure or determine. Alas, Dr. Beanland is, if anything, even more groggy and out of it than his patient. Because, apart from a two hour, half-dozen-units-of-chardonnay interlude at Joe's surprise! birthday party, this is the good doctor's 29th straight hour on casualty shift, and he knows he won't be getting home to his small tax-deductible farm outside Nullumbah much before lunch time tomorrow…

After only a brief exhaustion blackout, Dr. Beanland remembers to tell Joe that he's now on the list for an angioplasty- an operation that will balloon his blocked artery open and keep it that way thanks to the insertion of a small mesh cylinder called a 'stent'. Just when this life saving procedure will take place however, largely depends on the Rainbow Coast's only cardiologist getting back from his ski-ing holiday in Davos. The good news is that the artery expanding drugs will probably keep Joe alive until this happens. Unless another airline goes bust, or the cardio decides to continue on from Switzerland to the heart cloning conference in Acapulco.

Joe has a thousand and one questions to ask. Like: are stents safe? What if they rusted? Did they set off metal detectors at airports? And why *do* women with prominent noses always have such beautiful legs? But unfortunately, Dr. Beanland missed that anatomy lecture in third year, and staggers off to tend the burns of a fire stick twirler who had just ignited his vinyl waistcoat in Arcadia Park.

So the questions aren't asked, and the answers weren't given. And if the truth be known Dr. Beanland is beyond understanding them, let alone offering a coherent professional opinion. In fact, anything medically responsible from him will not be possible until he sleeps at least sixteen hours. Just when this might happen remains undetermined.

Inevitably, the valium that now kicks in on top of the aspirin, blood thinners and nitrates, combines to produce a certain, laissez-faire euphoria in Joe. Beautiful Day back on track…

Until suddenly…

…the walls, the ceiling, the clock, the railings on his cot- all go a bit blurry…

PULL FOCUS ON:

The Subcutaneous Cyst In The Middle Of Joe's Forehead

…as he slowly woozes in and out of consciousness…then

SHARPEN FOCUS AND ZOOM OUT TO:

9.29 pm, All Hallows Hospital, Friday 13th March

Amazingly, generously, Barbara is still there in close up. Arms folded. Shot from below with a commanding backlight. Lending her presence an awesome authority.

And again she is glancing at her watch. It could have been seven minutes, or an hour later. Maybe both. Because the clock on the wall is a clock set in Heaven and only as reliable as the many other colourfully unreliable clocks in town.

He is saying: "Barbara…"

But she cuts across him with: "Joe…you listen, but you do not hear. I'm leaving you. Okay? *Besseder*? You need help. You need professional help. And I can't give it to you. You've become downwardly mobile. It's called 'Amotivational Syndrome'. Mainly caused by dope. You have no 'umph' anymore. You lack direction, goals, pizzazz. What can I say? You *need* Personality Realignment Counselling. At least get a palm reading and a detox programme from Raiina Virago. Tell her your addictions are killing you."

"My only addiction is you."

But Barbara has no more time for this nonsense. She unfolds her arms and even frowns a little as he starts to lose consciousness a third or fourth time…

All he can manage to add is: "Barbara, I *refuse* to believe our feelings for each other are just the outcome of some biochemical reaction…"

…before falling once again into a delirium within a dream where he asks himself the question: if he does die now what *has* it all been about?

Him and Barbara? The fact that opposites attract?

That much is certain. Barbara loves life and embraces it with gusto. What got Joe's heart pumping (while it still worked properly) was a rainbow-clad sunset, or a pod of dolphins skylarking beside him in the surf. He stands back and watches from the sidelines, waiting. Like we all wait. Except people like Barbara. Who bungy jumped into life- abseiling and base jumping from one new experience to another.

What Joe wants to believe is: that this crisis in their relationship will force a new maturity, a bold reassessment of their value to each other and out of that will come a different understanding. A tolerance of each other and each other's faults (well, his faults, Barbara not having many)- that might, in itself, be quite charming. He would ask- no, beg- her forgiveness. Because, when the chips are down, you've got to believe (like she did, like Gra'eme did) that everybody is basically a good person. Not because we're created in some divine image, or because people are innately altruistic and generous. But because Gra'eme, the bastard, was also right when he said it was simply easier and less complicated if we don't go round killing, maiming and plundering each other. (If only he'd listened to his own advice.)

Because everyone *is* potentially noble and in control. We may all fall prey to some impossible dream, a yearning for something that never quite comes- like an honest politician, or the next public holiday. But who gets public holidays anymore? Public servants? Were there even any of *them* left, in an age of economic_irrationalism.com?

…Still, the yearning in itself is strangely touching. Especially for hopeless romantics like Joe. Love encourages desire, making people cautious and available. And of course, doomed to disappointment. Because in Jerusalem- or Heaven, or in any other holy city- there *is* no Messiah coming. It's as inevitable as it's disappointing and a little bit sad, but true. And as far as failing to solve the world's problems goes, we only ever have ourselves to blame…

When Joe notices Barbara again, remarkably, she's still there, and she's saying:

"We've been absent from each other, Joe. We lack…happiness."

This is not what he wants to hear right now, probably not what she really wanted to say, and deep down they both hope she doesn't mean it.

**BLUR FOCUS AND
RIPPLE DISSOLVE BACK TO:**

9.02pm, Travelling Ambulance, Friday 13th March (siren wailing)

Twenty seven minutes earlier. Night time in down town Heaven.

Streets are blurring past outside the window of some speeding vehicle. All Joe can see is a smudge of neon lights and the usual merry throng of bakpakahs and bar maids, tourists and tossers, ponces and peaceniks, greenies and groupies, hasbeens and wannabes- all the dense cultural mix of locals and interlopers from all over the world. Promenading up and down Angel Avenue, swamping Heaven's fragile sense of itself as a viable community and drowning the town under a tidal wave of short-term visitors. There's music and laughter and, inevitably, a great deal of fairly mind numbing (but spiritually liberating) percussion going on…

**PULL BACK AND
WIDEN TO DISCOVER:**

Barbara

She is in the vehicle beside him, and she is saying: "We're too out of sync with each other, Joe. We basically want different things."

"Opposites attract," he speculates- hoping anyway.

"Only if they're sub-atomic particles," she rejoinders cleverly.

Then relents a little with: "You never *go* anywhere, Joe. You potter around your little backyard as if it's the centre of the frigging world."

He throws his hands up in a gesture of surrender. "All right already! I'll come back with you to Israel. Losing everything I own just now has been the WAKE UP! call I needed. Finally. At last! I'm ready to travel."

"You *are* travelling…to hospital. This is an ambulance and it's saving your life."

There was a SIREN somewhere…

But is it an emergency in Heaven, or just another atrocity in Jeru-shalom?

RIPPLE DISSOLVE FORWARD TO:

9.20 pm, All Hallows Hospital, Friday 13th March

Joe WAKES UP! in a gurney in some hospital somewhere and is glad to see Barbara still there (side on from the horizontal). Like the guardian angel that she is. Yet his lover remains pale and washed-out looking. Her worst fears realised: the lifestyle induced heart attack she's constantly nagged him about and railed against, and even tried to rescue him from. He is woozy and he's losing both her and 'it' generally.

"Where have you been, Joe?" she seems to be asking from a long, long, way away.

It's a strange question, but like Mondeigo earlier (faced with why he had saved a complete stranger), Joe thinks about it and tries to answer honestly:

"Kate and I came to Heaven seeking the miracle cure. We didn't find it. But I stayed and now it's nearly finished me off too. I should have escaped as soon as I felt well again. Like you're supposed to. But why can't I ever feel like I'm properly cured? I just don't seem to be able to shake off this interminable depression."

"Precisely my point: you're *pretending* to be sick, so you can stay here. This mid-life nonsense is just an excuse. You know if you got better you'd *have* to move on. That's why you don't."

"Whatever doesn't kill you generally makes you stronger."

"I'd like to get a cardiologist's second opinion on that."

Joe appreciates her attempt at gallows humour. (On his behalf.) But she isn't smiling. Instead she is saying: "Your quest for the perfect day, Joe, is like a little stab at paradise, isn't it? A search for some sort of accidental utopia. A pining after heaven on earth- literally. Only, you see, it's not possible, mate. Not here on the Rainbow Coast or anywhere else you can find. You can't *have* the ideal in the real. By definition the two things are mutually exclusive."

"Barbara, all I know is: what you and I have got together, is so much better than what we have apart."

But she's already shaking her head. The contents of the plastic bag connected to the back of his left hand are running out on him, and so is Barbara. In fact Joe felt so low right now that he wanted to leave himself too. And possibly never come back. If only it was that simple. Or possible.

"People come to Heaven thinking they're escaping the pollution, stress and pointlessness of the city," she explains. "Hoping they'll find a solution to the emptiness that bottom-lines all our lives. Hoping to escape the daily humdrum that makes half the population want to commit slow suicide by smoking, or using mobile phones, or eating fast food. But in coming to the Rainbow Coast, Joe, they only seek an external solution to what is essentially an *internal* problem. And a few months, or a few years down the track the gloss wears off and the scales finally drop, and suddenly they realise they're in a pretty ordinary, rather small country town that's become a dreaded 'development opportunity'. With the added disadvantage of thousands of tourists clogging every queue and car park in sight. If they tried Personality Realignment they would *see* that the only thing which really matters lies in the *connections* between people. That's the clue to what drives any *real* community: being selfless and caring, and finding love *through* trust and friendship. Only by putting yourself out for other people does anyone achieve any sort of real happiness. So you've got to change, Joe, or it's over. But you can't can you? You can't let go of any of your far too many comfort zones."

He has to admit she had a point.

**BLUR FOCUS AND
WHITE OUT TO:**

9.29 pm, All Hallows Hospital, Friday 13th March

When Joe wakes and looks up again, he finds that the ceiling is moving. Or is he moving under it? He seems to be on some kind of trolley or conveyor belt rolling through the corridors of Nullumbah's tiny, inadequately funded, single storey hospital. The single story being Joe. And if there had been 6 million narratives in the *Naked City* this isn't one of them.

Barbara is walking beside the gurney. She is saying finally:

"I'm glad you had this heart attack because now you'll *have* to change, Joe. Otherwise it won't be a slow, it'll be a fast suicide. And either way, I won't be there to worry about it. Do you want to live? Then get healthy, stop smoking and lose weight. Start now!"

And he knows, as always, that Barbara is pretty well totally, incontrovertibly correct in all particulars. But Gra'eme had been right too. And now was definitely wrong. And if his accountant/guru could be fallible and was no longer to be trusted, could Barbara be wide of the mark also?

It is getting complicated. Again.

"There's nothing to be afraid of that can't be understood," is the last thing he remembers her saying.

All he can respond with is: "That's what Madame Curie said. And look what happened to her…"

BLUR OUT TO:

31

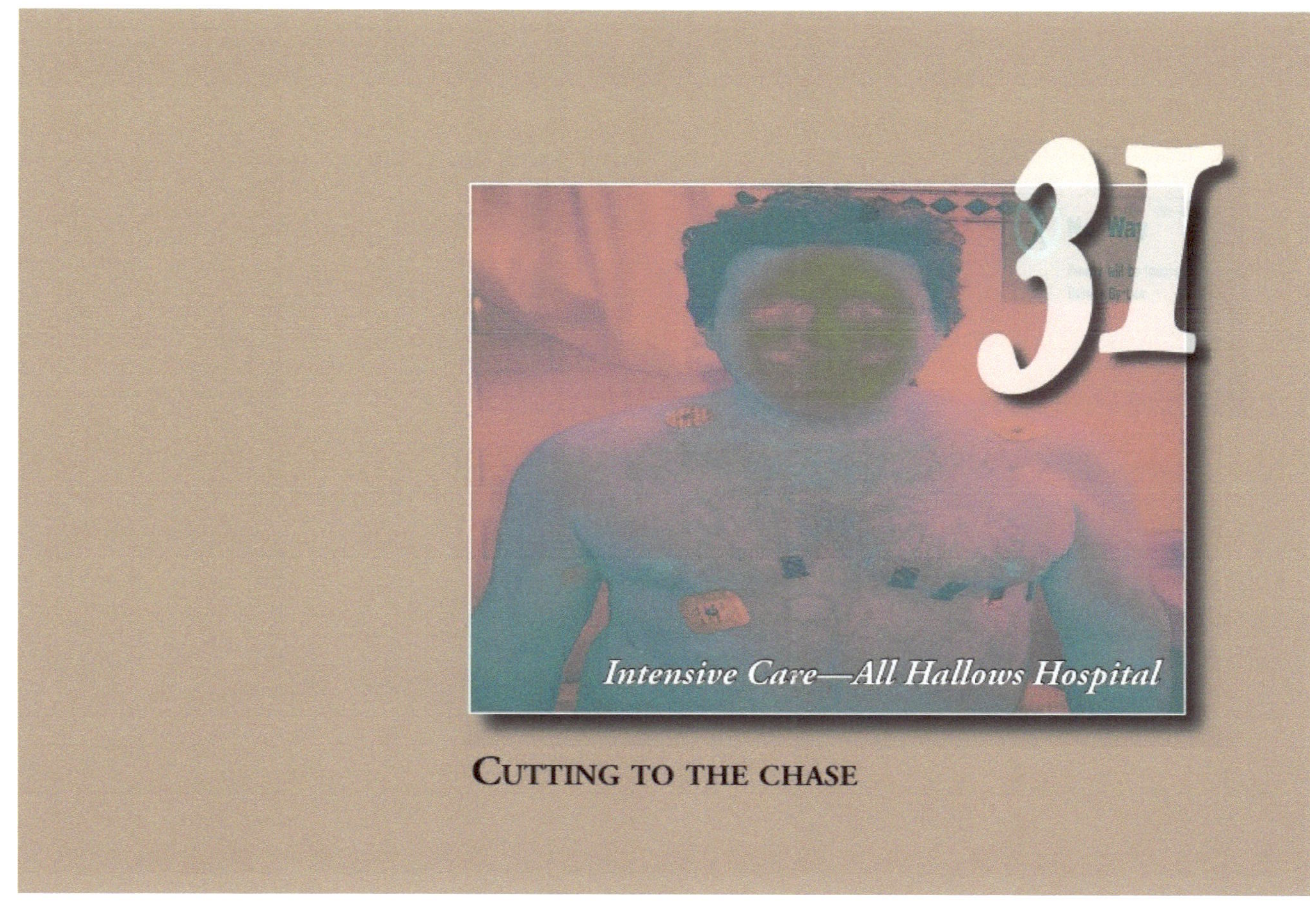

Intensive Care—All Hallows Hospital

CUTTING TO THE CHASE

Just another colourful but tragic outcome of the traditional
Western diet and lifestyle. Something easily remedied in
HEAVEN Ustraylia, with its organic water supply, pure salad
vegetables, fresh air and the combined healing energy of 238
unique local therapies developed with great skill over many
years by approximately half the population.

#31 of 33 Postcards from Heaven

printed on gently mulched, plantation-grown, organic bamboo fibre using
recycled greywater and bound with a biodegradable non-toxic glue

No animal or dolphin suffered in the making of this card
(apart from, of course, its author)

31
CUTTING TO THE CHASE

"Time and space have always been variable.
Look at the amount of sand on Purgatory Beach.
Hear the clock ticking in its lighthouse."
(Gra'eme *Laziness For Beginners*)

9.38 pm, All Hallows Hospital, Friday 13th March

Joe wakes UP! in a bed with rails along the sides like a metal cot (or small mobile prison), only to find all these wires connected to patches on his chest and fanning out, octopus-like, towards a machine that emits very strange sounds. The condition of his heart is playing on a monitor suspended from the ceiling. Every beat has a shape, and tells a story far more compelling for the ex-TV hack right now than any soap opera he could ever hope to scribble.

He peers attentively at the screen as if his life depends on it (which it does). Searching for any defect in the pattern, any telltale sign of ischaemic damage (which there is). But could it be described as a heart attack? Or just an attack of the heart?- watching his home and all his possessions reduced to a smouldering wreck. Knowing Barbara was leaving him forever- either of which would have been sufficient to bring on a fatal episode.

Joe lifts his head off a pillow virtually as uncomfortable as the one he provides for Barbara's house guests, and looks around. The hospital is deathly quiet. An unfortunate way for it to be he thinks, given his personal circumstances. He appears to be the only customer in All Hallows' only Intensive Care Ward, and he feels surprisingly well. Apart from the fact that some idiot is nailing roofing screws to the inside of his skull. Which Joe mistakenly ascribes to the inevitable hangover from too much bad wine and too little good food. This headache however, can still be sourced back to the large dose of Glyceryl Trinitrate injected into his arteries (ravaged through half a century of bad eating and not enough exercise) twenty nine minutes ago by a close to comatose Dr. Beanland.

Has Barbara already been there and left? He wonders. Or has he only dreamed she'd come?

Because now that Joe thinks about it, there *must've* been a conversation with Barbara. Here in this hospital- or possibly an ambulance. About…their relationship and his shortcomings. Or is that all part of the delirium that overtook him after the catastrophe of Da Groot's bulldozer and its bizarre tango with Casa del Fibro? It seems hard to separate fact from fantasy, dreamtime from wakefulness.

An electric clock on the wall opposite proclaims '9.38 pm'. Which probably means that there's only, around about, somewhere in the vicinity of eleven or so minutes to go before Barbara walks out of his life forever and leaves with Julie on the train to Sydney.

Joe decides that if he's going to be stuck like this, all wired up until the cardiologist gets back from either his ski-ing holiday in Switzerland and/or junket to Mexico, life could become about as boring as watching 'reality' (sic) television. And if that discussion about their lack of happiness *has* just taken place, then there was absolutely no way Joe could let Barbara depart on such a depressing note. That note was Z flat on the keyboard of their life together. Sincere, grovelling apologies had to be made and new resolutions offered. Soon! Like immediately.

Somehow, Joe manages to unbuckle one side of the metal cot, drop it down, and swing his legs over. Amazingly, he is also able to rotate himself up to a sitting position. Although this sudden exertion causes exaggerated seismic spikes to appear in the smooth line of heart beats on the monitor above him. Waves your body surfed to? he speculates.

Mercifully, the pattern quickly settles down into something resembling 'normal' (whatever that is)- just as soon as he stops moving. A nice, sleek, reassuring silhouette of peaks and troughs and little squiggly bits in between. It's okay, Joe tells himself. The universe he knows and loves is unfolding perfectly. Even his heartbeats. The low sensation thrill seeker takes the opportunity to glance down at a pair of filthy, mud-caked feet dangling below him. The shins attached are streaked by toxic asbestos ash. Both appendages seem a long, long way away. Almost separate from his body (if they are attached at all, and therefore technically 'his' to start with). From this angle, and with Joe's failing eyesight, it's hard to tell. But if these filthy limbs *do,* unfortunately belong to him, then obviously Sister Carmody hasn't had either the time, or the inclination to properly wash her patient before racing him into intensive care.

But that's okay, Joe reasons. Cleanliness may be next to godliness but staying alive always comes first. Besides which, he's upright at last, standing on somebody's two feet, and feeling remarkably okay- despite the strange woozy indifference he still feels about the world in general and parts of his own body in particular.

In fact, Joe feels so amazingly in the pink of health and on top of things generally, that he wonders why on earth (or in Heaven) he even needs to be where he is. (Again failing to connect such hubris with the wide spectrum of synthetic chemical help that has been injected into his body.) Hell, he thinks, there's nobody even looking after me! Monitoring me full time. It can't be all *that* bad. (Thereby also revealing his complete ignorance of the devastating effect on staffing levels at All Hallows of yet another dreaded Health Department 'restructure').

Even more worryingly, Dr. Beanland- Joe's first (and last) line of defence against the internal forces seeking to end his life (and paradoxically therefore their own)- has finally collapsed from exhaustion on a bench opposite the reception desk at the main entrance. Which is also unpersonned at this time of night, thanks again to the cut backs. It's the same item of public furniture that Julie, Joe and Barbara have all sat on at various high and low points throughout this fateful 50th birthday. Mostly low points.

Joe takes a halting step forward and, like a toddler standing up for the first time, is amazed he doesn't fall over. He unleashes a 'Look-Mum-I-can-walk!' sort of smile (prize-winning still), takes another step, and hears the thwack of plastic bags against metal from somewhere vaguely behind. Joe realises he's being followed…and swings round. Only to find the drip stand attempting to stroll along with him (on account of the fact that it was still connected to the large needle- or small UFO- going into the back of his left hand). Equally reluctant to let go are all the electrodes snaking out from his chest. Which, like an ersatz lover, are clawing him back to bed.

Wanting to end this waltz with inanimate objects, Joe rips the electrodes from the upper part of his body, taking a wide strip of fur off. (And geezus it hurt!) Which leaves Joe feeling intense pain and his chest looking as bereft of cover as a clear felled forest. This triggers an alarm somewhere that again, fortunately/unfortunately, nobody in All Hallows (if there is anybody) seems to take the slightest notice of.

Next, he wrenches the drip from his hand, and free at last, takes another step forward- away from the metal cot. Yet still no alarm bells ring, no flurry of health professionals arrive to restrain him. No doctors or nurses rush in from emergency surgery to urge him back to bed…Nobody even comes to take his order for dinner. And having unloaded all those partly digested saveloys on Da Groot's head, Joe realises his stomach has returned to empty and he's now officially starving. Again.

However, not for the first (or last) time that day, Joe is on a critical mission in an altered state- with only minutes to go before the *Nullumbah-Sydney Aurora* leaves Heaven's tiny railway station, heading south. Carrying his lover and her girlfriend away from him, possibly forever. Barely enough time to convey to Barbara all the things he has neglected to say in their unsatisfactory hospital (or ambulance) farewell of less than an hour ago. All the things that bound him to her (and her to him, and both of them to everything). All the things that would never let him let her go. (Assuming such an encounter had actually taken place, and wasn't also part of some fevered hallucination.) Which it could be. There was always that unfortunate/fortunate possibility.

Joe shuffles, hunchbacked, past the snoring form of Dr. Beanland sprawled uncomfortably on that same, recurring, hard bench. Then on past the main desk which should've had Sister Carmody behind it but she's too busy covering for Dr. Beanland in the operating theatre, tending to the fire twirler's third degree burns.

Joe glances down at the 'nil orally' tag dangling round his neck and hovers in the entrance foyer of the hospital, struggling to shake off a certain floating feeling while attempting, as much as he is intellectually capable, to take stock of the situation. He's leaving because Barbara is leaving. Therefore he has to find a door of some kind and go through it. Preferably one that would take him to an outside world- free of this persistent smell of drugs, bad food and disinfectant. It seemed simple enough. And not a big ask at all.

He lurches forward, scanning for exits…and suddenly freezes at the spectacle of a ghastly, deformed creature blocking his way. A horrifying sight with its haggard face and sickly grey skin. Once glorious curls are mattered with globs of stinking mud. Short, filthy legs protrude beneath a billowing pink smock that gives the pathetic life form a certain white-trash, drag queen effect. Especially when viewed from behind (with the monster's bottom clearly visible between the ties at the back). Blood gushes like a spring-fed waterfall from a wound in the thing's left paw, while the its nose also dribbles blood…

Huh? Something seems familiar about the nose bleed.

Joe leans forward and the creature mimics his gesture: leaning towards him, studying Joe closely. And then it hits the writer! Literally- as the cyst on his forehead bumps into cold glass! With night having fallen outside, All Hallows transparent front door has become a de facto mirror.

Nothing to worry about…it's just me again, Joe realises, to his slight relief and great disappointment.

JUMP CUT TO

9.47pm, Old Bogwater Road, Friday 13th March

Thirty eight seconds later, Joe pushes through All Hallows front door out into a (once again) moonlit, Heavenly evening. How wonderful the world looks, he realises. Even though, while his eyes adjust to the dark, Joe can see very little of it. If he really has had a heart attack, then he's been to the brink and come back. Alive! Reborn- literally. Ready, even eager, to continue. Here is life staring him in the face at last. Forget the feature screenplay, after today's events Joe will have enough material for a whole mini-series.

He glances over in time to see the *Aurora* arriving from Nullumbah. Bells ring and the giant arm of the road barrier comes down across Old Bogwater Road just as the big train hisses to a squeaking/screeching halt at Heaven's tiny railway station- not more than a hundred metres away from where Joe is currently swaying. Exactly the same distance he walks each morning for a surf. Not a big ask really, even for a recovering heart attack victim awaiting lifesaving angioplasty.

Only two things seem important: Barbara is going to board that train and Joe has to stop her. Or at least apologise profusely and grovel unrestrainedly on the platform beneath her. So far so good. Because nothing will stop him from having this final word with the last great love of his life. To beg her to stay. Or at best, come back- after a decent interval. However long it takes. He will be waiting. He just wants her to know. That's his mission. He'll even write a postcard tomorrow to confirm it.

As soon as Joe is able to shake the hospital's fluoro lights out of his retina, he sees that the storm front that washed out his BBQ has passed on through. And a clear, bright moon is sailing like a pirate ship in and out of clouds with silver linings. It hovers above the spiky silhouettes of the Norfolk pines strung with coloured lights along Salvation Strand- Heaven's seafront boulevard. The luminous jewel in the town's crown.

ZOOM DOWN TO:

Joe's Feet

…as they plop into the gutter. A pool of blood soon accumulates next to them. His blood. Still refusing to coagulate- thanks to all those artificial thinners Dr. Beanland has administered in both his semi-comatose state and Joe's. This heady mix of body fluids attracts a lost looking blue heeler. The same starving, homeless canine whose fateful path has already crossed Joe's several times today. Yet the recovering heart attack victim remains unaware of the dog. As 'unaware' as the hospital he's just escaped from. Where nobody has discovered their loss (or their gain as the case may be).

WIDEN TO DISCOVER:

Joe

He staggers on towards the railway station and his destiny.
Followed by the blue heeler, toward hers…

JUMP CUT TO:

9.56pm Railway Station, Heaven Friday 13th March

Close on:

Dark blood falling as light drizzle onto railway tracks as Joe steps around the flashing lights and clanging bells of Old Bogwater Road's lowered level crossing. He climbs up a ramp, approaching the platform from the wrong end.

ZOOM UP TO:

A sign declaring:

'NO WAY OUT'

It snarls back at him.
As if it's an omen. Or an existential manifesto.

WIDEN TO DISCOVER:

The blue heeler following

Grateful for Joe's bloody crumbs, and conveniently removing (like the birds in Hansel and Gretel) all evidence of the escapee's trail- if, for example, Sister Carmody or Sgt. Doreen Harris and her sniffer dogs should want to give chase. Followed closely by the Rainbow Coast's only Intensive Care Ambulance- assuming someone responsible could find it and deliver it to a place where it was urgently needed.

PAN ACROSS:

Heaven' s Tiny Commercial Hub, Friday 13th March

There is music coming from a cover band at the Pearly Gates Hotel. It booms out across the basin of the town from the pub's commanding heights on the back of Salvation Strand. Elsewhere, Joe's surprise! party winds down at Shangri La La Land. Where the stories about his flaws and foibles have just about run their tiresome, amusing course. Yet all of his friends, and more than a few of his enemies, have had a fabulous time at this birthday party without him.

All along Angel Avenue buskers, barefoot Indians, tarot readers and impromptu jewellery stalls are doing a roaring trade. German bakpakahs didgeridoo badly. Demented percussion penetrates everything. There's even a telescope where, for a silver coin donation, you can see the rings of Saturn or the moons of Jupiter. People queue six deep at *Heaven On A Cone*, the most popular shop open. While tribal folk sell angel wings, magic wands and healing crystals on blankets.

Luckily for Joe, this is the only small town in UStraylia where a decrepit and virtually naked hobo, barefoot in a pink muu muu, looking slightly deranged and bleeding, will barely raise a pierced eyebrow. There is much to be grateful for.

276

A hero in his own lunchtime, the couldabeen minor drongo hobbles painfully on, shambling Quasimodo-like alongside the hissing and steaming *Nullumbah-Sydney Aurora*. Almost worn out by his life threatening stagger from All Hallows Hospital. Desperately seeking Barbara. Pushing through the throng of thonged sufis and surfies, ferals and fortune tellers, bakpakahs and banana growers, pensioners and pot smokers, now climbing aboard the shiny metal express (sic). And already dreaming of breakfast somewhere else a long way away…

CLOSE ON:

The Station Clock
> …as it ticks over to:

9.59pm, Railway Station, Heaven, Friday 13th March

…leaving only sixty seconds of Heaven Time for Joe to redeem his relationship with Barbara and effectively salvage his thus far, fairly worthless life- what's left of it.

Four more sweeps of the lighthouse to either gain a future or lose a past.

When suddenly…

…the crowd parts and there she is- up the far end of the train, just stepping into carriage 'C'.

A lump catches Joe by the throat. But he flings it aside, adam's apple pumping. Clutching instead, a desperate hope, he barely manages to splutter out:

"Barbara!"

But it's too weak to travel the distance. So he slouches, hunchbacked, further along the platform, summoning some last reserves of energy, dignity in shreds. The lipid goitre round his middle puts a huge strain on the ties at the back of his hospital smock and exposes an even wider spectrum of hairy buttock.

"Barbara!" he croaks a second time, with nothing left to lose. Not even conscious of the spectacle he's making in front of a crowd of tired pensioners and bakpakahs.

All activity on the station comes to a complete halt. And people, when they finally notice Joe, step back a little, covering their noses against the acrid, rotten egg smell emanating from his muddy legs.

Ignoring their reaction, Joe shuffles on- through a gauntlet of disapproving, recoiling, apathetic faces. Finally, he reaches the window where Barbara and Julie are settling into their seats. For a gut wrenching nano-moment the (ex?)lover's eyes lock. Barbara braces herself and strides purposefully back down the aisle of the carriage to intercept Joe, and hold him at the doorway. Not wanting to embarrass herself in front of strangers she will have to share the next eleven hours with. Like everyone else, Joe's sole/soul mate frowns down at the disgraceful spectacle confronting her.

He smiles his pathetic gratitude for her meeting him halfway. Two columns of drool form at the edges his mouth, trembling slightly as they thin out and plunge earthwards. But Barbara is already shaking her head. He looks filthy and disgusting. The hole in his left hand (where the drip was torn out), continues to offer a wasted blood donation onto the platform.

Only the blue heeler hovers, awaiting her chance for another free sip. But pacing from side to side, not wanting to declare her interest in Joe's body fluids too openly. Fearing rejection.

As is Joe.

CRASH BLACKOUT TO:

Railway Station—Heaven

Just another colourful trainload of happy holiday-makers returning home from **HEAVEN US**traylia on the luxurious Nullumbah-Sydney *Aurora*. Why fly when you can always reach the Rainbow Coast at the speed of a family car built in the late 1920s? (Bridges and track maintenance permitting). Throw that carton of Stresseze™ away and rediscover the romance of rail while state funding lasts (which it won't).

Affix
stamp
here

#32 of 33 Postcards from Heaven

printed on gently mulched, plantation-grown, organic bamboo fibre using recycled greywater and bound with a biodegradable non-toxic glue

No animal or dolphin suffered in the making of this card
(apart from, of course, its author)

32

A HOLLYWOOD ENDING

"It's never a question of not grovelling.
It's only a matter of how much, and to whom."
(Gra'eme *How To Succeed At Anything Without Really Trying*)

Railway Station, Heaven, 11 seconds later ...

FADE IN:

The Nullumbah-Sydney Aurora

...as it huffs impatiently beside the platform. Passengers are already on board, wondering why they can't just leave now. Everyone keen to get on with it.

Everyone except Barbara who remains blocking the doorway of Car 'C', casting a despairing look back down at her former partner. Sensibly, the small crowd gathered to farewell friends and loved ones stand well back- wondering if someone should call the authorities. Preferably a professional cleaner with a lot of disinfectant, or a station master, for example. If stations still had them.

"Oh Joe..." she sighs, having virtually given up.

He looks down. "Yeah I know." And hangs there both humiliated and humiliating.

"Sorry, Barbara," he dithers.

Then it hits her: "What are you doing here!? You've just had a heart attack! Who the hell discharged you?"

"I escaped," he says, a touch sheepishly.

"Geezus."

"I know..."- completely ashamed of himself. But not really. In fact he feels so shithouse he's past caring about anything ever again.

Barbara throws a quick glance back inside the carriage to make sure Julie's okay. Then out at Joe again, still embarrassed that people might somehow connect this sad human being with herself.

Joe shifts uneasily on his stinking, filthy feet. Mondeigo's denials about the acid sulphate problem from *Dreamtime Beach* emphatically exposed for the noisome lie that they were.

"I just can't let you go off like this. Without..." - Joe's jaw starts its characteristic uncontrollable wobbling at moments of intense crisis. And he just hangs there unable to finish the sentence. His teeth clattering like a bad tap dancer. Forcing Barbara to draw it out of him.

"Go off like what?"

"Like we were the worst thing that ever happened to each other...without telling you how I really feel," he stammers, trying to sound convincing. But it's getting all jumbled up again. The self-styled word merchant has become technically speechless.

ZOOM UP TO:

The Station Clock

...as it finally ticks over to:

10.00pm, Railway Station, Heaven, Friday 13th March

There's a hiss of air as the *Aurora*'s powerful brakes release their steely, asbestos padded grip and the cover band at the Pearly Gates start their final number, a version of Bela Flek's sad, resigned but hopeful masterpiece, *'Sunset Road'*. Which carries a wistful, melancholy/ending sort of feeling out from the pub across virtually the whole of downtown Heaven- to the tiny platform on which Joe and Barbara stand, facing each other, transparently for the last time.

Someone in a uniform resembling what used to be a station master is hectoring towards both ends of the platform- more in desperation than in certainty, as he yells: "All aboard please, stand well back from the train, thank you."

Then double-checks his fob watch, fist tightening around a small green flag. Anxious lips pursing round a whistle. The train is supposed to leave now, yet nothing appears to be happening…

ZOOM UP TO:

The Station Clock

… as it clicks over again to:

10.01pm, Railway Station, Heaven, Friday 13th March

All 290 passengers in the *Aurora*'s eleven carriages are, not unreasonably, currently expecting to experience some kind of forward motion. But Barbara remains blocking Carriage 'C's doorway. Her future connection to Joe hanging in the balance. He's already regretting not having stopped to wash some of the putrid mud off at a tap in Arcadia Park, the one Heaven's tree dwelling ferals use for their domestic water supply.

Instead, he tries to distract attention away from himself by observing: "It's funny how a large slice of your life seems to move as slowly as a glacier and then, one day, you wake UP! And suddenly you're old and alone again, and all that stuff we did together- over the whole ten years of it, Barbara, seems like another place, a long time ago…"

"Too much information, Joe. Tell someone who cares."

"That hurts."

"It's meant to."

Joe winces. Feeling about as low as he can get. He deserved that. And she knew it. And he knew she knew he knew she knew it.

"Joe, please go back to the hospital and re-admit yourself," she pleads/urges him. "You could bring on another heart attack just standing here."

Again she flicks a quick, apprehensive glance back inside the carriage. But Julie is already buried in a trashy fashion magazine and, like everyone else, seems oblivious to the drama unfolding out on the platform.

"Barbara, I've lost the house," he blurts out as if it will make any difference. Still not feeling terribly good about it.

"What do you mean *lost* it?"

"I ran over it with a bulldozer and whatever wasn't crushed got burnt to the ground…"

"You're so *clumsy*, Joe!" she exasperates back at him. "And you know why!?" (A rhetorical question if ever there was one.) "Because you're almost permanently stoned- or drunk! Frequently both. You've got to get a grip, forgodsake."

Joe, pathetically: "I know." Then, as the full enormity of it takes hold: "Everything I ever produced is gone, Barbara. Like it never happened."

If he expects to garner any sympathy, let alone concern at this, then again he is both mistaken and disappointed. She's been nagging him for years! to get rid of all that paper junk. For Barbara this is only good news.

Joe becomes aware of other people glaring back at him. Even the German didge players have stopped (mercifully) and are listening. This is becoming embarrassing. And not only because of the way Joe looks and smells.

"Don't laugh I'm serious."

"Who's laughing ?" And she isn't.

For Joe there's too much to say and too little time to say it in. It seems to have been one minute past ten for much longer than sixty seconds and it was obvious the *Nullumbah-Sydney Aurora* should've been well gone by now. A conga line of lights snaking its way up beside Skypilot Drive, heading for the gap in the Xaviour's Shoot escarpment.

"All I've got left is the clothes I'm barely standing up in," he reflected, not inaccurately.

"And even that isn't yours."- but she couldn't help smiling as she took in the pink muu muu for the first time. His hairy buttocks protruding backwards out of it finally breaks all her resistance. And she laughs at him. Long and deep. Seeing the funny side. Finally.

It catapults Joe into a faint hope, grateful to have her chastising him again.

"Oh, and I probably killed someone…" he adds as a footnote.

Barbara frowns. He hastens to clarify: "But it was only Lech Da Groot."

Finally, Barbara is shocked. Joe had his audience back.

"You...what?!!"

"Yeah, I dunno...he flew out of the bulldozer. I'm pretty sure I didn't run over him. But he might have drowned in the quicksand. It was all too dark and blurry..." Joe drops his eyes, shuffling a little, not proud of the manslaughter- if that's what it was. Not even sure it had happened. Because nothing seems quite real now. Not even this conversation. But...what can he say? He didn't want to go into detail in public.

"Look, the bastard was trying to destroy an entire rainforest," Joe pleads, not unreasonably. "As well as me!"

As if that explained everything. Then, when it obviously doesn't:

"Somebody had to do *some*thing, Barbara."

She sighs, once again rolling her glorious, dark, almond shaped, Mediterranean eyes and shaking her head. Realising now she'll never change him. All part of her fate too, unfortunately.

"It was an accident forcrissake!" He blurts out, on the verge of tears. Again. Clearly losing all self-control and any shred of dignity he may still have left.

"Joe- you're *so*..."

But she's run out of negatives. And gives up. It's the first hopeful sign.

He bows his head, rubbing the cyst in the middle of his forehead. Looking down. Feeling at a loss himself. Unable to finish her sentence for her. There were too many adverse adjectives jostling for position. Including all the ones she's already used on him. And would continue to employ if she had to. Barbara *was* wise- as only a woman can be. And despite all the painkillers, Joe's trinitrate-induced headache continues to be excruciating. This is the chemical price he must pay for getting his life back...just as he seems to be losing it. Again.

"The point..." Joe almost catches another sob in this throat. But misses, and it wells up out of him anyway, rendering his personal spectacle even more demeaning.

"The point is, Barbara...this isn't just 'au revoir', is it? It's, it's...'good-bye'."

She doesn't deny it. She's heard enough clichés for one day. This embarrassment on the platform is the last straw for her. Like Julia this morning in the surf, Joe is Barbara's last straw man.

"It would've happened anyway," she shrugs, trying to make light of the ending of their decade long relationship. "Eventually...someday..." Then as a sort of concession: " Nothing lasts forever, Joe."

"But, Barbara, I can't go cold turkey from you. I told you, I'm addicted."

"You're addicted to many things, Joe, none of them is me."

That hurt. But it was meant to, even though it wasn't true. She is only being kind in order to be cruel (later on). There were many mind altering substances Joe has never taken and had no interest in touching. Not surprisingly he feels a faint, perhaps lethal stabbing in the heart. But the *Nullumbah-Sydney Aurora* still refuses to budge. So that, as the clock remains unaccountably stuck on:

CRASH ZOOM UP TO :

10.01pm

Even the *Aurora's* driver is leaning out of his cabin window, wondering why on earth nothing is happening. This is truly weird. And well beyond a joke. However, it would be hard to explain to the driver that some plots, even in Hollywood settings, seem willfully reluctant to move forward. Especially when they reach the compulsory farewell scene at the end- in front of as big a crowd as the budget will allow.

"What I'm trying to say, Barbara, is: no matter what happens, no matter what you decide. Whether you come back or not- I will always feel bound to you. Like a planet round its sun..."

"Great. I'm really glad I knew that, Joe. Your theory of human gravity. Thanks for the insight." Barbara stifles a yawn. It's late. For her too, an exhausting, emotionally turbulent and draining day. One she's really keen to draw the curtain on.

"Look, it's a much better explanation for what I feel than 'biochemical reaction'," he argues. Challenging her 'oxytocin' theory. Desperate for one last chance to keep her there, listening. And she hesitates long enough for him to pounce in with:

"This thing between us *is* a kind of inevitable attraction, Barbara. Precisely because it's also part of the Universal Force, binding everything. This inter-connectivity that ties couples together. It comes from somewhere out there…"

He's opening his arms, lifting them skywards, towards a set of stars rapidly being blocked out again by silver lined clouds.

But finally he's said it. Mission accomplished. It's all out in the open now: Joe's 'Theory of Relatively Everything'- getting wet like himself, as a second wave of thunder breaks in from the south west, and it starts to bucket down. Again.

ZOOM UP TO:

The Station Clock

… as it remains apparently permanently stuck on:

10.01pm

Two hundred and ninety passengers are peering out of windows and glancing round carriage doors, poking their heads this way and that, looking for an authority figure to protest to, and cause a nuisance of themselves with. If only someone like that was still paid to hang around and be picked on.

But is it just the clock that's stopped? Or has some larger, weirder, more mysterious stasis overtaken them all?- the passengers inquire of themselves and others without receiving any tangible answer.

In any case, it's a clock set in Heaven and like its iconic counterpart on Salvation Strand, it could be wrong most of the time if it felt like it. The station clock could even stop if wanted to, holding everything else up in its wake. Time will warp or stand still inside the Enchanted Triangle just so long as Bela Flek's sensational riffs continue to waft across from the pub to the station. Or there's another emotion to be explored and thereby exploited. Because it is all Heaven Time now and this was the Hollywood ending. Like Joe, it was a case of laying on maximum schmaltz.

"What I'm trying to say, Barbara, is that you and me- we're tied to each other by something that is greater than both of us…"- reaching out for her hand, and finding (strangely) that she lets him take it. He feels a warm inner glow- partly from the sub-tropical down pour now re-drenching him, partly from the trickle of urine down the inside of his left leg (a by-product of the three and a half bottles of chateau de migrainé that have come back to haunt him). But at last Barbara is fully listening and at least Joe is still feeling.

"I can't explain it, Barbara. I just know that we're born alone and we die alone…and in between we share the same space and breathe from the same atmosphere- like everyone else on the planet. Connected to all living things through every breath we take. Just as you and I are connected here on this platform. Even though you're leaving me."

There's a pause for her to deny it. Or change her plans. Barbara declines the opportunity. So he ploughs on with nothing left to lose:

"I just cherish the fact that our two paths crossed, for as long as we had together (discounting the six months every year you spent in Israel). What else can I say? You're my guardian angel. Barbara. You saved me from falling into a big black hole. And my life was blest through knowing you."

By now the station clock thinks it's probably heard enough of this stuff and finally ticks over to:

CRASH ZOOM UP TO:

10.02pm, Railway Station, Heaven, Friday 13th March

…making the alleged 'express' now officially late. Heaven's virtual station master can no longer ignore the obvious. He blows his whistle and waves his green flag. His daily ration of power.

A tremendous sigh of relief percolates through the train. Brakes hiss out their last bit of compressed air as the gleaming silver carriages stretch and test their connections before slowly clanking forward. People stop gawking out of windows and turn back to their various conversations and reading matter: tabloids bereft of news and gossip mags as empty of content as the brain of an Utta Bastard. Some are even naively expecting to sleep.

Barbara withdraws into the doorway of Carriage 'C'. A hand raised in farewell.

Yet the would-be local hero persists in shuffling, hunchbacked, alongside her- struggling to keep up. Completely failing to be Buddhist about it and let go. To let it all go! Even Barbara.

Joe splashes through puddles forming in dirty potholes on the unrepaired parts of the station's bitumen platform. Out in the open now, he's drenched by the renewed torrential downpour. His pink muu muu flapping dangerously in the breeze, threatening pubic exposure.

"Barbara, I can't live without you," he pants breathlessly, "I worship the ground you stand on."

They both look down at the floor of the carriage around Barbara's feet. A kind of sparkly, grimy, non-slip, synthetic surface.

"Well, maybe not that bit exactly… "

His gift for the right gag at the perfect moment finally breaks the ice and they both see the funny/tragic/funny side. At last!

But her shoulders drop as the train continues to whisk her away from him- sideways and fast. She's reached the end of her tether, he is rapidly reaching the end of the platform. A sickening two metre drop awaits him at its edge.

"So, all right, already! Then jump on this train and come with me!"- she caves-in, abandoning all common sense. Drawing a hand inwards, morphing her gesture of departure into an invitation.

Joe baulks, virtually jogging- painfully and dangerously (given his medical circumstances). He's pleading back at her: "But, Barbara, Heaven is my home!"

"Your home is gone, remember? Now you're free, finally! Of all that STUFF!" she triumphs. "You're healed, Joe. You don't *need* Heaven anymore. In fact, if you don't leave now you *will* get sick again. You said so yourself."

Barbara as always, cutting straight to the heart of the matter- literally. Sanmahdi-like. Finding the wise argument. The only one that mattered.

"Losing Casa del Fibro has a wonderful upside. It means you're like me now- everything I own in a single bakpak,"

She winces again at his flapping smock. "In your case not even that much…" Then she relents, and offers: "So come with me Joe Deegan, come 'home' to your sole/soul mate."

"What, and walk the world together? Barefoot, without possessions?"

He was starting to look doubtful, there would only be the land value of his property to live on. She can see the doubt, and he can see she can see he can see she can see it. So she makes another huge concession:

"Alright, already, one day you can come back here. Older, wiser, leaner."

"And know Heaven for the first time?" he recites, stealing from T.S. Eliot again, but trying not to sound too clever.

"Whatever turns you on…"

The barely recovering heart attack victim finds it hard to fault her logic. So he shrugs, virtually sprinting now and admits, singing tunelessly:

"I guess I must be just a goy who can't say 'no'."

They laugh again at his feeble musical/jewish joke just as her siren arms reach out to him like the best body surf imaginable- soft, warm and squishy. Offering him comfort, protection, and companionship. All anyone ever needed (apart from a tolerable bottle of chilled dry white around sundown).

Barbara's eyes are willing him on with that cheeky girlish twirl at the corner of her mouth, as if inviting him into a ravishing boudoir (instead of the doorway of some pretty run- down rolling stock.)

And, at that very moment- just as the platform finally ends- Joe makes the 'fate-al' leap up, onto the train and into Barbara's imploring, adorable embrace. Feeling her whole body press against him. Running his grubby hand along her familiar, but not very curved shape, with its little bumps and uniquenesses- as the lovers swivel and bend this way and that, kissing madly. His lips find hers and then her ear lobes and his tongue dabbles at the tip of her nose before swiping right across her forehead.

After which and at last! he breaks off and pulls back from her a little, enframing her face with those same grubby mitts that typed too much bad television- pointedly ignoring the blue heeler as it barks a mournful, begging reproach on the platform fast receding behind them.

And again, Joe has the cyclops view: Barbara's beautiful, semitic eyes melding into one, beholding his lover's inner 'I': the sum of the other two. Like a new born baby rapturously seeing its mother for the first time.

She smiles back and there's the delicious feeling of her hands shooting through his hair and getting all tangled up in those awful dreadlocked curls. (Which she will shampoo and condition as soon as they get to Julie's place in Newtown.) Then she runs her hands back down his face and kisses him in more than a dozen places, licking away a little crumb of dried blood from his nose.

Their heads drop towards each other, their foreheads bumping (with only his cyst in the way). And in the next instant Barbara's lips are finding Joe's again, forgiving him, wanting him, enfolding him. And him feeling the male/female thing in the peculiar straightness of her waist, the generosity of her breasts. A near perfect woman holding her pretty defective man. Opposites attracting. A couple united: the most unstoppable force in the universe- marching forward in harmony, facing a common destiny, glimpsing a future together. Two in one flesh. The ultimate, the only mystery…the thing that gets everyone through the night. (And most days as well.)

ROLL END CREDITS OVER:

10.10pm, *Nullumbah-Sydney Aurora*, Friday 13th March

The second storm front eventually passes over the town and a glorious, flooding moonlight again breaks through after all that rain.

Joe and Barbara's passionate embrace is still bracketed by the doorway of the *Nullumbah-Sydney Aurora* as it snakes its way up beside Skypilot Drive towards the saddle in the Xaviour's Shoot escarpment, through which it will pass.

The fairyland lights of Heaven are laid out below like some human colony on another planet. Like sparklers fallen from paradise. Flecks of gold and silver and red/blue neon pock mark the great, rolling black doona of the raging party town. Set at the back, along the curve of Salvation Strand, are strings of coloured bulbs threaded through the Norfolk pines, standing like coils of DNA on some cosmic runway. Inviting 'others' in.

And above it all, that jewel in the crown: the crystal-powered light from the house on Cape Surprise!. It's twin beacons carving out another kind of farewell. Always there, always turning, measuring out all the time that remains of Joe and Barbara's life together. And the Heaven Time that will now be 'lost' (or gained) until they return.

Until finally! Joe stands back from his lover, soon to be wife (their long pre-nuptial engagement officially concluded), and immediately realises how right she is: nobody needs a place more than they needed other people. And if his time in Heaven has seemed like a black hole in which Joe has achieved very little, then all that negativity is also coming to an end. It started with Kate's illness and ended with his heart attack. And included along the way that oh-so-debilitating crisis of artistic and personal self-confidence from which he was only now just emerging. Joe Deegan is finished with his mid-life crisis and cured of Gra'eme (whatever the man's surname might be.)

Instead, he is leaving Heaven UStraylia in the arms of the last great love of his life. Going with her up to Holy Jerusalem (via unholy Sydney). Where he will sit in some tiny flat near Nahlaot and write articles on the 'Immense Practicality Of The Rubber Thong In Subtropical Climates'. Or perhaps even the greatest unproduced UStraylian screenplay ever written. A work of towering genius.

Because only Jerusalem can be Jerusalem, just as only Heaven can be Heaven (and who cares about Sydney?). It was a critical mistake to confuse the two. To confuse Paradise with Urth. Utopia with Reality- as it existed in either place at any time in any dimension.

Above all else, Barbara has forgiven Joe for his lapse at *Seventh Heven* (if that's what it was- which it wasn't); and he is about to enter her life not only finally but fully. They've been married in spirit now they will get married in fact: a simple affair with a few close friends. Probably naked on a beach in Cyprus, since he isn't Jewish and therefore can't actually tie the knot with Barbara in Israel.

Their vows privately renewed, the lovers kiss again and the view is gone as the train rises up off the coastal plain and speeds on down the other side of Xaviour's Shoot through the dark winding valley of Elysium Creek, surging south. There is nothing left to background their hold on each other save some sleeping cows in a moonwashed landscape.

Framed by this, Joe falls headlong into Barbara as though cartwheeling into someone else's soul. And if Barbara is all he has, then that is all he needed. There is nothing more beautiful in the known universe than a mature human female he reasoned, and the only thing worth doing in life was making frequent and fairly passionate love to her- in as many delectable ways a sex god as talented as Joe could conjure.

At which point Barbara breaks off and stands back from him a little, weighing his thick pendulous jowls in both hands, whispering:

"I love you Joe Deegan."

And he answers:

"Oh yes, my darling. Yes and forever. Oui, ken, ja, aye, bien sur…"

Before falling once again, and not for the last time, through two glorious full lips into Barbara's wonderful mouth, as if into a dark, limpid pool at the bottom of some pristine waterfall.

Joe's sole/soul mate was a *good* woman. And the incurable romantic will hold on to her and love her and build the rest of his life around her. Paving a direct road- if not exactly to paradise on earth- then at least to some sort of ideal and truly balanced existence somewhere. Building on each day as if onto something even better than before. No matter where he happened to be, or what he pretended to be doing. He will, from now on, fill his days with purpose and meaning and do only *positive* things. Ennobling, uplifting things. Becoming more sharing and outgoing. Because Joe Deegan had at last found Barbara Solomon and Barbara, Joe.

Like two lost souls they cling together in the moonlight. Her lips melding into his as her tongue scrapes across calcified plaque and finds cavities in his mouth even Gail Divine didn't know existed…

RIPPLE DISSOLVE AND BLUR OUT TO:

33

THE PROBABLE (BUT FAIRLY ORDINARY) ENDING

Just another colourful, rainbow-clad, blue-sky dawn on perfect Purgatory Beach, glittering jewel in the crown of **HEAVEN US**traylia, capital of the Rainbow Coast, gateway to the Eternal Triangle.

Affix
stamp
here

#33 of 33 Postcards from Heaven

printed on gently mulched, plantation-grown, organic bamboo fibre using recycled greywater and bound with a biodegradable non-toxic glue

No animal or dolphin suffered in the making of this card
(apart from, of course, its author)

33
THE PROBABLE
(BUT FAIRLY ORDINARY)
ENDING

"Heaven is always just out there- waiting…
You only have to open your eyes to see it."
(Gra'eme *Stating The Obvious*)

6.41am, Casa del Fibro, Saturday 14th March.

A thick, scrofulous tongue with the flexibility and texture of wet sandpaper was plunging so deeply into Joe's mouth that it tickled the stumps of his long departed tonsils. His head was sprawled sideways on a cold, greasy, 'hotplate' (sic). Startled, he jerked awake and reared back, dry-retching, attempting to spit- giving the bitch responsible a terrible fright.

Geezus! He'd been dreaming of pashing Barbara and here was this filthy mutt taking complete advantage! His one chance to properly kiss his lover good-bye and he'd blown it. Badly.

Appalled, Joe wipes his mouth with a grimy hand, partly dislodging the thick wad of sausage fat that has congealed to the right hand side of his face, like a version of the Phantom mask in the Opera of the same name.

Joe was hungover and in pain. Looming illness surged through his body like bargain hunters through a turnstile. A sore throat heralded some virulent strain of flu contracted from sleeping in damp clothes all night. He didn't even want to think about how his immune system would be further compromised by the bacterial torrent that had just flooded into his oesophagus via the canine's septic tongue job.

Sodden remains from a party that didn't happen lay all around him like a sick joke. Washed out streamers trailed from the hills hoist onto damp grass. Plates of soggy and unnatural food stood about in bowls filled with water of many unnatural colours. It felt like more rain on his skin but was only 'pins and needles' from bad circulation. One glance up at the blue sky forming above him confirmed it.

Joe Deegan was officially and irredeemably fifty. The same age as Hitler when he started World War Two. Only not quite so confidant and in control of things. In fact, Joe was alone again. And Barbara nowhere to be seen!

Below him, the blue heeler adopted a wretched, rejected, appropriately hang-dog look. She had only been expressing her love for Joe (while scoffing half cooked saveloys from the hotplate). It was hardly her fault she'd worked her tongue across to express her appreciation more personally on Joe's greasy face. Which conveniently, happened to be lying there- side on, like a stricken Gulliver. The dribble of blood from his nose leading the way- encouraging the heeler on. Indeed, some congealed vomit on Joe's hair and crunchy bits of sleep from his eyes even provided a nice salty aftertaste to all that cold meat…

It finally dawned on the scriptwriter (both literally and metaphorically) that he must have passed out last night- right here, kneeling over the hotplate. Like an aging altar boy in some open air cathedral: the temple of his BBQ, his head sprawled sideways, resembling nothing so much as one of Old Frank's greyhounds that had been cranially unbalanced by Vasuda Devi. Not even the disciplined piety of boarding school (all those countless, lost years spent genuflecting at masses, rosaries, benedictions and stations of the cross) could have prepared his knees for being knelt on all night- especially at their age.

Out on Cape Surprise! the lighthouse automatically switched itself off, separating one of the more fascinating Nights in Heaven from another, full-of-potential, Heavenly Day. Through a haze of pain and in growing daylight, Joe tries to recall his last coherent thought- any reliable detail at all from yesterday. It was no mean feat. To make matters worse, a deafening cacophony of birdlife had just broken out, adding to the torture and home renovations going on inside his cranium…

Joe felt defeated, depressed, diseased, and rather deflated as it finally sank in that Barbara had gone. Consoled only by the thought that he'd managed at least, to make it to the station, to say good-bye...

...after his heart attack...

...brought on by the destruction of his house and all its contents...

Huh?

Joe glanced over towards Casa del Fibro, already warming nicely in the early autumn sun. It stood miraculously unscathed. He swung quickly round, peering over the back fence. That vital, thin green line of rainforest also remained intact. With no evidence whatsoever of any earthmoving equipment primed to destroy it...or any feet from a developer's corpse poking up through quicksand.

"Excuse me?" He asked himself redundantly. Had it all been a *dream* of some kind?

Da Groot, the bulldozer, destroying his house, having a heart attack, staggering after Barbara to the station in a backless pink smock with stinking feet...must all have been some sort of feverish nightmare. A nasty amalgam of the thoughts and fears plaguing yesterday. Joe punched a fist into his hand and laughed out loud with such exploding relief that the stray dog again scampered away in fright. This time however, he quickly pulled the bitch back towards him and, risking fleas, gave it a weak pat.

"Were you the one, eh, mate?" he asked the blue heeler. "That silly canine I kept bumping into yesterday, all around town?"

She whimpered assent. Smiling back. Tail wagging happily at this new development in their relationship, admitting to anything for another pat.

"It's all, all right," Joe chuckled warmly, flem rising from the sore throat, coughing and talking to an animal at last.

"The whole nightmare was just a figment of my overactive and infrequently talented imagination!" He concluded to no one in particular. "The ambulance, intensive care, that insane attempt to defend this last bit of forest against Da Groot's bulldozer, crushing and burning all my precious tapes, films and scripts, chasing Barbara to the station, and then imagining I had somehow entwined myself in her beautiful arms..."

His happy mood evaporated.

Geezus, he'd missed Barbara and Julie's departure completely! Instead he'd fallen asleep- here at home. Ninety minutes before their train left. He'd just *dreamed* he'd said good-bye. Now she'd never come back.

Joe was racked once more by feelings of shame, remorse, guilt and failure. A last chance to redeem himself and he'd fluffed it. He struggled to get a grip on his mid-term memory. As usual, it was slipperier than an eel in a bubble bath.

Just when, exactly, had yesterday's reverie started? Where was that always tenuous line between the familiar, tangible world and some sort of waking (or sleeping) delirium? A demarcation sometimes as vague and permeable as a Muddled Eastern border. Had Gra'eme really betrayed him? And did *Infinity Ltd* exist, for example? Or was that also just more rumours built on lies, gossip and half truths, spread by mendacious types who should never be trusted...

But of course, that was the thing about dreams. You don't know it's a fantasy while you're actually dreaming it. Inside the surreal, sometimes perverted world of the subconscious mind you can 'imagine' you've woken up while you're still in some kind of deluded catatonia or waking coma. You can even dream dreams- smudging 'reality' out to a kind of seamless, subjective, inner/outer self-awareness. Indeed, was this morning, here with this dog, in his perfectly intact backyard, actually happening or...was Joe merely dreaming that it was? In other words...when did he fall asleep exactly, and was he even properly awake! yet?

To which the answers seemed to be:

      a) he hadn't clue and

      b) how could he properly tell?

Joe pinched himself and it hurt. Good. He was awake now. No doubt about that.

Except...of course, he could be dreaming that it hurt.

And did this prove what the Immortalists always believed: that life itself was a dream from which one day, we're all going to WAKE UP!?

Joe began to panic. What *was* the last, seriously normal, demonstrably tangible thing about the debacle of Friday 13th March which he could actually, concretely remember? And which he probably should have just fast-forwarded through (as was his original intention). Perhaps, in some bizarre way, he *had* fast-forwarded through it after all? And this was the morning that he wanted yesterday but couldn't quite get at the time…? So where was the rewind button? How to sensibly review yesterday from the position of today? If that's what they were, in that order.

He collapsed onto a milk crate (spread around for his guests- the ones that failed to show) and tried to focus his mind on the only thing about yesterday that was at all important: his miserable failure with Barbara.

Joe sighed and looked around for something to take the edge off his hangover. Medication perhaps. Or more alcohol? There was only warm cask wine to chose from. He'd have to get it into the freezer quickly for that to be at all an option.

In any case, nothing would remove the pain of knowing that he had failed to turn up at the station to offer Barbara a dignified 'au revoir'- or 'good-bye' as indeed the case may now be. Betrayal was one thing, unpunctuality and forgetfulness a sign of serious moral disarray.

The only upside to all of which was: the knowledge that His Smarmyness had lost all purchase with Joe through his treacherous and insulting liaison with Mondeigo and Co. That much about yesterday had to be true. Either way, Heaven's most expensive Oracle was never to be trusted again. Another small, halting, personal leap forward for the newly liberated ex-disciple from the overall debacle of his 50th birthday.

The blue heeler's cold, wet nose snuggled into Joe's groin. And while Heaven's newest quintogenarian still recoiled a bit at such intimacy (and dog saliva generally), he also couldn't avoid patting and scratching the pathetic, abandoned creature- who seemed so extraordinarily grateful. Patting its head was the one thing it couldn't do for itself. Something that bound dogs to humans in the first place. A mutual, inter-species dependency. Unfettered love, companionship and a lot of barking at strangers, in exchange for a few crumbs and the occasional walk with a tennis ball. First, the saveloys, vomit, and sleep from Joe's eyes, and now a bit of gratuitous frottage from a potential new master. At least the heeler's day was looking up.

Joe had rarely even touched a dog before. Some canine phobia obviously. Yet another unconscious injury buried inside his damaged childhood- like a favourite bone…

The bitch lifted her head and looked straight up into Joe with such sad, adoring eyes. Windows of a soul as innocent and trusting as it was possible to get without actually bunging it on.

He smiled back down at her. Dogs weren't so bad, he accepted. If only they didn't smell. And leave a lot of shit lying around. Speaking of which, he would take the poor thing to the beach later with a plastic bag and an old frisbee to frolic with her among the shallows as this divine Heavenly morning curved toward perfection- as it was bound so to do- especially after all that overnight rain.

Joe would have another fabulous surf while the dog waited patiently on the shore, perhaps menacing a seagull or two. Afterwards, he would shower them both off under the hose and let his naked body dry slowly in the hammock. If he wanted to make this morning's swaying meditation fairly useful he'd hose the garden as he oscillated back and forth.

The lifelong observer of human nature was pretty sure now that this must be the same dog he'd seen pulling delinquents on skateboards round town, and hanging out with the ferals and hobos in Arcadia Park. Then he'd nearly tripped over it outside *Heaven On A Cone* and later at *Kingdom Come Inc*. In fact, he'd almost *run* over it on his bike while careering down Skypilot Drive from Mondeigo's place. Last night, at the station, she'd turned up again- following Joe's blood line, carrying on like she'd been abandoned and stranded on the platform by some heartless owner who'd just caught the *Aurora* to Sydney and absconded out of the dog's life forever. Looking much like Joe himself had felt when first deposited at St. Patrick's boarding college as a tender seven year old. Left to the not so tender mercies of large men in black frocks.

But hang on a sec…

…the station bit, pleading with Barbara, proposing (and accepting) marriage- was all part of the nightmare surely? Had the dog somehow penetrated Joe's delirium? Just as she had literally and, quite unapologetically, penetrated his mouth? Causing him to WAKE UP! from the dream of last night. And maybe, the whole delusion of his first 50 years? Such progress would qualify any day in Heaven as Fabulous all by itself. Even better than Beautiful.

Joe gazed around his backyard and began to laugh out loud. A tremendous sighing relief surged up out of him. Letting it all go. Most of the worst bits of yesterday *were* only a nightmare! Getting today right should be a breeze. About as gentle and achievable as the angel's breath of a north-westerly that now teased the Bethlehem chimes into their wonderful, surf-predicting melody.

His joy and delight built and resonated out across the corrugated back fence where it mingled with a chorus of early morning bird song, including the Kookaburra gang- who picked up on Joe's laughter and echoed it out across the magnificently intact rainforest now stirring awake itself in the same gentle, early morning breeze. Joe took the dog back in his arms and, risking fleas, caressed and patted…?

What would he call it?

Joe was so ignorant of animals and domestic pets generally, that he got its gender all wrong by weighing up names like 'Bluey' or 'Pat' (in memory of his old school); but they seemed either too obvious or too silly. Then it hit him: 'Gra'eme'.

Yes. He would call the dog 'Graeme' (without the pretentious apostrophe in the middle- making it sound more exotic than it really was). So that he would only ever use the name from now on in relation to something dumber, smaller and humbler than himself. A creature Joe could look down on and give orders to. Train even, in certain useful ways- such as fetching his stubby from the back fridge, or bringing his thongs over to the hammock after a post-surf shower.

'Graeme!' Joe commanded, laughing and growling as he fondled the dog's ears, patting her playfully and tugging her upper body this way and that, virtually adopting her on the spot. All of which she enjoyed with unrestrained delight, taking this as her cue to start the nuzzling, adoration thing again. Going for the groin. Which Joe resisted, pushing her back, laughing.

Seeking serious protein to pacify his new 'mate', (and still in urgent need of saveloys himself) Joe headed into the kitchen. In fact, with no serious red meat for 24 hours he was now practically anaemic (even discounting the nosebleed). Ravenous, he went straight for the fridge and it was the first thing he noticed on its door:

To the line: 'This relationship is fucked',

had been added the word: 'almost'.

'This relationship is *almost* fucked'.

Barbara! She had come back after all! He started breathing fast, his heart approaching mid-brain, shut-down phase without hardly trying. She'd come back and offered him another chance. 'Almost' was almost the most beautiful word in the English language. Resonant with qualification. Deliciously vague and open-ended.

Under the spare magnet was scrawled a message. It read:

"You looked so totally wasted and out of it I left you pissed and dribbling on the BBQ hotplate. Will call from Newtown- B."

Then a ps:

"Your surprise party at Shangri La La Land was a big hit."

Joe was staggered. His crazy dream had actually predicted what must've happened. Among all the doubts and fears plaguing yesterday his inner clairvoyant had virtually premonitioned that Barbara would organise a proper 50th bash for him somewhere…and he'd missed it!

There was even a 'pps':

> "If you don't get below 87 kilos in the next three months I won't be coming back."

No kisses or hugs or affectionate little heart shapes with noughts and crosses, just 'B' and the 'ps' and 'pps'.

But- '*almost* fucked'! Joe could dare to dream again. Barbara *would* return. She would call from Newtown and be really pissed off with him (as she had every right so to be). But he would see her again. As far as their relationship went there was nowhere to go but up. Or out… So long as he could get the fat off. That would be the hard part.

And it would be the first thing he'd put to Raiina Virago as soon as he saw the beautiful young witch (hopefully later this very morning). He knew he needed a cleansing, full throttle, Wicca diet- fast. Perhaps red or yellow food only. No more procrastinating. Joe would phone Raiina today and make an appointment (if she had one- or beg for a cancellation if she hadn't). He'd lay all his cards on her tarot table and come clean about the appalling state of his physical ill being. He would seek from Raiina (in the absence of any better 'guru') the immune boosting cure. (Although he realised that just making the call was tantamount to being 99% cured.) In fact he would make that call NOW!…straight after today's early morning tantric body surf.

After which, Joe would switch on his computer (as always at 7.47 am) and finally start that long delayed feature screenplay. A story so outstanding and personal it would will Barbara back to him. Even if it never got made. (Which it probably wouldn't). And she would see how much he cared (when she read it) no matter what he actually weighed. It would have nothing to do with cosmic interference by wayward comets, but would instead, be grounded firmly in the magick and sparkle of human nature- the most tantalising, surprising and impenetrable subject of all. He would simultaneously abandon all his ruinous addictions, detox completely (starting with a full colonic). And from then on, losing flab would become a pushover. The ugly goitre round his middle would simply melt away.

Joe might even change to someone who tucked his shirt *in* for a change. And not leave it dangling around his midriff in a pathetic attempt to hide the obvious. He would go so far as wearing underpants again and, although he knew growing old amounted to an increasingly dysfunctional prostate, he would certainly refrain from urinating in public places- no matter how urgent the need (and always under a tree or near a bush). He might even lower his standards, abandon the Dunlop Volleys, and submit to wearing thongs full time, finally accepting their versatility and usefulness in a sandy, subtropical environment. As his future freelance magazine articles would demonstrate.

In short, Joe Deegan would give Barbara Solomon absolutely *nothing* to complain about. And enjoy her consequent frustration (when she couldn't find any serious fault with him). Allowing her to finally mellow out at last and shed some of her own, bi-polar, A-type, behaviour.

Joe was irrevocably part of her life just as Barbara was part of his. They were *familiar*- in the sense of being 'like a family'- albeit a rather odd one. They would always be 'there' for each other. Even though Barbara frequently wasn't. And still wouldn't be.

Certainly theirs was a curious but not unfriendly relationship; and maybe, in our crazy fucked up world, not all that unusual. Because, all we had in the end, Joe realised, when it all boils down, was the love of a man for a woman, and a woman for a man (or a man for a man or a woman for a woman or a person for an animal). This intangible bond. This friendship, mateship, through thick and thin-ship sort of thing. A strange sharing/going together. This stranglehold of emotional blackmail called an ordinary human 'relationship'. This centre of everything…

Joe grabbed a hat and earplugs, speedos, towel, plastic bag for the doggy do, and an old frisbee. Then he and 'Graeme' ambled the 100 grassy metres down Redemption Road's footpath and on through the still intact strip of pristine rainforest bordering the beach- to emerge finally, out onto its frontal dune.

Here Joe found a suitable patch of sand, knelt down, formed a supporting triangle with his forearms, and stood on his head to marvel (upside down again), at the wonderful panorama of time and space opening up before him. Like a gift from above (or below)- which it was. Always. The miracle of life. Thanks be to Gaia. Mother of all things.

And as he stood like an inverted, pear shaped spear for an impressive fifty six seconds, Joe Deegan sensed immediately that here was another chance to get the Beautiful Day even better. In the best place imaginable.

It was the first morning of the rest of his life and it would begin with his inaugural surf as a demi-centenarian. Then later this morning, he would write Barbara a deeply apologetic postcard willing her back to him and post it off immediately- in time for it to arrive in Jerusalem (via the Rainbow Coast's erratic mail system) just before she herself did. In about three months time.

Kate might be gone. But Barbara would come back. There was hope. He was happy. Life in Heaven was a hell of a thing, but *some*body had to do it.

SLOW FADE TO BLACK…

Glossary
of terms, names and places

A

A-list, the
a bunch of idle, freeloading wannabes, neverwillbes and hasbeens who run all of Heaven's rumour mills and generate its main conspiracy theories; includes architects, pulp novelists, journalists, glass blowers, lawyers' and doctors' wives, boutique shopkeepers, idle philosophers etc

A-types
clinical name for a person with an aggressive, pushy, demanding personality, usually the result of a testosterone imbalance and/or superiority complex

abseil
to senselessly risk one's life descending incredibly steep cliffs, sides of buildings, electric power poles etc, solely by means of ropes, see also "hang gliding," "surfing with sharks," "walking through brown snake infected long grass" etc

acid sulphate
ghastly toxic substance released when wetlands mud is disturbed through agricultural or building practices

acid flashback
the future price paid for ingestion of LSD in one's carefree youth, involving random hallucination and recurring mental instability often involving the presence of people who are not really there

aliyah
Hebrew for "*to go up*," to "*be ascended*" usually to holy (sic) Jerusalem, also: to migrate to Israel

All Hallows Hospital Heaven's chronically underfunded, rural hospital, run virtually single-handedly by the heroic Sister Carmody

Al'l'ah
Muslim name for *God*

Aloha
a five-foot-ten-inch slab of ditoxopolyphenalcarbate used as a surfboard with a half life of 25,000 years

Alternative Everything, The
a kind of permanent garage sale down the quiet end of Angel Avenue owned and run by the inventor Ronnie Rainbows, a former Professor of Botany

altitudinally challenged
pretentious, politically-correct-speak for a person who is of short stature

amotivational syndrome
a tendency not to do or achieve anything much, often associated with excessive cannabis use, membership of the fishing class or an upper house of parliament

Angel Avenue
Heaven's main street (Cardo) running from Salvation Strand at its Purgatory Beach end and intersecting with Saint Street (Decumanus) at Repentance Roundabout (see map of Heaven postcard #25)

anger management
a form of psychological counseling designed to curb deep inner anxieties and frustrations—often unsuccessfully

arboricide
the killing of trees by naturephobes and psychopathic environmental vandals or property developers

Arcadia Park
the only public open space in Heaven as yet un-optioned for private development by its corrupt Shire Manager

Armageddon
final battle at the end of history, taken from the name of a plain in northern Israel and its nearby tel, *Megido*

Astarte, Krystal
an astrologer prophesying for the *Valhalla Times*

au naturel
naked, dressed in one's 'birthday suit'
aura cleanser
spiritual healer who de-frags the meta-light emissions unique to each individual and visible only in the 49th dimension
Aussie douleurs
UStraylia's permanently undervalued local currency, won by genuine locals often to the accompaniment of blood, perspiration, tears and several other bodily fluids
Avalon Meadows
Carlos Mondeigo subdivision on Heaven's old quarry site (illegally rezoned from Industrial to Freehold Residential by a corrupt Shire Manager)
Avalon Motors
Heaven's only service station, specializing in home-made, solar powered vehicles
avgas
aviation gasoline, a form of purified kerosene
ayurvedic yogi
a master of traditional Hindu medicine

B
Baal
ancient Canaanite god believed to encourage child sacrifice
bad karma
actions offending against the good order of the universe generally, and Gaia's masterplan for the Urth in particular
bakpak
ad-speak for *back pack*, a form of luggage worn on the back, and a form of language that is, like its milieu, largely synthetic
bakpakah
ad-speak for a twenty-something traveler, who will work illegally for food and shelter, seeks adventure, altered states, sex etc before returning home to a career in data processing or civil engineering
banana lounge
a soft plastic deckchair/bed where both ends are adjustable up or down
Barbaraism
certainly *not* a repugnant act of moral depravity typical of heathens, but rather something wise and sensible such as only Barbara Solomon would say
bangalows
palm trees native to the Rainbow Coast
bastard
UStraylian term of affection for someone usually less fortunate or older than oneself
BBQ hotplate
see *the Curse of*; Joe Deegan's backyard cooking implement caught in the grip of a meteorological curse placed upon it by persons or forces unknown possibly emanating from the 49th dimension
Beatification Beauty Parlour
Heaven's only hairdressing salon; manicures, eyelash grooming and facials available
Beautiful Day, The
Joe Deegan's ideal daily routine for achieving heaven on Urth involving minimum 'work', several little lie downs, and as much tantric body surfing as possible
Bedouins
see also 'beduins,' Arab desert dwellers, nomadic people of the Muddled East
Be'er Ada
an ancient well situated in a wadi (dry creek bed) in the southern Negev Desert
Ben Gurion
name of Israel's main international airport, honouring the country's founding Prime Minister
Benny the Process Server

freelance servant of the Property With Little Amenity Tribunal and other local courts, licensed to carry firearms
besseder
Hebrew for 'okay'
beta-blocked
from *beta blockers*, a pharmaceutical preparation used to calm concert musicians, heart attack victims, examinees, athletes and anxious people generally
Big C
avoidance-speak for *cancer*
Big Favour
something somebody does for you that will involve an excessive amount of future obligation
Big Idea
major insight capable of being fashioned into a marketable feature screenplay
Big Mistake
serious miscalculation, usually detrimental, often terminal
Big Move
a seminal journey in one's lifetime where residency is changed for self-conscious reasons not to do with earning a viable income or having a real career, family etc
Big Picture
an entire philosophy, the situation looked at as a whole
Bigtime
a major amount, usually owed to somebody for favours previously done and impossible to repay
bilum
New Guinea string bag, native artifact capable of expanding to hold all of a woman's health, mothering and cosmetic needs with plenty of room still left for shopping
bio-tech futures
a form of 'investment' [*sic*] where money changes hands for no apparent physical or discernable reason to do with economics or making any sort of profit and therefore hardly worth the paper they're not written on
blabbermouth
person given to talking a lot, betrayer of secrets, generally untrustworthy and usually foolish
Blessed Boulevard
local nickname for the meandering forest bikepath linking the south end of Purgatory beach to Heaven's tiny commercial hub
Blissed Out Bakpakah Academy
a highly successful tourist business, bicycle rental company and accommodation provider which has cornered the gap year market by masquerading as an educational institution in order to bypass Council regulations governing the number of bodies allowable per room - thanks to a corrupt planning department. It offers courses in basic numeracy, literacy, surfing history, snorkeling, bushwalking, skydiving, kite surfing, mountain biking, ocean kayaking, wake boarding, hang gliding, abseiling, skindiving etc, including worthless certification procedures and an opportunity to share cones (spliffs, joints, bongs) with people your own age from all over the world
blokey
UStraylian for someone who carries on in the manner of an UStraylian male: democratic, fair, easy-going, familiar, passionate about sport, shy about their real talent, not given to skiting
blue
UStraylian for *fight, brawl, conflict*; see also *feeling down, depressed* etc
blue heeler
an UStraylian mongrel of kelpie–dingo origin
Blue Sky Bowls Club
Heaven's local 'bowlo', an entertainment hub and gambling centre where occasionally the game of lawn bowls may be played
blurb
a short, mass-produced piece of blanket marketing involving text and (sometimes) images

Blu-tack(ed)
to stick (have stuck) something on a wall or vertical surface using a blue, rubbery synthetic adhesive; from the brand name *Blu-tack*
body bomb
to flop into water stomach first, creating a big splash, and considerable embarrassment, especially if overweight
boganish
in the manner of a bogan—a uniquely UStraylian male (or female) of limited cognitive ability and poor ratiocination skills while possessing some cunning in relation to bodily needs, usually presents with a flannel shirt, a tragically bad haircut, thin jeans and thongs or ugg boots (in winter)
Bogwater Creek
original name for the radiotoxic coastal swampland on which the village of Heaven now stands
bomb out
UStraylian for to *fail spectacularly*, to *go down in a heap*
bong
see also *bong water*; an implement for consuming cannabis involving smoke passing through various cooling fluids prior to inhalation
bottle'n'fronta me
inebriate-speak for *having a bottle of alcoholic beverage close to hand*; see *frontal lobotomy*
bouncinette
small, netted, reclining seat for babies which can be bounced up and down with a seated parents' foot
bovva boy
British slang for uncouth young man, generally given to making a complete arsehole of himself especially when in the company of similar types at sporting features; see also *larger loons*, *legless idiots*, *ill-mannered morons*, *bogans* etc)
Breatharian
resident of Nullumbah Shire who sincerely believes that food and drink are unnecessary and humans need only consume air in order to survive
Brett Whiteleys
paintings by the artist Brett Whiteley, usually involving lots of squiggles, scenes of Sydney Harbour and/or strands of the artist's hair
Brewers Shoot
a high escarpment overlooking the village of Heaven, originally the place where logs from the Rainbow Coast's ancient rainforests were assembled and 'shot' down to the coast for export on a type of flying fox
bristle pudding
the act of 'blowing raspberries' into the soft young tummy of a boarding-school pupil whilst scraping beard stubble from side to side—a game often played by Brother Carol with sub-juniors during private anatomy tutorials at St Patrick's College, Nullumbah
budgie smuggler
UStraylian for a skimpy nylon swimming costume covering the buttocks and groin of a male swimmer, sometimes worn by prime ministers (where they morph into pelican smugglers); see also "Speedos"
bunging it on
from the UStraylian verb to *bung on*; pretending, over-acting slightly, trying too hard
bungy jump
to risk death by mindlessly flinging oneself upside down from some suspension bridge or other high structure with only a length of flexible cord to prevent one's brain from being pulped on the ground below
bumpf
UStraylian for material of little importance, usually written; see also *useless crap*

Byron Pay
a town situated just outside the Rainbow Coast region and almost completely destroyed by criminally wanton over-development, now one of the most expensive places to have a holiday anywhere in UStraylia with dysfunctional infrastructure, devastated natural capital, degraded environment, rising street violence, and an almost constant traffic jam through its single main street—and thus little to show for the millions made by developers once their boom was all over (as it so quickly always is)

C

cab sav
UStraylian for *cabernet sauvignon*—a form of dry red wine
Café Celestial
gathering place for local indignation and conspiracy-theory hatching, disguised as a popular sidewalk bistro serving Heaven's best skinny cappuccinos
Canonisation Court
an early subdivision of Carlos Mondeigo's carried out on what used to be Heaven's public golf course until virtually handed to the wealthy developer for a song (actually an old Nazi marching ballad) by a corrupt local Shire Manager
cantankered
from the adjective *cantankerous*; to bluster with obvious irritation, compulsorily argumentative
Cape Surprise!
a rocky promontory at the northern end of Purgatory Beach supporting Heaven's historic, iconic and much over-photographed lighthouse (see map on card #25)
capton wiring
the electrical wiring in most jetliners, subject to corrosion and unable to be adequately monitored producing a high probability of future structural failure
Cardo
Latin for 'the heart' or main street of any ancient Roman town (normally built at right angles to the Decumanus): see 'Angel Avenue'
carks it
UStraylian for *dies*—usually with some contortion involved, e.g. gasping for air, being throttled by someone larger etc
Carlton Light
brand of low-alcohol beer brewed in Victoria, see also *Victoria Bitter*
Carmody, Sister
a woman of prodigious energy and stoic dedication who, as a result of recent cutbacks, now virtually runs All Hallows Hospital single handedly; see "Heaven's chronically underfunded rural hospital"
Carol, Brother
middle-aged member of a notionally religious order and personally exhibiting anger management problems compounded by the vow of celibacy; also infamous for his 'bristle puddings' and personally responsible for sending Joe's best mate Dennis Hogan deaf while giving Joe himself a permanent fear of large men in long black frocks
Casa del Fibro
Joe and Barbara Solomon's one-bedroom home situated at 13 Redemption Road, South Heaven composed mostly of fibro asbestos sheeting
Cause, The
an apparently almost endlessly doomed attempt to achieve some modicum of Common Good at the expense of vested Private Interest
cement box/brutalist style
a form of architecture borrowed from blueprints of Nazi bunkers found in an old Gestapo file and since reproduced globally on some of the world's most expensive shorelines using only building materials that are neither natural nor organic; see *Surface Paradox*, *Byron Pay* etc)
chai
sweet, milky tea

---

chakra
energy lines in the body (or the Urth) that channel one's essential spirit or *chi* through the 49th dimension

channeler
person who, for a small (or large) fee, pretends to be the conduit between this life and some other in any number of dimensions

chardy
UStraylian for a variety of dry white wine also known as *chardonnay*—the legally trademarked name belonging to a region of France which vigorously sues for product copyright the moment another country attempts to use the term

Chastity, the vow of
a form of religious-based celibacy implicated in the systemic failure of Joe's alma mater, St Patrick's Boarding College for boys with mums and dads who'd prefer not to be

Chateau de Migrainé
a brand of cheap wine guaranteed to bring on a dreadful headache the following day

Cherubim's Hot Chookery
a popular bakpakah eatery, specialising in organic, free-range, gently killed poultry

Chi
'energy' that 'channels' through the body's chakras, also a form of milky, spiced tea

chippie
an UStraylian carpenter, specially trained to be always late to start a job and always slow to finish

chum
British UStraylian for *close friend*, someone capable of being exploited for personal gain

cinch
UStraylian for a *certainty, easy to achieve, guaranteed outcome*

Circumflex
short for *Circumflex Artery*—the one circling the heart and vital to its proper function

cirrocumulus
a form of high-altitude, streaky cloud

clamber
to crawl over an obstacle with little skill or balance

clobber
UStraylian for *clothes*

cobber
UStraylian for *good friend*, mate, someone you'd die for—either before or after you've thoroughly exploited them

cockup
UStraylian for *big mistake, major maladministration, systemic failure* etc

cognoscenti
literally *people in the know*; see *A list, superiority complex*

Cold Coast
a thin, twenty-kilometre long strip of badly planned highrise towers built in a cement/brutalist style with garish colours mostly on the fragile frontal dune system of a once pristine sub-tropical coast, with little public infrastructure or amenity, soaring crime rates, and a boom/bust economy based on its fickle real estate market; see also *Surface Paradox*

colonic irrigationist
person who performs a detoxification procedure by flushing the colon with fluids, enemas etc producing a brownish grey fluid extract containing peas and pieces of carrot

Common Good
a nostalgic and once valid concept, now largely discarded in favour of vested Private Self Interest

Common Sense
an ability to behave in the most obvious, normal way, requiring the least effort, damage or hassle, now notable mainly by its absence

common stuttering frog
a paradoxically rare and endangered species of amphibian rapidly becoming distinctly uncommon
compos mentis
as in *non compos mentis*, i.e. not of sound mind
conk
UStraylian for *to hit*; to stop something dead in its unfortunate tracks
copper scrubber
a mesh of copper wire used for scouring dishes, cutlery etc
Cosmic Bodyworx
Heaven's only gym, built inside a coldroom of the former Bogwater Fishermen's Co-op
Cosmic Time
a concept of time measured in billions of years and encompassing the life spans of universes both within and beyond the 49th dimension
couldabeen
lazy UStraylian for *could have been*
crackers
UStraylian for *fireworks*: gunpowder wrapped in a solid cardboard cylinder; see also *biscuits*
alternatively may also refer to a mentally unbalanced state, exhibiting a propensity to do silly things
cranially rebalanced
a healing practice involving realignment of the head and neck muscles for no particular reason or health benefit
crap
UStraylian for excrement, thing of little value
crapping on
UStraylian for talking a whole lot of rubbish, generally to the annoyance of one's listeners
crim de la crim
a potent, evil individual, someone generally to be avoided
cryogenic suspension
deep freeze designed to preserve the body from decomposition
crystallographer
a master (or mistress) of crystals and their curative powers, able to deploy certain combinations of vibrations to achieve healing and deep emotional change, particularly in the 49th dimension
Curie, Madam
pioneering French nuclear scientist who died of cancer caused by her research into enriched uranium
currawong
an aggressive black-and-white UStraylian bird, similar to a magpie, known to drive less powerful species to either distraction or extinction
current squeeze
current girlfriend, common-law wife, mistress etc
CV
acronym for the Latin *curriculum vitae*: the lies, fudges and half-truths of a person's professional working achievements

D
DA
acronym for *Development Application, Devious Architecture, Destruction Application*: a process whereby a (usually divided) local council and the majority of a small town's residents are hoodwinked into thinking some massive over-development—which cleverly contorts numerous local planning rules—won't have any negative effect on their public infrastructure, traffic congestion, social amenity or natural capital; and which, if it fails at the first hurdle, can always be rescued by the proponents at the Property With Little Amenity Tribunal stage

Da Groot, Lech
tall, thin, sub-optimal example of the get-rich-quick brigade, with lank, shoulder-length hair, beady, snake-like eyes, a heart of pure roadbase, and an IQ somewhat shy of his shoe size, believed to be a Hungarian national who illegally migrated to UStraylia from Eastern Europe just before the collapse of the East German communist regime where he worked as an in-house torturer for the Stasi (secret police)

Daliesque
in the manner of the satirical Spanish painter Salvador Dali

Damien
(Prendergast) a professional lifesaver, one of the twelve main scheming, bronzed, manipulative, good-looking, dim-witted characters in the television drama serial *On Golden Sands*

dandysoychino
liver-cleansing beverage made from boiled dandelion root and soy milk

DDT
acronym for *DichloroDiphenylTrichlorothene*—a deadly poison once used widely in the dairying and cattle industry (see *dip site*) and believed to be implicated in the current pandemic of cancer in the red-meat-eating percentile of the population

D9
an extremely large bulldozer capable of leveling a rainforest or refugee camp within hours

death adder
a black-skinned UStraylian snake whose bite like so many other UStraylian snakes is generally lethal

decaf cappuccino
decaffeinated coffee with frothy milk often ordered in the mistaken belief that it's better for you

Deegan, Joe
lover, dreamer, Piscean, incurable romantic, tantric body surfer, hack scriptwriter-cum-scribbler-for-a-living, low-sensation thrill seeker, couldabeen minor playwright, word-merchant, dialogue cruncher, the people's emissary, born-again green hero and neo-Luddite eternally chasing after his modest version of the Beautiful Day; while partly redeemed by Barbara Solomon, Joe continues to endure an apparently interminable mid-life crisis brought about by the death of his parents and his wife Kate in quick succession nearly a decade earlier

Dentalcam
a miniature camera used to produce digital pictures of damaged teeth

derro
UStraylian for a 'derelict': a homeless (usually male) alcoholic often presenting as a kind of down-beat Santa Claus

desponded
past tense of the verb 'to despond', to indulge in one's depression almost willfully, expecting sympathy, rarely getting it

Devi, Vasuda
a self-anointed witch highly skilled at separating gullible bakpakahs from their euros, yen, pesos, shekels, krona and francs through tarot reading, cranial rebalancing, and aura cleansing—all performed under uninsured conditions at the semi-permanent Happy Hunting Ground Teepee

dial
UStraylian for *face*

didgeridoo
long (usually wooden, sometimes plastic) pipe of Aboriginal origin, capable of making deep, sustained notes; often taken up enthusiastically (for some mysterious reason) by itinerant, tone-deaf German bakpakahs

dingbat
UStraylian for a person of low intelligence, unstable mental shape, in probable need of substantial Personality Realignment see also *drongo*

dings
knocks or chips (usually out of a surfboard or car—frequently both)

dip site
a former cattle-drenching trench irredeemably and tragically saturated with toxic poisons such as DDT in a vain attempt to remove ticks from cattle, never properly cleaned up by the dairy and beef industry who profited therefrom and subsequently compromising for all time the immune systems of both vegetarians and carnivores unfortunate enough to come anywhere within 10 kilometres of the place

ditoxopolyphenalcarbonate
an extremely durable and highly poisonous plastic foam used for making surfboards; unlikely to biodegrade inside the next 250,000 years

Divine, Gail
Joe's very sensible dentist and holistic health advisor

Divine Dental Surgery, The
a dental practice overlooking Purgatory Beach at the south end of Salvation Strand (laughing gas a specialty, a wide range of exogesic therapies and gum restoration strategies also available)

DIY furniture
household goods that come in flat packs where the purchaser, upon opening, is confronted with a box full of disconnected parts and an incomprehensible set of 'assembly plans' written without language but using icons that remain bewilderingly meaningless along with tools that are utterly without any mechanical point or obvious function

DNA
life's building block, an essential and increasingly traceable bio-data processing facility within the genetic taxi of the human body (fueled by hormones and driven by a biological computer compromised by prior disorders) and responsible for the genetic make up of everyone alive (and quite a few who have passed on and may only have been pretending)

D-9
an extremely large bulldozer capable of leveling an endangered rainforest, olive grove, or refugee camp in a mere few hours

dob in
UStraylian for *betray*, to reveal someone's petty crime or misdemeanor to the police, tax authorities, headmaster/mistress etc

doctor-speak
a series of euphemisms designed to offer hope where there generally is none

Donne, John
18th-century metaphysical poet, creator par excellence of erotic verse, and former Anglican clergyman

douleurs
French for *sadnesses* and UStraylian for its own undervalued and over-sweated local currency

down chunder
corruption of *down under*, a British skinhead/barmy army put-down of UStraylia and its fair-minded people, offering a pretty clear indication of where these sad Pommie yahoos and their priorities as tourists are coming from

Dreamtime Beach Estate
proposed 11-hectare subdivision by Carlos Mondeigo involving the construction of 238 pink and lilac medium-density, cement/brutalist townhouses on a degraded, radiotoxic and flood-prone former sandmining wasteland, tucked away inside the middle of a rare remnant of otherwise untouched littoral rainforest

drizzle
light rain, or flecks of perspiration, blood, olive oil etc dropping as a kind of misty spray

drongo
affectionate UStraylian for *no-hoper*, person of little merit or capability, but still basically a good bloke/and or drinking companion

Druid
ancient Celtic priest prone to wearing tall conical hats and white flowing robes while holding small tree branches

Dr Who
a television philosopher who travels in time and space via a British phone box in order to defeat a number of constantly reappearing mobile garbage bins
Dunlop Volleys
an 'all natural' white (or black) sandshoe designed—and once manufactured—in UStraylia, consisting of a canvas upper glued to a rubber sole/soul
Dux
Latin for *leader*; literally *first in class*; see St Pat's Boarding College, Nullumbah

E

Eaton, Christabel
a Nullumbah Shire Councilor, elected on a pro-environment, sustainable-development package, generally outnumbered when it comes to the vote in Council by a solid bloc of dairy farmers, ex-real estate agents and the mayor's casting vote, casting a shadow over everything
economic_irrationalism.com
both a web site and a system of regulating any national economy whereby power and money increasingly ends up in the hands of fewer and fewer people
ecovandal
someone hell-bent on destroying the natural environment; see *enviro-nazi, fascist nutcase, Lech Da Groot* etc.
Ecstatic Dance Workshop
a gathering of women warriors in which pathogenic male energy centres are ruptured and made ineffectual through exaggerated, jerky movements to an obsessive, tranquillising, percussive beat
Eden
Carlos Mondeigo's palatial enclave built illegally on the Xaviours Shoot escarpment
'em
UStraylian abbreviation of *them*
Elysium Creek/Valley
a small stream and its surrounding hills running inland from the Xaviours Shoot escarpment
Enchanted Triangle
a special precinct within the Rainbow Coast bounded by the locus points of Mt. Lookout!, Cape Surprise! and Paradise Point, an area which contains the villages of Heaven and Nullumbah and which lies directly across one of the seven global chakras; a place of intense spiritual energy generated by the giant crystal located deep inside Mt. Lookout!
Endangered Habitat
the highest form of zoning that a block of land can receive in order to protect it against any kind of willful destruction—until a developer applies to the Property With Little Amenity Tribunal for permission to utterly devastate the site and build on it in his chosen cement/brutalist style
endless bikie party
what constitutes night-time diversion for Joe's extremely loud neighbours, the Utta Bastards Motor Psychle Club
en*light*enment
a state of consciousness in which one is able to comprehend, for example, Joe Deegan's 'Theory of Relatively Everything' or even one of Gra'eme's pamphlets.
entitlements
something a salaried employee used to get at the end of their working life, now mainly diverted towards the corporate auditor's fees required when their current employer is liquidated as a viable company just prior to the employee's retirement
enviro-nazi
see *property developer, bulldozing contractor, demolition company, Lech Da Groot*
Ep 1113
the fatal episode of *On Golden Sands* where Joe realises just how low he's sunk professionally and it becomes blindingly clear that his cushy working life is over
Esogesic Colourpuncture

concentrated light vibrating at the 49th degree, applied to certain acupuncture points on the body and believed to heal diseased gums, even possibly to restore tooth enamel
Essenes
members of an ancient Jewish sect who exiled themselves from Jerusalem and set up an early form of monastery in the vicinity of the Dead Sea around 2000 years ago
exasperate
to speak with an air of losing impatience and possibly all respect for one's listeners cognitive abilities
exorcist
a priest or holy person empowered to drive away devils and/or other malevolent spirits

F

Falcon station wagon
iconic UStraylian motor car
fate-al
a rather mixed concept/metaphor involving fœtal, fatal and fate-full
Feng Shui
an approach to house design which allows an occupant to see who's coming through the front door
ferals
latter day pagans and members of a self-identifying nomadic 'tribe' of young, homeless people attracted to living self-sustainably in treehouses, and vigorously protective of all groves, forests and places sacred to Gaia
ferchrissake/ferkerrissake
lazy UStraylian for *for Christ's sake*; an expression of frustration, desperately appealing to Common Sense or some higher rational entity if there is one which there usually isn't
'fess
lazy UStraylian for *confess*, as in *'fess up*
fibbed
past tense of the UStraylian verb to *fib*, to tell an untruth, bend the facts, quote statistics, read from a political party's manifesto etc
Filthy Mick
piratical chieftain of the Utta Bastards Motor Psychle Club apparently unaware of his considerable personal cleanliness issues
fire sticks
pieces of wood with kerosene-soaked pads at either end that are set alight and twirled, usually dangerously close to people with thick, matted, flammable hair see *ferals*
flatulate
to *pass wind*; coincidentally also the sound made by any large, noisy motor bike or musical instrument played badly
Flek, Bela
American jazz musician, songwriter, master of the banjo
flesh pleasurer
pretentious UStraylian for *masseuse*
fluff
common UStraylian for *fail something badly* in a demeaning and public way—usually something easy, also to 'break wind' 'bottom whisper' 'fart'
fluoro lights
UStraylian for *fluorescent lights* vibrating at an intensity dangerous for epileptics
fœtal attraction
an attempt to explain the apparent irrationality of close male/female relationships
franked dividends
income from shares that is effectively tax free, thus embodying the most effective and desirable form of financial return for members of the banking class
Freehold Residential

the zoning process whereby a developer becomes virtually immune from any planning constraints unless compelled by a higher authority such as a mining company or transport industry lobby pushing for a new freeway

Freud, Sigmund
aka 'the great Sigmund', pioneer of psychoanalysis, the 'talking cure'

Frida Kahloesque
in the manner of Frida Kahlo, an iconic and long suffering Mexican self-portraitist whose style has been imitated and emulated by countless amateur painters over too many years

frontal dune system
the high dune between a beach proper and the (usually swamp) land behind it; a vital buffer in the prevention of flooding from high tides, almost invariably appropriated and built upon by unscrupulous developers in a myopic attempt to maximise sea views, little realizing that this will eventually cause the dune itself to collapse during some future king tide—taking with it some of the most expensive ex-real estate no longer in the country

frottage
the erotic rubbing of skin on skin (or skin on hide, rubber, steak, banana peels, mango pulp etc)

full-caff skinny cap
pretentious UStraylian for a full-strength coffee diluted with steamed, frothy, low-fat milk

furry
adjective derived form the noun *fur*; see *furry ice*

G

gab, gift of the
an ability with words, a natural tendency to be articulate and convincing; see *Joe Deegan's 'Irish genes'*

gagabytes
a jaw-droppingly enormous amount of computer memory not yet fully understood and too impossibly enormous to be useful

Gaia
see *mother of all things*; the divine spirit said to animate planet Urth, effectively its main protector, and capable of destroying any species which threatens the whole

gawk
to look with dim or slow-dawning intelligence; to regard something unselfconsciously

geezus
low UStraylian for *Jesus*, an expression of some frustration; see also *geezuskerrist*

geezuskerrist
low UStraylian for *Jesus Christ*, an expression of even more frustration

Geogharty, Mrs. Edith
(aka Mrs. Gaa Gaa, the wholly ghost etc) an Aries and an octogenarian member of the Nullumbah Shire Protection Society, a longtime resident of Heaven who suffers from a extremely garrulous condition known as diarrhœa verbosia

galoot
UStraylian for *silly person*; someone of feeble mind or limited understanding

Gandhi Room
a private enclave within the *Seventh Heven* pleasure complex, dedicated to peaceful aromatic floatation and vegetarian massage

gingivitis
a disease of the gums characterised by excessive bleeding which, if left untreated, can result in both in tooth loss and/or serious, potentially fatal infection

gi-normous
low UStraylian for an enormously long or large thing or shlong

gloomering
becoming gloomy, taking on a dark mood with depressing intent

Gnaspuri
a holy town in unholy India

Gnome Liberation Front
a little-known horrorist group dedicated to protecting Gnomes from inappropriate use (such as a mail box); their motto: 'decapitation before humiliation'
God's Glass Blowing Studio
one of the many colourful artist precincts in Heaven
godspot
that part of the brain responsible for spiritual and other-worldly feelings
goluptuous
the state of being euphorically satiated by a rush of endorphin-fed pleasure
Good News Agent, The
Heaven's only newsagent and lottery sales outlet to its largely poker-machine-deprived community
goof
to act with extreme silliness and little self control
gotta
UStraylian for *got to*
GP
short for *General Practitioner*, a medical doctor; see *Dr Beanland*
Gra'eme
a disgraced former corporate auditor, Life Coach, oracle, the Apostle of Time, Joe's Mentor, His Master's Voice, the Wise One, the Great Man, His Smarmyness, a Leo and a prolific author of 61 'purple pamphlets' on Speculative Philosophy and economic_irrationalism see
Gra'emeism
an extremely wise saying, probably attributable to Gra'eme
Gravitron
a former Luna Park amusement ride in which participants were stuck to the sides of a large steel cylinder by centrifugal forces produced when the cylinder is rotated at high speed
Great Leveller
aka Death, the Dark One, Grim Reaper, politician etc
Green Police, the
shadowy group of eco-horrorists, tree huggers and self-appointed foot soldiers in Gaia's equally shadowy army; see Gra'eme's *Global Triumvirate: The Three Cartels that Rule World Trade and How to Stop Them*
grump
to dismiss with evident distaste, to self-indulge in one's bad mood
Guardian Angel
a being existing only in the 49th vibration and generally believed to exhibit a protective relationship towards humans; detectable by the presence of certain unaccountable aromas or a sudden rise in temperature, sometimes glimpsed as a disembodied sigh but always there and unaccountably always looking after you
guestroom/study/library/archive
a converted garage containing Joe Deegan's working office, manuscript archive, library storage and *Casa del Fibro*'s guest room
Gulf War I
the first British/American re-invasion of Iraq in a failed attempt to lower the price of oil
guru
professional spiritual guide, a person usually of great insight and experience charging only a modest fee for something that is essentially priceless
Gus
(Renshaw) Nullumbah Council's always difficult-to-locate compliance officer, irresponsible for keeping an eye on the excesses of local developers

H

hack
an inferior writer, someone who creates scripts or stories to a given formula; see *pre-emptive buckle*, *Joe Deegan teledramatist* etc

Hades
aka Hell, Ghenna, Tartarus, The Bottomless Pit, Netherworld, Melbourne in winter (or summer)
Hail Mary
prayer to the Virgin Mother of God asking for help from her son, Jesus
Hallelujah Hall
Heaven's only community gathering space; used for netball Saturdays, choir Fridays, Yogalates
Mondays
Happy Hunting Ground Teepee
a tent-like structure, borrowed from an original Native American design, consisting of a number of
poles lashed together towards the top and covered with woven hemp material; used as a nomadic
clinic by Heaven's original white witch, Vasuda Devi; see *cranial rebalancer*, *tarot reader*, *aura
cleanser* etc
hankering
unfulfilled desire, vague unarticulated longing
Harris, Sgt Doreen
Heaven's senior law enforcer; an honorary member of the Utta Bastards Motor Psychle Club as
well as the proud owner and chief disciplinarian of several champion sniffer dogs
Hav-a-Hart
ironically heart-shaped, chocolate coated, icecream confection popular in Queensland and the
Rainbow Coast during the 1960s and responsible for initiating a subsequently catastrophic epidemic
of cardiac disease in baby boomers generally
Hawaiian shirt
a colourful cotton shirt displaying floral and coastal motifs
Heaven, UStraylia
a small and increasingly popular town situated at the very heart of the Rainbow Coast, boasting an
historic lighthouse, pristine beach, zero crime rate, clean water, cheap real estate and an unspoilt
hinterland of national parks and rolling grassy hills; clearly a hallowed and blessed spot living on
borrowed time
Heavenians
any one of the 1138 troubled and semi-impermanent, mostly conscious, residents of Heaven
UStraylia
Heaven On A Cone
the town's only organic icecreamery (cholesterol depth charges a specialty); third most successful
business in town
Heaven Time
a strange, sometimes woozy, often dreamlike state in which reality as it is generally understood
tends to become somewhat rubbery—if not actually impossible to find, certainly outside either the
49th dimension
head honcho
UStraylian for *leader, chieftain, alpha male, prime minister* etc
Heartless Bank
Heaven's one remaining bank agency just barely remaining open
high-carb (low fat)
healthy diet with a lot of complex carbohydrate, fruit, vegetables etc
Hills Hoist
a circular, umbrella-like arrangement of tubes and wires, uniquely UStraylian and designed to rotate
drying laundry
Himmel's Hot Pies
Heaven's only bakery, fortunately run by a family of talented Vietnamese refugees trained in
French cuisine
Ho Chi Minh
iconic poet and revolutionary leader of Vietnam during its war with the USA and others (like
ourselves)

Hogan, Denis
Joe's best friend at St Pat's, sent deaf by Brother Carol when hit on the side of the head with a covered tennis racket
Holy Ghost
third member of the allegedly monotheistic Christian divinity, and a nickname for the Brother from Adelaide who they kept moving from school to school—but only after parents actually complained although the archbishop still claims he never knew
hoon
common UStraylian term for an emotionally stunted young fellow of limited intelligence who is generally hell-bent on some act of mindless destruction upon either animate or inanimate objects— usually both (not excluding himself)
hopeless drongo
yet another sub-optimal example of the male gender
Horrorism, the War On
a feeble and apparently doomed attempt to remove offensive material and/or certain recurring personalities from current-affairs television
Hosannah's Herbarium
Heaven's local nursery and garden centre
hullabaloo
UStraylian for an unnecessary over-reaction, a big fuss over very little
humbugged
to have drawn attention to one's inadequacies in a loud, embarrassing way that one will later deeply regret
hydro power
electric power produced by moving water, readily globally available and potentially inexhaustible

I

Iced Vo Vos
a confection of congealed pink-and-white icing spread over a sweet biscuit base, cardiovascular disease guaranteed
ID
acronym for one's proof of *identity*— usually in the form of a card: such as a drivers licence, passport etc
id
the inner you, the bit left after your ego and super ego are subtracted which they rarely are
IDF
acronym for *Israeli Defence Force* which, paradoxically, has largely spent its time attacking other people and their various countries
Immortalist
a member of the Rainbow Coast sect founded on the belief that most life forms can (or soon will) live forever
'income-producing'
an elaborate tax scam designed to claim deductions with the appearance of legality
Inferno
aka Hell; see also *Hades*, the *Netherworld*, Melbourne in summer (or winter) etc
inner-feelinged
verb formed from the adjective and noun *inner feelings*
inside drum
UStraylian for *secret knowledge*, hidden private information
interlocutors
people who are engaged in some type of formal discussion or exchange of views
iridologist
a healer who diagnoses illness simply by observation of damage to the iris of the eye

J

jacuzzi
a large bath of hot, bubbling water creating an ideal soup for a plethora of self-generating bacteria and other pathogens
Jason
a merchant banker character in the television soap opera *On Golden Sands*
Jehovah
oblique and respectful name for *G–d*
Jeru-shalom
spelling of Israel's capital city drawing attention to the 'peace' aspect, paradoxically
Jung, Karl
pioneering psychiatrist, lover, interpreter of dreams, discoverer of the collective unconscious

K

kamikazi act
a suicidal mission (literally Japanese for *divine wind*)
kerrist
UStraylian for *Christ*; see *geezuskerrist*, another expression of impotent frustration incorporating the idea of the Christian prophet as well as a former UStraylian Governor General
karma
something that either offends against (bad *k…*) or reinforces (good *k…*) the proper order of the universe; one of Gaia's many controlling agencies
Kietel, Bryce
Heaven's colourful 'unReal estate agent'; a dynamic and successful salesman, Bryce always gets the best price, even if it involves indictable criminal behaviour and frequent bribing of public officials—obviously atypical of his profession
kinesiologist
healer who uses touch and movement to effect a cure
Kingdom Come Inc
Heaven's only stupormarket and consequently one of the most expensive places in town to buy virtually anything
King of Siam
current Monarch of Thailand
Krishna
a Hindu God

L

LAD
Left Anterior Descending artery, critical to the heart's proper function, 90 per cent blocked in Joe Deegan's case (without his realising it)
laissez faire
French for *allow to happen, what will be will be*; a relaxed attitude to any sort of control, self or otherwise; also a synonym for laziness or surrender to unrestrained market forces
'Lake Lethe'
(English/Greek) a local joke name for the artificial pond, to the north of Heaven, left behind by sandmining; originally a river in Hades, Lethe produced an intense forgetfulness of the past; a reference to the general ignorance of sandmining's devastating impact on the environment by the town's current residents
larrikin
common UStraylian for a rowdy, undisciplined, anti-authoritarian but basically likeable bloke
Latrun
a crusader monastery (12th century) situated at the base of the road leading up to Jerusalem from the Mediterranean coast
layabouts
inactive, disgruntled youth, destined to end in tears (either theirs or others, frequently both)

Leggo blocks
tiny plastic toy bricks used to construct bridges, buildings, people, space vehicles etc
Libby
Julie's lover, cause of much heartbreak, currently a roadie with an all-women's heavy-metal band;
soon to join a mono-gender circus
Libscombe, Bernie
dentist in Nullumbah who no one seems to want to go to
lifeplan
a kind of macro-diary for macho people
lifestyle jazz
Joe Deegan's freewheeling, improvised daily quest for a pretty near perfect way to exist
Lighthouse, The
a century-old wooden tower on Cape Surprise!, rapidly becoming an iconic and much over-
photographed tourist emblem for the 'en*light*enment' so readily available in the town of Heaven
below
Limbo Creek
a pleasant spring-fed babbling brook draining most of Heaven's remaining wetlands, soon to be
dredged and straightened as a 'waterfront' canal for expensive pleasure craft
Limbo Creek Fever
a virulent and incurable muscle-wasting disease often causing a painful death and commonly found
among newer residents of Heaven lacking the immunity afforded by long-term exposure
Limerance factor
that rush of blood to the head at the start of any new relationship in which patterns of behaviour that
will later be seen as diabolical, nagging flaws, are initially perceived as cute little foibles
lino
common UStraylian for a form of plastic/rubberised floor covering; abbreviation of *linoleum*
lite
ad-speak for *light*, as in (generally) low-fat products; see also *lite gardening*, *lite snooze*, *lite
workload* etc
Little Lie Down
the spiritual high point of nearly every one of Joe Deegan's Beautiful Mornings
littoral
literally *coastal*, adjacent to the sea; see *littoral rainforest*
live blood analysis
process of earning money by diagnosing illnesses from fresh, vampire-ready blood
Logie
an UStraylian television award, determined by popular vote, verifying Gra'eme's perception that
the more things stay the same the more they don't change
loofah
a semi-firm sea-sponge used to abrade the skin
loom
to look down on someone with malign intent
lorikeet
brilliant rainbow-coloured native UStraylian bird, displaying vivid red, blue and green feathers
Loyal Traveler Miles
the elaborate marketing strategy whereby a commercial airline befuddles customers into a
monopolistic commitment to their services by awarding points towards a free ticket on some future
flight where there are never any seats available
LSD
lysergic acid diethylamide: a crystalline solid prepared by degradation of ergot alkaloids, which
produces temporary hallucinations and a schizophrenia-like psychotic state known as 'tripping'
lugging
carrying greater weights than necessary—with evident distress
Luna Park

iconic timber construction in St Kilda, Melbourne, built in 1914 and still offering unlimited fun at the far end of a large smiling mouth

M

M-16
a devastating, semi-automatic military rifle used primarily as a National Rifle Association sanctioned form of population control in most US states and cities with massacres now occurring on an almost weekly basis in schools, cinemas, libraries, university campuses, shopping centres etc.

macrobiotic zenburger
a bland tofu patty crushed between slices of mouldy, organic wholemeal bread

Madonna-like
resembling the Blessed Virgin Mary, as depicted in any one of the many Renaissance interpretations of the iconic motif of a Mother with Child

magick
ancient, Druidic healing practice based on a broad understanding of how to harness energy to the 49th vibration

magnetic poetry
not so much attention-grabbing verse, as a set of odd words and letters with magnetic backing used to make nonsense, temporary sentences and bizarre statements on fridge doors

mallee bull
an extremely fit form of semi-arid-dwelling bovine of the male gender

Malvern Star
a popular brand of bicycle once produced in the Melbourne suburb of Malvern

Martyr's Meats
Heaven's popular butcher shop, struggling to survive against ruthless competition from the meat section at the globally franchised Kingdom Come Inc. stupormarket

Marx, Groucho
a highly influential socio-economic philosopher

Marx, Karl
a well known humourist

masseusee
some lucky devil in receipt of a massage

Master's Voice, His
see Gra'eme: thoughts, pronouncements, musings

maximum schmaltz
a thick layer of naïve romanticism overlaid with a cynical manipulation of emotion; something taken to the level of a high art form in, say, most Hollywood movies

Mayan
ancient South American civilisation virtually destroyed by Christian-European deceit and introduced disease

mea culpa
Latin for *my fault*; see *mea maxima culpa* (trans: 'I'm really in deep shit now')

Mehane Yehuda
the Jewish market in West Jerusalem

Melbourne
largest city in the world facing Antarctica, with only tiny Tasmania to protect it from the prevailing south-westerly gales; the general depression produced from the resulting unbroken leaden skies has resulted in a well recognised angst that 'animates' [*sic*] the city's many intellectuals and coffee drinkers

ménage à trios
a triangular love relationship inviting the hope of peace but delivering almost inevitably the certainty of conflict

Men In Suits
a cabal of former used-car salesmen who run the television Network Joe Deegan currently hacks for; see also *The Suits Upstairs*

Messiah Meadows
a gated community subdivided and speculatively built by Carlos Mondeigo on Heaven's last remaining public caravan park which was virtually handed to him on a plate by a corrupt Shire Manager
metagenician
a healing therapist who uses genetic manipulation in order to harness 'chi' to the 49th vibration
middens
sites of ancient Aboriginal encampments, consisting of mounds of shellfish, bones etc discarded over millennia and subsequently raided and destroyed by a cement industry ravenous for free lime
mid-life crisis
an affliction assailing (mostly) forty-something males and involving a sudden, apparently unaccountable plunging of their lives into a miasma of failure and withdrawal; often associated with jealousy of younger generations and a concurrent acute awareness of their personal, mental and biological degradation, sometimes treated (ineffectually) by the purchase of a large throbbing automobile/motor bike and/or the acquisition of a younger spouse/partner
mikva
Jewish ritual bath designed to achieve spiritual and literal cleansing
Milo
brand-name for a sweet chocolate flavoured beverage usually made with warm milk, especially at bedtime
Mitchell's snail
rare and endangered species of gastropod mollusc common to the Rainbow Coast
mitts
common UStraylian for *hands*
Mobile Yoga
an obscure form of occidental Yoga based on a series of constantly moving tantric stretches and a headstand designed to cleanse the internal organs
Mondeigo and Co
see also *Infinity Ltd*; a loose confederation of building contractors, corrupt public servants, real estate agents and property developers brought together via a mysterious, weekly poker game on Bryce Keitel's back deck (but not in any traceable way connected to Carlos Mondeigo, either financially or legally)
Mondeigo, Carlos José Henrique
(aka Shaftinundra, Chuck McPhee, Andy Searsburg, Bagwashanti, Ron Meadows, Sheik Rattle'n'Roll) the penniless second son of a Portuguese count, who arrived in UStraylia as an economic refugee fleeing the socialist government that confiscated his family's dynastic, robber-baron estate on the Estremadura coast north of Lisbon in 1975
Moonshadow
Helen Strongfeather's baby daughter, father or fathers unknown
moon-washed
dazzling, ethereal, nocturnal landscape caught in a full moon and doused with magikal qualities
morphing
changing physical form (usually computer-generated)
***mort*-gaged**
literally *constrained until dead*; a form of financial slavery in which borrowers willing indenture themselves for life to some monolithic global financial entity in the vain hope of finding shelter for themselves and their offspring (at least until the will is read)
mozzies
onomatopoeic UStraylian for *mosquitos*
Mother Theresa Terrace
another of Heaven's half-dozen streets named by a clever town planner many years ago in honour of famous spiritual people

Mt Lookout!
a volcano extinct for 29 million years and said to contain at its core the planet's largest crystal—
clearly the source of so much of the Rainbow Coast's healing energy and an appropriate spiritual
cornerstone of the Enchanted Triangle
Muktananda
an Indian sadhu, or holy man
Muddled East
Joe Deegan's corruption of *Middle East*, a place of some confusion and despair where the enemies
of my friends are sometimes also the friends of my enemies and therefore both friend and foe at the
same time, and sometimes friends with other friends and enemies also - but in different places for
different reasons requiring separate alliances prone to breaking down at any moment
mugachino
a large cappuccino served in a mug
mugged
robbed by mugs
Murphy, Father
the 'good' father, a semi-retired priest and Virgo, living out his days as chaplain to St Patrick's
boarding college, displaying a tendency to get tired and emotional in confession after too many
chalices containing the 'blood of Christ' imbibed during early morning mass
must-go-tos
a key opportunity for any member of a town's *A list* to discuss real estate prices while obtaining
free alcohol and finger food at occasions such as fashion parades, gallery or shop openings, product
launches, first nights at the theatre, sneak film previews, house warmings etc
muu-muu
a billowing, shapeless, tent-like garment, unaccountably popular in the early 1960s
muzak
a form of white noise designed to deaden the brain and lull it into a false sense of consumer
vigilance by using barely recognisable musical sounds pitched at the 49th vibration
Mystic Medicine
Heaven's boutique Wicca Craft shop
N
Nahlaot
a suburb in West Jerusalem, adjacent to the Jewish market
Naked City
an American cop show of the 1960s which started a craze for low angle camera shots and pork pie
hats, purportedly bent on making six million episodes
naked gardening
a wake-up call informing the gardener in question that some Personality Realignment is long
overdue
narrative cure
a form of self-healing that starts with self-loathing and evolves to actually writing down the worst
parts of some tragically unexpected bit of bad luck or illness that overtakes one; "the best self-
medication money can't buy"; see Gra'eme's *Watching A Cloud Go By—Very Fast*
Nature
Mother Gaia in one of her many organic forms
Negative Social Impact
something that inevitably follows in the wake of unrestrained over-development such as is generally
unleashed by the Property Without Any Amenity Tribunal as soon as a developer appeals to it
neo-Luddite
a person with little trust in any of the many forms of 'modern' technology, believing, quite sensibly,
that older, less complicated and more organic systems are better for all concerned
neo-Noosa
a building style developed on Queensland's (cancer causing) Sunshine Coast involving tile roofs
and garish colours, in a low-rise version of the cement/brutalist style

Neptune
Roman God of the sea
Network, The
collective noun for the cabal of former used-car salesmen who own the (publicly granted) right to charge enormous amounts of money for advertisements beamed to approximately a quarter of the nation's population, the only requirement being that they must also produce vacuous local drama series like *On Golden Sands*
New Resolve
one of Joe Deegan's many (usually hopeless) attempts to turn his personal and artistic life around to something more positive and outgoing
Nirvana News
one of Heaven's two popular local newspapers run by talented idealists
no-hoper
common UStraylian for unemployed layabout, with few skills and even less self-respect
Normal Bob
pro-active member of the Nullumbah Shire Protection Society, so severely ordinary and average that no one can quite work out what hell he's doing living in a place like Heaven
no probs
lazy UStraylian for *no problem*; see also *she'll be right, mate*; an optimistic assertion, usually baseless or lacking any real proof, especially when uttered by anyone connected with a building trade
NSPS
acronym for *Nullumbah Shire Protection Society*, sadly, the Rainbow Coast's only organised grass-roots resistance to the tidal wave of over-development about to descend upon the whole region and destroy the last vestiges of its social and natural amenity
Nullum'
lazy UStraylian abbreviation of *Nullumbah*
Nullumbah red-wing butterfly
endangered species of Lepidoptera found only on a small segment of the Rainbow Coast
Nullumbah Shire
local-government area encompassing the villages of Heaven and Nullumbah, including a twenty-kilometre arc of pristine bays and empty beaches fanning out from the base of Mt Lookout!; now known as the Rainbow Coast
Nullumbah–Sydney *Aurora*
Heaven's one daily rail connection to the outside world, constantly threatened with closure
nuts-and-boltsy
UStraylian for getting down to basics, the intimate details
nyet
Russian for *no*

O

O'Flannery, Lynton
the Nullumbah Shire Protection Society's 'honorary solicitor', still to win his first case before the Property With Little Amenity Tribunal
Old Frank
Joe's neighbour, a retired mechanic and greyhound breeder with an uncanny knack of choosing slow dogs and fast women, forced to accept as rent-free tenants, a constantly changing number of Utta Bastards in part payment of an old gambling debt
oka yoga
an odd form of oriental-style yoga based on a series of tantric stretches and headstands
On Golden Sands
a soap opera shot in the left-over sets from a reality TV series set on the Cold Coast, now entering its ninth bewildering year on air with still no end in sight, its only saving feature the provision of a living-of-sorts for the likes of Joe Deegan (albeit not for much longer)

Onecoat Kev
a Gemini, and slapdash local handyman, police informant, gossip monger and contract postman, always arriving later than promised to do a job, and never leaving earlier than hoped for, happy to admit that he's never found the need to apply two coats of paint to any wall, fence or piece of roofing iron
Otto
UStraylian for a large, wheeled garbage bin
oui, ken, ja, aye, bien sur, beseda gamore
French, Hebrew, German, Scottish, French, Hebrew for *yes*
outta
UStraylian for 'out of'

P
PA
acronym for *Public Address* system or *personal assistant*
paperkrieg
a towering pile of reports, analyses, memos and other impenetrable documentation designed to confuse and baffle a democratically elected Shire Councilor in order to hide the truth about some devious agenda being pursued by the corrupt public servant responsible for preparing it (in the interests of his/her blackmailer or developer mates)
papoose
a leather sheath, of Native American origin, designed to carry babies
pash
common UStraylian verb for *to kiss with serious intent*, generally involving more than labial contact and possibly a binding commitment with the possibility of children further down the line
Pathsandras
followers of the cult of the Smiling Swami, and dedicated to the idea of self-pleasuring in all its many varied and wonderful local forms
pearls, little
short for "*little pearls of wisdom*," something such as Gra'eme might say, or used to as the case may now be
Pearly Gates Hotel
Heaven's favourite watering hole, a beautiful old weatherboard building built on the back of the town's frontal dune system with wide, breezy verandahs and stunning sea views north-west to Mt Lookout!
pearly whites
UStraylian for *teeth*; see also *the pearly white gates of Heaven*
peepers
UStraylian for *eyes*; (as in the verb *to peep*: to sneak a look at)
Perpetual Moment
the eternity inside each tick of the clock
Perpetual Motion
Ronnie Rainbows' solar- and wind-powered 'car' [*sic*] consisting of two bicycles welded parallel to each other with plastic chairs in between and solar panels on top (designed to charge batteries under the car's seats)
personal journey
one's ordinary lifespan, capable of going in many directions but almost invariably involving a bumpy ride
Personality Realignment
a form of counseling where men (particularly) are forced to confront their fundamentally selfish natures, acknowledging the suffering caused to their partners by this, and thereby effect deep personal change through some kind of remedial action and/or self denial (regular maintenance sessions also highly recommended)

Phelan, Bruce
corrupt Mayor of Nullumbah Shire, a monarchist and fundamentalist Christian banana farmer,
rumored to be on an unbroken, year-long winning streak at the mysterious weekly poker game held
on Bryce Keitel's back deck—usually in company with interstate investor/developers and local
building contractors
phumpt
the sound a head makes as it whacks padded leather, and vice versa
phutt
the sound a blockage in one's chakras makes when released by karmic massage
physio/spiritual
all the known (and some of the unknown) aspects of a given life form
Piggot, Alistair
president of the Nullumbah Shire Protection Society and chair of the Rainbow Coast's UFO
committee
Piper, Wal
Nullumbah's corrupt Shire Manager, a former Sydney drug-squad-detective-turned-security-
consultant prior to being handed the Shire Manager's job ahead of a number of better qualified
applicants (also believed to be on a near permanent winning streak at the weekly poker game with
local real estate agents, developers and contractors etc on Bryce Keitel's back deck)
playdough
brightly coloured synthetic putty, generally given to toddlers so they can make a complete mess of
themselves and others with toxic materials
plonk
low UStraylian for 'cheap' or 'fortified' wine
plonked
common UStraylian for to *put down*; to *drop in place*
Poet's Breakfast
a casual, 3PM-ish daily gathering of Heaven's colourful poets, philosophers and artisans round a
chilled wine or three at Shangri La La Land
Point Paradise
mysterious broken headland at the southern end of Purgatory Beach which encompasses The Three
Sisters; a trio of small, rocky islets that are themselves the subject of a powerful local myth
Pompeii
ancient Roman coastal town destroyed by an erupting volcano (Mt Vesuvius)
pong
UStraylian for *bad smell*
Post Office, the
Heaven's tiny mail exchange, stationery retailer and gambling outlet for lottery tickets, now
struggling to cope with several new poker machines installed nearby at the Pearly Gates Hotel; it
also sell postcards and locally produced trinkets to visiting bakpakahs which can be posted to an
external world never closer than two months away at the ordinary surface/airlifted rate
postprandial
literally *after lunch*: a time for reflection, relaxation and renewal involving a serious lie down; see
Joe Deegan's *Beautiful Day*
power dress
the application of clothing to make one look more important or influential than one actually is
pre-emptive buckle
a process of giving in before being asked to do so; see *hack writer*, television scribe, Joe Deegan etc
premonitioned
to premonition, to predict future events in a way not fully understood by either the predictor or
predictee

Private Enterprise
a scheme of socially and politically sanctioned plunder in which a very large proportion of the
population is exploited by a very small one whereby funds all go in the one direction from the
majority to an increasingly small core
Private Interest
something that replaced the Common Good a long time ago
Probity, the Age of
an apparently fictional time and state when there appeared to be honesty and a corresponding trust
evident in most forms of public life
property developer
practitioner of the dark art of defrauding small, usually defenseless, sometimes gullible
communities of their natural capital and social amenity; almost always Leos or Capricorns; see
enviro-nazi, greed brigade, cement/brutalist style etc
Property Skyrocket
that early phase in any real estate cycle where abnormally low prices begin to increase at an
exponential and clearly unsustainable rate
Property With Little Amenity Tribunal, The
a state-government watchdog on the probity of planning and building decisions taken at local
council level, still to make its first finding in favour of the Nullumbah Shire Protection Society
against some Private Developer
pterodactyls
prehistoric form of flying dinosaur
punters
UStraylian for *gamblers*, ordinary people, pensioners, dupes etc
Purgatory Beach
Heaven's main beach, a beautiful curve of fine golden sand stretching from Paradise Point with its
Three Sisters in the south, to Cape Surprise! and the lighthouse five kilometres away at its northern
tip

Q
Quasimodo-like
similar to the fearful and pathetic spectacle of Quasimodo, the damaged title character in the film
The Hunchback of Notre Dame
quintogenarian
person aged in their fifties
Qumran
site of an Essene monastery east of Jerusalem and the place where the Dead Sea scrolls were found

R
RAD
Right Anterior Descending artery, critical to a heart's function
Rainbow Coast
a twenty-kilometre stretch of largely undeveloped golden beaches and rocky headlands somewhere
around the middle of UStraylia's east coast
Rainbow Coast UFO Committee
a loose coalition of locals concerned about the coming destruction of Urth from a rogue asteroid
hiding a spacecraft behind it believed to be from the planet Zylathon in the Quahilian nebula
Rainbows, Ronnie
inventor, botanist, owner of the Alternative Everything, and creator of *Perpetual Motion*,
Nullumbah Shire's first solar- and wind-powered 'car'
R&R
short for *Rest and Recreation*—usually for soldiers from the battlefield (see *Vietnam War*) and
something most people deserve a lot of the time
rankled
from the verb *to rankle*: to complain with irritation and perhaps a slight raising of the voice

Reality Check,
Joe Deegan's private term for his own personal WAKE UP! call
Reality [*sic*] TV
a genre of television comedy which exposes the folly of human behaviour by using discreet cameras
to capture private, revelatory moments (usually of an embarrassing kind and generally hyped or
faked by the attention-seeking participants, hoping to become celebrities as a result of being
allegedly 'imprisoned' in some artificial house or on some 'island')
real job
a full-time, permanent position—just about extinct in today's economy
rebirther
a healer and counselor who uses an extreme hyperventilation technique to find closure for a
patient's current emotional problems by taking them back to the exact moment of their emergence
from the womb—presumably in order to start all over again (probably with the same disappointing
end result)
Redemption Road
a small gravel track at the south end of Purgatory Beach; site of *Casa del Fibro* (#13), Joe and
Barbara's modest, one-bedroom home
Redneck FM
Nullumbah's only commercial radio station, with a number of schlok-jocks catering to the lowest
common denominator and a playlist consisting entirely of both country *and* western music
reggo
low UStraylian for *car registration*
reggo check
a series of annual mechanical tests required to keep car manufacturers and petrol stations profitable
by finding non-existent faults with hapless motorists' expensive to repair automobiles
reiki specialist
a person who uses physical touch as a method of transferring healing energy
Relatively Everything
see *Joe Deegan's theory of——*; Joe's personal account of the unaccountable attraction of men for
women and women for men (or men for men and women for women) based on a kind of universal
gravitational/animal force
release script
final version of a teledramatic script before its actual production in which its inherent faults and
flaws are reduced to a point where it is finally viable to show it to all the others involved
Repentance Roundabout
Heaven's main traffic-calming device, situated at the intersection of Angel Avenue and Saint Street,
technically the geographical centre of town
rescue remedy
a Grade R poison used to cure depression and anxiety
Riuyku
astrologer writing for the *Nirvana News*
Rugby
a form of mobile wrestling involving a single, oval shaped football, four padded posts, and thirty
large men in sweaty clothing
Rusty
Joe and Barbara's failing Datsun 1600, currently undergoing a not-so-slow dissolve in Heaven's
humid, salty atmosphere; unlikely to pass next year's reggo check

S

Saint Street
Heaven's second main thoroughfare, meeting Angel Avenue at Repentance Roundabout (see map
Card #25)
Salvation Strand
a wide gutterless boulevard running parallel to Purgatory Beach at the top of Angel Avenue with a
magnificent stand of Norfolk pines decorated on festive evenings with strings of coloured bulbs

St Barbara
Joe's joke name for his lover: a reference to her extraordinary generosity and goodness
St Mary's
Joe's primary school, run by the 'Sisters'
St Patrick's College
Joe's boarding school (from age 7 onwards), a systemically dysfunctional educational (sic) institution run by the 'Brothers'
St Peter's Pizza
Heaven's macrobiotic pizza parlour with its famous blinking statue of the primary apostle urging customers to 'come along and eat before we both starve'
St Vinnies
lazy UStraylian for *St Vincents*; a religious charity funded by recycling clothing to the poor and fashion-conscious
Samantha
a Taurus and merchant banker character in *On Golden Sands*
Sanmahdi
Hindu for *wise one*, the creative energy of Lord Shiva; see also *Barbara Solomon*
sarcast
to *speak with sarcasm*; a mocking, haughty response to some person or thing
saveloy
a purportedly meat-based product containing the mashed remains of both cloven-hoofed and uncloven-hoofed herbivores, popular at children's birthday parties when boiled for hours and drowned in tomato sauce
Savage, Carmel
daughter of a wealthy East Sydney stockbroker with connections to the Network that produces *On Golden Sands*, and determined to clear the show's active [*sic*] writers' list of people as old and blokey as Joe Deegan
schlep
to travel or carry oneself with some effort and considerable disgruntlement
schmiel
Yiddish for *fall guy*; a comic character of low status, often the unlikely real hero
scoff
(1) to pour scorn on, to speak mockingly of
scoff
(2) UStraylian for to *eat with insufficient mastication*, resulting in heartburn, dyspepsia etc
scoot
to move quickly away from, to dash off in a covert, sometimes cowardly manner
screenplaywright
deluded fool who lives in constant hope of actually seeing the fruit of his/her labours realised on a big screen somewhere see also *teledramatist*
second body surf
the mid plank of Joe's Beautiful Day, usually just before (or after) a lite brunch and Little Lie Down
septic tank
a small, domestic means of treating raw human sewage, often inadequately
sequester to remove money or chattels from someone by judicial—but not necessarily just or even strictly legal—means
Seraphim Surf Shop
boards and bikinis, bangles and bandanas, shorts and shirts, Speedos and sunglasses: one of Heaven's most successful businesses (along with the Pearly Gates Hotel and Heaven On A Cone)
session in the hammock
a regular feature and generally another 'high' point of Joe's Beautiful Day
Seventh Heven
an establishment devoted to pampering all the known (and some unknown) physical senses with aromatherapy, massage, float tanks, esogesic colourpuncture, colonic irrigation, life counseling etc

shaman
a wise/holy man, teacher and healer, able to travel to the dark side and emerge with a whole new recipe for the Common Good
shambolic
from the UStraylian verb *to shamble*, to stagger forward in an apparently aimless, probably inebriated or mentally challenged manner
Shangri La La Land
an Amerikanised bar in Heaven, serves cocktails and tapas 24/7
shebang
UStraylian for *project*, *undertaking*, usually of a calamitous nature
sheoak
native UStraylian tree of the genus casuarina
shopaholic
compulsive consumer of useless goods, unable to resist a bargain that they don't need, usually overweight and under-primed in the grey-matter department
shopping bikeride
Joe's daily burn-fat-not-oil programme
Sheik Rattle'n'Roll
one of Carlos Mondeigo's many aliases
sic
Latin for *thus* (i.e. used, supplied or spelled/written the way it is represented); indicates deliberate, ironic, ignorant or even arrogant misspelling (see also Spelt InCorrectly)
Shiva
main Hindu God, source of all creative energy
shitheap
person or thing of little value
shithouse
low UStraylian for *bad* or *terrible*, of no worth, excremental
short and curlies
UStraylian for pubic—and sometimes also unfortunately, public—hair
shrink
a witchdoctor skilled in treating mental illness, sometimes with actual medical qualifications
Sinead O'Connery
in the manner of the Irish singer/songwriter Sinead O'Connor
sink the boot in
UStraylian for low tactics excessively used on an opponent who is clearly beaten
Sinners Street
a street in South Heaven which veers off from Redemption Road and appropriately enough dead ends at Lake Lethe see map on card #25
skinny cap
a cappuccino made with frothy, low-fat milk
skiting (see also **"skyting"**)
UStraylian from the verb to *skite*, boasting of one's prowess or abilities without any real backup or proof
slagging off
to run down, denigrate, point out someone's faults—unnecessarily in most cases
slavering greed brigade
a cabal of property developers intent on wrenching a profit from real estate development no matter what the devastating consequences may be for the local community unfortunate enough to be living next to it
Slawter and Pryce
an unscrupulous Sydney legal firm, former colleagues of Gra'eme's, and almost singlehandedly responsible for forcing everyone else's public liability insurance up by 187 per cent in the last twelve months

slog
hard, menial or repetitive work, usually in an office with bad lighting
Smiling Swami
former corrupt Burmese general who found a way of sanctioning a hedonistic lifestyle by setting up the (tax-deductible) 'Church' [*sic*] of Pathsandra, subsequently garnering a fortune from gullible Californians who flocked to his programme of self-pleasuring and overindulgence in all its many forms
smoko
UStraylian for the short break and tiny amount of relaxation available on a worker's shift, extending as long as it takes to consume a cigarette and or other combustible material
snow job
a form of bureaucratic fraud whereby public officers conceal illegal activities under a paperkrieg of misinformation; see *paperkrieg*
soap opera
serial television drama programmed in half-hour episodes with continuous stories but not necessarily continuous actors or even characters
Social Security, Department of
a front organisation by which various governments pretend to be doing beneficial things for people in need, with no detectable outcome or visible improvement in the alleged recipients' lives
Solomon, Barbara
Joe's lover of nine years, a traveler, teacher, guide, counselor, best friend, networker, activist, surrogate mother, nature worshipper, Jerusalem Syndrome victim, Capricorn and unanointed saint; see also *Sanmahdi*: the wise one
sook
UStraylian for a soft, spongy cry-baby: any male lacking in backbone or resilience, usually a source of constant complaint and self indulgence; see also *wuss*
sound-bitey
in the manner of a 'sound-bite': a quantum of misinformation condensed to a couple of sentences for the purposes of endless regurgitation on various massed media
soutane
a long, black frock/coat worn by the 'Brothers', and useful for secreting various instruments of punishment such as straps, rosary beads, wooden crosses, missals etc
South Nullumbah Sewerage Treatment Plant
Heaven's ailing and technically constipated public sewerage system, soon to be condemned by the Environmental Protection Authority before being resurrected and resanctioned by the developer-friendly Property With Little Amenity Tribunal
special deal
offer from a door-to-door salesperson that always seems to end in the householder paying more than normal
Speedos
UStraylian brand name of a skimpy nylon- or lycra-based swimming costume; see *budgie smugglers, pelican wranglers*
Spikemilliganly
in the manner of the Irish satirist Spike Milligan; surreal Irish humour loaded with puns
spirituo/physical tandem
part of the ongoing mystery of male/female relationships
spliff
UStraylian for a small cannabis cigarette
sponger
UStraylian for lazy son of a bitch who thinks the world owes him/her a living
spot-on
absolutely correct in all particulars
spotted quoll
small, endangered carnivorous marsupial

squatters chair
a solid, wooden lounge-style chair with extended arms for resting one's legs or drinks on
(frequently both)
stent
a small mesh cylinder 80 per cent successful in keeping blocked arteries open
stairway to heaven
a ribbon of light dancing on waves; generic description for the shimmering band of broken light that
emanates from a rising moon over water, also subject of a popular song
'Stranger', The
chameleon-like developer's spy present at all NSPS meetings, usually distinguished by long grey
hair gathered in a tight pony tail at the back
'Straylyin
lazy UStraylian for *'UStraylian'*; a form of antipodean English best understood when uttered with
closed lips (to keep the flies out)
Strongfeather, Helen
a scarred thirty-something single mother of three or more children (fathers unknown), barmaid,
cleaner and brilliant masseuse
stubbies
UStraylian for small bottles of beer; see also *pair of shorts*
subcutaneous
beneath the skin; see Joe Deegan's *subcutaneous cyst*
subluxation
manipulation of the vertebrae by chiropractic means
subtroppo
a form of mental illness fueled by an intense humidity and copious amounts of alcohol, producing a
sudden realisation that one's life is increasingly going nowhere (while usually hopelessly self-
medicated with even more alcohol)
suck
UStraylian verb for *flatter*; to please or coax in a self-demeaning way; see also *suck up to*
Suits Upstairs
see *Men In Suits*; the mysterious and rarely seen cabal of former used-car salesmen who, between
expensive tax-deductible lunches, run the Network Joe currently does casual, contract-based work
for without any conditions or superannuation
'Sun'day
a non-pun on *Sunday*, i.e. a day in the sun at the beach, usually at the weekend - but not necessarily
super
UStraylian for *superannuation*; normally part of a worker's 'entitlements' due at the end of a hard,
stressful lifetime of slavish dedication to his/her job, and allegedly existing in an account supervised
by some large institutional investment conglomerate which always seems to go mysteriously broke
just before the aforesaid worker retires, thus condemning the poor bugger to attendance at a series
of decades-long creditors' meetings from which they extract almost nothing owed to them because
the directors of the aforesaid conglomerate have invariably long since purchased foreign citizenship
in a small island state and disappeared there along with the untold missing millions
super/natural
spiritual/cosmic/religio-physical reality, of this world but not of this world
Surface Paradox
capital of the Cold Coast, a place totally obsessed with its own self-image, yet 'paradoxically' now
monumentally unattractive as a result of a decades-long open slather of unrestrained
overdevelopment by the get-rich-quick brigade
suss
UStraylian for *suspicious*; of dubious quality
swagger
to carry on like a *pork chop*, to boast with no legitimate grounds for same

swig
UStraylian for *mouthful*; see also the verb to *swig*: to *drink*
Sydney
a largely out-of-control conurbation of dangerously overpriced real estate built around a polluted
harbour and now filling most of the coastal plain of central eastern UStraylia; a place often stricken
with poisonous drinking water, violent crime, corrupt law enforcement and bad design in the
cement/brutalist tradition, thus causing its residents to adopt a near terminal and unfounded sense of
smug superiority
Sydney silk
a barrister from Sydney, charging fees commensurate with survival in a badly overheated property
market
Sympathy Orchestra
any unusual gathering of relatives and friends brought about by adverse personal circumstances
sync
see *in sync*; going together, parallel to one another, in step, coherent

T

Tai Chi
a series of continuous, balanced movements of arms and legs known as katas
tantric body surfing
a form of catching waves aided only by Speedos, gravity and an ability to paddle hard, producing a
feeling of karmic and ecstatic at-oneness with the known cosmos—including rainbows, dolphins,
whales etc closer to home
tarot table
a piece of furniture designed for the laying out of picture cards that are used to summon angels,
predict future events, and separate gullible customers from their hard-won douleurs
teatree/titree
native UStraylian tree commonly found in coastal areas, its leaves resembling that of the tea plant
and capable of healing many skin conditions
teetotalers
people who drink tea in preference to alcohol, with consequent low self esteem and little zest for
life
telco
any one of a number of telecommunications companies devoted to charging a fortune for phone
calls that cost almost nothing to produce, once owned by the UStraylian people and returning a
healthy profit to the public coffers but now largely in private hands
Temple of Sin
Joe's ad-hoc, jokey nickname for *Seventh Heven*
Terminal Travel Agency
Bryce Keitel's partially insured booking service for all non-returnable, tax deductible holidays
terror firma
a pun on *terra firma*, Latin for *firm ground*: a piece of dirt, 'secure' real estate—all owned by
nobody because nobody can own the land, the land owns *us*
terra nullius
land owned by nobody: virtually every square inch of dry ground on planet Urth
Tezza
nickname for an earlier boyfriend of Helen Strongfeather (possibly Moonshadow's father?)
THC
delta–9–*TetraHydroCannabinol*: the active ingredient in grass/pot/dope/ganja
theo-philosophical
see *theo-philosophical anomalies*; confusing, and sometimes even contradictory forms of abstract
thought questioning the existence of God(s) and the meaning or even the possibility of an individual
consciousness
Three Sisters, The

small rocky islets just to the east of Point Paradise, named after a famous and cautionary local myth about tantric body surfing

thwack
sound made by plastic hospital drip bags as they hit their metal support (coincidentally similar to a Brother's strap hitting a small child's upturned palm)

time
a concept of orderly progression based largely on various imperfect mechanical measurements such as numbers on a circle, vibrations in a crystal, sand through an hour glass etc; alleged to be constant, yet constantly changing, expanding and contracting (especially on the Rainbow Coast)

tofu pie
a pastry filled with chunks of congealed bean curd in an over-spiced and priced glutinous sauce

togs
UStraylian for a "swimming costume"; see also *Speedos, budgie smugglers, bum thong* etc

tomorrow
something that always seems to lie ahead and quite often fails to turn up

tottered
from the verb to *totter*, i.e. to lean with a clear intent to fall

tradie
UStraylian for *tradesman* or skilled worker who is contracted by the hour and almost always arrives later than promised and never leaves earlier than predicted

Transcendent Light Centre
a place of tender loving care, with fully certified professional counselors available 11AM–3PM Tuesdays and Thursdays only

t-shirt
a cotton undergarment often worn by itself, somewhat over-represented in Joe Deegan's wardrobe [*sic*]

Twelve Apostles
Joe's cryptic name for his technically illegal but well camouflaged annual hemp crop

twenty winks
a short snooze, aka *a little lie down*, power nap etc

two bob each way
UStraylian for having a bet that includes alternative choices—hard to lose, but not risking much

U

UFO
acronym for *Unidentified Flying Object*; something seen quite frequently on the Rainbow Coast, possibly because of its 'Enchanted Triangle'; see *planet's largest crystal*

Ultimate Banker
aka *Death, The Grim Weeper, Satan's Selector, Tantric Terminator* etc to which we are all personally mort-gaged

unadulterous
not containing any elements or admissible evidence of extramarital relations such as could be used in divorce proceedings

unbiodegradable
not capable of being broken down into anything with a half-life less than 724,000 years

unfrank
not truthful; see also anybody but a person named *Frank*

UnReal Estate
a property-acquisition vehicle posing as a real estate agency, partly owned by Bryce Keitel and his mysterious 'partners' connected only through their attendance at a weekly poker game on his back deck

Urth
a planet not unlike earth

ute
lazy UStraylian for *utility*: a two-door vehicle with a large tray at the back; mostly used by
tradesmen, farmers, fishermen etc
Utopia
Gra'eme's private retreat and technically illegal holiday accommodation complex incorporating
(literally) a tax-deductible hobby farm commanding a large section of the eastern slope of Mt
Lookout! with attendant remarkable views
Utta Bastards Motor Psychle Club
a recreational club of middle-aged Vietnam Vets drawn together by their shared interest in
enormous, noisy machines, mind-altering substances and not-terribly-bright young women
Uzi
a light machine gun made in Israel and available online to both approved and unapproved regimes
throughout the world

V

Valhalla Times
Heaven's other popular local newspaper
Vasuda Devi
a spiritual healer, skilled in tarot reading, cranial rebalancing and aura cleansing, runs the Happy
Hunting Ground Tepee
Venice of the Southern Hemisphere
aka *Surface Paradox*, a place of many canals, doomed like its namesake to an under-watery future
thanks to the greedy acquisition and destruction of its frontal dune system by overseas based
investors and fund managers
Virago, Raiina
a white witch and mistress of Wicca Craft, an ancient, nature-based healing regime involving
incantations, curses, potions, small animal sacrifice and food of certain colours only (i.e. red,
yellow, blue, mauve etc)
Virtue, Cassandra
a woman warrior and entirely capable secretary/activist of the Nullumbah Shire Protection Society

W

Waif, the
a young twenty-something, deep-green activist dedicated to self-punishing acts of resistance to
patriarchal domination and nature rape, seeking a future planet ruled only by Gaian principles
WAKE UP!
a constant, self-urging mantra devised by Gra'eme for free downloading to any of his many
workshop participants
wannabe
a jealous failure
warlock
a male witch (either white or black)
Whole-In-One Estate
a subdivision built by Carlos Mondeigo on Heaven's former publicly owned golf course
wimp out
to retreat in a cowardly way, to give up, find a poor excuse for not doing something
Wicca Craft
the practice of healing through the casting of spells and the preparation of ancient herbal
concoctions for an agreed amount of gold and/or precious stones (ancient coins with runic
inscriptions also accepted)
Wicca Guide
a column in the *Nirvana News* devoted to advertisements for the practice and supplies of general
witchcraft
willy nilly
randomly
Wilson, Wayne

unemployed youth and primary school drop-out, will surf for money and save lives almost without thinking

wimmin
plural of womin

Wise One, the
see *Gra'eme* and all he implies

Whirling Dervish
follower of a mystical branch of Islam where people spin themselves into a trance-like state for hours on end, channeling grace from above to below

woozy
a state of semi-consciousness, involving feelings of light-headedness combined with a loss of balance and possibly self-control (also potentially the early symptoms of a heart attack, embolism or stroke)

wordsmith
poor deluded fool who seeks to write for a living in a country as sports mad and culturally blind as UStraylia—thus ensuring for him/herself a lifetime loss of ego, including ritual humiliation from directors, actors, editors, publishers, producers etc; see also *first person blamed for the failure of any film, play or book*

work
something that should never take up an excessive amount of any Beautiful Day

write-off
UStraylian for *useless*, *good-for-nothing*, unusable etc

wORKS-oF-aRT
outcomes, processes and/or medical procedures that challenge current aesthetic conventions expressed as a form of dada-ist semiotics

wuss (see also **wuus, woos**)
UStraylian for a character of little backbone, weak, insipid, afraid or unable to act, probably never played rugby or trained as a cage fighter

X

Xaviour
respectful form of *Saviour*

Xaviour's Shoot
a high escarpment overlooking the village of Heaven, and a place where logs from the Rainbow Coast's ancient rainforests were assembled before being 'shot' down on a type of flying fox to Purgatory beach where they were floated out to ships for export to make the floorboards of Sydney and Melbourne

Xmas
respectful form of *Christmas*

XXXX
not a double double cross, or an attempt to cover up bad language but a popular beer brewed in Queensland

Y

Yogalates
a combination of traditional yoga and pilates: a series of exercises designed to remedy back problems and strengthen tummy muscles (sometimes successfully)

Z

zephyr
a light wind similar to an angel's breath or lover's sigh

Zen
a religio/philosophical approach to being in the moment and milking it for all it's worth

zenburger
a macrobiotic snack consisting of fried tempe and salad inside an organic stone ground wholemeal bun

Zeus
Roman god of suspect virtue, prone to excessive use of divine power responsible for murder and general senseless slaughter (like most deities)
Zion
a fortress originally built to protect Jerusalem on its northern side, since appropriated to encompass certain wider religio-political agenda and associated strategies
zilch
very little, almost nothing, dramatically and completely bereft
Zylathon
a planet belonging to the Quahilion nebula and of some growing concern for members of the Rainbow Coast's UFO Committee

Gra'eme - Towards a Purple Pamphletology

Every now and Zen
Reflections in a third I
The point of pointlessness
Is it really wedding bells or just a
bad case of tinnitus?
The ten plagues of a real estate
boom
Prisoners of the imagination
Buyer logical warfare
The great forgetfulness
Practice random acts of sarcasm
and senseless brilliance
Cars = carnage
The bloke who spoke in jokes
'Minding' the body temple
An excessory after the act
Bad/calmer
Towards a stock exchange of
principles
The disinformation age
Smart money
Nail biting for cannibals
12 steps to true happiness
Guilty bystanders
Save the shark
Just because you're paranoid
doesn't mean the bastards
aren't out to get you
A man who lived without
television
The outer game of tennis
There are no answers only
alternatives
Touching base with your inner
puritan
Acting the mongrel
My chiropractor always cracks
me up
Overcoming your fear of fearing
fear itself
Instant gratifications
Prophecy for dummies
Weapons of mass distraction
Life's too short to drink bad
coffee

Today's news = tomorrow's fish
and chip wrapper
Having your life and living it too
Watching a cloud go by—very fast
One small stagger forward for
wo/man, one hopeless shamble
for wo/mankind
How not to blow a kiss
Ageing disgracefully
Stop me if you've heard this one
before
Cemeteries are for the living
A towering work of incomparable
genius
Time, space and the whole damn
thing
Getting real and how to stay there
Life's a bastard, then you
discover your real dad
Alien dialogues
The war on horrorism
The rat in history
Recovery recipes for diet victims
Never trust anyone under forty
Power is the only drug—all the
rest are flowers
Money doesn't talk, it swears
Pleasure is a two-way street
Success is a journey, never a
destination
An Irishman's fear of Vikings
Everything you need to know
you've already been told
Laziness for beginners
How to succeed at anything
without really trying
Stating the obvious
Global triumvirate: The three
cartels that rule world trade
and how to stop them
Whatever happened to the vision
in television?
Who Am I? Why am I here?
What's it all about?

for
Caz Howard
a bright shining star

Paul Davies is an award winning playwright best known for his early site-specific works staged in trams, boats and houses. These were a key feature of Melbourne's revolutionary 'location theatre' movement in the 1980s, which is the subject of his new book, *Really Moving Drama*. Paul has also written a number of films including the short feature *Exits*, and just over a hundred episodes of a dozen TV series from *Homicide* to *Something in the Air*. Other forthcoming books include his collection of plays, *Beyond the 7th Wall* and articles on the screen trade, *Scribbling for a Living*.